Nina Milne has always dreamed of writing for Mills & Boon—ever since she played libraries with her mother's stacks of Mills & Boon romances as a child. On her way to this dream Nina acquired an English degree, a hero of her own, three gorgeous children and—somehow!—an accountancy qualification. She lives in Brighton and has filled her house with stacks of books—her very own *real* library.

Teresa Southwick lives with her husband in Las Vegas, the city that reinvents itself every day. An avid fan of romance novels, she is delighted to be living out her dream of writing for Mills & Boon.

Discover more at millsandboon.co.uk

HIRED GIRLFRIEND, PREGNANT FIANCÉE?

NINA MILNE

AN UNEXPECTED PARTNERSHIP

TERESA SOUTHWICK

MILLS & BOON

First Published in Great Britain 2019
by Mills & Boon, an imprint of HarperCollinsPublishers,
1 London Bridge Street, London, SE1 9GF

Hired Girlfriend, Pregnant Fiancée? © 2019 Nina Milne
An Unexpected Partnership © 2019 Teresa Southwick

ISBN: 978-0-263-27230-7

0419

MIX
Paper from responsible sources
FSC® C007454

This book is produced from independently certified FSC™ paper to ensure responsible forest management.

For more information visit: www.harpercollins.co.uk/green

Printed and bound in Spain
by CPI, Barcelona

HIRED GIRLFRIEND, PREGNANT FIANCÉE?

NINA MILNE

**To Clara—for being a fabulous friend *and* for
reading all of my books in a very short space of time!**

CHAPTER ONE

WHAT ON EARTH was she doing here? Gabby Johnson forced a smile to her face and her nerves into submission as the word *mistake* flashed through her mind in neon. *Get a grip, Gabby*. This was supposed to be fun, for heaven's sake—a hen weekend, friends together for two days of female solidarity and a good time to be had by all.

The problem was it depended on your definition of a good time.

'Right!' The maid of honour, to whom Gabby had just been introduced, a vivacious petite redhead called Lorna, clapped her hands together. 'Ladies, I have a timetable of fun activities planned to celebrate the upcoming wedding of our very lovely friend Charlotte.'

Gabby relaxed slightly as everyone cheered. She reminded herself that this *was* a celebration—that it had been *kind* of Charlotte to include Gabby. They had been friends in college, lost touch and then reignited a friendship of sorts after bumping into each other a few months ago.

'OK,' Lorna continued. 'So here we are in the lovely city of Bath, in this fantastic house right in the centre, and this is our plan for the evening. I promise that cocktails will be involved later. But first, I have a fun activity planned. Before I explain that, it's time to have a glass of bubbly whilst we all get changed.' Lorna turned around and gestured to seven luminous pink bags. 'These are all named, and I hope I have got the sizes roughly right.'

Gabby stepped forward with everyone else and took her designated bag, watching as everyone else peered into theirs, listening to their shrieks of laughter. Panic began to shrivel the edges of her introverted soul.

Come on, Gabby. Woman up. How bad can it be?

The pops of champagne corks as everyone pulled mini bottles from their bags should have reassured her, but then...

'It's a bunny suit!' one of the women exclaimed. 'I have always wanted to try one of these on.'

A bunny suit? Somehow she'd expected a more low-key affair. Dinner and drinks. Maybe a cocktail. Bunny suits hadn't figured anywhere in the equation. Now she was going to spend the evening in one.

Why, oh, why couldn't she be like all the other women in the room, who seemed enthused by the whole idea? She would have sold her rapidly contracting soul in exchange for some of the palpable joie de vivre and confidence that filled the room.

Gazing into the contents of the bag, she forced herself to maintain a smile as she tugged the costume out. A bright pink corset, a pom-pom tail, bunny ears, sheer tights... Now she understood why she'd been asked to bring a pair of pink stilettos.

Ideas streamed through her mind: perhaps she could fake illness, perhaps she could object on the grounds of political correctness...? *Get a grip, Gabby.* There was nothing worse than a party pooper, so all she could do was exchange her jeans and T-shirt for the bunny outfit.

Somehow she had to loosen up. Her childhood mantra ran through her head—*in twenty-four hours it will be over.* It came from the times when she'd been scared, hiding in whatever sanctuary she'd been able to find whilst her mother partied.

Even aged three she'd known with chilling certainty that her mother would not be able to keep her safe, would be too far under the influence of drugs and alcohol. So she had always scoped out a place to conceal herself—in a cupboard, under a bed... And wherever she'd been she'd kept telling herself that she would get through it, that at this time tomorrow it would be over. Comparatively speaking, parading the streets in a bunny suit would be a doddle.

'You OK?' Charlotte had moved next to her in her bridal bunny costume. 'I know this probably isn't your cup of tea, but...'

'Don't be silly. It's a laugh,' Gabby managed and adjusted her bunny ears with an enthusiasm she hoped came across as genuine.

Time to douse her inner cringe. Irritation threshed at her nerves—*why* couldn't she take this in the right spirit and have fun? It wouldn't be that bad; she was in a group of eight, all dressed the same—she could just fade into the background. After all, that was one of her best skills.

'OK, ladies. Gather round!' Lorna called as she produced her next exhibit—a pink top hat. 'This hat contains eight challenges. Each of us will take one and then off we'll go to attempt the challenges. We'll pretty much stick together, but I do require photographic proof that the challenges have been completed!'

Fabulous. Even her fade-into-the-background skills would struggle to provide invisibility in this situation. And what sort of challenge?

Panic began to twist in her tummy. Gabby might chafe against her introvert nature, but she accepted it as a cast-iron personality trait. Acknowledged that it had helped keep her invisible and under the radar when she'd most needed to, and had kept her safe amidst the chaos of her mother's lifestyle. Then later, after the horror of her mum's death—the result of an overdose—Gabby's quietness, her 'invisibility', had meant she had been allowed to live with her grandparents despite her social worker's concerns about their ages.

'Read it! Read it! Read it!'

The chant pulled Gabby back to the here and now and she realised that someone had pulled the first challenge from the hat.

'"Exchange an item of clothing with a man you don't know."'

Gabby looked on as everyone laughed, and felt anxiety tornado as Lorna held the hat out to her.

Breathe. In twenty-four hours this will be over. Her dignity would be in tatters, but it would be over.

Inwardly praying, she pulled out a slip of paper and looked down at it. Someone, somewhere *had* to be kidding.

'Read it! Read it! Read it!'

Stomach hollow, she did just that. '"Find a hot stranger and get a kiss on camera."'

This caused much merriment and Gabby forced herself to join in, etching a smile on her face in a gallant attempt to join in the spirit of the occasion. Time to channel personality trait number two—the art of faking it. Throughout childhood she'd made sure she'd played a part—whatever part she'd needed to play to survive.

A couple of hours later, as afternoon segued into the beginning of evening, her cheek muscles ached and her panic had escalated to the point of a need for a paper bag to breathe into. All around her Kate, Charlotte, Lorna, et al. had danced and spun through their challenges, and soon it would be only Gabby left. She would be the focus of attention.

Moisture sheened her neck, even as she maintained the smile and her brain raced.

At that moment Lorna moved over to her, a friendly smile on her face. 'Gabby, it's just you now. How can we help? Or if you want to give it a miss, it's no big deal. I should have known that this wouldn't be everyone's thing. If you want to skip it, then it's not a problem. We can head straight to the cocktail place.'

For a moment Gabby nearly collapsed in relief at the opt-out clause—but then sheer annoyance at herself surfaced. Did she want to be the one person on this hen do who didn't complete her challenge? The one person who didn't provide a photograph for the album Lorna would be putting together for Charlotte to look back on? Dammit— she *had* to try.

Keeping her lips upturned and her body relaxed, she even managed a laugh that hopefully held insouciance.

'Actually, would it be OK if I slip off by myself and give it a go? I could meet you at the cocktail place after.'

'Sure. That works.'

So, challenge in her hand, tugging at the ridiculous bunny suit, Gabby Johnson ventured forth into the dusk.

Zander Grosvenor looked around the table and reminded himself that he was an ultrasuccessful multimillionaire, not a scrubby schoolboy any more. Yet, as he surveyed the faces of his mother and two elder sisters, it was hard to hold on to that fact.

His father had clearly had the right idea when he'd absconded to the golf course This felt way too reminiscent of those awful sit-down chats from when he *had* been a schoolboy—and a very unsuccessful one at that. For a moment the remembered burn of frustrated humiliation, the sting of failure, pinged his nerves. He remembered the knowledge of his own stupidity, the knowledge that he couldn't live up to the bar set by his sisters however hard he tried. Hell, he couldn't even manage to read a baby book.

Enough. That was the past. And it had been resolved when eventually he had been diagnosed with dyslexia. So simple an explanation, and yet it had occurred to no one. And that was why they were sitting here now—the Grosvenor family.

His mother had been racked with guilt that she hadn't realised sooner and, once the diagnosis had been made, had supported him every step of the way—as had his father. Julia, his eldest sister—ten years his senior—was now a successful human rights lawyer, divorced with two children, one of whom had just been diagnosed with dyslexia, too. Gemma was a successful surgeon, four years older than Zander, and engaged to Alessio Bravanti, internationally successful racing driver and Zander's best friend.

The four of them had gathered here to discuss the fundraiser he had organised and would host to raise money for and awareness of dyslexia. For a minute the reminder of his duties as host, the need to make a speech, twanged his nerves with anxiety. *Not now, Zander.* He'd manage it; he'd tamed his fear of public speaking and it wouldn't get the better of him at such an important event.

It was an event his family all wanted to be a part of, and he was grateful for that. Yet as he looked around the table he had the distinct impression of a hidden agenda.

'OK, everyone. It's a week until the event, so I thought we should go through any last-minute details.'

'Good idea,' his mother said breezily. 'I've invited Brenda Davison to the gala. She's just back from two years in Oz. She had an incredible time there and she is *such* a well-rounded person. Really interesting. I think you'd like her, Zan.'

Gemma beamed at him. 'And of course you remember Louise Martin. I asked her to attend the gala, but she's busy that day so I've asked her to the wedding instead. She's exactly your type.'

Zander blinked. 'That wasn't the sort of last-minute detail I had in mind,' he said sharply. Aware that he might have raised his voice a touch more than necessary, he tried a smile. 'I'd like to look down the auction list, talk about the caterers—not listen to a staged intervention on my love life.'

'It's not an "intervention on your love life" because you don't *have* one,' Julia pointed out gently. 'We're not trying to interfere. We want to help.'

'I don't need help.' Reminding himself that his family had the best intentions, that he loved them dearly and that love was mutual, Zander tried to keep his voice even.

His mother let out a small sigh and he could see the worry in her grey eyes. 'Sweetheart, Claudia wouldn't have wanted you to never have another relationship. It's been five years now since she died.'

'I know that.' Aware of the tautness of his tone, he tried to soften it. 'I am fine, Mum. Truly.'

Laura Grosvenor shook her head. 'We're not suggesting you remarry or enter into a long-term relationship...'

'Our suggestion is just to go out there and date...Have some fun,' Gemma said.

'When I want to do that, I will.'

Julia leant forward, blonde hair swinging, and touched his arm. 'We just hate to see you still grieving so much. We know you loved Claudia, and none of us will ever forget her, but we all think it's time for you to move on.'

For a second he closed his eyes, couldn't meet ' ily's gaze as the guilt stabbed him.

Yes, he had loved Claudia; they ha'

sweethearts and he had worshipped the ground she'd walked on. They had swept into marriage aged twenty, full of optimism and hope for the future. But it had turned out their visions of that future were polar opposites, and soon Zander had known that they had made a mistake—that *he* had made a mistake.

It was a knowledge he had never shared—not with Claudia, not with his family, not with anyone. Because he would never have reneged on the vows he had made. Because whilst *his* feelings had changed, Claudia's hadn't. And then illness and tragedy had struck.

And after Claudia's death what had he done? Zander Grosvenor, grieving widower, had decided to follow his vision of the future, pursued his own dream and achieved phenomenal success. Accomplished a life and found fulfilment he would never have experienced if his wife had lived.

Sensing the heaviness of the silence, he opened his eyes. 'Look. I appreciate your concerns. I really do. But truly I am happy with my love life as it is.' *As in non-existent.* 'So, please, no more worrying. And no more matchmaking, OK?'

'OK…'

Three heads nodded, two blonde and one dark, but Zander didn't believe a word of it. Pushing his chair back, he rose to his feet. 'I'll be back soon—I need to go to the shops. Anyone want anything?'

Minutes later, he strode towards Bath's town centre, hoping the exercise would dispel the fumes of guilt, but knowing they wouldn't.

His family cared about him, but how he wished they would respect his decision to eschew the world of relationships. In their defence, they didn't understand the truth. Of course he grieved for Claudia—grieved the loss of life young, the tragic waste, the loss of the girl he had once loved. But it was a tainted grief, besmirched by the cold, hard knowledge that if Claudia had lived, he wouldn't be the person he was today.

On impulse he turned towards the abbey, made his way through the throng of people and headed for a place of cool walls and sanctuary. A place to look at the architecture, think of history and seek assuagement of the emotional turmoil that thoughts of Claudia still evoked five years since her death.

As he approached the imposing grandeur of the sandstone spires, touched by the orange rays of the setting sun, a flash of pink distracted him. A woman stood irresolute in the courtyard—a woman clad in a pink bunny suit. Not the usual garb for a visit to the abbey.

In the shadow of the abbey walls he could see her serious expression, her enormous hazel eyes filled with doubt, a straight nose, generous mouth. Glossy chestnut hair topped by pink bunny ears fell in a sleek curtain to her shoulders.

As if deciding to abandon her plan for entry, she turned and recognition jolted his brain. He wasn't sure why— who *was* she?

Her gaze met his in a fleeting skim; he saw an answering recognition and then she ducked her head and made to step past him. Just as memory kicked in.

'Gabby?' She'd been in the year below him and Claudia at high school.

For a moment he thought she'd deny it, and then she gave a small reluctant nod. 'Yes. I'm surprised you remember me.'

The memory came back. A young Zander, seventeen years old, walking down the school corridor as a tall slim girl with glossy chestnut hair came towards him, a pile of books clutched to her chest. As she'd passed, the books had cascaded to the floor and he'd automatically bent down to pick them up. He'd recognised the title of one, more from familiarity than an ability to decipher the words, but at least he'd seen the film.

They'd engaged in a conversation. He'd played the cool kid, one who didn't bother with books because films were way better, and she'd been so earnest in her disagreement that he could still recall her expression. Then Claudia had suddenly appeared. He'd later found out she had been alerted by a 'well-wishing friend'. Within seconds the chestnut-haired girl had been graciously dismissed and Zander had been swept away.

His attempts at remonstrance had been met with a shake of the head.

Dropped her books by accident? Don't be stupid, Zan. That girl—Gabby Johnson—likes you. I know I've got nothing to worry about, but she's a bit of a dark horse. No one knows much about her except that she lives with her grandparents. I just wanted her to know you're taken.

In the here and now, he decided there was little point in reliving the details. 'I do,' he settled for saying. 'So, how have you been?'

'Fine. I'm sorry about Claudia.' The words were simple but sincere, and, to his relief, she left it at that. No intrusive questions or additional sympathy.

'Thank you.'

'Right, well. Nice to see you again. I'll leave you to go in.'

As she moved forward, a piece of paper fluttered from her hand and she looked down at it, made to reach for it and then clearly recalled that she was wearing a bunny suit.

'We must stop meeting like this.' Zander squatted down and rose. He handed her the paper, his gaze inadvertently taking in the words. *Challenge No. 8.* The penny dropped. 'Hen party?'

'No,' she said, deadpan. 'I usually parade around Bath dressed like this.'

'Lucky Bath.' OK. That was *not* what he had meant to say. But somewhere between his brain and his mouth, that was what had come out.

Gabby stared at him. 'No. *Not* lucky Bath—and definitely not lucky me. Would *you* like to parade the streets dressed like this? Or the male equivalent, whatever that is. How about in a pair of tighty-whities?'

There was a silence as they both contemplated the scenario. Her face turned pink and her look of appraisal morphed into one of confusion. 'And bunny ears,' she added.

'Probably not many women's fantasy.' *Another vocal miscue.* 'Not, of course, that a bunny suit features in *my* fantasies. At all.' *And that was worse.* It was obvious that it had been a long time since he'd interacted socially with a woman. Time for a subject change. 'Anyway—did you manage the challenge?'

'Nope. Not yet. I thought I'd come to the abbey and have a bit of time out…maybe come up with a strategy. Or even some courage would do. But I don't feel comfortable going in dressed like this. It doesn't seem right. Plus I'm nearly out of time, so I'd better get going.'

'Maybe I can help?'

This caused her to pause. 'Why would you want to help?'

'I'm a nice guy. I wouldn't like you to fail a challenge. Old times' sake. Take your pick. So, what is the challenge?'

Reluctance warred with the hope on her face.

'I need to get a photo of myself kissing a h—a…a stranger.'

Ah. This was what happened when you started a social interaction with a woman dressed in a bunny suit. Not that it was a problem; a simple peck on the cheek and they could both go their separate ways. Yet his awareness of her ratcheted up. His gaze skimmed the smattering of freckles on the bridge of her nose, the impossible density and length of her eyelashes, the glossy lushness of those kissable lips.

Stop. What was the matter with him? He quite simply didn't look at women like this—hadn't done since Claudia. The sooner he got this over with the better.

'OK. I'll help. I know we aren't technically strangers, but it's close enough.'

Uncertainty touched her features and then she expelled a sigh. 'OK. Let's get it over with.'

Despite the echo of his own sentiment, he felt irrational chagrin touch him.

As if she sensed his reaction, she reached out and touched his arm. 'Sorry. That came out wrong. This is just a highly embarrassing situation for me. I'm a university librarian. An introvert. Being dressed like this... Asking someone to kiss me for a selfie is... I feel like an idiot. That's what I meant. But what I *should* have said is thank you—I really appreciate this.'

'No worries—and it's not a big deal. Where shall we pose?'

They moved to the side of the entrance.

'Here is fine.' Reaching into her small clutch bag, she pulled out her phone. 'OK. I'm ready.'

Zander leant forward and aimed for her cheek, ridiculously aware of her elusive flower scent, the smoothness of her skin and the glint of the chestnut sheen of her hair. Then at the last second she moved slightly, presumably in an attempt to position the shot, and instead of her cheek, his lips brushed hers.

Of course the right thing to do—the sensible action, the gentlemanly option—would have been to draw back. But that didn't happen. Instead he froze, caught in a sudden surge of sensation, tantalised, yearning, preternaturally aware.

Gabby drew in the slightest of breaths, and that triggered something else. Did he pull her forward? Did she step towards him? He didn't know and it didn't matter. Because all he could think about was the imperative need to deepen the kiss.

Her lips were soft, pliant against his, and somehow—impossibly—it felt as though they were the only two beings bathed in the last rays of sunshine that hazed around them and added magic to the ambience. Strands of desire twined together into a knot of longing in his gut as Gabby gave a small moan, pressed against him, looped her hands round his waist.

Until the spell was broken as a teenager jostled them, then jumped back with an embarrassed muttered apology.

Gabby, too, moved backwards in a jerky movement, hazel eyes wide in shock, her breathing fast. 'I…I…'

But clearly speech had deserted her, and without another word she spun round and walked away, her pace rapid. For a moment he opened his mouth to call her back—and then closed it again.

Bad idea. Bad move. Since Claudia's death Zander had eschewed the whole dating scene for a reason. Too complex. Too confusing. Too *complicated*. Just like that kiss had been.

And so he stood still and watched Gabby walk away.

CHAPTER TWO

GABBY HAD NEVER been so glad to see Monday morning arrive, and as soon as she entered the university library the world felt a better place. The feeling was further enhanced by the fact that she was dressed in cropped navy trousers and a cream blouse, her hair caught up in a ponytail, without so much as a vestige of pink, let alone any bunny motifs, in sight. Even better, she was surrounded by the familiar dense quiet of her workplace—a blanket of calm after the neon pink of the weekend.

Sure, she'd enjoyed herself, but it had been overwhelming, as well. The fact she didn't really know the other women very well but they knew each other had been an eerie reminder of her early life. As a child she had always been the outsider looking in—too shy, too awkward, too scared to try to join in. Cliques and friendship groups had formed and she'd missed the boat.

But those days were behind her, and as she walked towards her office, the library environment offered a comforting mix of technology and history, computers mingled with shelves of books—all enough to propel the weekend into the dim and dark recess of her memory.

Well, most of it anyway.

It would take a while before that kiss ceased to haunt her—days later she'd swear her lips still tingled. Ironically, the only physical evidence that the kiss had even happened—the sole picture she'd managed to take—had come out so blurry as to be useless. On her way back to the party she'd entered an upmarket fashion store, located a mannequin and he'd been her 'hot stranger'. If only she'd thought of that earlier.

However, even if she *had* snapped That Kiss, and had the guts to display it, she'd have been disqualified anyway—kissing your teenage hero probably didn't count as a 'hot stranger'.

Back in high school she had liked Zander Grosvenor—but not because of his looks or his rebellious cool kid image or even his prowess on the sporting field. It had never occurred to her that she could have a chance with him and that had been fine with her. Admiration from afar had suited her, because perversely she'd liked him because of his evident loyalty to his girlfriend. True, Claudia had been one of the prettiest, most popular girls in school but nonetheless...he had never so much as glanced at anyone else.

And she'd admired that; the traits she still valued were loyalty and trust. So she hadn't acknowledged that her interest in him was a crush, even though his presence had always brought on her nerves and she'd had to fight the impulse to try to 'accidentally' be wherever he was. The one time she had genuinely bumped into him by mistake had been so nerve-racking she'd dropped her books and actually had a conversation with him.

Enough. That was the dim and distant past and now she needed to banish Zander Grosvenor from her mind—and her lips, for that matter. At twenty-nine she was way too old to crush on anyone, let alone a man like the one Zander had become. Rich, successful...not her type at all. Time to focus on work.

Her day was divided between a reclassification project, a stint on the front desk and work on an online course she was putting together to help students access relevant information—more than enough to absorb her attention. So, apart from the occasional memory lapse to Planet Kiss, she was on her way back to 'Gabby as normal'. Enough so that at the end of the day she was able to close down her computer and look forward to a quiet evening at home.

The actual library was still open, and as she walked through the book-lined area she exchanged pleasantries with a few of the students. She stopped at one of the tables to pick up a couple of books that had been left, turned—and her sandal-clad feet screeched to a halt. Surely it couldn't be…? *Zander Grosvenor?* Her imagination must be messing with her head.

But then, there he was.

'Hi, Gabby.'

'Zander,' she said, and her voice echoed as hollow as her tummy.

For an insane second Gabby considered a dive beneath the table—though what she hoped *that* would achieve she had no idea. She needed to remember that she was no longer a cowering three-year-old, caught up in her mother's chaotic lifestyle, nor even a scared nine-year-old, terrified she would be taken from her grandparents. Back then, hiding had been her go-to strategy and she'd built dens wherever she could, cocooned herself away from the world.

But it really was not an option in the present situation, so she forced herself to stand tall and face him. Unfortunately, that necessitated looking at him, and her hormones did a flip before standing at attention.

Today Zander was suited and booted—the suit a faintly pinstriped charcoal grey, the shirt a pristine white. The whole ensemble epitomised wealth and success and a wow factor she really could do without. Dark blonde hair, just a little bit too long, blue-grey eyes that pierced…and suddenly the vast library seemed to shrink around her.

Eventually she located her vocal cords. 'What a surprise. Were you looking for me?' *Please let this be some strange coincidence.*

'Yes. You mentioned you worked as a university librarian—I did a bit of research and here I am.'

It occurred to her that despite the suave suit, he was uncomfortable; something in his expression indicated that the expensive shirt felt constrictive round his throat and the square jaw held a hint of tension.

'So, how can I help?'

'I was wondering if…if you'd have dinner with me.'

For a moment she couldn't hold back the instinct to smile. She felt a bubble of anticipation at the idea that their encounter had sparked this—a desire to follow up. Though something warned her that her reaction was misplaced and she dialled down the smile—an instinct justified by his next words.

'I've got a business proposition I want to discuss.'

Of course. How foolish of her to think it could be anything else. She could only hope he hadn't clocked her initial response. Especially idiotic because even if he *had* asked her on a date she would have refused. Zander was not her type—in so much as she *had* a type…which she didn't. But in the unlikely event that she ever figured out love and relationships she'd want someone ordinary, and Zander wasn't that. Being with Zander would be too much—too intense. He was too gorgeous, too rich, too successful…just too *everything*.

'You need a librarian?' Could he have a collection of books that needed cataloguing? It seemed unlikely.

'Nope.' He rubbed the back of his neck. 'It's complicated.'

The word should have her running for the sanctuary of her apartment. Gabby was a big fan of simplicity. Yet curiosity surfaced—what on earth could he have in mind? Hesitation stretched the silence and then she shrugged. After all, the point was that this wasn't a date—this was business.

So… 'OK. I'm intrigued. Dinner sounds good.'

'Great. Are you finished or shall we meet somewhere later?'

'I'm good to go.'

As they exited the university, Zander wondered if he had completely lost every vestige of common sense. Sitting at his desk earlier he had thought his idea made perfect sense, verging on genius. The problem was now he'd seen Gabby again he'd remembered the major flaw in the whole concept. In a nutshell—the Attraction Factor. One second in her presence was all it had taken for any ideas of business to desert him at supersonic speed. To be replaced by a near-overwhelming urge to cross the room and try for a repeat of that kiss.

But now, out in the fresh dusk-laden air, he sought perspective. Reminded himself that the attraction wasn't a problem as long as he didn't act on it.

'I thought we'd eat at Lothario's.'

One of Bath's most prestigious restaurants, it would provide a persuasive backdrop to explain his proposition. Yet she didn't look impressed; in fact she didn't even look enthusiastic.

'Unless you'd prefer somewhere else?'

'Actually, I would rather go somewhere more low-key, if that's OK with you.'

'Sure.' So much for the dazzling-her-into-acceptance plan.

'There's a really good pizza place not far from here. How about we go there?'

Ten minutes later they entered a small cosy Italian restaurant from which wafted out the tantalising aroma of tomato, garlic and a hint of oregano. Most of the tables were occupied with an eclectic mix of diners, and the low-lit room exuded a lively ambience without being loud. The tables were a mixture of sizes and shapes and were cheerfully hung with red tablecloths. The chefs tossed pizza bases into the air with verve and pizzazz.

A waiter stepped forward, led them to a table without fuss and left them with a smile and the menus.

Gabby gave hers a perfunctory glance and placed it on the table. 'I already know what I'm having,' she explained. 'Artichokes, capers, goat's cheese and olives. I always have that.'

'Always?'

'Yup. I don't eat out often, so I like to know for sure that I'll enjoy it.'

'But maybe you could swap something out? Have extra mozzarella instead of capers? Ham instead of artichokes? Or why not try the special? You may find something you like better.'

Zander stopped at the sight of Gabby's frown. For Pete's sake. What was *wrong* with him? The answer was not one he liked: discomfort. This was the first time he'd gone out with a woman since Claudia's death and he was assailed by an onslaught of nerves.

Zander hauled in a breath, reminded himself that this was a business dinner and it was time to put things on to that footing. 'Sorry. I didn't mean to sound so didactic. Especially over pizza toppings.'

'Apology accepted.'

Zander checked the menu, focused on the words and realised the irony of his own criticism. As a child, restaurants had been a nightmare for him—unable to decode the menus, he had simply pointed randomly to items with a varied degree of success. Or requested a staple generic dish that he knew would be on the menu.

The waiter returned with a long wooden board that held bread and three slender bottles of olive oil. 'Rosemary, chilli and plain,' he explained, then took their order and departed.

As she helped herself, Gabby glanced across at him. 'So,' she said, 'I'm intrigued. To be honest, I can't imagine what kind of business you have in mind.'

A sudden heat touched her cheekbones and she looked down at the piece of bread she held. A flash of insight told him with complete certainty that she had suddenly been hit with exactly the sort of business he currently had in mind.

Say something, Zander. Before the silence stretches so taut it snaps.

'Before we go any further, I need to know if you are in a relationship.'

'I can't see how that could possibly pertain to a business proposition.'

Her voice had a definite chill factor and he couldn't blame her.

'Humour me. Please. Just a simple yes or no will suffice. Then I'll explain.'

Gabby narrowed her eyes but then shrugged. 'No.'

Out-of-all-proportion relief touched him that his assumption had been correct. It was an assumption based purely on the sheer intensity of the kiss they had shared. Somehow he'd been sure that if Gabby was seeing someone, she wouldn't have kissed him like that.

'So explain,' she said flatly.

'It all started with that kiss. There were some rather unfortunate repercussions.'

The waiter reappeared with their wine, and the interlude gave him time to gather his thoughts and marshal them into coherence.

She tilted her head, waited for him to continue.

'You know my circumstances?'

'Sure. You run a highly successful consultancy company, with offices in London, Germany and Ireland, you made your first million by the time you were twenty-seven, and you started your business from a rented garage whilst you slept in an ancient caravan because you gambled everything.'

Guilt delivered another sucker punch. He'd done all of that. His wife had died and it had kick-started his route to a success she would never see—a success that would not have happened had she lived.

It's not that I don't believe in you, Zan. It's just not worth the risk. What's wrong with what we have now? If you do something like that, I'll never see you. I want us to be together, have a family, not risk losing the roof over our heads.

Claudia's words were so clear in his head, but there was no point pursuing that path. Right or wrong, he'd done what he'd done.

'All that is correct,' he said. 'But I meant my personal circumstances.' Though he couldn't blame Gabby for citing his business ones. This was supposed to be all about business.

'I know that you were widowed. And as I said on Saturday I'm so very sorry. You must have been devastated.'

How to explain it? Explain that he had been blasted with grief—grief at the loss of a life so young, grief that the girl he'd fallen in love with aged sixteen should have been taken, grief at the waste, the sadness, the sheer horror of watching someone you cared about fight and lose, slowly get weaker and fade away.

'It was difficult,' he said.

He waited as their pizzas arrived, black pepper and parmesan were dispensed. Then he continued, aware of the intent concentration of her expression, grateful for the lack of question or comment. Gabby was letting him tell the story as he wanted.

'Since Claudia's death I haven't had another relationship, and to be honest I am good with that. I haven't wanted one and I still don't. However, my family have different ideas. They are worried about me, think I need to move forward…and they spend way too much of their time trying to set me up.' He paused to sample the pizza and nodded. 'You're right. This is incredible.'

'Glad you like it.' She paused to pour chilli oil over her pizza. 'It's nice that your family cares.'

For a second he saw wistfulness cross her face.

'Yes. But on Saturday, after our…encounter, I went back to Mum and Dad's and everyone fell on me with joy.'

'Why?'

He sighed. 'We were spotted by one of my mum's friends. Edna Harris, if you want to know full details.' The woman had an uncanny ability to nose out secrets, to be in the 'right' place at the 'right' time. 'She headed straight for Casa Grosvenor to share the glad tidings and my family are thrilled.'

Gabby's face held bemusement. 'OK. But I'm still not seeing this. All you had to do was explain you were helping out an old schoolmate with a hen challenge. End of.'

'Given the detail Edna went into about what she saw, it would have been a tricky explanation.'

Gabby speared an artichoke heart and shook her head. 'Yes, but…'

'You're right. I could have explained it. I decided not to.'

'Because…?'

The artichoke was halted, halfway to her mouth, and for a moment his gaze snagged on her lips. He remembered their feel, the taste of her, the sheer unexpected passion and desire that kiss had evoked…

Deep breath. He decided he might as well go for it. 'Because I thought it would be a great idea to pretend you are my girlfriend.'

The artichoke heart fell from her fork.

'That's why I'm here. I want to hire you to be my fake girlfriend.'

CHAPTER THREE

GABBY WATCHED THE descent of the artichoke heart on to the tomato sauce of her pizza as her brain scrambled for a response to his words...questioned whether she could have heard them correctly. Perhaps this was Zander Grosvenor's idea of some sort of bizarre joke. Perhaps her tomato-splattering response was being recorded by an unseen camera. If so, the image could be labelled *The Personification of Stupefaction*. Or maybe she had misheard him?

Trying not to gibber, she surveyed his expression—outwardly calm, with a hint of tension in his jawline.

Eventually her brain decided on a single syllable. 'Why?' Immediate hindsight suggested a simple no would have been a better choice, followed by a rapid exit.

Zander sipped his wine, then placed the glass down, his fingers still around the base. For a second she studied his hand—its size, its strength, the very faint smattering of hair, the sturdiness of his wrist—and a funny little thrill shot through her.

Wrenching her gaze away, she looked up. 'Why would you want to hire a fake girlfriend? If you need a girlfriend, I'm pretty sure you could muster up a real one.' The man was gorgeous and loaded and—oh, God, had she just given him the wrong idea? 'Not me, obvs. But I'm sure there would be plenty of women who would go out with you for nothing.'

'I don't want a real girlfriend. I don't want a real relationship. Not right now.' The words *or ever* seemed to hover unspoken over the table, implicit in his tone, and Gabby could have kicked herself around the restaurant. The man was a widower, either still in love with his wife or not yet ready to move on. She'd been so inappropriately focused on his damn hand she'd lost the plot.

'I'm sorry, Zander. I didn't mean any disrespect to Claudia.'

'None taken.'

'But I still don't get why on earth you would want a pretend girlfriend.'

'Because it would make my family happy.' His sigh contained exasperation, but affection and warmth, as well. 'They were genuinely so thrilled that I might have found someone.'

'Did Edna Harris mention the bunny suit?'

'Yup. But I don't think they would have cared if you were naked.'

Had he really said that? *Naked?* The two syllables resonated in the air, evoking images he quickly censored. *Move along.*

'My sisters were happy I'd lightened up and met someone "fun". My mum was happy I'd met *anyone*, because she's worried I'll never get over Claudia.'

Do you think you will? She bit back the question. None of her business. God knew she didn't like discussing her own personal circumstances, her own losses and how she'd dealt with them. So instead she picked up a piece of pizza and contemplated him over the rim.

'I get that you want to make your family happy.'

Hell, she'd do anything for her grandmother. *Anything at all.* The familiar twinge of intertwined love, guilt and worry twinged her nerves. Her grandparents had used up their pension, the equity in their house on her—the cost of bringing up a child as they'd entered their seventies had taken a huge financial toll on them. Then, when her grandfather had died, his pension had stopped.

And now... Well, Gabby squirrelled away as much of

her salary as she could for the future that she knew was imminent—the time when her grandmother would need more and more help at home to retain her independence. A time when there might be no choice but to find a residential care home. After all, Lucille had turned ninety the previous month.

Gabby would be more than happy to move in with her grandmother right now, but Lucille flatly refused, informing her that she didn't need to be tied to an old lady—she needed to be living her life and enjoying her youth. Nothing would budge her.

'Gabby?'

'Sorry. The thing is that, however much you love your family, faking a relationship is a little extreme. Plus... surely it's wrong.'

'Wrong in what way?'

'Well, it's an outright lie, for a start. But it's not only a factual lie. It goes deeper. You want to make them believe that you're getting over Claudia, that you're moving forward, when you aren't.'

'I *have* got over Claudia. In the sense that I am not still in love with her or her memory. But my family won't accept that—they want proof, and the only proof I can offer them is a girlfriend.'

Gabby shook her head. 'But if you're over her, why not open yourself up to the idea of a *real* relationship? With someone you really like as opposed to a virtual stranger whom you kissed to help her out.'

For a treacherous instant the kiss returned to her mind, replayed in full neon pink bunny-suited glory. And in that instant a small voice from the deep recesses of her brain screamed at her to shut up! Questioned why she was having some sort of moral, intellectual discussion about this.

Hell, if this man wanted a fake girlfriend, so what? She should take the opportunity and run with it.

Run where? interjected the voice of reason. *Towards more kisses?* That would be plain stupid.

'My reasons for not wanting another relationship are personal. My objective here is to combat my family's worries. And, from an entirely selfish viewpoint, I'd like them to cease their matchmaking efforts, which, frankly, are driving me nuts.'

'But…it won't *work*.'

'Why not?'

'Because presumably you don't want to continue this fiction for ever. So what happens a few months down the line when we split up? They'll start worrying again. Even more than they are now. Because if you dump the fake girlfriend—FG for short—then they'll think it's because of Claudia. And if FG dumps *you*, they'll be worried that you're heartbroken. Lose-lose.'

'I've thought of that. I'd make it clear from the get-go that the relationship isn't serious for either of us. You *or* me. It'll be a bit of fun, an interlude…a first step on the relationship ladder.'

To her surprise she felt a pang of hurt at the implication that that was all she could be. *Get real, Gabby—talk about oversensitivity.* This was a fictional, hypothetical scenario. Yet the idea of playing the role of 'an interlude' didn't appeal. Shades of her childhood. To her mother she had been an unfortunate interlude, not a commitment.

Aware of his scrutiny, the small crease on his forehead, she shook her head. 'There is no "us"—this is a hypothetical question about you and FG.'

He raised a hand in mock surrender. 'Fair enough. But I have thought this through. This fake relationship will be a fun, strings-free one. Me putting my toe back in the relationship waters with someone not after commitment. That way my family won't try to gather FG into their bosom, but they will feel happy I am "moving forward". They will also stop trying to set me up with every female of their acquaintance. Win-win. It *will* work. So I need a real fake girlfriend. I need *you*. All you have to do is attend a few events with me, some family functions, be seen with me for a few months… And, of course, I'll pay you. So what do you think?'

'I think it's mad and you're madder.'

Suddenly he smiled. 'So you'll do it, then?'

For a moment the smile literally rendered her speechless. The usual gravity of his face had lightened, his eyes seemed flecked with wicked charm, and for a moment she almost entered the bubble of insanity and agreed.

As if he sensed her hesitation, he said, 'Come on Gabby. It might even be fun.'

Fun. Still under the spell of that smile, her brain was exhibiting interest in the whole ridiculous idea. Perhaps it was a bit like the urge to poke an aching tooth or prod a bruise. Plus he'd said he would pay her—so in truth this would be a *job*, a business transaction, a chance to put away a little extra money for her grandmother.

'What sort of events?'

'My sister is getting married in a couple of months in Bath—at the actual Roman Baths. And I'm hosting a charity gala next week in London. We'll need to have a few meals out, or other date-like activities in between. Smile for a few photos. There may be an interview or a few questions from reporters.'

The last words were said in such a casual tone that at first she didn't comprehend their meaning. And then suddenly a whole lot of dots were joined up. 'Exactly *who* is your sister marrying?'

'Alessio Bravanti.'

'The racing driver?' Just to be absolutely sure.

'That's the one.'

'And this charity gala—you don't mean a knees-up in the village hall? You're talking a full-on function? The type covered in celeb magazines?'

'Yes.' He eyed her, no doubt noting the horror that etched her features. 'Is that a problem?'

'Yes. I'm sorry, but you've got the wrong girl—the wrong candidate for the role.' Pushing her plate away, she shook her head, aware of a pulse of frustration-tinged regret. 'I wish I was the sort of woman who would jump at this, but I'm not. The whole thought of being watched and judged makes me come up in hives.'

'No one will judge you.'

'That's not true and you know it. Your family will definitely judge me, and I won't blame them for that. They care about you. But it won't only be them. What about all the guests at the wedding and the charity function? The reporters...the public...?'

'Why does it matter what they think?'

'Because words can hurt just as much as sticks and stones, and the wounds can take longer to heal.'

Gabby could still feel the pain she'd felt when her mother had been discussing her with her boyfriend du jour.

Yes, the kid's a pain...a drag. I know. I'll see if I can dump her with my parents again.

That sting would always be with her—the knowledge that she was nothing more than an encumbrance.

'And people's opinions *do* matter.'

Sometimes they could even be life-changing. Social workers had watched her throughout her childhood, assessed her, assessed her grandparents, formed opinions, and Gabby had made damn sure she'd conformed to whatever they wanted.

She had been the child they'd needed her to be: quiet, invisible, polite, grateful… Whatever it took to jump the regulation hurdles and stay with her grandparents after her mother's death from an overdose. And she was still that person—the kind who shunned the limelight, the one who had never wanted to be anything like the 'party girl' her mother had been, the one who just wanted an ordinary life.

'So I'm sorry, Zander, but I can't do this. It wouldn't work.'

Perhaps she was mad, given that he would pay her and she would love the chance to add to her savings. But it wouldn't be fair to either of them when she knew she couldn't pull it off.

'I'm not the type of person who could act as your girlfriend—someone who goes to glittering events on the arm of a multimillionaire. You'll have to find some-one else.' He opened his mouth and quickly she stood up. 'Bathroom break,' she said.

And on the way to the bathroom she'd pay the bill, say goodbye and leave. Because for some daft reason she felt bad—bad that she was refusing the job and bad that she was too chicken to take on a role that most people would kill for. But she knew it was the right decision. Gabby knew her limitations and this was definitely one of them. This role was beyond her abilities.

Five minutes later Zander watched as Gabby headed back to the table, her stride purposeful, the doubts he'd sensed earlier clearly dispelled. This was a woman on a mission to say farewell and leave as soon as possible. *Well, tough.*

She halted, looked down and frowned.

'I ordered dessert,' he explained. 'It's the house special, and according to the staff it's what you always have.'

The frown deepened. 'I... How on earth do they remember that?'

Her surprise was genuine, and Zander realised that Gabby really had no idea how memorable she was. He wasn't sure he could put his finger on it himself. She was undoubtedly pretty, but it went deeper than that. Perhaps it was the depth of expression in her hazel eyes, a sense of vulnerability...some elusive facet that etched her on people's memory banks.

'Anyway, I wasn't planning on staying.'

'But it would be a shame to waste it,' he said smoothly. 'And also I didn't have a chance to mention an important part of my proposition.'

There was a hesitation and then she sighed and sat down, picking up her spoon with an expression that indicated a determination to speed eat her way through the tiramisu.

'I didn't mention the fee.'

Now she looked up. 'The fee is irrelevant—because I'm not applying for the role.'

'I understand that, but if you were to agree to this I'm willing to pay you one hundred thousand pounds plus expenses.'

The spoon clattered to the table. 'Are you *nuts*?'

'Nope.'

'I guarantee you can get someone a lot cheaper than that.'

'I don't want someone else. I want you.'

Silence stretched taut as awareness joined the party— an awareness that swirled itself around them as he realised the truth of the words. He did want her. Right now he wanted to lean across the table and kiss her, taste the chocolate on her lips, entwine his fingers in the glossy sheen of chestnut hair, and then he wanted to...

Stop!

'You are the obvious choice.' The words sounded

forced, his voice hoarse, and he picked up his espresso. 'You are the woman I kissed. The woman Edna saw.'

Gabby took her time replying, her cheeks still flushed as if she was able to read his mind. 'I doubt Edna could pick me out in an identity parade.'

'Maybe not, but I'd rather not risk it. I get that this isn't your sort of gig, but think what you could do with the money.'

A dreamy look entered her eyes and she caught her bottom lip between her teeth in clear indecision. Then, 'You're right. The money would be great. But I can't accept the job because it wouldn't be fair. I couldn't pull it off. It's not only the limelight factor.' Pushing her empty bowl away, she leant forward. 'In real life I wouldn't go out with you. So how on earth could I fake it? No one will believe it.'

To his surprise, chagrin punched his chest at her words. 'Why wouldn't you go out with me?'

'Does it matter?'

'Yes. Because if you tell me then I can work out if we can overcome it or not.'

'For a start, I would never agree to a temporary, fun, strings-free relationship.'

'Because you're looking for a happy-ever-after?' Try as he might he couldn't keep the wariness from his voice.

She reached out to cover his arm in an instinctive gesture of comfort. 'I'm sorry. I know your happy-ever-after ended in tragedy, and I understand why you may want a temporary relationship, but I…I still want a shot at it. One day.'

'So you won't embark on any relationship unless it's with Mr Right?'

'Let's say I don't want to embark on a deliberate relationship with someone who is definitely Mr *Wrong*.'

'Fair enough. But you wouldn't be. This would be a fake relationship.'

'But I would find it hard to maintain a pretence that goes against my character and my beliefs. That's hardly going to be easy to pull off, especially when I will be so far out of my depth I'll be in constant danger of drowning. You're a "catch." I'm ordinary and my ideal man is ordinary. You aren't that.'

A dark memory crossed his soul. Again Claudia's voice echoed in his imagination.

Why can't you be happy with what we have, Zan? With what you *have? Be happy to be ordinary instead of striving after an extraordinary dream that may ruin us.*

As she studied his expression Gabby shook her head. 'I didn't mean it as an insult. I just want to explain why you aren't my type.'

He couldn't let her get away with that. 'Don't you remember that kiss?'

Her lips parted and he wondered if she'd have the gall to deny any memory, to say *What kiss?* But instead, she shook her hair forward slightly to hide her face.

'Of course I do. But that didn't mean anything. It was just an anomaly.'

'Then why don't we try it again?'

'Excuse me?'

'You heard me.' Zander wasn't a hundred percent sure where he was going with this but… 'Why don't we try it again? Another kiss?'

'That is a ridiculous idea.'

'No, it isn't. Because *I* don't think it *was* an anomaly. On a physical level I think I *am* your type, and I know you're mine. And that is exactly why we can pull this off.'

'Relationships are about more than the physical.'

'Sure. But without a physical attraction there is no relationship. And in the case of a fun-filled interlude the physical aspect is the most important.'

'I am not kissing you *now*.' Gabby glanced around, then

narrowed her eyes at him. 'I bring my *grandma* here, for goodness' sake.' Her forehead scrunched into a scowl. 'In fact I am not kissing you ever. If you think you can pay me to—'

'No!' How could he, Zander Grosvenor, king of the boardroom, dealmaker extraordinaire, be making such a hash of this? 'That isn't what I meant. I don't want to have a *real* physical relationship with you.'

Liar, liar, whole suit on fire!

Deep breath. 'I just want to demonstrate that whether we like it or not, act on it or not, there is a real physical attraction between us—and that means I think we could pull this off. Convince everyone that we are in a real relationship. Even though we won't be. On any level.' He leant back. 'Can you look me in the eye and tell me this attraction is a figment of my imagination?'

Against all odds her eyes scrunched further shut, and then she expelled a sigh. 'I can't do that. But believe me, I wish I could.'

Bingo! 'Then I respect your reservations, and I appreciate your honesty, but I believe we *can* do this. If I'm wrong that's my bad—not yours. So what do you think? A few social events and you pocket a hundred grand?'

Indecision hovered on her face, etched her forehead with a crease. She closed her eyes as if picturing the cash.

Finally she opened them and gave a small, decisive nod. 'OK. I'll do it. But only if I can tell my grandmother the truth.'

Zander hesitated.

'She won't tell a soul. I give you my word. Also, it's a non-negotiable condition.'

'Then so be it. You can tell your grandmother. Now, do we have a deal?'

'We have a deal.'

CHAPTER FOUR

'SO THAT'S HOW I made a deal with Zander Grosvenor.' Gabby summoned reassurance and a smile as she came to the end of her edited explanation to her grandmother.

Lucille had interspersed the recital with questions aplenty, and now her expression tended more towards dubious than joyful. 'I don't like it, Gabby. I especially don't like it that you are doing this for money to look after *me*.'

Gabby grinned. 'So if I was doing it for money for me, that would be all right?'

'It would be better!' Lucille settled back on the chair and tucked her shawl over her knees.

'It's not exactly a hardship. Most women would volunteer for the job, forget getting paid for it!'

'You aren't "most women" and I am sure you have no wish to have a temporary fling with a man just because he is good-looking and rich.'

'But I'm *not* having a fling with him, Gran. I'm *pretending* to.'

'Gabrielle. I may be old, but I am not stupid. I understand that this is a pretence. But it isn't one I approve of. It's a lie, and it's a lie you won't enjoy enacting. A gentleman wouldn't ask you to do that.'

'But his motivations are good.'

'Would your granddad have liked him?'

'Yes.' The answer came from her gut, even though she wasn't sure where the conviction came from. 'He married his childhood sweetheart and he has remained loyal to her memory. He loves his family enough to concoct an illusion, possibly *delusion*, of a relationship for them.'

Lucille shook her head, her still bright blue eyes clouded with trouble. 'It seems to me he'd be better to face his family head-on.' Sadness touched her features. 'Though what do *I* know about family relationships?'

'Don't say that, Gran.' Gabby knew that Lucille still grieved for her daughter—would always blame herself for the path Karen had taken. That was why, all her life, Gabby had striven to be the polar opposite of her mother. 'You and Gramps understood all about relationships, and I couldn't have asked for more caring people to bring me up.'

'Thank you, darling.' For a second she smiled, then took Gabby's hand and squeezed gently. 'Promise me you'll be careful.'

Sensing her grandmother was tired, Gabby nodded. 'I promise.'

'Don't get your heart broken. He's a good-looking, charming, successful man.'

'He may be all those things, but Zander Grosvenor is not my type at all. In the slightest.'

Lucille raised one delicately pencilled brow and Gabby reminded herself that she had downplayed the kiss and utterly omitted even a mention of any attraction.

'I'm in this for the money and I am in no danger at all of falling for the boss!'

The words were nothing but the truth. The attraction was an annoyance, an irritation, a problem she intended to solve. Even if she hadn't figured out how yet.

And perhaps her scowl carried conviction, because Lucille nodded. 'OK. Then enjoy yourself, darling.'

Yeah, right. The prospect of the next weeks showed a vista that crossed so far into her discomfort zone her eyes crossed at the mere thought. But she wouldn't add to Lucille's worry by sharing that.

'I will—and I will give you regular updates as to my

progress. Right now I'm off to meet Zander to sort out the small print. We're going boating on the river...'

Fifteen minutes later, Gabby approached the boat hire company based on the banks of the River Avon. It had seemed a suitable date-like activity, and Zander had pointed out they could speak without fear of being overheard in a boat. As a bonus, she sincerely hoped open air and wide outdoor spaces would act as a deterrent to their attraction.

It was a hope that lasted precisely as long as it took for her to spot Zander. As he rose from the riverside bench her tummy flipped. He was dressed in stonewashed jeans, a white T-shirt and trainers. The simple outfit showcased his sheer masculinity, the hard curve of his muscles, and threw her hormones into disarray. Yet she forced her feet to maintain pace as she walked towards him.

'Hey.'

His voice rippled over her skin as he stepped forward, his hands outstretched.

'Hey.' Belatedly she realised that they were now in role. She placed her hands in his and her skin goosebumped despite the warmth of the late-spring sunshine. 'Are we being watched?'

'Let's say I wouldn't put it past any of my family to be lurking behind a tree somewhere.'

'So you told them?'

At least her voice appeared to work, even though every one of her senses was focused on the strength of his grip, the feel of his skin against hers.

'Yes...' Zander, too, seemed mesmerised by their clasped fingers, until in an abrupt movement he dropped her hand. 'So it's probably best if we continue this conversation once we are on the river.'

'Good plan.'

It was an activity to focus on, and for a moment she did exactly that. Studied the row of wooden boats bobbing on the water—punts, skiffs and canoes.

'Which one shall we hire?'

'A skiff. I'm happy to row, or we can take turns.'

'You go first and then I'll try, depending on how easy it is. I don't want to capsize.'

Ten minutes later they climbed on to a long, varnished wooden boat and Gabby could see the owner had been right. The graceful slender craft was built for speed, but was also wide enough for stability and comfort.

Zander sat in the centre, an oar in each hand, and she settled herself against the traditional wicker backrest and tried to visualise the instructions they had been given. 'So I can help steer by using these lines?'

'Yup. They're connected to the rudder. But don't worry about it too much. When I came here with my sisters, their attempts at steering nearly capsized us.'

'Hmm… Well, I'll do my best—though, to be honest, I'm quite happy to just keep a lookout for otters.'

In reality, for the next five minutes, her gaze was focused exclusively on observing Zander row, watching the flex of his muscular forearms, the strength and sculpt of his biceps. She tried to tell herself that her entrancement was due to the necessity for study, for learning the technique for when she came to take the oars herself. She knew that theory held not an iota of truth—she could only hope she wasn't drooling.

Enough. Time to recall exactly why they were here. 'So, how did your family take the news about "us"?'

'They were all thrilled.'

Try as she might, she couldn't interpret either his expression or his tone—relief, ruefulness, regret or all three? 'That's good, right?'

'Yes. They are happy, and they have abandoned their plans to hook me up with every female of their acquaintance.'

'I sense a *but*.'

'Not a *but*, exactly. More of a realisation that I've rolled the dice and the game has begun. Now it is imperative that we make this work.'

'Yes.'

Gabby could hear the fervour in her own voice. After all, she knew how it felt to build up a fantasy world that collapsed about you in a rubble of disillusionment. When she had been small, and her mother had constantly left her with her grandparents, appearing and reappearing in her life with bewildering uncertainty, Gabby hadn't understood why.

Her grandparents had wanted to spare her pain and so had allowed Gabby to believe in the scenarios she'd created. That her mother was ill but missed her so very much. Or was away working somewhere where children weren't allowed. Occasionally her imagination went into fantastical overdrive and she made her mother a princess, a mermaid...

Eventually, though, the bubble had burst, and the grim reality of the time she spent with her mother—the dirt, the grime, the empty alcohol bottles and drug paraphernalia—were all things she couldn't weave into her fantasies. So she'd confronted her grandparents and forced them to tell her the truth. It had truly shattered her world. Made her feel stupid, angry and sad, and hurt by the deceit. The feelings had been made all the worse because she hadn't been able to express them to her grandparents, afraid she would lose them, too.

'Gabby?'

'Sorry.' Gabby tried to push away the onslaught of qualms and concentrated on the swish of the oars in the water. This illusion bore no similarity to those of her childhood. Yet... 'Are you sure about this, Zander? Maybe you should come clean now. Before this goes further. If they find out, they'll feel hurt and stupid.'

For a second he hesitated, his dark eyes serious as he considered her words, and then he shook his head. 'No. The die is cast. Now we need to play our parts with conviction.'

'Then let's get to work. If we want to make this believable, the detail is important. We have to fabricate this so well that *we* almost believe it's true.'

That was a fact. Sometimes she even wondered if her whole personality was based on a part she had played for so long that it had become the truth.

'What exactly did you tell your family about me? I need to figure out what they're expecting.'

'I said I bumped into you in town, remembered you from school. We got chatting, had a coffee and things went from there. I said that we both agree we're not looking for anything serious, just some uncomplicated fun. Mum and Dad are pleased. Julia is worried you're after my money—that you staged the meeting—and Gemma hopes it will turn serious. That's because Julia is a cynic and Gemma is a romantic.'

'Great. So Julia will check my bag for a gold-digging shovel and Gemma will expect me to fall at your feet adoringly.'

'Nope. I sorted it. I told them neither scenario is the truth—that you aren't after my wallet or my heart, just my body.'

Gabby closed her eyes in silent horror.

'And I wiggled my eyebrows.'

'Suggestively, no doubt? So they now think I'll rip your clothes off in public?'

Nice one, Gabs. With any luck she'd be tipped overboard and get swallowed up by the depths of the river.

'You could try it and see.'

Was he laughing at her? *Yup.* Her mortification had triggered an upward quirk of his lips and his eyes had a wicked glint that turned her knees wobbly.

'In your dreams!'

'Probably,' he agreed, and her cheeks heated as she narrowed her eyes at him.

'You need to take this seriously!'

Yet it wasn't possible not to smile back, not to revel in the flirtatious undertones, the shimmer of attraction that vested their conversation with a thrill.

'I am. This is part of getting in character—you said we need to almost believe it ourselves. Two people in a fun, flirty relationship where we kick back and enjoy ourselves. Have a bit of banter. That's what a fun fling is all about, isn't it?'

'I wouldn't know.' To her own irritation she could hear wistfulness in her voice.

His lips twisted ruefully. 'Neither would I.'

Realisation dawned on her that he wouldn't. This guy was a one-woman man, and that in itself sent a cascade of emotion through her, a glow not of desire but warmth. *Stop!* Lust was bad enough. Warmth was not an affordable emotion.

Before she could stop herself she asked, 'So since Claudia you really haven't dated anyone? Or seen anyone? Or…done anything with anyone?' *Very subtle, Gabs.*

'No, I haven't.' He leant the oars against the side of the boat, that amused glint back in his eyes. 'If you're asking what I think you're asking—no, I haven't. Slept with anyone.'

'Oh.'

Gabby *knew* she should leave it, but she was having a little difficulty with the whole concept.

'I understand that you loved Claudia very much and you want to remain faithful to her memory…'

The boat jolted as Zander resumed rowing, his actions jerkier than before, the amused glint vanished.

'But surely you don't plan to remain celibate all your life? I mean, *why* haven't you had a fun fling? For real? Or a one-night stand?'

For a moment she wasn't sure he'd answer, wasn't sure she should have asked. Then he shrugged.

'I've been busy. These past five years I've put all my energy into my business. It hasn't been a deliberate choice as such to avoid women, but I haven't had the time or the inclination to indulge in any sort of a relationship.'

The word was said as if it were a contagious disease rather than an indulgence.

'So that's me. What about you? I gather you aren't a fan of fun flings. But what about past relationships?'

Damn. Now she really regretted asking him anything, because she could hardly refuse to reciprocate. Though she could at least prevaricate…

'My turn to row, I think.'

'Sure.'

It was only then that she realised her mistake, because now they had to swap places, manoeuvre past each other. Rising, she tried to steady herself as the skiff bobbed on the water, and for a moment she wondered if she'd topple over. Then, in one lithe movement, Zander stood up, somehow balanced his weight so that the skiff itself seemed to steady, and his hands were on her waist, steadying her.

Chill, Gabby.

Zander was holding her for practical reasons, to help her get her balance. But, *hell*, it didn't feel like that. Her body's reaction was downright *personal*, and the cotton of her T-shirt was a flimsy barrier as they carefully edged their way round in a circle, their bodies close. Her heartbeat echoed in her ears. It was a Herculean effort not to close the gap between them.

Finally he released her, and she lowered herself into the vacated seat and picked up the oars. She watched the ripples in the water and glanced at the trees that fringed the lake, their branches swaying in the slight breeze, the different shades of green redolent of new beginnings and growth. She looked anywhere but at Zander until she had her breathing back under control.

'Right. Past relationships. There are two. Steve and Miles. Neither worked out.'

Sometimes she still wasn't sure why. It was as though at some point someone had handed out a rule book when she hadn't been there and no one had bothered to send it to her. No matter how hard she tried she hadn't been able to figure out how to play her part right, and the harder she'd tried, the more clingy and insecure she'd become.

Both Steve and Miles had been good, solid, ordinary blokes, and both had ended the relationship, citing the whole "it's not you, it's me" argument, having met someone else. Steve had explained that when he'd met his new love there had been a spark that had been lacking with Gabby. Miles had used terminology such as 'fizzled out'. Gabby was no fool and she could spot a pattern—in the context of relationship fireworks, she was a damp squib. So she had decided to leave the display and opt for singledom.

'So I've put relationships on hold.' Until maybe someday when that rule book arrived.

'So for you a fun fling would be out of the question on principle?'

Well, didn't *that* make her sound boring? And suddenly for a minute, as the sun glinted on the water and the sound of the oars swished in her ears, she wished she could throw caution to the wind and be the sort of person who could kick back and enjoy herself.

'It's not a principle. It just doesn't work for me.' Her mum had seen parenting as a short-term, temporary thing. Had worshipped at the altar of fun. 'Short-term makes me feel like I'm not up to scratch. Not good enough to be permanent.'

Even as she said the words she regretted them—better to be judged boring than pathetic.

'Not me personally,' she added. 'I mean in general.'

The slight quirk of his eyebrow indicated doubt. 'But surely that is only if the fling isn't on equal terms? If you want it to be more permanent and the other person doesn't then, yes, I get that. But if you *both* agree you want something temporary then that isn't a judgement on either of you.'

'I guess I just don't *do* temporary.' There had been way too much of that in her life. Temporary stints with her mother, temporary stays with her grandparents. The fear of going into temporary care. As far as she was concerned, temporary sucked, and it smacked of not being good enough. After all, she hadn't been good enough for her mum to change her lifestyle.

'Whoa! Slow down, Gabby.'

Huh?

'Oh.' Belatedly she realised that she was moving them along at breakneck speed. Worse, there was a boat headed towards them and she seemed to have rowed straight on to a collision course. 'Sorry.'

Zander steered and she rowed and, to her relief, the two crafts squeaked past each other without mishap.

'You OK?'

'I'm fine.' But it was time to get back on track. 'Anyway, it's going to be really hard to get *anyone* to believe either of us is up for a fun fling, let alone your family. So we need to get down to the nitty-gritty detail.' She glanced round the boat. 'I need to take notes, so perhaps we should stop at a riverside pub and see if we can find a secluded corner...'

CHAPTER FIVE

TWENTY MINUTES LATER Zander handed Gabby the orange juice she'd requested and seated himself opposite her in the shade of a willow tree in a corner of the pub garden.

'Right…'

As she pushed a stray tendril of glossy hair away she looked endearingly pretty, and he squashed the urge to lean over and tuck another escaped strand behind her ear.

'First, tell me about this charity event.'

'Its aim is to raise funds for a dyslexia awareness charity, and help promote the need for early recognition in schools.'

'I see.' But both her frown and her tone indicated surprise. 'I assumed that it would be connected to Claudia?'

Zander shook his head. 'I donate privately to a cancer charity and I have set up a medical scholarship in Claudia's name.'

Of course he had considered hosting fundraisers in Claudia's memory, but in truth he'd bottled it. Unable to face the sympathy, the need to relive those last months of her life, the complexities of his emotions around his marriage and her death.

'So why dyslexia?'

'Because, whilst it isn't a life-threatening illness, its impact can be devastating.'

Her hazel eyes surveyed him. 'That sounds like a knowledge born of experience.'

'It is. I'm dyslexic. I was diagnosed very late, and for a long time I believed I was stupid.'

His stomach hollowed in memory of the awful gnaw

in its pit as his childhood self had stared at the jumble of shapes in front of him, desperately trying to rearrange them, to work out what they meant. Of the shameful, humiliating knowledge that around him everyone else could do it. Could see it. Could manage it. Could read and write. But he couldn't.

'I'm sorry.'

Sincerity shone from her eyes and he suspected his attempt at a neutral expression and factual tone had backfired.

'I'm not dyslexic, so I can't understand how that feels and I won't pretend to understand. But I *do* know how it feels to believe you're stupid, and it sucks. For a variety of reasons I missed a lot of school, and by the time my attendance became regular I was far behind everyone else. I dreaded every lesson, knew my ignorance would be exposed. In the end my grandparents paid for a private tutor and I caught up. I know it's not the same, but I know it must have been tough for you.'

He sensed she didn't usually share this information, and without thought he reached out and covered her hand in his. 'It sounds like it was tough for us both.'

Her proximity, the softness of her hand under his, the slenderness of her wrist, the warmth in her eyes, the almost impossible length of her eyelashes, the curve of her lips all combined to throw him for a loop.

Focus. Under the pretext of drinking his coffee, he lifted his hand from hers.

As if that had broken the spell, she frowned. 'How old were you when you were diagnosed? I don't remember you being dyslexic at school. I *do* remember you being cool and popular.'

'I worked at it. And I made sure I excelled at sports.'

He had been on every possible school team. Plus, over

the years he'd learnt to mask his dyslexia—persuaded friends to write his essays, made out he didn't care that he was failing, messed around in class to be cool, figured out ways to slip under the radar.

'And then I got lucky. When I was seventeen, at college, with hardly any GCSEs to my name, my football coach figured it out—and I got diagnosed with dyslexia. Late, but not too late. Not everyone is so lucky.'

Enough of his life story.

'So I thought I'd organise a fundraiser. My family have all pitched in to help. Alessio can't be there, as he has an event, but he has donated his yacht as the venue. The tickets have all been purchased. There will be an auction and a four-course dinner, music and dancing, and *Glossip* is writing it up.'

He'd swear she'd turned a greyish shade of pale, but she gave a small determined nod.

'I'll do my best to play my part. Could you let me have a copy of the guest list?'

'No problem.'

'And could you tell me more about your family? Just some background and a quick character sketch.'

'My mum was a nurse. She retired a couple of years ago. She always said she would have loved to be a doctor, but her family didn't support that. She had a difficult start in life, and as a result she wasn't in a position to get into medical school. My dad is an electrician, also retired, and has discovered a late-life interest and talent for golf. There wasn't a lot of money when I was growing up, but there was a lot of encouragement and heaps of expectation. My sisters thrived—Julia is a human rights lawyer and Gemma is a surgeon.'

Gabby looked slightly daunted and he couldn't blame

her. As a child that was how *he'd* felt. Two high-achieving siblings and then there was Zander. The Failure.

'We grew up in Bath and my parents still live here. Julia, Gemma and I all live and work in London, but we come back to visit often. Julia is divorced with two kids, and somehow manages to juggle everything because she's scarily efficient. Gemma is the one getting married in a few weeks. She's very career-oriented and we didn't think she would ever want to settle down. Then Alessio swept her off her feet.'

'He's your best friend, right? Does that bother you? Your best mate and your sister?'

'Nope.'

In truth, it terrified him, because he no longer believed in happy-ever-after. He knew with bone-deep certainty that people changed, that love could wither away. But it was an opinion he couldn't share. Not without bursting the illusory bubble of his own happy-ever-after. The only consolation was that at least Claudia had never suspected his doubts, his frustration, the cold, growing realisation that he had made a mistake. He didn't want that for his friend or his sister; hoped it wouldn't happen to them.

'I'm happy for them.'

Expression intent, Gabby scribbled in her notebook, her handwriting a series of loops and generous curves. 'Tell me a bit about your sister's children.'

'Freddy is seven and Heidi is five, and they're small balls of energy who never stop talking and are interested in everything. I looked after them for a weekend last month and by the end of it I was a wreck. Good for nothing but a cup of cocoa and a nine o'clock bedtime.'

He could hear the affection in his own voice, and clearly so could Gabby.

'Sounds like you're a great uncle. You're lucky. Your

family sounds amazing.' The wistfulness in her voice was unmistakable.

'They are.' Zander hesitated and then continued. 'What about you? Are you an only child? I don't know the details, but at school Claudia did mention that you lived with your grandparents.'

'Yes.' Her voice was flat. 'My parents died. My grandparents were wonderful and they agreed to take me on. They were brilliant. Truly brilliant. At the time Gran was seventy and Gramps was seventy-two. It would have been completely understandable if they had decided it was too much. Instead they gave me security and love. I owe them a great deal. Gramps died several years ago. I still miss him, but obviously Gran was devastated. They were married for over sixty-five years.' Her voice was soft now, and a look of admiration touched with sorrow filled her eyes. 'They married when Gran was nineteen and Gramps was twenty-one. How incredible is that?'

'That *is* incredible.'

Sadness touched him now—at the knowledge that it was possible to grow old together, to marry young but make it through. But not for him. He knew that now. Because he was governed by an ambition that took precedence over everything and everyone—even now, when he had achieved so much, he wanted more. To grow the business, make it global, show everyone that he was the best. That was his priority, and he *knew* any relationship couldn't compete.

'I'm sorry.' Her voice was soft. 'I didn't mean to remind you of the chance you lost.' She hesitated. 'I asked Gran once whether if Gramps had died younger there could have been anyone else.'

'What did she say?'

'She said yes. She said that even now, aged ninety, she wouldn't ever discount the chance to love. She said that it would have been a different love, because it would have been with a different person, but that love is always worth having. That if she had gone first she would have wanted Gramps to be happy and would have hoped he'd find love again.'

'I understand that. For me, though, I am truly happier on my own. Not because I disagree with your gran, but because I am a different person now and a relationship is no longer what I want.'

'For ever? What about children? The way you spoke about Freddy and Heidi... You clearly love them.'

'I do. But that doesn't make me good father material.'

That was an absolute. Claudia had wanted children but Zander had prevaricated. Had put his business ambitions first. With the result that Claudia had missed out on motherhood.

'I am a self-confessed workaholic. There's no point having a family you never see.'

Time to shift focus away from him; this wasn't a discussion he wanted to get into.

'What about you? Do you want the whole package? Mr Right and 2.4 kids? With a white picket fence thrown in?'

'Yes. I do want children. But only with Mr Right. I know there is no guarantee of either, but that's my aim. If I have children I want to believe I can give them everything. Security, love, a brilliant dad and a stable family life.'

Further evidence, if any were needed, that he and Gabby were poles apart in their life goals.

Gabby blinked, picked up her pen and clicked the end. 'We seem to have got distracted.'

Zander shook his head. 'Not really. If we were really having a fun fling, we would have discussed all this. To make sure neither of us had false expectations of the other. I'd need you to know I'm not your Mr Right.'

'I think I'd have figured that out by now. So, now we need to convince everyone that we are Mr and Ms Right for Now but Not Right for Ever.' A smile curved her lips. 'It's not very catchy, is it?'

His gaze snagged on her mouth and he forced himself to focus on his coffee. He sipped it and almost welcomed the bitter coldness of the dregs. 'So what next?'

'I need to look the part. I have no idea what fun flings wear.'

'I don't think there is a dress code.' Seeing her hazel eyes cloud in genuine worry, he was aware that he wanted that smile back and clicked his fingers. 'I've got it! Get that bunny suit back and we're set. I'll even wear a matching pink bow tie and socks.'

Her eyes widened and he gave a sudden crack of laughter. 'If you could see your face! I'm not serious.'

'Thank goodness. But could you imagine it?' There was a moment of contemplation and then she gave a small, delicious gurgle of laughter. 'You could go for matching bunny ears. That would convince your family you'd gone bonkers.'

He had a sudden vision of his family's bemused expressions and joined in her laughter. When was the last time he'd laughed like this? Dammit—he couldn't remember.

Eventually she subsided, and worry shadowed those hazel eyes again. 'Seriously, though, I don't want to look wrong.'

'You won't.' And he meant it. Sitting opposite him, her make-up-free face touched by sunshine and laughter, her glossy chestnut hair gleaming and dappled, she looked beautiful. 'Whatever you wear you'll be…' *Beautiful.* 'Fine.'

'It's not that simple. I don't want to stand out… I—' Breaking off, she shook her head. 'Don't worry. This isn't your problem. I'll do some research and figure out how to fit in.' *Deep breath.* 'But it's not just about clothes. It's about how we act around each other. Should we be lovey-dovey? Hold hands and gaze at each other in adoration? Or opt for smouldering?'

Momentary panic touched him—a sudden realisation of what he had got himself into—and he could see the echo of anxiety cloud her eyes. The thought of love and adoration, even of the counterfeit variety, made him cringe. But it was too late for reservations now—the whole point of this charade was that it had to carry conviction.

'Option three is our best bet, I think. This is all about attraction.'

Now the clouds in her eyes stormed. 'You make it sound so easy. It isn't. When we walk on to this yacht peopled by celebrities and your family, no one will believe this. I could smoulder all I want—all that will happen is my dress will scorch. *No one* is going to buy this.'

Panic escalated in her voice, shone from her wide hazel eyes, and he recognised the signs of a person about to back out of a deal. 'Gabby? Slow down. Listen to me. I really don't think we'll have a problem. I could probably get people to invest in our smoulder factor.'

'You don't understand…'

'Maybe not. But I do understand this.'

Instinct took over and he twisted his chair to face her, angled himself into exactly the right position to lean forward and claim her lips.

A small gasp escaped her, and then without hesitation she pressed against him, her lips parted and her hands twined round his neck. Then he was lost, the last vestiges of common sense fled, and all he could think about was the moment, the vanilla scent of her hair that tickled his cheek with exquisite softness, the tang of citrus on her lips, the fierceness of his desire for her. For Gabby.

The intensity was too much—until the sound of laughter from a group of people as they sat down at a nearby table penetrated the fog, pulled him back to reality and the realisation that if they didn't stop he wouldn't be able to. Even so, pulling away was way harder than it should be, and the level of reluctance blared a klaxon of warning.

This was meant to be fake. The kiss was supposed to have been a tactical exercise to keep Gabby at the table, in the deal.

They sat for a moment and simply gazed at each other, until she gave a small half laugh followed by a muttered curse. 'I don't know what else to say. That was…'

'Awesome?'

'An awesome mistake.'

'Why?'

'Because neither of us wants to make this real.' She touched her lips as if in wonder. 'And that was real. A more important reality, though, is that you don't want the complication of any sort of relationship with anyone, and I'm—'

'Waiting for Mr Right.'

And she didn't do temporary. Both absolutely excellent reasons why that kiss should never have happened. Gabby had made it more than clear that she didn't want a purely physical relationship. She was holding out for the real thing. What her grandparents had had. What he knew he couldn't offer. Hell, what he didn't even *want* to offer. So…

'You're right. I shouldn't have kissed you.'

Yet it was nigh on impossible for him to regret it.

'Hey. There are two of us at the table. But it can't happen again.'

'You're right. No more kisses.' A nascent emotion that he knew to be regret surfaced and he pushed it down. 'But we will have to play our parts, and that will necessitate a certain level of closeness.' *Heaven help him.*

'I understand that.'

Somehow he had to get this back on to a business footing, because right now—*dammit*—he wanted to kiss her again. *Madness.*

'Then we're good to go. You need to give me your bank details. This…arrangement…will continue until my sister's wedding in three months, so I'll pay you in three monthly instalments. I'll also set out a schedule of our dates, starting with the charity event on Friday.'

Gabby clicked her pen again, the sound a signal of her relief at the turn of the conversation. 'OK. Shall I meet you there?'

'No. Seeing as the gala is in London, it will be easier and look better if you come to my flat before. You can get ready there and stay the night after. I have two spare rooms you can choose from, which will make it less awkward than our staying in a hotel—if that's OK with you.'

The idea of Gabby in his apartment already felt heavy with awkward portent. The idea of *any* woman there filled him with unease; the idea of *Gabby* there gave him a severe case of the collywobbles.

And, although she nodded in agreement, the agitated *click-click-click* of her pen indicated that the collywobbles were mutual.

CHAPTER SIX

GABBY STOOD OUTSIDE the imposing block that overlooked the Thames—the whole edifice was ridiculously over-whelming. The thought of the combined worth of all the apartments made her eyes cross.

The butterflies that had occupied her tummy for the better part of the day swooped and dived. For most of the week she had toyed with the idea of backing out, all the while knowing she wouldn't. She couldn't walk away from the money for her grandmother's sake, and wouldn't renege on a deal for the sake of her own pride. Yet the knowledge that in a moment she would enter a penthouse apartment on the edge of the Thames, and would then attend a celebrity charity gala with Zander, felt madly surreal. Too much.

Her arm felt heavy as she buzzed for entry, then pushed the communal door open, entered the state-of-the-art lift and pressed the button for the sixth floor.

Seconds later the lift door opened and Zander stood outside, clad in jeans and a T-shirt, barefoot, his dark blonde hair shower-damp. Her heartbeat escalated.

'Hey.'

'Hey. Come on in.'

The words were polite, but she sensed a reluctance that matched her own as he led her to his flat and pushed open the heavy-looking door. Somehow the act of stepping over the threshold felt stupidly personal, an invasion of his privacy.

Shaking off the sensation—this was all Zander's idea, after all—she looked around with burgeoning curiosity.

The hall stretched forward in its immensity, with rooms off to the sides. Yet it wasn't just the size she noted—it was the utter starkness of the decor, the swathes of beige on the wall not enlivened by a mirror, a picture—anything. The luxurious cream carpet ran clear, with hardly any furniture to impede its length.

'Would you like a cup of tea, coffee—something stronger?'

'No. Thank you.' Suddenly the sheer size of the apartment combined with his presence brought on a desire to escape. 'It's probably best if I go straight to get ready. I don't want to make us late.'

A quick nod of his head and he set off down the hall before pausing outside a door. 'Here you go.'

An hour later Gabby paced up and down the bedroom— the size at least allowed scope for long strides—and paused in front of the mirror. *Again.* Stared at her reflection. *Again.* Wondered whether she'd got this all wrong. *Again.*

Panic at the idea of all those guests—the rich and famous, the reporters from *Glossip*, the photographers and Zander's family—*everyone* watching her, twisted her insides. They would all see through her. They would know that she was an impostor. Especially in this dress. What had she been thinking?

Chill out. Hopefully the herbal remedy she'd taken to calm her anxiety would soon kick in. The concoction bought from her local health food shop had come highly recommended by a student who suffered from exam nerves, and Gabby had figured she might as well give it a try.

Resisting the urge to recommence the pacing, she studied her image instead and started to talk herself off the ledge of anxiety, exactly as her childhood self had done.

First, she looked at her surroundings, focused on objects and decor—an exercise in grounding. The bedroom continued the beige theme, and the room was furnished as if from a tick list. Double bed, wardrobe, bedside cabinets. *The End.* The room had an unused feel to it, and she couldn't help but wonder if she was its first ever occupant.

Next she turned her attention back to her reflection. The dress was fine—it suited her and muted her, would hopefully allow her to fade away into the background. For better or worse, she'd decided to go the high-street route. She had visited the most exclusive boutique in Bath and been unable to justify the prices, despite the generous expenses allowance Zander had transferred into her account. She'd donated most of it to the dyslexia charity Zander was supporting.

In truth, it hadn't all been altruism—the thought of wearing one of those expensive designer dresses had brought the aphorism 'mutton dressed as lamb' to mind. Although she knew in theory she would fit in better if she wore the same sort of thing as the other guests, in reality she knew it wouldn't work like that—in some way she would still be recognised as an impostor. Better to remain true to herself, play the part of a temporary fling who didn't want to be dressed by her...lover.

Lover. The word brought the panic back in a waterfall of nerves, and she focused on the dress itself.

Black. Strapless. Long. Bodice boning ensured the top half contoured her curves. The satin skirt fell to the floor in a satisfying sweep and swish of elegance and modesty. Her hair fell in a simple curtain to her bare shoulders, her make-up was a study in the art of discretion.

Somehow she would get through the evening, pull off

this nonsensical fantasy and *this time tomorrow it will all be over.* Plus, she had a new secondary mantra in place now—*think of the money.*

The reminder steadied her. Because at the end of the day, no matter what personal humiliation or social anxiety she had to endure, she'd get to walk away with enough money to ensure her grandmother would get the care she deserved. So she would hold nerves at bay and go and do the job she had agreed to do.

After all, she'd played a role before when the stakes had been way higher—the part of a well-adjusted child when she'd been an inner wreck. So this would be fine.

Yet the knock at the bedroom door triggered a further burst of butterflies, along with a stupid thrill of anticipation. *Ridiculous.*

She pulled the door open and stepped outside into the hall. The anticipation was justified—one look at him and all her brain could think was, *Yum.* Every instinct told her to use her arms to pull him up close and personal. Every instinct except the one of self-preservation. But Zander looked gorgeous—the tuxedo emphasised every lithe muscle, added a devil-may-care twist to his dark good looks, emphasised by the glint of his dark blonde hair.

The silence lengthened and she stepped backwards, reminding herself that they could not let physical attraction overcome common sense. And yet a deep yearning sparked inside her, curiosity as to what it would be like simply to succumb. To grasp the lapels of his tux, drag him towards her, kiss him senseless and pull him into the bedroom.

As if. That would be so far out of character that she would suspect she'd been possessed. So instead she said, with a brightness that rung false, 'Hey!'

'Hey…'

It occurred to her that despite the aura of drop-dead gorgeousness he was nervous—acting as awkwardly as it was possible for Zander Grosvenor to be. *Oh, God.* Had he taken one look at her and realised what she'd been trying to tell him all along? That she couldn't cut the mustard—or any other condiment for that matter? That no one would believe this ridiculous charade?

'You look great,' he said eventually.

Yet she didn't believe him as he shifted his weight from foot to foot, his stance the epitome of discomfort. Was it her? She needed to know the truth.

'If I don't look right you need to tell me. We can't make this work if I look wrong.' If she was not a plausible date for Zander Grosvenor.

Zander frowned, gave his head a small shake and then he looked at her—properly looked at her—and her skin rippled with a shiver of desire.

'You don't look wrong. You look fantastic.' A small smile tipped his lips. 'I promise. This will work. We've *got* this.'

His voice deep, full of promise of a different type, and there it was again, that desire to close the gap and kiss him. But that way lay a road she would not walk—she could not be an interlude, a temporary rung on his ladder to getting over Claudia.

Claudia. The reminder was stark—and needed.

'Thank you. Now, we'd better go.'

We've got *this... We've* got *this... We've* got *this.*

As Zander drove with easy competence through the London streets Gabby concentrated on the role she would play. This was no different from her careful preparations before each social worker's visit, her daily preparations when she'd first moved in with her grandparents. She'd moulded herself a persona back then and she would use those skills to pull this off.

But once they'd parked, left the car and made their way to their destination, doubts began to slip into her conviction. And as she saw the looming yacht docked in the river she could feel her confidence seep away, escape into the night air and be blown away by the cool breeze.

This was not her milieu—the vessel was too enormous, too redolent of wealth as it glittered and illuminated the water of the Thames and the surrounding London landscape. But this was the world Zander inhabited and was comfortable in.

A glance sideways at him and there it was: the palpable shiver of desire. Suddenly the zing of attraction seemed stark in its utter stupidity, and a swell of panic washed over her at the enormity of the deception they had embarked upon. But it was too late now to turn and run, so somehow she'd have to tough it out.

This time tomorrow it will all be over. Think of the money.

Side by side they boarded the yacht and she braced herself, feeling the warmth of his hand on the small of her back. The heat of his touch through the thin material of her dress sent a message to her whole body, almost like a brand, as she gazed round in wonder.

The enormous wood-decked function room was bathed in light. Chandeliers and fairy lights combined to cast a magical glow of illumination. Glass-topped tables were strategically placed and suited waiters and elegant waitresses were ready to be deployed, standing next to a long table that sparkled with champagne glasses and carried silver trays of canapés.

Then the surroundings faded into irrelevance as a group of people approached them.

The Grosvenor family.

Smile. Remember your role. Play the part.

'Mum, Dad, Julia, Gemma… This is Gabby. Gabby, this is my mum, Laura, my dad, Frank, and my two sisters, Julia and Gemma.'

Gabby looked at each of them in turn, saw the appraisal in their eyes, homed in on each and every nuance. She knew she would need to read them effectively. 'It's lovely to meet you.'

Keep it cool. Talk, but not too much. Listen carefully and say what they want to hear.

All the old rules were still in play.

'And you, Gabby. We've been looking forward to it.'

Zander stepped forward. 'OK. As we discussed, there'll be plenty of time to talk later. But now it's all men and women to the pumps. I'll greet the guests as they arrive— the rest of you mingle and make sure everyone's happy. Any glitches, come and find me. Also, do your best to promote the auction items—subtly.' As they had prearranged, he glanced at Gabby. 'Will you be all right?'

'Of course, darling.'

The word was said as naturally as if she used it every day. *Damn*, she still had it. She could still play a part even if it made her nerves sizzle with anxiety. Even if this was a part that went against every particle of her character.

'You go—and if there's anything I can do to help just shout. Don't worry about me.'

A brief nod and he disappeared. Gabby took a deep breath and turned to face the Grosvenors.

'Have you had a chance to look at the auction details?' Frank asked.

She heard the kindness in his voice and knew he was trying to set her at ease. 'Yes, and I think the list is incredible.'

Items included a luxury weekend break in Portugal, a painting by a famous artist, a share in a yacht, a designer necklace from one of London's most prestigious jewellers and an afternoon driving a racing car with Alessio Bravanti himself. Each item was another reminder of the wealth of the guest list.

'I'll definitely do my best to promote it, but I think it will speak for itself.'

Now Laura smiled. 'I'm sure you'll do a great job.'

Before she could say more, a couple came towards them with cries of greeting, and both Laura and Frank stepped forward.

'I hope we have time to talk more later, Gabby,' said Laura.

'That leaves you with us.' Julia smiled at Gabby. Her tone was friendly but her smile didn't reach her ice-blue eyes.

Gemma darted a frown at her sister and chimed in. 'Zander asked us to make sure you're OK whilst he greets the guests, and we thought we could use the time to get to know each other better, too.'

A waiter eased by, offering a tray of champagne cocktails, and Gabby took one, pretty sure that fun flings didn't ask for orange juice or a nice cup of tea at events such as this. Though she'd make sure she stuck to non-alcoholic beverages after this one—she had no intention of risking letting the mask slip.

'So…' Julia said, and Gabby tried and failed not to feel intimidated.

Julia Grosvenor would be formidable in court. Zander's eldest sister was scarily elegant, her blonde hair swept into an immaculate chignon, the ice-blue dress a vivid echo of her eye colour and a perfect showcase for her figure.

She studied Gabby with disconcerting appraisal. 'Zander tells me the two of you met recently and hit it off.'

'Yes. We were at school together, though I was in the year below him. We bumped into each other in Bath and things went from there.'

'A chance meeting?' The question was civil, but the faintest stress on the word *chance* indicated waves of scepticism.

'Come on, Jules,' Gemma interpolated. 'This isn't a courtroom and we haven't got time for a whole series of questions. Why don't we cut to the chase?'

Like Zander, Gemma was dark blonde, tall and slender, and tonight she was dressed in a deep red gown.

'We all want to know what your intentions are.'

The direct approach—Gabby welcomed it. 'I don't have any,' she said. 'We've only just started to see each other. I like Zander and he likes me, but neither of us is looking for anything serious.'

Stop there. Don't overdo it.

Both women were looking at her—two super successful, intelligent women, used to judging and evaluating people in their different fields. Yet she had told them nothing but the slightly shaded truth.

Julia studied her for a long moment. 'If that's true, then go for it,' she said. 'Zander deserves some fun.'

Gemma smiled. 'On that note, as you have probably noticed my brother is a workaholic. Anything you can do to persuade him away from the office would be much appreciated! Now, we need to mingle...'

Soon enough they were engulfed, and Gabby's plans to embrace invisibility were scuppered by people eager to meet Zander Grosvenor's date. Panic threatened again, but Gabby combated it with a steely determination not to make a fool of herself *or* Zander. He'd trusted her to hold her own and she would play her part.

Yet her nerves twisted and tied into knots, and as the evening progressed the scenario felt more and more surreal. The pop of champagne corks, the glitter of the women's jewellery in the light of the chandeliers, the flash of expensive watches under the sleeves of designer tuxes, the conversations with their casual mention of royalty, celebrities and share portfolios made her dizzy.

To her relief, though, most people, whilst clearly curious, were also courteous—until...

Gabby sensed trouble as a red-haired woman glided towards her with a speculative, near-malicious smile on her lips.

'Hello, Gabby. I just *had* to meet you. The woman who has lured Zander Grosvenor from his monk's cell.'

Gabby tensed; she recognised the woman as a grown-up version of the playground girls who had made her life miserable as a child, with their loaded comments and taunts.

'I'm Melanie Kilton. So, tell me all about yourself— and how on earth you managed to catch Zander.'

Melanie had a smile on her lips and icicles in her blue eyes. She also had a figure to die for and a plummy voice that spoke of the fact that she'd been born to grace events like this—preferably on the arm of a man like Zander.

'I'm a librarian—' Gabby began, before realising the stupidity of her answer.

Melanie's laughter tinkled. 'How...*stereotypical*. Perhaps you and Zander will be like one of those cheesy romances where the librarian heroine falls in love with the handsome hero?'

Gabby willed her brain to come up with a witty comeback. But in the mirror of her childhood, she stood there, with the sting of humiliation behind her eyelids, willing the ground to open up and swallow her.

'I think you may be mixing up cheesy romance with classic fiction.'

Gabby turned at the sound of Zander's deep voice, half in relief, half in exasperation that she hadn't thought of the riposte herself.

'Hello, Melanie,' he continued. 'I see you haven't changed a bit.'

It seemed clear it wasn't a compliment as the redhead flushed slightly and narrowed her eyes. 'It seems that *you* have,' she said, and flicked a venomous glance at Gabby. 'And your standards have definitely dropped.'

With that she swivelled on a pointy stiletto and walked away. Gabby knew it was irrational, but the words had stung with a poison that made her insides twist.

Your standards have definitely dropped. Was everyone thinking that? Comparing her to Claudia? She knew it was petty, irrational, stupid and unnecessary to make the comparison, but she was. All those feelings of not being good enough resurfaced. But she was damned if she would let anyone see it.

'I'm sorry.' Zander's voice was level.

'What for? All you did was come to my rescue. A rescue I shouldn't have needed. You have nothing to apologise for.'

Dammit, she was snapping at him. Closing her eyes, she inhaled deeply. This wasn't Zander's fault. The issue here was that she was a fish out of water, the mutton in the flock of lambs, the woman who should never have taken the job.

'My turn to say sorry.'

'Forget it. I came to tell you the auction is going to kick off soon.'

She was sure she heard the smallest strain in his voice,

so slight she wouldn't have heard it if her own sensitivities hadn't been so heightened.

'Is something wrong?' she asked. 'Was it what Melanie said about you changing?'

If the words had upset *her*, of course they must have been a hundred times more difficult for him to hear.

'This must be hard for you—everyone believing you're with another woman.'

Especially one who didn't measure up. How many people at this dazzling high-society event were whispering behind their hands, wondering why on earth Zander was with someone so ordinary?

There was a silence, and she couldn't read the expression on his face. Then, 'We need to talk.'

Hand on the small of her back again, he gently ushered her into a secluded corner, shielded from the flow of guests by an exotic arrangement of verdant green potted plants.

Zander stared down into Gabby's hazel eyes, saw the vulnerability he knew she was trying to hide, and knew Melanie's words had hurt her. He knew he couldn't let her believe he was racked with guilt because he felt he was betraying Claudia's memory.

'You're right—something *is* bothering me, but it is nothing to do with Claudia.'

Gabby's forehead creased in bemusement and question. If he prevaricated she wouldn't believe him, so he needed to tell her the truth—how hard could it be? It wouldn't kill him to admit weakness. *Much.*

'I'm nervous.'

Her eyes widened. 'Why?'

'I don't like giving speeches.'

It reminded him too much of being asked to read out

loud at school—the weight of imminent humiliation as the teacher went round the class, the horrible knowledge that it would be his turn next. The fear of having to mark other people's work, his mind and body constantly geared up for fight or flight.

'As in *really* don't like it.'

As in it caused a sensation of nausea, a clamminess-inducing anxiety, a sheer funk that he loathed and had barely tamed into reluctant snarling submission.

To his relief Gabby didn't laugh; instead her expression softened.

'That sucks,' she said. 'How do you manage at work?'

'Avoidance where I can, but at work it is a little easier. I know what I'm doing and I'm the boss.' The last words were stated in a deep drawl, but she didn't smile, clearly recognising the bravado as fake.

'You know what you're doing here, as well. You know it better than anyone. What it feels like and what may help others. I know the facts and the figures—I researched those and the numbers matter—but I don't know what it feels like inside. To be that child, that young adult, that adult with dyslexia. You *do*. That's what you can bring to your audience and they will listen because you care, not because *you da boss*.'

The small smile she gave, the warmth of her voice, the sheer belief in her eyes touched him. Even if it was a touch misplaced. Because his speech focused on facts and figures; he had no intention of making it personal.

But before he could explain that she reached into her small beaded evening bag. 'You could try this, as well.'

'What's that?'

'It's a herbal remedy for anxiety—it helps calm you down. It's new, completely full of natural good things.

Just a couple of drops work wonders. Really. I used it tonight and I'm sure it helps.'

'I need all the help I can get.' Taking the bottle, he took a couple of drops, handed it back.

She placed her hand on his arm. 'You hide it really well,' she said. 'I would never have imagined you were capable of even the tiniest amount of nerves and neither will anyone else.'

'It's more than a tiny amount.' The all-too-familiar flotilla of butterflies looped the loop in his gut. No amount of logic could quell them. 'I'm terrified. Bricking it. Scared. Here. Feel my heart rate.'

Taking her hand, he put it over his chest. *Bad move.* Because as she looked up at him the moment caught light, shimmered around them, and his whole being was preternaturally aware of the feather-light touch of her fingers that seemed to burn through the silk softness of his shirt. Now his heart rate ratcheted up, and this time it was nothing to do with nerves.

'Maybe *I* can help.'

Her voice was a near whisper as she stood on tiptoe and placed her other hand on his chest to steady herself before pressing her lips against his.

The lightest of butterfly kisses skimmed his lips and he closed his eyes and pulled her closer, his hands at her waist. Just as the sound of a throat being cleared caused Gabby to leap backwards so fast she nearly fell over.

Gemma grinned at him. 'Sorry to interrupt, little bro, but it's auction time.'

Zander rolled his eyes at his sister. 'We're on our way.' He waited pointedly until she'd vanished and then looked down at Gabby. 'You OK?'

'Embarrassed—but yes, I'm OK.' Her gaze met his

full-on. 'Right now you need to go and knock them dead. I know you can.'

'Thank you.'

On some level alarm bells clamoured in his head—the idea that events were running away out of his control made his unease torrent. By his reckoning that was kiss number three—and, oddly, it had been more potent even than the two before.

But Gabby was right—he would consider those ramifications later. Now he had a job to do. A speech to make and an auction to run.

They made their way back to their table. Out of the corner of his eye he saw Gemma in conference with their mother, saw their quick speculative looks across at them. On the plus side, at least that kiss should have solidified the illusion that he and Gabby were in a relationship.

Hoping Gabby was correct in her analysis that not a single one of the guests would have so much as an inkling of the nervous energy that coursed through his veins, Zander went and stood on the podium, smiled and began.

He kept his speech measured, his words evenly paced as he focused on the content he had memorised and practised until he was word-perfect. He ensured his words matched the prepared presentation, carefully colour-coded so his brain could decipher and interpret the words his audience could read with ease. He went through the facts and figures, the case studies, hoping his voice was infused with the passion he felt for this subject, and then he did an audience participation exercise in which he handed out notes written in Chinese and asked people to try to read them.

As he came to an end, Gabby's voice echoed in his head. *I don't know what it feels like inside. To be that child, that young adult, that adult with dyslexia. You* do. *That's what you can bring to your audience and they will listen.*

Before he knew it, unrehearsed words began to form in his brain and spill from his mouth.

'Before I wind up, I'd like to make this a little more personal. I have dyslexia myself, and I wasn't diagnosed until my late teens.'

The change in the audience was electric—a low hum that generated a charged silence. Suppressing the urge to gulp, he let the words continue.

'I know exactly what it is like to feel stupid, to feel humiliated, to feel small and awful inside. I was lucky. I got a diagnosis and my family helped me to cope with it. A lot of children don't have that. Equally, though, if I had been diagnosed earlier, it would have made my childhood a much happier, easier place to be. I want other children out there to be given a chance. So dig deep into your wallets—because it's time for the auction!'

Gabby watched as Zander began the auction with the sale of a beautiful landscape painting—a kaleidoscope of colours that evoked the English countryside in such detail that she almost felt she could step into it. But she realised it was *his* pitch that called attention to and emphasised the merit of the artist, made her want to buy the picture, made her appreciate every stroke the artist had touched to the canvas.

He talked, caused laughter and a friendly competitive spirit, encouraged people to bid without being aggressive— it was a masterly performance, made all the more admirable by the speech he had made earlier.

Gabby hugged the knowledge to herself that she and only she knew what it had cost him, the emotions he'd had to master. She realised that she was proud of him.

Whoa. Careful, Gabs.

But right now she didn't want to be careful—and there was nothing wrong with admiration anyway. There were numerous people she admired. Winston Churchill, Mother Teresa, her grandparents… Problem was, she didn't think she'd be studying the way Winston's hair curled on the nape of his neck, or the lithe grace with which he moved. Whereas as she looked at Zander, her tummy was tied in knots of desire.

Next to her, Julia cleared her throat, and Gabby could only pray she hadn't been drooling.

'He's doing a pretty good job, isn't he?'

Turning, Gabby attempted what she hoped was a casual smile. 'Definitely. You have to admire that passion in someone—I think Winston Churchill was the same.'

Had she really said that?

Julia looked slightly puzzled, clearly wondering the same thing, and Gabby hurried on. 'Anyway, it's fantastic to see people having fun and bidding so much.'

As she spoke, the gavel pounded to indicate the painting had gone for an exorbitant sum and Zander moved on.

'Next up is an incredible trip to the sunny climes of Portugal. A romantic three-night trip in…'

Julia nodded. 'I'm not sure if Zander told you, but the reason he decided to do this event wasn't only because of his own dyslexia. It's because my son, Freddy, was diagnosed with it recently, and that seemed to trigger Zander into an absolute determination to do something. He said he wants to show Freddy it's nothing to be ashamed of.'

Great! Something else to admire about the man. Just what Gabby needed. But it was impossible not to appreciate the gesture, the drive to do more than simply offer personal support.

'Freddy's lucky, really—early diagnosis makes an enormous difference. I don't think Mum will ever forgive herself for not working it out sooner with Zander. You see, Gemma and I were high achievers academically and she expected Zander to be the same. To be honest, she was baffled when he wasn't. Never unkind, but her pep talks and lectures and the muted disappointment must have been hard for him. Of course, he's achieved a lot now!'

'Yes. And Zander certainly doesn't seem to blame anyone.'

'We feel guilty all the same. I used to tease him sometimes. Now, when I look at my Freddy and imagine people teasing him, it makes me so mad I could spit.'

Before Gabby could respond, a cheer went up and they looked to the podium as Laura Grosvenor stepped up on to the stage.

'Oh. Mum's won the holiday! She must have got it for her and Dad's anniversary.' Julia smiled fondly at her parents. 'Dad is really quiet, but I don't know what Mum would do without him. He is her rock. I'll just go and congratulate them…'

The rest of the auction items went for equally exorbitant sums, and the gavel pounded a final time to much applause. But before Zander could step down, Laura Grosvenor climbed on to the stage again and took the microphone.

'Sorry, everyone. One last thing. Zander—I am very proud of all you have achieved, tonight and throughout your life. And it occurs to me that you deserve a holiday. So here you go—this is for you. A three-day break to Portugal. And I'm sure we *all* know who you'll be taking!'

As the whole room turned to look at her, Gabby strove to fix a smile of surprise and delight on her lips, even as her brain churned in incoherent panic.

CHAPTER SEVEN

SOMEHOW GABBY REMAINED in role, smile in place, as she watched the scene play itself out on the podium. After a split second of shock, Zander thanked his mother with apparent sincere appreciation, cracked a couple of jokes with an aplomb she could only envy, and then he and his mother descended from the stage.

Stay in role.

Horribly conscious of all the eyes on her, she rose and walked towards Laura, hand outstretched.

'Thank you *so* much. That is amazingly kind of you—though you really shouldn't have included me.'

Laura's gaze went from one to the other of them. 'Why ever not? I've had a look at the conditions and you can go as early as next week if you like.'

Her blue gaze was disconcertingly perceptive—but, charade or no charade, Gabby knew she had to try to wriggle out of this somehow. She might not have been listening completely to the description, but words like *sun-kissed*, *romantic*, *cosy* and *perfect for two* lingered in her memory.

'I feel a little guilty accepting such a generous gift. I mean, you hardly know me.'

'Yes, but I *do* know Zander. And I know he hasn't had a holiday in five years.' The implication hovered in the air. *Since Claudia.* 'All he has done is work. So I would love for him to have some downtime, and now seems like the perfect opportunity.' Laura glanced from one face to the other. 'I'm counting on you, Gabby, to convince Zander that all work and no play is *not* a good thing!'

'I'll try,' Gabby said and wondered if her nose was having a Pinocchio moment. 'But if I can't, then you must promise me that you will accept the holiday back for you and your husband.'

'We came back from a cruise just recently.'

'And *we* don't want it.' Gemma and Julia had materialised.

Gemma continued, 'I've got a wedding to plan and my honeymoon is already booked.'

'I have work commitments, no one to go with and the kids to think of,' Julia pointed out. 'So it's all yours.'

Any more protest would only fuel the suspicion that was already on the verge of sparking, so Gabby tucked her hand into Zander's arm. 'Then all I can do is thank you.'

'You're very welcome.'

The rest of the evening passed in a blur. Zander's proximity as they sat through dinner was both a solace and a menace. Not even the food—marinated salmon, truffle potatoes, a fillet of beef so rare and tender it made sense of the melt-in-the-mouth cliché—could completely distract from her body's reaction to his proximity or the sense of impending doom that the idea of Portugal had brought on.

But Gabby did her best to focus on the job at hand, striving to consolidate the illusion of a relationship and to make the event a success. She told herself that, between them, she and Zander would work out a way to mitigate or better yet wipe out the Portugal disaster.

Finally the last guest departed, the last goodbye was said and only the family were left.

Julia stepped forward and gave Zander a hug. 'Well done, little bro. This was a fabulous event and thank you for doing it. I'll show Freddy the pictures.'

'You do that—and tell him I'll be round soon.'

Turning to Gabby with a smile that made her seem way less scary, Julia added, 'Gabby, it was great to meet you—and if I don't see you before, I'll see you at the wedding. Have a fabulous time in Portugal.'

Gabby smiled, watching the remaining farewells and witnessing the sheer warmth and affection that existed in the Grosvenor family. A part of her felt a yearning for that sort of family closeness. Lord knew she loved her grandmother, but Lucille was all she had. And that meant one day, in the scheme of things, she would be alone. The thought cloaked her in sadness.

Goodbyes finally finished, they made their way to the car. Gabby waited until they were inside, seat belts secured, before she spoke. 'What are we going to do?'

'Drive back to my apartment?'

'I meant about Portugal.'

'I know. I suggest we both try to figure out a strategy and we can talk about it when we get back. But first— thank you for everything you did tonight. You played your part to perfection, but you also did a fantastic job of talking to people about dyslexia. That wasn't part of the deal and I appreciate it.'

'I wanted to help. It's not a topic I've really thought about very much until recently, but the research I did showed me how important a topic it is. And you did, too.'

'I really do believe the more people discuss it and raise awareness the better. So thank you.'

He turned to flash her a quick smile and her tummy flip-flopped, tiredness suddenly forgotten as awareness simmered. And this was in a *car*—what would happen on a romantic beach getaway?

Determinedly closing her eyes, she leant her head back and tried to think of a strategy, a way out. But her brain refused to cooperate; instead, images drifted through her mind of herself and Zander on a beach, sitting on the sand, his fingers massaging sun cream into her back...

'Gabby? We're here.'

Sitting upright, she opened her eyes, blinked fiercely to dispel the lingering stupid fantasy and opened the car door.

They walked through the lobby, into the lift and out again, then into the apartment, and this time she followed him into an enormous living area.

More neutrality here, mixed with a minimalist feel that didn't look like a design choice. It looked like the result of utter disinterest. Two large leather sofas, two chairs, a flat-screen television. A coffee table. More empty walls. No pictures, no photographs, no clutter, no cushions. Bland mixed with impersonal.

It was enough to temporarily distract her from the urgency of the Portugal fiasco and prompt a question. 'Did you only move in recently?'

He looked puzzled as he glanced around the room, as if seeing it through her eyes. 'A couple of years ago. Once I was sure that the business was secure, I figured it made more sense to own than to rent. Alessio persuaded me that a penthouse apartment was what I needed, and it seemed like a good enough investment.'

As he spoke, he tugged off his tie and unbuttoned the top button of his shirt with an exhalation of relief. Gabby's gaze fell on the small triangle of exposed skin and her breath caught in her throat. Her fingers itched with an insane desire to step forward and unbutton the next button, and the next. A reaction presumably brought on by panic and tiredness and his sheer proximity.

'Did you choose the furniture?' It was the best small talk she could conjure up as her gaze focused on his hands, studied the strength of his fingers, the broad wrists, the way he pushed his shirtsleeves up to reveal his muscled forearms.

'Yes.' He frowned. 'I just ordered online. I seem to

spend more time in the office or travelling on business anyway, so this is more than enough for my needs. It's just a place to eat and sleep, really.' As if sensing her bemusement, he folded his arms in an almost defensive position. 'I take it you disagree?'

'It's not that I disagree—it's more that I don't get it. My flat is where I eat and sleep, but I think of it as more than that. It's my *home*.' Her sanctuary. She utterly loved the security, the familiarity, the fact that it existed, was there every day. 'I have a lovely landlord who has let me decorate and paint how I want to. I scoured the markets and charity shops in Bath and I've picked up and restored some gorgeous furniture.'

'So you rent?'

'Yes.'

If she wanted, she could buy rather than rent, but the deposit needed would take all her savings—which were earmarked for care for Lucille. Plus a certain amount of her salary went each month on providing a home help for her gran. But that wasn't something she wanted to discuss with Zander.

She sat down on the armchair, which despite its *meh*-ness was at least comfortable. 'Anyway, we have more important things to discuss. What are we going to do? About Portugal?'

He walked over to a drinks cabinet in the corner of the room. 'Drink?' The suggestion was accompanied by a rueful smile that, despite the situation, made her tummy dip.

'Ha ha!'

'Obviously I am not suggesting drink as an answer to the problem, but I think it may help deaden the pain of my answer. I can offer you whisky or wine.'

'Red wine would be lovely.'

Minutes later he handed her a glass and then sat opposite her. 'We'll have to go.'

'Go?' Her voice reached an octave she'd hitherto thought impossible, and she sipped the rich ruby wine as a palliative.

'Yes.'

To her irrational chagrin, his voice held no enthusiasm. But it did hold conviction.

'Unless you have an idea that would get us out of it without hurting my mother's feelings and unmasking us as impostors.'

'Can't you have a work emergency?'

'Not on a permanent basis.'

'But if we do go…'

Her voice trailed off. If they did go, *what*? They'd end up in bed together? That was ridiculous—she was a grown woman, not an adolescent. Yes, she was attracted to Zander, but surely she could get through three days without actually jumping him?

'Won't it be awkward?'

'It doesn't have to be awkward. Yes, it is meant to be a romantic break, but there won't be anyone watching us. We can spend our time however we like. I was planning on a working weekend, but I can work from anywhere.'

Hurt pinged, along with a sudden sense of outrage that he could be so unaffected, could imagine sitting there and working rather than spending time with her.

But you know he's right.

After all, every time they spent any amount of time in close proximity they ended up in a clinch. Plus, this was a fake romance—so why would he *want* to spend time with her?

Another sip of wine and she studied his expression, wondering if there was just a hint of a clench to his jawline as she told herself that his solution was the correct one. Go to Portugal and spend their time separately. And yet...

'I don't think a working weekend will work. Your family will ask questions when we get back...expect some photographs of us together. Julia strikes me as a woman who likes evidence. More to the point, your mum gave you this holiday in good faith. She wants you to have a break. Surely you owe her at least a credible pretence that you've done that?'

Colour touched his cheekbones and then he nodded. 'You're right. I should have thought of that.' Now his expression was rueful. 'I guess I'm so used to working weekends I've forgotten how to even *fake* a break.' He reached forward and picked up the brochure and the details about the trip. 'I guess we will have to spend some time together after all.'

Well done, Gabby. She'd now persuaded him to spend time with her. A little voice questioned her motives—maybe that was what she actually wanted?

Holding out her hand, she forced her expression to remain cool. 'If you like, I'll do a bit of research...figure out the best things to do.' That way at least she could retain some semblance of control.

'Sure. That would be good.'

Taking care not to so much as brush against his fingers, she took the folder and rose to her feet. 'Now that's settled, if it's OK with you, I'll hit your spare room. I'll be out of your hair first thing tomorrow morning.'

Literally—her plan was to sneak out at daybreak.

'Then, next stop—Portugal.'

A week later, Zander glanced across at Gabby as she clicked her seat belt on and settled back in the luxurious first-class seat. Simply dressed in cropped linen trousers and a blue-and-cream-striped T-shirt, she looked utterly gorgeous.

Over the past days he'd immersed himself in work, taken some time out to spend with his niece and nephew, caught a beer with Alessio—but Gabby had popped into his head with a persistent, disconcerting frequency.

Logic told him that it was all to do with physical attraction, and further informed him that, however mutual the attraction, it would be a bad idea to succumb.

Instinct warned that it would bring complications of the type he didn't want. Gabby had made it more than clear that a short-term relationship was not what she wanted. She wanted a relationship like her grandparents had had. He respected that, but he knew he couldn't offer it. So the best way forward was to keep a lid on the attraction.

He opened his netbook and settled down to work—yet he couldn't resist the occasional glimpse out of the corner of his eye. The gloss of her chestnut hair, the length of her long slim legs, the small frown of concentration that creased her forehead as she read her book...

The two-hour flight was achieved in near silence, broken only by polite banalities over the quality of the food. Gabby had clearly decided the best way to get through their 'romantic break' was the use of platitudes to combat the danger of proximity. It seemed as good a strategy as any.

'Nice airport,' he said as they alighted from the aircraft.

'I don't have a lot of airport experience, but I'm sure you know what you're talking about.'

Their discussion on airports and Tarmac was sustained through customs and baggage control and then segued seamlessly into comments on the hire car.

Once they were en route to Sintra, he sensed Gabby relax, as if now his focus was on driving and navigation she could afford to drop her guard and enjoy the scenery and the heat of the Portuguese sunshine as they made their way to their destination.

And what a destination it was.

Gabby gave a small gasp as they arrived. 'This is... *amazing*. I knew Sintra was in a natural park, with beautiful scenery, but I didn't realise it would be like this.'

Neither had he. Hills covered in lush forest contrasted with a rugged coastline. Verdant greens, azure blues, rich browns all combined in a kaleidoscopic panorama of vibrant colour.

'The villa is on the outskirts of Sintra, so thankfully we don't have to drive through town. The owner recommended walking and using public transport.'

But despite the factual nature of his words, Zander could feel himself relax, too, almost against his will. The scent of eucalyptus and the inexplicable sense of time slowed down pervaded the very air in the car, and for a moment he almost wished this was a real break, a real holiday. That he and Gabby were a real...

He wrenched his thoughts from the impossible and focused on navigating the narrow winding country road that led to the villa.

'Holy moly...' Gabby whispered as they climbed out of the car. Her hazel eyes were wide with wonder, her lips slightly parted. 'It's...fantastical, phantasmal—I mean, I can't believe it's real.'

It truly was idyllic. Whitewashed stone walls, a low roof, a doorway trailing with plants, wooden framed windows that gleamed pristinely, a mosaic patio garden. The scent of pine, the drone of bees, sun-dappled greenery. The villa could have been lifted from a book of fairy tales.

'And look!'

Her hand landed on Zander's bare forearm and the touch sent an instant ripple of sensation over his skin, a tantalising hint of a promise that he knew couldn't be kept.

The expression on her face was so alight with enthusiasm and awe that he found it hard to take his eyes from her and follow the direction of her gaze. But he did, taking in the magnificence of the view, the steep descent of the valley, the shine of the sea in the late-morning sunshine, the medieval walls of the Moorish castle that overlooked the town.

'Breathtaking.'

Yet even now he wasn't sure if it was Gabby or the scene before him that had caused his lungs to constrict, and he turned back to the villa.

'Shall we make sure it's solid and look inside?'

Gabby nodded and together they approached the aquamarine front door, where he halted, leant down and retrieved a key from under a flowerpot.

'The owner should have left full instructions and some provisions inside.' Turning the key, he pushed the door open and they stepped inside.

The stone walls were unpainted, a higgledy-piggledy pattern of shades of cream and brown and grey. The living area was small but comfortably furnished, with a white love seat scattered with scarlet cushions and two plump armchairs in cool cream. There was a small kitchen area in the background, with a display cabinet holding an array of brightly patterned plates, cheerful curtains at the window. Tucked away was the bathroom—a small room cleverly designed to include a marble sink and a state-of-the-art shower. A winding staircase led the way up to a mezzanine level under the gables where a double bed sat.

'You can have the bed,' he said. 'I can easily manage down here.'

'How?' They both scanned the size of the sofa. 'There is no way you'll fit on that.'

'Yes, but neither will you.'

'Then we'll take turns,' she said firmly.

'Well, you have upstairs tonight and then we'll see.'

He followed her up the winding wooden stairs, lined with bright red iron banisters wrought in thin wavy lines. Once on the mezzanine, they stood in silence. The entire area was dominated by the double bed, which had an ornate curved headboard and was tucked snugly under eaves and gables.

Turning away from it, she said, 'What a beautiful bed.' Instantly heat touched her face. 'That is *not* what I meant. I meant to say view. What a beautiful *view*.'

'It is.' He couldn't help it. He kept his gaze focused on her face and her blush deepened.

'Out there,' she said, and he followed the pointing of her finger.

Gabby was right. The window framed a burst of flowers, a kaleidoscope of colours and scents that wafted inside. Yet right now he'd prefer to look at Gabby. *Not good.*

He headed for the stairs.

Once downstairs, Gabby sat on one of the armchairs. 'Right. As discussed, I did some research and...' She paused. 'What?'

He realised that without meaning to he had started grinning. '"I'll do a bit of research." It's the Gabby Johnson catchphrase.'

'Go figure.' But she was smiling, too. 'I *like* research. I like to have a plan. And, honestly, I enjoyed it. Sintra is an incredible place—there's so much to do. A palace, a medieval castle, and it all looks so very magical. I wish—' She broke off and regrouped. 'I've basically come up with a few things we can do, take some photos and garner enough information so that we can make sure your family believe we had a proper romantic break. *And* you will still have time to work.'

'Perfect. I'll make coffee, then we can figure out what to do next.'

CHAPTER EIGHT

As HE SCOOPED coffee into the cafetière, Zander pushed down a sudden, inexplicable, *ridiculous* sense of regret. There was nothing *to* regret—this was an enforced break and he needed to work. Yet Gabby's enthusiasm, her sense of the magical, had infused him with an unmistakable tint of dissatisfaction at the prospect of work, and with an urge to explore Sintra and see it through Gabby's eyes. *Daft.* He'd never been one for beach holidays or romantic breaks and now was definitely not the time to start.

With a shake of his head he poured the coffee and returned to the lounge area, where Gabby sat on the sofa, laptop resting on her knees.

'OK. So what's the plan?' Handing her a mug, he sat down in the other armchair.

'Well, there is so much that we can do it's been quite hard to narrow it down. This place is like a tourist treasure trove—fairy-tale castles, beaches, fishing villages…'

As he watched her, something tugged in his chest. Her enthusiasm, the way she described the places, was still doing something strange to him.

'You choose—I'm good with any of them.'

'Nope. It's important *you* choose.' Her face was serious now. 'The whole point of this charade is to make your family happy, so we need to do this properly. What would you *like* to do? Apart from work.'

It occurred to him that he had no idea. 'I really don't mind.'

She frowned, hesitated. 'What sort of holidays did you and Claudia go on?'

'We mostly holidayed with her parents. They'd bought an old chateau out in France and we spent the holidays helping them renovate it.' He hadn't enjoyed those holidays—he'd known Claudia's parents didn't really approve of him, though he'd never been sure as to why. Perhaps they had seen something he hadn't been able to—had known that in reality he and Claudia weren't suited.

'So even that was a sort of working holiday?' Gabby asked. 'What about family holidays when you were young?'

'We used to go down to Cornwall and Devon and camp mostly. Money was tight, but we still had a wonderful time. I spent loads of time swimming in the sea and trying to make surfboards out of driftwood.'

It was a long time since he had thought back to those holidays, those hours of happiness away from school, away from the scent of failure and humiliation. Free to be himself, free to swim and run and think and plan how one day, somehow, he would prove to the world that he wasn't stupid.

'Then I have the perfect thing for you to do. You can go surfing! Why not have a lesson? On a real surfboard?'

For a moment he was tempted, but then he shook his head. 'No point. I haven't the time or the inclination to take it up as a hobby, so why bother?'

'Because it might be *fun*! No one is going to demand a commitment from you to take it up as a lifestyle. Plus, if you enjoy it, why *not* take it up as a hobby? You surely can't work all the time, every weekend.'

'Surfing sounds like a time-consuming hobby and I don't have the time.' Right or wrong, his entire focus was on his business and that was the way he liked it.

'OK. But one afternoon surfing won't impact your company, will it?'

Put like that, he realised how absurd he sounded, and wondered at his own reluctance to kick back and enjoy something other than work. 'Of course not.'

'Good. Then that's decided. I'll call them and book you in.'

'What about you?'

'Uh-uh.' She shook her head. 'No way. Not my thing at all. I wish it was—I mean, the idea of mastering the waves is obviously incredible—but I can't imagine doing it. I wish I was that sort of person but I'm not. I'll sit on the sand and watch.'

He frowned. When he'd first met her hadn't she said the same?

I wish I was the sort of woman who would jump at this, but I'm not.

'How do you know? Have you tried it before?'

'No. I don't need to. The whole idea leaves me cold—or rather shaking with terror.'

'Can you swim?'

'Yes. In a pool I'm pretty competent, but the thought of swimming in the sea doesn't appeal. Too scary.'

'But you might be a natural—you might love it.'

'Or I might drown.'

'Unlikely on a summer day, on a safe beach with an instructor *and* me there. I think you should give it a try.'

'Well, I appreciate your thought, but I don't want to.'

'But if you try it and find it too frightening, you can always stop.' Perhaps *he* should stop, but he sensed that deep down she did want to do this.

'I'm already finding it too frightening and I'm on dry land, miles away from the sea.'

'But—'

'Stop with the *buts*. The idea of falling in, of the waves sucking me in, pulling me away, of drowning, of choking, not being able to breathe, not coming back… *That* is too frightening.'

Her knuckles had tightened white against the brown enamel of the coffee mug and he reached out and gently took it from her clasp.

'Back off, OK?'

'OK. I'm sorry. I didn't realise it was such a deep-rooted fear.'

'And I'm sorry. I didn't mean to snap.' She closed her eyes and inhaled deeply, then reopened them. 'It's OK. To be honest, I hadn't realised myself how much it would still affect me. It's silly, really. I just have a vividly overactive imagination. My grandfather loved swimming in the sea. Really loved it. But it terrified me. We'd often go to the coast on weekends and I'd watch him go out further and further, getting smaller and smaller, and I'd get more and more scared. Because I realised that the sea didn't understand or care that he was one of only two people I had in the world to look after me. I would imagine the sea as the enemy, luring him away from me, away from the shore until he wouldn't be able to get back.'

Her arms wrapped defensively over her stomach, as if she could feel the same twist of hollow dread now.

The image hit his brain with shocking clarity. A young Gabby sitting on a beach, watching, dreading, hoping… And, given the loss of her parents, her fear would have had a horrible validity—her reliance on her grandparents must have been absolute.

'But he came back,' he said gently.

'Yes, he did. Every time. It should have made the anxiety lessen, but it didn't. Each time I figured the probability had increased that *this* time would be the one when it all went tragic. I'd make so many bargains in my head. If he comes back, I'll give up chocolate…make straight

As… I never told him how scared I was because I knew how much he loved swimming in the sea and I didn't want to spoil it for him.' She reached for her cup. 'I'd changed his life enough.'

The last words had been said so softly he suspected she wasn't even aware she'd spoken the thought aloud.

'Anyway—lesson learnt. The sea is not for me.'

'Maybe.' Zander leant forward. 'But perhaps your fear was that you would lose your grandfather, not a fear of the sea *per se*.'

'Perhaps. But the bottom line is I can live without surfing quite happily. My life won't be blighted if I don't book myself in for a lesson.'

'I understand that, but your life might well be enhanced if you *do*.'

'Why does this matter to you?'

'Because fear is debilitating. I spent my whole childhood afraid that I was stupid, scared of books and of being found out. For years I devised strategies so that people would think I could read. If I hadn't been so scared I think I would have asked for help. If there is one thing I've learnt it's that I don't like being scared and that fear can change you. Facing fear can change your life. I'm not saying surfing will change your life, but in some ways not being afraid of the sea will make your life better.'

'How?'

'Let's say you've met Mr Right and one day you're on the beach with him and your two kids. Do you want to pass your fear on, or do you want to swim with your family in the sea?'

Gabby narrowed her eyes. 'No fair.'

'The end justifies the means. Come on, Gabby. Book us both a surfing lesson for later today. Then let's go down to the beach and have a go at swimming in the sea.'

'Now?'

'Yup. There's no time like the present.'

Panic widened her eyes and she shook her head. 'Hang on. If I have to move out of my comfort zone, so do you.'

'OK. Name it. What do you want me to do?' Even as he spoke the words he had a vague inkling of their stupidity.

'You take a *real* holiday. No more work.'

The tables had turned so fast he hadn't seen the edges coming for him. 'I can't do that.'

'Why not? Would your whole business collapse if you took a break?'

Again, put like that it sounded absurd, and yet the idea of no work... It *scared* him.

Her lips tipped in the tiniest of smirks. 'If the idea scares you, you should face up to that fear. Or we can give up on the whole idea. You work—I stay clear of the sea. Deal?'

Zander hesitated. Work kept him sane, gave him purpose, satisfied his need for success. It was his drive. But it was nuts that the idea of a break *scared* him. Time to put his money where his mouth was and face the fear down.

'No. No way. I'll take a break and you'll swim in the sea and *then* we are going to surf. Deal?'

Silence and then she nodded. 'Deal.'

'And...' Whilst he was at it he would face down the fear of spending time with Gabby, too—the fear that he couldn't control the attraction factor. 'If I'm taking a break, then maybe we could spend some time together. As friends.'

'Friends?'

He could hear the doubt, and an echoing inner voice questioned the sanity of the suggestion. It appeared that he was launching from stupidity to stupidity in an ever-increasing circle.

'Yes, friends. Why not? We both accept that physical

attraction exists and can't be acted on, but that doesn't mean we have to be afraid of it. We should face it down.'

'Combat it with friendship? I guess it's worth a try...'

'Friends it is.' He held out his hand. 'Deal?'

'Deal,' she echoed and placed her hand in his.

The simple touch called the whole pact into question, causing a temptation to hold on, to circle his thumb round the tender pad of her palm. Instead he shook it and dropped it.

'I'll call the office.'

'I'll call the surf school.'

Gabby tried and failed to subdue the odd buzz of anticipation that laced her veins as they left the house and headed for Sintra and the tram station. True, there was a knot of anxiety in the pit of her tummy at the thought of the forthcoming swim, sea and surf experience, but her nerves were overlaid by the reassurance offered in the sheer bulk of Zander at her side. Perhaps they were also helped by the drops of herbal remedy she'd hastily taken whilst changing.

The idea of the next few days caused a fizz inside her she knew she should subdue. *Three days with Mr Wrong— remember, Gabby?* But the reminder did nothing to dispel the bubble of happiness. And why not? It was OK to enjoy the company of a friend. And friendship was a *good* thing. Plus, maybe getting to know each other better would help dilute their physical attraction.

Inside her that little voice of reality dissolved into hysterical laughter. *Yeah, right*, it jeered, but Gabby refused to acknowledge it. This would work.

And so she revelled in the sunshine as it soaked her skin, and in the feel of the streets under her sandals—as if she could absorb the historic beauty of Sintra through its cobbles.

Central to the town, the Gothic National Palace was a monument to history, with its whitewashed rambling walls and the iconic coned chimneys that reached for the unending blue of the sky.

'Apparently Hans Christian Andersen said they looked like champagne bottles,' she told Zander, suddenly happy that she could talk to him as if to a friend, no longer using the words as small talk.

He glanced down at her and suddenly he smiled—a smile that scorched her and sent all thoughts of friendship rushing into the shadows.

'More research?' he asked.

'Absolutely. The history of the palace is fascinating. I've always loved history. I nearly did it at uni.'

'What stopped you?'

'Not vocational enough. I wasn't really sure what I would do with a history degree—and I really didn't want to come out of university with a massive student loan.' Gabby had always known that her priority was her grandparents—ensuring she could care for them. 'So I decided to skip uni—go a different route. I worked in a library and studied for a diploma in librarianship at the same time, and luckily I love it. And I get to keep history as a hobby.'

'So tell me about the palace.'

She frowned. 'Why?'

'Because I'm interested and because I like the way your face lights up when you talk about things that interest you.'

They were words a friend might use, but it didn't feel like that. His eyes held warmth and his gaze caressed her skin.

'OK. Um…' For a moment all her research deserted her, but then finally memory kicked in. 'The palace was built on the site of a Moorish fortress way back in medieval times, and Portuguese royals used it as their home. Some of them were born and died here. One of the best stories about it is that in 1582 four ambassadors from Japan visited Europe and came to Sintra—how brilliant is that? Wherever they went they were treated with respect; they were seen as a living letter from Japan. I think that's wonderful—that centuries ago people showed respect to other cultures…cultures that must have been so different.'

Gabby came to a stop, aware that her voice had quickened into a torrent of words.

'Sorry. Too much information.'

'Nope. I'm genuinely interested.'

And still his gaze rested on her with a glint that quickened her pulse.

'The tram station is this way.'

They walked onwards, and, as luck would have it, within minutes of their arrival a bright-coloured, old-fashioned tram trundled in. They joined the throng of people and squashed on to a wooden seat, but it was no matter that the carriage was crowded. In fact her body almost whooped at the chance to be legitimately pressed up close to Zander, to breathe in his scent, to feel his hard, muscular thigh against hers as they undertook the slow, noisy journey from town to coastline.

Three-quarters of an hour later they alighted at the beach, and suddenly she began to question the wisdom of her decision. A glance at the sea with its calm majesty should have reassured her, but somehow its vast expanse triggered anxiety and her footsteps slowed, her tummy churned.

And there was another issue to contend with. Like it or

not, she had to take off her blue-and-white floral summer dress and reveal the swimsuit underneath. A completely serviceable plain black swimsuit, chosen for its simplicity. Yet self-consciousness engulfed her as she pulled out the changing towel from her bag and began some complicated manoeuvring.

Zander observed her for a moment and then, without a shred of embarrassment, tugged his T-shirt over his head, leaving him standing on the sand patiently in his board shorts.

A deep breath and her dress dropped in a silky puddle to the sand, leaving her with the towel still covering her. *Right.* She wriggled out of it with as much nonchalance as possible, feeling the heat of the sun's rays warm her skin, trying not to feel exposed as she stared at the waves.

He held out his hand. 'Let's paddle to start.'

A moment of hesitation and then she placed her hand in his, told herself that friends held hands, that it was a gesture of reassurance. Nothing more.

Yet as they walked towards the gently lapping waves it *felt* like more. Skin against skin was a safe anchor, for sure, but it held an added overtone of awareness, made more acute by her sideways glimpses at his muscular chest, the smooth sculpture of his shoulders, and heightened by the fear of the water ahead of her and the crunch of the sand underfoot as each step took her closer.

Then cool waves washed over her feet, snaked around her calves, and she halted.

'Standing here, all my fears seem groundless,' she said. 'The sea seems so innocent. But when I look out there I remember that in fact all I have to do is go out of my depth and I could drown.' She shrugged. 'I guess it's a pretty apt life analogy, isn't it?'

'No. Because it is possible to go out of your depth and

not drown. Some people swim the Channel. Or you can go by boat.'

'At greater risk. It's safer to stick to paddling.'

'But then you never get to leave the shore.'

Sensing that there was something more in his words, something deeper than the superficial, she turned to him, studied his expression. 'Some people are happy on the shore.'

'Yes. They are.'

Now his eyes were definitely clouded, and the words held an unhappiness that was palpable—almost a self-reproach that she didn't understand.

'Are you?' he asked.

'I…' She looked out to sea, unsure how to answer. There were so many times when she yearned to be a different person, someone willing to take risks, someone braver, more extroverted, more… Just *more*. But she was who she was. 'Of course,' she said. 'And there is nothing wrong with that.'

'No,' he agreed quietly. 'There isn't. If you don't want to swim in the sea you don't have to. You've kept your part of the bargain. You're here. In the water.' Zander ran a hand over his face. 'You don't have to do this,' he said. 'I shouldn't have made you, and if you don't feel comfortable, then don't do it.'

His tone of voice was so at odds with the Zander of earlier that it jolted her out of her funk and she turned to face him, studying his face and noting the shadow that crossed his eyes.

It was he who now faced the waves, his body shifting away from hers. 'I have a bad habit of bulldozing people into doing what suits *me*. And I have no right to do that.'

'You didn't bulldoze me. I agreed to do this. But there's no point fibbing. I *am* terrified.'

Gabby caught her bottom lip between her teeth and glared at the sea, wishing she could will it into submission. Life didn't work like that, though. Zander hadn't been able to will his dyslexia into submission—he'd had to face the fear and work at it, learn to live with it.

Now she had a choice to make: she could take the easy option—turn away from this, tell herself there was no need to swim in the sea. Or she could try. She could swim away from the shore. And come back.

'I am going to try. Show me. You swim out. But not too far.'

'Sure.'

There was no hesitation, not even a sliver of the anxiety that instantly consumed her as he strode forward into the water, increasing his pace. And then he was swimming with strong, sure strokes, cleaving through the water until he flipped over on to his back, then floating for a moment and treading water to face her and wave.

The panic began to swirl. That urge to call him back rose, and she swallowed it down. The sea was calm. There were no rip tides or currents; they had checked. It was safe. But she wanted him to come back.

As if he knew that Zander reversed course, and minutes later he was beside her again. Water dripped from his dark blonde hair, glinted in the sunlight. His features were relaxed; he looked younger, happier...exhilarated. *Gorgeous*. A man who didn't live on the metaphorical shore.

'Right. What's the best way to do this?' she asked.

'First you need to remember that you can swim—of course it's different than a pool, but it's still water. You do have the ability to navigate the sea as long as you respect it. Respect is healthy. Also, remember we've done all the safety checks on tides and currents. Next, you need to get used to the temperature—come in a little further, get a feel for it.'

His calm deep tones helped and Gabby nodded, stepped forward, felt the resistance of the water against her legs. She was relieved that the water, though cold, was already sun warmed in the late afternoon as she tried to absorb and define the swirl of the current.

'Watch your breathing,' Zander said. 'It's easy when you're a bit anxious and in water to breathe shallowly. Better to focus on deeper breaths—inhale and feel your diaphragm move.'

Now it wasn't only his voice but his presence that helped. She walked a little further, feeling the sand rougher now between her toes, and she looked down, wondered what lurked in the swirling turquoise depths.

'It's OK. Let's just swim out a little way—a few strokes, slowly and methodically. Then we'll flip over on to our backs and you can look at the sky and float. Does that sound OK? I'll be right next to you.'

She made the first few strokes and then fear, unfamiliarity and the idea of the unknown segued into panic. Even the ability to swim, to breathe seemed to desert her. Then came his voice.

'Now on to your back. It's fine, Gabby.'

On automatic, she managed to turn over, her panic assuaged by the feel of his hands under her, offering support, and she concentrated on breathing and floating. Then he released her and she gazed up at the still, intense blue of the sky, open and vast and oddly calming. She was doing it—actually being carried by the waves—and disbelief fought with sheer exhilaration.

'You're doing great. You ready to head back to shore? Or do you want to go a little further?'

One last look at the sky and Gabby switched to treading water. She looked at the shore—the sandy curve was still not too far away—and turned her head to look out at the sea. There were other swimmers out further...a few surfers along the waves.

'Let's go a little further. I'd like to actually swim.'

'How about twenty-five strokes and then we'll turn and head back? Make sure you breathe on both sides if you're doing front crawl—and maybe swap to breaststroke if you feel panicked. That way you can see where you're going better.'

Again Zander struck the right tone—acceptance without question, an assumption that she could do it alongside common sense and practical advice. That and the knowledge that he'd be there right beside her enabled Gabby to turn away from the shore and strike out, counting the strokes in her head, keeping time, feeling the cleave of the water against her limbs.

She reached twenty-five and stopped, turned and looked back at the shore, now peopled by what looked like the equivalent of toy figures. She could feel the rise of panic; the growing idea that she wouldn't make it back. She saw an image of Lucille, left all alone, Gabby's promise to her grandfather to look after her broken by a stupid urge to try to be different, to change her personality.

Suddenly the limbs that had felt so strong, so buoyant just seconds before trembled, her lungs refused to cooperate, and an urgent need for oxygen caused her ears to pound.

'Gabby. It's fine. You're doing fine. Twenty-five more strokes and you'll be back in touching distance of the shore. You *will* make it back.'

She opened eyes she hadn't even known she'd closed and looked at Zander's expression. He was serious, his belief in his own words so strong she could swear they formed an aura. Every fibre of her being wanted to ask him to tow her back, and she knew he would do so without question or censure. But something deeper told her that was the easy option and one she would regret taking.

'Let's go.'

This time it was harder, each stroke more of an effort, but eventually she hit twenty-five, surfaced—and saw the shoreline! A few more strokes and she could stand. Her questing toes found and crunched on the seabed and she waded towards the shore, reached it, turned and looked back out to sea.

'I did it! I swam out and I came back!'

'You did it and came back. Your grandfather would be proud of you.'

Turning to Zander, Gabby smiled at the thought. Imagined her much-loved gramps patting her on the shoulder, a beaming smile on his face.

'I did it!' she repeated. 'I did it. I did it. *I did it!*'

And before either of them knew what was happening Zander had caught her around the waist and was twirling her round and round, both of them laughing like loons. Eventually he placed her on the sand gently and looked down into her eyes.

Heaven help her, all she wanted to do was kiss him. But she knew she mustn't. Even though right now, in the moment, she couldn't remember why it was bad idea. Adrenaline rush—that was all it was.

Who knew whether common sense would have prevailed? It wasn't put to the test, because a man approached them. Young, long hair, tanned, a happy smile, a surfboard under his arm.

'Gabby? I am Pedro. We spoke earlier. I am your surf instructor.'

'Fantastic! Hi, Pedro. This is Zander.'

'Pleased to meet you.'

A few preliminaries later and Pedro smiled again. 'Right. Time to choose your board and get you wetsuited up.'

Exhilaration still rushed through Gabby's whole body as she listened to him, still hardly able to believe that she had swum in the sea and was about to go back in.

Pedro was speaking. 'Before we go into the water, there are various techniques you need to practise on the sand. Paddling out. Popping up. Then we will move into the water, and I hope by the end of the afternoon you'll have caught your first wave!'

All her worries seemed to have dissipated—even the idea of catching a wave didn't faze her.

Her jubilation continued throughout the lesson, enhanced by watching Zander, his lithe movements and natural affinity for the surfboard. Something warmed inside her as she saw how carefree he looked, saw the look of concentration on his face, the smile that heated her skin with an intensity equal to the afternoon sun's rays, his deft, impatient movements as he pushed his hand through his sea-sprayed hair.

All of it gave her a funny little thrill of happiness, a sense of freedom—as if just for the day she was a different Gabby, one who had shed worry and caution.

The finale came when Pedro took them further out into the waves to put everything they had learnt into action. Zander lay on his board, his dark eyes intent and focused on the waves in assessment as he paddled. He bobbed, and then Pedro gave a small grunt of appreciation as Zander spotted the white-water wave, rode it and popped up.

'Like a pro, Zander! Way to go!' Pedro fist-pumped the air as Zander rode the wave in and then he turned to Gabby. 'Are you ready?'

'Yes!' Whether she was able was a different matter.

Zander grinned at her, reached out and took her hand in his. 'You've got this. I know you have.'

His voice was deep and genuine and his touch imbued her with confidence. The glint of appreciation in his blue eyes pumped her veins with a belief that she could do anything.

Grabbing her board, she headed out into the water, the sea swirling around her calves and then her thighs. She stood and let some white-water roll by, then closed her eyes as she tried to do as Pedro had instructed—get a feel for the rhythm and power of the waves. She held her surfboard in position, nose towards the waves.

OK. Now do this thing.

She identified a suitable incoming block of white water, took a deep breath and turned to face the shore. She lay on her board and paddled, focused. As the wave took the board and surged forward she stopped paddling, put her hands on the board, pushed up and popped her feet beneath her and did her best to stand and balance her weight.

As the surfboard washed on to shore she half fell, half leapt off, her muscle ache defeated by sheer exhilaration. 'I did it. I did it. I did it! *Again!*'

Pedro high-fived her and Gabby made no attempt to disguise her happiness, turning to Zander.

'At the risk of repeating myself—I did it! I did it! I did it! I did it! I caught a wave!'

'You did. You were amazing. Utterly incredible. How about we celebrate with a picnic on the beach?'

She looked around her. The rays of the setting sun cast a miasma of orange on the sand, their glow in direct contrast to the darkening dusky blue of the sea. Music emitted from the restaurants that lined the promenade above them, and the hum of conversation and laughter vibrated in the air. Lights twinkled into being, more than sufficient to combat the incoming dusk and cast an ambient illumination.

The whole idea of a picnic was impossibly romantic. With the emphasis on impossibly. The day might have had a dreamlike quality, but Zander was not the man of her dreams—not her Mr Right. Her Mr Right was a nice, ordinary bloke, not a drop-dead gorgeous, immensely successful multimillionaire.

Zander had been unattainable when she was a teenager and he was even more unattainable now. He was too good-looking, too rich…too *much*. His world was not hers. His goal in life was to achieve even more wealth and boardroom triumph. His aura, his presence, would overwhelm her.

But today he had proved himself a friend—so, whilst romance wasn't on the cards, surely there was no danger in the enjoyment of each other's company.

'A picnic sounds awesome.'

'Leave it with me. Once we've changed, I'll sort it.'

CHAPTER NINE

ZANDER LOOKED AROUND the small but excellently stocked supermarket Pedro had recommended, chose his items carefully, then added a bottle of full-bodied red and two plastic wine glasses to his basket. He wondered why he had suggested a picnic at all.

He tried to tell himself it was simply a ploy to put off their return to the villa, where he might be tempted to check in with the office. But deep down he knew that he was only kidding himself. Standing there on the beach, seeing Gabby's joy in her achievements, still buzzing himself from the thrill of riding the waves, he had wanted to prolong the moment for as long as he could.

Friends had picnics all the time. One picnic—what could be the harm in that?

The answer arrived all too soon. As he made his way back to the beach, down the rickety wooden stairs towards where Gabby sat in the dusk, he stopped and caught his breath. Right now he wished with a deep gut-wrenching twist of desire that this was a fun fling for real, that the charade could be true.

But that wasn't possible. So instead he'd try to be a fun friend.

Arriving next to her, he placed the bags down and retrieved the newly purchased tartan picnic blanket, shaking it out with a theatrical flourish.

'I have come laden with food and drink, so I hope you're hungry.'

She rose to her feet and gave an exaggerated wince. 'I

am definitely ravenous—and muscles I never knew existed ache! This looks incredible.'

Minutes later they had unpacked olives and bread, cold meats—*presunto* and *paio*, which the lady in the shop had explained to be smoked ham and smoked pork loin—a selection of cheese and some sardine pâté. *Batatas fritas*—chips—and pastries completed the spread.

Zander poured the wine and raised his glass. 'What shall we drink to?'

'To today. It's been amazing. I'm still buzzing.'

'Me, too.'

The feel of the sun on his skin, the cold salt spray of the water, the challenge of trying to master the surfboard and the waves had brought a surge of adrenaline that differed from the thrill of work, the buzz of a business deal. But, more than that, he'd felt pride in Gabby, in the way she'd faced, tackled and taken down her fears.

'Would you do it again?'

Her face clouded a little as she took a contemplative bite of a gleaming black olive. 'I don't know. Today feels like stolen time in some ways—as though it wasn't real. Wasn't me. Those feelings when I swam in the sea, when I caught the wave... *Exhilaration* doesn't do it justice as a description. There was that total sense of freedom, and for a transient second feeling in control of nature. I felt invincible.'

'A natural high?' Not the right words; he knew that immediately as her eyes dimmed in the evening light.

'I hadn't thought of it like that.' The idea clearly troubled her.

He frowned. 'There's nothing wrong with that. It's a great feeling.'

'That gets harder to achieve each time you seek it.' Her voice soft now. 'To start with, it's something small, and then that's not enough any more, so you need more and more to get that high. I'd have to swim the Channel, surf the most dangerous coast. And that's not me—I'm happy I managed to catch a wave. I think I'll stop there.' She spread some pâté on bread. 'What about you?' Her smile held a hint of sadness. 'Have you changed your mind? Are you going to set your sights on becoming a champion surfer?'

'No. I loved it, but I really don't have time to surf regularly.' Though now, sitting there, he felt a sudden uncharacteristic regret strike and had to remind himself. 'I get a buzz, a natural high, from success—from winning a deal, helping a client to succeed. I'll stick to that.'

'But, like I said, each time that goal becomes harder, and you need to achieve more to get that buzz. Surely in the end nothing will satisfy that craving except global domination?'

'You make ambition sound like an addiction. Maybe it is—but not a destructive one. Yes, I *would* like to achieve global success—I don't think that's a problem.' Not any more. But it had been once. His ambition had shown up the flaws his relationship with Claudia, but it would never be a problem again—he would never hurt anyone again—he'd make sure of that. 'I love my job and I am proud of my company. For me ambition, moving the goalposts, is a *good* thing. Else you stagnate.'

'Being content with what you have is not stagnation. I am happy with where I am, with what I have. I couldn't keep up with your level of ambition, your drive to succeed.'

Further confirmation that relationships and ambition didn't mix. 'We all have different contentment levels and different motivations.'

'That's true. And I'm sorry—I truly didn't mean to

criticise your achievements. Your success is phenomenal.' A sudden smile illuminated her face. 'Tell me about it. How you did it.'

'Too dull.'

'No, it isn't. I want to know.'

Her voice sounded sincere, her enormous hazel eyes were focused on his face, and he figured, *Why not?*

'I wanted to succeed, but I also wanted to help other people set up their own businesses. Anyone. Not just people with expensive college backgrounds and loads of money. Anyone with an idea and the drive to achieve it. I'd been working in a bank. I went straight there after A levels.'

A levels had been incredibly hard for him and his learning curve as he'd tried to figure out dyslexia and a whole new world of study. But he'd got straight As—an achievement he still felt proud about.

'I decided university wasn't for me. And, given Claudia and I were already engaged, work seemed a sensible option.'

'Do you regret not going to university?'

'I'm not sure. I don't think it has impacted my life dramatically, but I would have liked the opportunity to spend three years studying something I felt passionate about. But at the time it seemed like a step too far.'

She nodded in understanding. 'So what happened next?'

'I did well at the bank. I'd always found numbers easy and I was interested in the business side of it all. But what I learnt was how many people there were out there who couldn't get a loan because they didn't have enough capital or a guarantor, or their ideas were too risky. That didn't seem right to me. So what I wanted to do was set up a consultancy firm that helped them—and, at the risk of sounding arrogant, I knew I would be able to make a go of it.'

After Claudia died. After those terrible months when the sickness had moved in with inexorable, insidious finality.

'I decided to try to do just that. So I liquidated everything and worked out of—and lived in—a tiny rented garage.'

Of course his parents and his sisters had offered him a roof and help, but it had seemed vital to him that he achieve it all on his own.

'It was a lot…but it worked. I'd found a niche. There are so many people out there with innovative, fantastic ideas. I provided finance and advice and help, and it took off. I worked every hour I could, so I could fit around different time zones. It was a mad time.'

'And a confusing one, I imagine. A lot of that drive and energy must have been fuelled by grief.'

'Mostly I think I was driven by my own ambition.'

'I don't believe that. Claudia's illness, the tragedy of losing her, must have been beyond awful.'

'It was hard.'

He'd been there for her every minute, taken unpaid compassionate leave, tried to do everything he could to somehow mitigate the sheer tragedy. To help Claudia come to terms with her illness and navigate the acceptance that she had only months to live.

'I did my best. She wanted to live the time she had left to the fullest, but it was hard as she got weaker. We tried. I took her to Paris because we'd never been, and to Disneyland. We watched all the films she'd always wanted to.'

As he spoke he realised he'd never shared those bittersweet, tragic months with anyone—hadn't been able to, given the aftermath of his betrayal. But now, sitting on the green-and-orange-plaid rug in the moonlight, it felt cathartic, and he knew it was something to do with Gabby, with her ability to listen and her warmth.

'It sounds like you made her last months happy.'

He shook his head. 'Then weeks after she died I started my business. I'm not proud of that, but there it is.'

'You *should* be proud—Claudia would be, I'm sure. I wish she could have seen it, been part of it,' she said simply. 'I hope that somehow, somewhere, she can.'

'It wouldn't make her proud. Why *would* it?' The words were tinged with bitterness and he sipped his wine, hoped the rich spiciness would remove the taste, but knew nothing could.

'Because she loved you. She'd want you to be happy, to have achieved your dream.'

Suddenly he couldn't let her believe that. He wouldn't share the whole truth—couldn't betray Claudia's memory—but he could at least burst the bubble that painted him as someone he wasn't.

'It wasn't her dream,' he stated. The words had never before been uttered, and they felt full of portent. 'Claudia didn't share this dream, this ambition. And so it took her death for me to get all my wealth and success. The worst thing of all is that I have enjoyed it—every step of my path to success. I've loved it all. So what sort of man does that make me? No need to answer that. It makes me a number-one bastard.'

There was a long silence. He kept his eyes on the sea, rougher now, the dark waves crested by moonlight.

Then, 'No, it doesn't.'

'That's easy for you to say.'

'Actually, it isn't easy. Because I know how you feel. I *know*.'

Her voice was low, the words caught by the light evening breeze. The dusk had deepened and the warm night air held a different scent now. Cooking smells, sea spray, deeper and stronger.

'I know how it feels for a life to benefit from a death.'

Her tone was weighted with sadness and he moved closer to her so they sat shoulder to shoulder.

'*My* life. My mother was an addict. Drink, drugs… She was the all-time party girl. And becoming a parent didn't make any difference to her at all. She just took me along for the ride. My father was a drug dealer, a criminal… He eventually died in a prison brawl. Not that I ever knew him. My mother had moved on by then. She broke my grandparents' hearts—only came home when she needed money or when she needed somewhere to dump me. Sometimes it was a day, sometimes a week, sometimes a month.'

Zander was sure he heard the crack of his heart as a surge of impotent anger coursed through his body for tiny Gabby, tossed from pillar to post, never knowing where she would be from one minute to the next. No wonder she craved security.

'Anyway… When I was seven she left me with Gran and Gramps and she didn't come back. Eventually we were told that she'd died—overdosed. And you know what stinks? When I found out, my first emotion, my first thought, was, maybe I can stay here. With my grandparents. Where there is food and safety and security. So if *you're* a bastard, what does that make me?'

The words froze him in his tracks. They were an echo of his own feelings, only so very different.

'It makes you *human*. Gabby, you were a child. Your mother—the one person in the world who should have put you first, cared for you—didn't or couldn't give you the fundamental safety you deserved. It was a completely natural reaction. There is no fault.'

'That is logic speaking—but it doesn't change the burn

of guilt inside me. For better or worse she was my mother, but her death benefited me. Gave me security, love and a home. So I understand how you feel about Claudia and it's a sucky feeling. But I'm sure that Claudia wouldn't begrudge you your success or blame you for it. She loved you and you loved her. Nothing is more important than that. I'm not sure my mother and I even had that.'

Only Gabby still didn't know the full truth. Once he and Claudia *had* loved each other, but his love had faded, withered, had not been strong enough to withstand their different approaches to life. But that was his cross to bear, and more important right now was Gabby—Gabby, who must have had such complex feelings for her mother.

He knew empty platitudes would be rightly rejected as inadequate, and he thought carefully before he spoke. 'I can't pretend to know how your mother felt, but addiction is a very terrible thing. It changes people—changes their priorities, their very nature. It can make them choose actions they know to be wrong.'

She nodded. 'I know. I've done a lot of research into it. But I do wish I'd been worth enough to her for her to try to turn it all around. Wish I'd been good enough'

'No one could have been good enough—it wasn't a flaw in you, it was a fault in her.'

'It didn't feel like that.'

He wondered if it still didn't.

'And still I wish that my first reaction to her death had been different.'

'I think that your mother would have understood, and she'd be happy that you ended up with love and security. I don't think she would begrudge you that, either.'

'Thank you. I mean that.' She shook her head. 'I can't believe I'm even talking about her. I never do, really. It upsets Gran and it makes me feel guilty.'

'You told me to make me feel better, and I appreciate that. Thank you.'

For a long moment they sat, and slowly the atmosphere began to morph and shimmer. His whole being was acutely aware of her closeness, her warmth and beauty.

She caught her breath. 'That's what friends are for.'

'Yes.' He turned to look at her, her chestnut hair sheened by moonlight, her features dappled by the beams casting them into shade and brightness. 'Problem is, right now I don't feel like just a friend.'

Her hazel eyes were luminous in the moonbeams as she twisted a strand of hair around her finger. 'So...like a friend...with benefits?'

Her voice was small, but clear, her gaze unwavering, and now the awareness that had simmered, muted by the sheer emotional warmth of their conversation, shifted, almost as if the moon's haze had cast a sparkling net of magical awareness around them.

'What sort of benefits did you have in mind?'

Now she smiled—a slow, almost languorous smile. 'I'm thinking of the exact type of benefits *you* have in mind.'

All he wanted to do was kiss her, but some innate sense of honour pulled him back, kept him still.

'Unless I've got this all wrong?' Hurt, fear of rejection, crossed her eyes.

She made to move backwards and instantly he reached out, covering her hand in his.

'No! You haven't got it wrong. *Jeez.* I want this. I want you more than I can say. But I need to be sure you want it, too. You said that fun flings aren't your thing, that you don't want to feel second-best. I don't want you to feel like that.'

'I don't. This isn't about being second-best—this is

about what we both want in the here and now.' Her hand picked up some sand, trickled it through her fingers. 'For once I don't want to be cautious—the one who clings to the shore, who won't take a risk, won't have fun. For once I want to let go. Just for a weekend. I want to break free from common sense and reason and all the shibboleths and worries that govern my life. One weekend. That doesn't complicate anything.'

His brain made a last-ditch attempt to tell him that it wasn't that easy—that this would complicate everything—but he shut it down. One weekend—what could be wrong with that?

'Are you sure?' His breath caught in his lungs as he waited for her answer. 'Sure this is what you want?

CHAPTER TEN

GABBY STARED INTO his eyes, then glanced around the beach, wanting to imprint it for ever on her memory. Then she looked back at Zander. Took in every detail. The darkness of his blue-grey eyes, the contained, controlled aura of desire that she knew was for her, and revelled in that knowledge.

'I'm sure. One hundred per cent.' She could see doubt fighting desire in his stance. 'You can be my Mr Right for the Weekend.'

For a second inexplicable sadness touched her, but then she pushed it away. Zander could not be her Mr Right for Ever. His life goals were utterly different from hers—and, of more importance perhaps, she couldn't keep up with him. She wasn't in his league and it wasn't a league she wanted to be in—not a world she wanted to be part of. Lord knew she loved her niche, the place in the world she'd forged and carved out for herself. Secure, safe... A place where she could be content.

But right now that didn't matter—nothing mattered except the here and now, and for once she was going to grab the moment. And him.

'I want this. I want *you*.'

And finally he smiled and her heart soared.

'Then what are we waiting for? It would be my pleasure. *Our* pleasure, in fact.'

She could hear the rough edge of desire in his voice and it thrilled her. His eyes, molten in the moonlight, were completely focused on her as he leant forward and brushed his lips across hers with a tantalising slowness, caressing her shoulders. Her skin shivered under his touch and desire surged inside her in a swirling vortex of need that only he could assuage.

She couldn't hold back the moan of protest when he pulled away.

'We need to go. Get back to the villa.'

Together, their fingers made clumsy by the sheer need for speed, they cleared away the remnants of their picnic, rolled up the rug and half walked, half ran up the beach to where the lighted streets still showed couples out for a stroll, bars lit up and where there was the sound of late-night diners, laughter and the hum of conversation.

Within minutes he'd found a taxi, tugged her towards it and their journey began. A silent journey, broken only by a few courteous platitudes to the driver. There was no need for words to each other, nothing to say that could eclipse the mounting anticipation inside her. Not a single doubt was allowed to surface—she knew that she couldn't stop now, propelled by a desire so deep, so consuming, it wouldn't be possible to deny it.

As she alighted from the taxi she felt as though she was walking through a sea of sensation. Every sound was magnified, every chirp of a cricket, every rustle of a tree's branches in the wind. The breeze lifted her hair against the nape. Her skin was supersensitive. Her heartbeat pounded in her ears as Zander pulled her into his arms and kissed her—a deep searing kiss in which their mutual passion met and matched, a kiss that branded her very soul.

Time lost meaning, and it could have been minutes or hours that they stood lip-locked, surrounded by the late-night garden scents. But finally he took her hand and they walked unsteadily towards the front door.

Once inside they wasted no time, practically sprinting for the stairs, and she gave a small laugh of relief as they reached the mezzanine level—until he dropped an expletive.

'What?'

'I haven't got any protection...'

'It doesn't matter. I'm on the pill.'

She had remained on it after her split with Steve, as it regulated her periods. It was a decision she had been unsure about, but now she welcomed it with a wash of relief, matched by Zander's and shown in the force of his answer when she explained.

And then the need for words was over; his expression said it all, and he was utterly focused, almost reverent, as he gently pushed the straps of her dress down, bent his head and whispered kisses across her shoulder. How was it possible to feel boneless, to be so caught up, so focused on the thrills that ricocheted through her?

She reached out in wonder. Finally this was allowed—to slide her hands under the soft fabric of his T-shirt and feel the muscular solidity of his chest, to rest her palm over the accelerated beat of his heart. And then he was kissing her again, and Gabby gave herself up to the sensory onslaught...

Zander opened his eyes and stared up at the whitewashed ceiling, aware of the rays of bright sunshine that filtered through the slatted blinds they had forgotten to close properly. A feeling of immense well-being filled him—an urge to throw open the windows and sing. Instead he shifted slightly, aware that next to him Gabby still slept.

For a long moment he looked down at her and marvelled at the sheer joy they had experienced just hours before. Passion, laughter, discovery and a generosity that still startled him. Now she lay curled on her side, her

impossibly long eyelashes on show, one hand tucked
under her cheek.

As quietly as he could, he slipped from the bed, closed
the shutters so she could sleep on and tiptoed downstairs,
determined to produce a spectacular breakfast.

Half an hour later her head appeared over the banister.
'That smells divine!'

'Bacon, eggs, pastries, coffee, toast. They stocked the
kitchen in style. I figure we burned off a whole load of
calories. I also figure we need a whole load more energy
for what I have in mind.'

An endearing blush and a wicked smile greeted this,
and she padded downstairs dressed in an oversized T-shirt.
Her hair cascaded wildly to her shoulders and his heart
did a funny little dip.

Whoa, Zander. Any other bit of his anatomy, sure, but
his heart really did *not* need to get involved.

Turning away, he concentrated on breakfast and on
the plunge of the cafetière, and the sheer unfamiliarity
of cooking for two smote him. It was a reminder that this
was not normal—it was a capsule of time outside reality
and away from the usual slipstream of their lives.

'So.' He placed a heaped plate in front of her. 'What's
our plan for the day?'

'Well, we could follow our old plan—visit the fairy-tale
castle or the palace…' Reaching out, she concentrated on
buttering a piece of toast, her eyes on the knife as if the
whole enterprise was a complicated military strategy. 'Or
we could stay here. Play board games, read books, drink
coffee, cook…and anything else that takes our fancy.'
A small shrug. 'Have a complete break from the world.'

The phrase was an echo of his earlier thoughts.

Zander poured more coffee, shocked at how very much
the idea appealed. Never before had he embraced the idea

of doing nothing, let alone doing it wrapped in cosy intimacy.

A small alarm bell started to sound. 'Are you sure? I saw yesterday how enthusiastic you were about the castle and the whole history of Sintra.'

'I was. I am. But...'

Her cheeks flushed and he couldn't help but smile. 'But you figure there are better activities on offer than sightseeing?'

'Well...now that you mention it...'

His brain shut off the growing siren that urged caution and his vocal cords jumped into action. 'A complete break from the world sounds good. The castle will be there another day.'

Whereas whatever was happening here had a time limit. It was a reminder to himself—a justification as to *why* he wanted to spend the next two days cocooned with Gabby in the villa. After all, once they went back to England normal life would resume. The opening of an office in New York, deals and clients and business growth—that was where his focus had to be. But suddenly he didn't want to think about that.

'I vote we stay right here. And I have a brilliant idea. Let's go back to bed.'

'Works for me.'

And so started a day unlike any Zander had experienced before—a day when time seemed to lose meaning as they alternated between conversations about films and books and comfortable silence, as they played Monopoly and ate gigantic ham-and-cheese toasties in bed.

'It's been an amazing day,' he said softly as the night drew in and he opened a bottle of champagne.

'Yes, it has. I'll definitely be putting this day in my treasure trove.'

Handing her a frothing glass, he settled next to where she was curled up on the sofa, dressed in a fluffy dressing gown. 'Treasure trove?'

'It's something Gran came up with when I was a child. It was hard, knowing that the time I spent with her and Gramps could be snatched away at any time. And I never knew if Mum would bring me back again or not. So Gran said we should make a treasure trove of memories. Special things that I could treasure and take out and remember when I needed them. It was a brilliant idea. When things were tough I'd imagine opening the treasure trove and there they'd be. I'd lose myself in the memories.'

Her eyes were looking into the past now, and he wondered how bad it had been. 'I'm guessing it was pretty tough,' he said.

'Yes, sometimes it was.' Her voice was flat, matter-of-fact, and then she smiled. 'But there were some good memories, and that's where the treasure trove came in. When good things happened I'd make sure to imprint every second on my mind and I'd imagine putting the memory into a special box. And now it's a habit I've got into. It helps sometimes—when things go wrong it's good to remember there were happy times. Sometimes Gran and I sit and remember Gramps, look into our treasure troves of memories of him.'

Zander watched Gabby and saw the affection on her face. 'Your gran sounds like a really special person.'

'She is. I'd do anything for her. Gran is the best person I know. And Gramps was pretty impressive, too. Life wasn't always easy for them but they never gave up, never despaired. Gran says it's because they had each other. She says Gramps was her rock, and the knowledge that their love was indestructible gave them both strength in the dark times. One day I hope I can find that kind of love, but I realise it's probably a pipe dream.'

'Why?' Conflicting emotions hit him. Right now the idea of Gabby with the love of her life didn't sit well with him—in fact the idea of Gabby with *anyone* else caused a knot of anger in his gut. Dog in the manger, or what? He told himself that of *course* he wanted her to have what she wanted.

'You're only twenty-nine. There's plenty of time to find Mr Right.'

'Even if I find him I'd have to figure out how to keep him, how to maintain the relationship.'

'You make it sound like a car.'

'A relationship *is* like a car—Gran told me she and Gramps had to work at theirs. Sometimes it needs fuel, sometimes it needs fine-tuning, sometimes it needs a polish.'

'So you *do* know what you're doing?'

'Nope.' She shook her head, chestnut strands shaking in emphasis. 'In real life I have no clue how to look after a car, and I don't have any idea with relationships, either. Been there and have the T-shirt.'

'What went wrong?'

'I think I wanted it to work *too* much. Then I couldn't figure out how to *make* it work, and the harder I tried the more panicked I became. That had a knock-on effect and made me madly insecure and needy. That made both Steve *and* Miles run for the hills—or rather run to other women.'

Her tone was light, but he knew how hurt she must have been. 'Whoa… Hold on a minute. That was their fault—they were the ones who were wrong, not you.'

'I know. I get that. And to be fair they got that, too—they both did feel really bad about their behaviour. They accepted complete responsibility…gave me the whole "it's not you, it's me" spiel.'

'They got *that* right,' he pointed out and heard the anger in his voice. It was an anger aimed not at Gabby, but at the unknown Steve and Miles. Anger at how they must have made her feel. Gabby's mother had made her feel not good enough, and they had added to that. 'They were schmucks. They weren't worth it and they weren't worthy of you. You're well rid of them.'

'I tell myself that, but I do also accept that it's possible that there isn't a Mr Right out there for me. Both Steve and Miles seemed so right—good, normal, ordinary blokes.' She sipped her champagne and then smiled. 'Don't get me wrong—I'm happy on my own. I love my job and I have security, a home, food on the table, consistency. And I have Gran—which is amazing, given she's ninety. I'm lucky and I know that.'

Yet once her grandmother passed on, and in the scheme of things that could happen sooner rather than later, Gabby would be alone. No wonder she wanted a family, and had wanted her relationships with Steve and Miles to work out too much.

Without thought, Zander shifted a little closer to her and she rested her head on his shoulder.

'Anyway,' she said. 'Enough about me. Let's talk about you.'

'What do you want to know?'

'What were you like as a child? What did you want to be when you grew up?'

'That's easy. I wanted to be a success. Simple as that. I didn't care how I did it or what I did—I wanted success.'

She frowned. 'So you were always ambitious? It's funny—I don't remember that about you at school.'

'Sixth form was a strange time for me.'

It was the time when he'd just started seeing Claudia. He had been unable to read, but had been incredibly popular—a success on the sporting field, a cool kid, a rebel who had hardly any qualifications but seemingly didn't care. A kid on the path to success of the wrong type. Then had come the dyslexia diagnosis—a turning point and a time when everything had changed for him. A vista of possibilities had opened up, and his determination and drive had been focused around conquering the written word.

His relationship with Claudia had deepened at a time when his ambition had been muted, and with hindsight he could see that perhaps it meant Claudia hadn't known the real Zander. And perhaps he hadn't known the real Claudia—he had been grateful she had gone out with him, someone 'stupid', but in reality she had been happy to go out with someone cool. But that didn't answer Gabby's question.

'I was always determined to succeed. I think because my sisters had set the bar so high and I hated being the stupid one. I was always intent on equalling them.'

Her forehead creased in thought and then she sighed. 'Yet you gave up that dream for Claudia because you loved her. You were happy to accept that her dreams were different. *That* is how relationships work—two people willing to compromise. You obviously understood the maintenance manual. That's why you truly don't need to feel guilt because you achieved success after her death.'

The words hit him like individual pellets and he had to force himself not to wince with each blow. Yet she sensed something; it clearly hadn't been possible to keep the tension from his body.

'I'm sorry. I shouldn't have reminded you.' Her voice

was small, sounding suddenly almost defeated. 'Of what you've lost.'

Jeez. Each word poured salt into the wound, and for a moment he hesitated, wondered if he could admit the truth, air his guilt and the baseness of his soul to her. But that wasn't the issue. Sharing his flaws meant a betrayal of Claudia. It would humiliate her memory.

'You haven't.'

How to explain that he couldn't talk about Claudia? Not without conjuring up all his guilt and sadness…not without confessing that in fact he'd had no idea at all about relationship maintenance or compromise. That in fact his love hadn't survived marriage, living together, a real relationship.

He could see compassion in Gabby's eyes, along with a frisson of sadness, and then she shifted, moved in and kissed him softly on the lips. Her sympathy was so wrong he moved away. Then he saw hurt in her eyes and wished it were possible to kick himself round the whole of Sintra.

'Gabby…?'

'It's fine. Really.'

It wasn't, but he didn't have a clue how to make it better. Whatever he said would make it worse, because he couldn't tell her the truth.

'What did you want to be when you grew up?' As a question it was abrupt, gauche, stupid, but it was all he could come up with. 'Did you always want to be a librarian?'

For a moment he thought she wouldn't answer, then she shrugged, accepted the conversational gambit. 'I wanted to be safe. I still do. You want success—I want security. As a child I don't think I much cared how I got it, but as I grew older I did realise I had a choice. My priority was and is a regular income. Though I did once toy with the idea of being a writer.' She said it as though the idea was a crazy one.

'What did you want to write?'

'Happy stories,' she said without hesitation. 'But also stories that make you think. For kids. Books were an incredible solace for me, growing up—they allowed me to escape from a difficult world into a fantasy one. I used to imagine the pages literally swallowing me up. And I was glad of it. I'm sorry that you didn't have that.'

He shrugged. 'Some people say you can't miss what you never had, but I think what's worse is desperately wanting something you *can't* have. I used to think I'd wish away my soul if I could just decipher the meaningless jumble of shapes that everyone else could read.'

Gabby moved back closer to him, so close a silken strand of her hair brushed his cheek. 'That truly sucks.'

'Yeah. But, hey, somehow the conversation seems to have come back to me. What about you? Do you still want to write a book?'

'No. There wouldn't be any point.'

'Why not?'

'Because I'd rather focus on a job that brings me money.' She paused. 'Like this one.'

It was a timely reminder to them both that this was a job—that these few days were not real.

He took a breath. 'Perhaps writing a book would make you money.'

'Unlikely. The chance of success in the current competitive market is minuscule.'

'But if you don't try you won't succeed for sure. Why not write in your spare time? Not for the money, but for the kudos of publication. You already have a job and security.'

'Exactly. I've achieved the important things. The whole "write a children's book" thing was just a daft dream.'

'Dreams are important.'

'Sure they are—but not dreams that can't be achieved and will most likely open you up to rejection.'

'But you might get accepted.'

'Unlikely—and getting rejected sucks. So I can't see the point of inviting it.'

'But—'

'There is no *but*. Subject closed. Let's not spoil this with a pointless argument.'

Stop. Quit.

Gabby was right. Yet he couldn't shake the idea that he was missing something, and he asked a question on instinct. 'You've already written it, haven't you?'

There was a silence. Then a shrug. 'Yes. Though I don't know how you figured that out.'

Instinct, and the knowledge of Gabby he had somehow garnered. 'Then why not send it out?'

'I didn't write it for publication. I wrote it for me.' A small shrug and then, 'Maybe if I ever figure out relationships and have children, I'll read it to them.'

Children. The word was another reminder of just how different he and Gabby were. Gabby could picture a world where she was a parent—she actively wanted that responsibility. Zander couldn't and didn't. But right now that didn't matter.

'Anyway...' She said the word with finality. 'Can we change the subject?'

He bit down on his instinct to urge her to send her story off, to do what *he* would do—strive after success. Gabby had been deemed not good enough by her mother, not good enough to give up her lifestyle for. She had been terrified she wouldn't be good enough to be kept by her grandparents, and she believed she had played a part in both her relationships ending in infidelity. Perhaps it was no wonder she didn't want to risk being judged not good enough again.

No wonder she wanted to settle for an 'ordinary' bloke. Maybe the best thing he could do was tell her that *he* thought she was good enough.

'Yes, we can. But first I want to say I believe that those children of yours will be really lucky. To have the chance to listen to your story, but most of all to have you as a mum.'

For a second he'd have sworn a tear glistened on the end of one of those impossibly long eyelashes, but then she pulled him towards her and her generous lips curved into a smile of sheer beauty.

'You say the loveliest things. But now I think it's time to stop talking.'

He laughed, 'And show you some action?'

'Absolutely.'

CHAPTER ELEVEN

GABBY ROLLED OVER, felt the last vestige of sleep slip away from her and tried to hold on to it. She knew that she didn't want to wake up just yet.

Drowsily she reached out a hand, expecting to encounter Zander's warm, comforting bulk next to her. Instead her hand met cool sheets and now she *did* open her eyes. Remembered. This was it. The morning of their flight back. She needed to be up and packing. It was over.

A queasily familiar sense of impending unhappiness washed over her but she forced herself to jump out of bed instantly, to infuse her movements with purpose even as memory strummed a chord. This was akin to how she'd felt as a child, when her mother had returned to pick her up from her grandparents'. She'd packed her suitcase then with the same dread, with the knowledge that her safe time was over and she didn't know when or even if it would come again.

To her horror, this was actually *worse*. Back then there had been hope—even the probability that she would return, perhaps in days, perhaps in months. But this was different. This would never happen again. She'd asked him to be her Mr Right for the Weekend—and the weekend was over.

But she would not, *could* not regret it. Their moment had been joyous and joyful—and, dammit, she'd had *fun*. So now she would act with dignity and she would not repine.

Gabby snapped her suitcase shut and switched on her

brightest smile, preparing to descend from the mezzanine and face him.

'Good morning!' Her words came out too cheerful, too shiny and bright, but he didn't comment.

'Good morning.'

His voice was pleasant, courteous—and so formal. Hurt twanged her nerves. The man she had come to know over the past forty-eight hours had vanished as completely as a mirage in the desert. That Zander had gone and she would never see that aspect of him again.

'I've made coffee if you would like some.'

'Thank you.'

For a moment she wondered if he'd ask if she took milk or sugar—perhaps the past two days had been a figment of her fevered imagination. He handed her the mug with exaggerated care, careful to avoid even a brush of their fingers. On the table his netbook was open, and she had little doubt he had already been in contact with his office.

The silence held a cloud of awkwardness and she forced herself to fill it. 'Hopefully the flight won't be delayed.'

'Hopefully not. We should leave within the next half hour, if that's OK with you.'

'Traffic shouldn't be too bad,' she stated, as if she had *any* knowledge of traffic congestion in Portugal. Oh, God—they'd gone full circle. Their break had started with stilted conversation and so it would end. As if the middle had been no more substantial than a dream.

They left the villa in silence and she forced herself to walk to the car without a backward glance. Better for it be preserved in her treasure trove of memories as a magical place untouched by shadows of regret.

The whole car journey consisted of her fight to remain still, to contain her agitation and to focus on the scenery as it whizzed past rather than on Zander. Yet she couldn't resist the occasional glance at his profile. His expression was unreadable—not even a hint of the man who'd just hours ago held her in his arms.

Anger suddenly sparked that he could be so calm, so uncaring—that he could switch off his emotions so easily. But then again his emotions hadn't been engaged, and in theory neither had hers. She shifted on her seat again, realising that now Zander's fingers were drumming a tattoo on the steering wheel. An apology hovered on her lips but she bit it back—she had nothing to apologise for.

Then in a smooth movement Zander put on the indicator and pulled into a lay-by. 'Is something wrong with the car?'

'No.'

He unclicked his seat belt and turned to face her. 'But *something* feels wrong. On the beach we decided to change the parameters of our relationship for the weekend, but we didn't stop to think about what would happen next. And now we're acting like strangers.' His shoulders lifted in a shrug as his lips tipped up ruefully. 'I'm not sure I even understand why, but I don't like it.'

Relief touched her that he didn't want this stilted awkwardness, either. 'I guess we need to figure out how to go back to friendship.' *Right, Gabs. Because that worked out so well last time.* 'Or to a working relationship at least. You're paying me for a reason. We don't want to blow it now.' The reminder tasted bitter on her tongue.

He nodded but made no attempt to restart the car. Instead, his fingers continued to drum the wheel as he gazed ahead at the dusty vista of the road.

'There is another way,' he said finally. 'An option that has nothing to do with money. Whatever we decide I will pay you the agreed sum, because I'm paying you to convince my family that I have moved on. But, given that we are going to see a lot of each other until the wedding, we *could* make this into a *real* fun fling. Just for the next few weeks.'

'I…'

Yes! Hurry up and say yes, urged every instinct. *For heaven's sake, please don't think about it.* Even her brain chimed in. *Go on, it makes sense.*

She had made the decision on those sands to grab the moment. This was her chance to extend it. To continue to enjoy the benefits that she knew with every millimetre of her body were infinitely pleasurable.

Only her gut urged caution, informing her that it was too dangerous, that it would be too much.

But it was too late for that consideration. For the next few weeks their relationship charade had to continue regardless. That necessitated her being with Zander, and it would take a person with more willpower than she had to turn down the option of more time in his arms and in his bed.

'That would make sense,' she said, keeping her voice cool and calm, as if they were simply negotiating a simple additional clause to their deal. Though her tummy somersaulted with doubt and anticipation, relief and anxiety in equal measure.

'Good.'

His smile was warm, his body language relaxed—a return to the Zander she'd got to know over the past three days and she smiled back.

Now he did start the engine, and pulled out on to the road. They resumed their journey, still in silence, but this time it was a silence that spoke of relief, and of a disinclination to start any conversation that might convince them of the sheer idiocy of their decision.

Four days later

'Do I look all right? Does this work for a Grosvenor family lunch?' Gabby surveyed her reflection in the mirror in Zander's bedroom and then turned to look at Zander, who stood by the bed, smiling at her.

It occurred to Gabby that they'd both smiled a lot since she'd arrived the previous evening, and an illogical frisson of unease touched her. *Daft.* Smiling was a *good* thing, right?

'Hmm… I think I need to take a closer look.'

As he advanced towards her, she gestured at the simple patterned drop-waisted dress. 'I've gone for a casual, I've-tried-hard-but-not-too-hard look,' she explained.

He raised his eyebrows in genuine bemusement. 'You know that makes no sense, right?'

'It does to me. The point is, will your family think it's OK?'

'My family doesn't have a dress code.'

Now his smile had deepened, and she looked at him with a hint of suspicion as he stepped closer.

'But let me quickly check something on the back of your dress.'

She swivelled round and in one swift movement, he'd slipped the straps off her shoulders and bent down to kiss the nape of her neck.

'I think I'd better inspect *exactly* how you look,' he murmured, and now he tugged the zipper down.

Desire washed over her and without hesitation she turned and shimmied out of the dress…

Half an hour later Gabby shook her head as she tugged the dress back on, grabbed a pair of heels and slipped them on, too. 'I can't *believe* we did that. If we're late it is all *your* fault.' She regarded her reflection and groaned. 'Do you think they'll guess that we just…?' She waved a hand at the rumpled sheets.

Zander buttoned his shirt. 'We won't be late—and if they do, they do. It all adds verisimilitude to the charade.'

'Yes. Of course.' All inclination to laugh left her. Had he instigated the whole thing to enhance the charade?

His blue-grey eyes held concern. 'Gabs… That wasn't planned. It just happened.'

'I get that.'

But she wasn't sure she did—suddenly wasn't sure if she was overthinking, on the way to insecurity or neediness.

Rising, she glanced at her watch. 'We'd better go. I don't know London that well but, according to my phone app, it will take us at least forty-five minutes to get to Gemma's.'

In fact, the journey across London took just under that, and they pulled up outside Gemma's three-storey London house at the same time as Julia and her children.

'Hey, little bro,' she said.

But before Zander could reply, Freddy and Heidi tumbled out of the car.

'Uncle Zan-Zan! Look at my new game—it helps me read and it means I get to use a tablet.'

'Uncle Zan-Zan, tell Mum that isn't fair.' The little girl folded her arms. 'I think I should have one, too.'

Zander grinned, and as both children ran towards him he scooped Heidi up. 'You'll have to manage without, Heidi. How about I play a game with you later?'

Heidi squealed with laughter as he tickled her, and nodded. 'Hide and seek, Uncle Zan-Zan—and Monopoly. Please.' Turning, she looked across at Gabby. 'Are you Gabby?'

Gabby nodded.

'Are you Uncle Zan-Zan's girlfriend?'

'Yes, sweetheart, she is—and, now, enough questions. We need to go inside.'

With that, Julia swept everyone towards the front door, and minutes later they were inside. Unlike Zander's apartment, the house had a lived-in feel and a definite sense of personal taste. Gemma clearly favoured bold abstracts and warm wooden flooring. The hall held a collage of family photographs in black and white, and for a sudden moment Gabby felt a sense of aloneness, a stab of emotion that she acknowledged as envy.

Before she could dwell further, she saw Laura Grosvenor heading towards her. 'Gabby, how lovely to see you. You look fantastic—positively glowing! The sun has done you both good and I love your dress.'

'Thank you.'

Gabby returned the hug and again emotion swelled inside her—a sense of being an outsider looking in. She wanted *this*—the clear affection that existed in this family, the easy camaraderie, the jokes and the banter. Yearning tugged inside her, but she blinked it away. One day she would find Mr Right and she'd create this—have children, laughter, family holidays, Christmases with a turkey large enough to feed an army.

Once they were all seated around the large wooden table in the state-of-the-art kitchen, Gemma grinned at Gabby. 'OK. So tell us all about Sintra. Was it fantastic?'

'It was absolutely amazing,' Gabby said, and now there was no need to act her part. All she had to do was tell the truth. 'Magical, in fact.'

'We even went surfing.' Zander held his arms out and gestured for applause. 'Gabby and I caught our first waves.'

'No way.'

'*Yes*, way.'

'And how many hours did he spend on his laptop or talking to the office?'

'None,' Zander said.

'*Definitely* no way.'

'Yup. Gabby will vouch for me.' Zander was relaxed, his arm around her shoulders, and she felt a bubble of happiness because for a moment she truly felt she belonged.

'It's the truth. And he even came home early from the office yesterday to meet me.'

'In that case we all need to drink to you, Gabby.' Gemma rose to her feet and lifted her glass. 'To Gabby, who has achieved the impossible. Cheers!'

And when Gaby saw the look of happiness on his mother's face, she understood why Zander had initiated the whole illusion.

The hours flew by. They ate a delicious simple home-cooked lasagne and a green salad, followed by a sumptuous cake that Gemma happily admitted was from the local patisserie. A boisterous game of hide-and-seek ensued, followed by a fiercely competitive game of Monopoly. Then the children were allowed to watch a film whilst the adults sat on the circle of sofas in the enormous living area.

'So,' Gemma said. 'Have you bought a dress for the wedding yet?'

'Not yet,' Gabby said and smiled. 'But that's not important—it's *your* dress that everyone will be interested in.'

Gemma shook her head. 'You wouldn't believe the fuss—all because Alessio can drive a car fast.'

Zander laughed, '*That* is a master understatement.'

'Pah!' Gemma waved a dismissive hand. 'Anyway, the point I was making is that the dress has been a massive drama. Loads of designers want the job! One up-

and-coming woman—Hannah Colter—even sent me a free sample dress. Not a wedding dress, but it's beautiful. Actually—' she looked Gabby over with a critical eye '—it would be perfect for *you*.'

'I couldn't possibly…'

'Yes, you could. Hannah would be stoked at the publicity. Just come and look.'

Gabby glanced at Zander but he laughed and shook his head. 'No use appealing to me—I've never been able to get Gem to give up on an idea.'

Succumbing to the inevitable, Gabby followed Gemma up the stairs to a large and messy spare bedroom.

'This is the wedding room—or *wedding dumping ground* might be a better description.' Gemma headed to a large wardrobe, tugged the doors open, reached inside and pulled out a transparent zippered dress bag, through which Gabby could see the sparkle of shimmering material.

Qualms began to surface. Instinct informed her that the dress was most definitely not suitable—not her type, not her style. Not *her*. Too visible.

Oblivious to her dilemma, Gemma pulled the dress out and Gabby held back a small gasp. Hundreds of adjectives flooded her brain. *Magical, shimmery, delicate, gorgeous.*

'Right. Let's try it on,' Gemma stated.

And somehow, ten minutes later, Gabby was wearing it, staring at her reflection with shell-shocked eyes. Sleek and sleeveless, the dress left her shoulders and neckline bare, emphasising the slenderness of her waist before falling in a silvery, sparkling, sculpted waterfall to the floor.

'I…'

'You look like a fairy-tale princess. Decision made. It's yours.'

But this wasn't who she was—clad in designer gear, glittering for every eye to see. And yet… The wedding would mark the end of her time with Zander and, damn it—how did she want him to remember her? Like this or muted and neutral? The answer was absolute. Let his final memory of her be a dazzling one. Just once let her risk coming out of her shell for the occasion. Because after the wedding she would return to life as normal. It would be her final show and she'd make it a good one.

'If you're sure, then thank you.'

'I'm sure.' Gemma packed the dress back into its bag and handed it to her. 'Here you go. You may as well take it now.'

With that they returned downstairs, and soon after that the party dispersed.

'Your family are wonderful,' Gabby said as Zander started the car. 'I can see why you want to make them happy.'

By faking a relationship. With each moment it seemed increasingly important to remind herself of that. Fact and fiction were beginning to blur and she had to ensure she could see the defining line.

'So,' she said. 'What now? If you drop me at a Tube station, I can head back home. It's not that late.'

There was a pause as Zander drummed the steering wheel with his fingers—it was a trait she now recognised as his thinking trait.

'Actually…why not make a weekend of it?' he suggested slowly.

Gabby hesitated as instincts warred within her. Then, 'That sounds great. If we stop at a supermarket on the way back, I'll even cook dinner, if you want. I do a great fish pie and salad.'

She closed her eyes in silent despair. *Fish pie and salad?* This was a man who could afford to dine out on caviar every night of the week.

But Zander smiled. 'Fish pie and salad sounds perfect.'

* * *

Zander pushed the trolley around the supermarket as Gabby chose items, enjoying the intent expression on her face, her ability to imbue such an everyday chore with interest.

'Do you have any dill?' she asked.

'I think you should work on the assumption that my cupboards are bare.'

Gabby looked up from the potatoes she was assessing. 'So how does *that* work? Presumably you need to eat. You don't have some sort of superpower that enables you to subsist on air?'

'Unfortunately not. I mostly eat out or get food delivered to the office. Also, every so often Mum descends and fills my freezer with homemade meals I can just heat up. I go to the local shop as and when I need staple items.'

Gabby grinned suddenly. 'Well, it doesn't seem to have done you any harm.'

The smile lit her face and tugged at his gut, causing an urge to pull her into his arms in the middle of aisle three and kiss her. *Not a good idea.* It was worrying enough that he'd suggested extending the weekend, decided to abandon the office in favour of her company.

So instead he said, 'Do you want me to look for anything?'

Gabby shook her head. 'I'm nearly done. All I need are ingredients for the salad.'

'Leave that to me.'

Half an hour later they carried the loaded bags into his kitchen, unpacked the ingredients and set to work.

'This is Gramps's recipe and I love it,' Gabby said as she selected a knife from the block and started to chop onions. 'When I was a kid I'd have it with ketchup and baked beans, but as I got older I figured out it was better without!' Reaching for the garlic, she looked up at him. 'What was *your* favourite childhood dish?'

'My mum's chicken casserole, closely followed by Dad's pork chops in cream with potato dauphinoise. We always ate together, so mealtimes were pretty noisy affairs.'

'Like today at Gemma's?'

'Yes.'

'You were lucky,' she said quietly, as the smell of sizzling onions pervaded the air. 'Sometimes I wished so hard for siblings, to be part of a "normal" family. And then I'd feel guilty, or I'd worry the social workers would think I'd be better off somewhere else.'

'Was that ever a possibility?'

'Gran and Gramps were in their seventies and there were concerns. So many visits and meetings and whispered conversations… I was constantly petrified I'd be taken away. Luckily we jumped through all the hoops, I played my part and there was a happy ending.'

Zander's heart went out to her. 'Did you *have* to play a part?'

'Yes! It was incredibly important that I came across as quiet and well-adjusted—a child who wouldn't cause any issues at all. Perhaps it was a good thing—it taught me to push down anger and grief and focus on the positive, on my goals in life. In truth it wasn't only the social workers I needed to convince—it was Gran and Gramps, as well.'

Zander frowned. 'But there must have been times when you didn't feel quiet or well-adjusted?'

'Sure, but I wasn't only worried about convincing the social workers. I was scared that they were right—that I would be too much for my grandparents, or that I would remind them too much of my mum. I was scared they would change their minds, and I was grateful they took me in. So I knew I had to be perfect.'

'Didn't you ever feel like being loud and noisy and letting your hair down?'

'Maybe years ago, but not any more. It's not in my nature now. I'm quite happy looking on whilst other people do that.'

Zander didn't believe her—he sensed that along with her grief and anger, Gabby had also stifled her joie de vivre and her sense of adventure.

'I've got an idea.' He glanced at his watch. 'How long does your fish pie need in the oven?'

'An hour.'

'Perfect. Then once you have it in, why don't we pop out for a predinner drink in the pub?'

'Sure. That sounds nice.'

As he mashed potatoes and shelled hard-boiled eggs, mixed a salad dressing and loaded the dishwasher, he hummed under his breath.

Gabby's eyes scrunched in suspicion. 'You look like Freddy did earlier, when he was planning on mischief.'

'*Moi?*' He opened his eyes wide in simulated surprise. 'What mischief could I possibly be planning?'

'I don't know…' Opening the oven, she popped the fish pie in and he gestured to the door.

'Let's go.'

They walked the tree-lined streets, inhaling the smell of the nearby river, until he spotted what he was looking for—a pub a colleague had mentioned.

'Here we are.'

The pub exuded warmth. People had spilled out on to the street, glasses in hand, and the sound of music tumbled out to mix with the chatter and laughter. Once inside they headed to the bar, and Zander beamed as he saw the stage against one of the walls, plastered with posters of local bands.

'Look at that,' he said. 'Turns out it's karaoke night. Why don't we give it a go?'

Gabby stared at him. 'Uh-uh. No way.'

'Why not?'

She waited as he ordered their drinks and accepted her gin and tonic with perfunctory thanks as they found a tiny unoccupied table. 'Well, for a start, I can't sing.'

'Yes, you can. I heard you in the shower this morning and you sounded fine.'

'That is completely different. I will *not* stand up there and make an idiot of myself.'

'So there isn't even a tiny bit of you that wants to do it?'

'There is a tiny bit of me that wishes I was the sort of person who wants to do it, but I'm not. End of.'

'We could do it together.'

'Is this why you brought me here?'

'Yes. I even brought this to help you.' He showed her the herbal anxiety remedy he'd picked up on their way out. 'Obviously you don't have to do it if you don't want to. But I think you do. Maybe years ago you didn't just suppress grief and anger... Maybe you supressed a bit of the real you, as well.'

Her forehead creased in a frown. 'And maybe that bit is so buried it can't be retrieved. Because I really can't do this.'

'What's holding you back?'

'Fear of making a fool of myself—fear of being watched, noticed, the centre of attention.'

'But if you do it—face that fear—you'll feel good.'

'Possibly...' The admission was quiet and wrenched out of her.

'Then let's do it. After all it's only five minutes of your

life. In five minutes it will be over and we can leave the pub, never to return.'

'OK. Sign me up.'

The words were blurted out, and she looked as if she regretted them instantly, but he was out of his seat before she could recant.

They waited, and listened to the two people before them. He watched as she twisted her hands together, ran her finger through a splash of water on the table to make a pattern, picked her drink up and put it back down again untouched…

'This is nuts. Why can those people just stand up and sing and I can't?'

'You can.' He stood up. 'Come on. We're up next.'

It was only as he ascended the stage that it occurred to him that he hadn't thought this through. He was going to have to read lyrics on a flickering screen from the stage, which in essence made this on a par with public speaking. It also meant it would be harder for him to help Gabby. A co-singer who couldn't read was hardly ideal.

He muttered a curse under his breath.

'What's wrong?'

'Nothing.'

Gabby looked white-faced with anxiety as it was, and he reached out for her hand, tried not to wince as she squeezed it. Somehow he'd have to wing it—hope he knew enough of the lyrics to manage.

The music started and Zander gave himself up to the whole experience—after all this *wasn't* public speaking. It didn't matter if he tanked. But the words on the flickering screen were hard to decipher, and eventually he resorted to *la-la-la* in place of the words.

Gabby had remained silent, but as she realised his predicament she turned, glanced at him, squeezed his hand even tighter, then turned back towards the audience and began to sing. Softly at first, almost as if she were trying to prompt him, and then her volume increased—and *then* her foot started to tap to the rhythm and she began to belt it out!

At the final note the audience clapped and they descended from the stage, making way for the next singers. Gabby turned to look up at him.

'I did it,' she said quietly, almost as if she couldn't believe it.

'You did.'

'Thank you, Zander. For putting yourself through that for me.' And, standing on tiptoe, she brushed her lips against his.

'You're welcome. Now, let's head home for that fish pie.'

She smiled. 'And after dinner I'll show you how grateful I am.' She wiggled her eyebrows. 'Maybe shed a few more inhibitions.'

'Now, *there's* a plan I like the sound of.'

CHAPTER TWELVE

Six weeks later

GABBY SMILED AT her grandmother, making her usual surreptitious check on how well she looked.

But today Lucille returned her scrutiny with interest. 'You look peaky,' she said. 'Is everything all right?'

'Of course. I've just been busy at work and...' *Busy with Zander, stacking up a whole pile of treasure trove memories...*

'Busy with Zander?'

Sometimes she wondered if her grandmother could read her mind. 'Yes.'

'How are you feeling about the wedding?'

Gabby knew how she *should* feel: relieved. Relieved because the wedding would mark the end of an interlude she knew couldn't continue. Already the lines had been blurred too much. The fun fling was no longer a charade, but it was still a temporary job with an end date. That date had almost arrived and it was better this way—to end on a high note before the inevitable fizzle-out factored in.

But now she needed to answer Lucille's question. 'Nervous. But relieved that the charade is coming to an end.'

Lucille raised a delicately arched brow and her blue eyes clouded with sudden worry. 'You're sure that the charade is still a charade?' she asked, her voice gentle.

'Of course. Zander will pay me the final instalment after the wedding and that will be that.'

The idea caused her more than a touch of discomfort.

A part of her wanted to refuse to accept it; another part knew she couldn't. Not when it was her grandmother's well-being at stake. Plus the money grounded her, made her remember that it was a job.

Her grandmother poured the tea, a lapsang souchong blend, into delicate blue-and-white china cups and Gabby reached out to accept hers. She looked into the light brown depths and suddenly her stomach gave a small lurch. Frowning, she put the cup down. This was her favourite tea—a smell and taste she associated with her grandmother and long, happy chats. But now it smelt...*wrong*. And her tummy definitely told her not to imbibe.

'You do look peaky. A bit pale and—'

'Excuse me, Gran.' Gabby bolted for the bathroom, sat on the loo seat and fought the nausea. She looked across at the gilt-enamelled mirror—she did look peaky. Pasty, even. With a very unattractive green tinge to her pallor. *Nice*.

Touching her tummy, she thought back over what she'd eaten in the past day—nothing that would cause this.

A small strand of an idea began to niggle at the edges of her brain. A shadow of doubt wriggled and writhed as she did some frantic calculations. *Not possible.* She hadn't had a period for a while, but she was on the pill so she could not be pregnant—the possibility was not worthy of any thought. She'd assumed it was simply due to her normal life being tilted on its axis.

No period.

Feeling sick.

Coincidence.

Yet the doubt persisted through the ensuing conversation with her grandmother, through the rest of the day, and through the supermarket trip where the jars of pick-led eggs seemed to call to her.

For God's sake.

Pausing in the pharmacy aisle, she picked out a pregnancy-testing kit.

Zander stood outside the Roman Baths, one of the city's most enduring historical spots, where Gemma and Alessio's wedding ceremony and reception were to take place, and reminded himself that today was a happy day. A day when his sister would wed his best friend.

But it was also the day that marked the end of his fling with Gabby. They'd decided to enjoy it and then stay at her place for their final night together.

Although... A stray thought entered his head—a thought that kept wriggling its insidious way past logic and common sense. Did it *have* to end today? Yes, the job had ended...but could they extend the fling? Prolong their time together for real?

Bad idea.

Gabby wanted love, marriage, Mr Right, a family—and God knew she deserved that chance. *He* couldn't offer her any of that.

The limousine pulled up and he stepped forward to open the door. Gabby climbed out—literally stopping him in his tracks.

'Wow. *Wow.* Just...wow.' The dress—a miasma of silver and white, a tapestry of lines that accentuated her slender shape—fell to the pavement in a swirl of elegance. Her chestnut hair was swept up in what he suspected was a deceptively simple chignon, her hazel eyes enormous in a delicately made-up face. 'And wow again.'

Her generous lips, enhanced by a deep red-brown colour, turned up in a smile. 'Right back at you,' she said. 'James Bond, eat your heart out.'

Her tone was light, but he frowned, suddenly sure that something was off. Was she a little pale? 'Are you nervous?'

Another smile, and yet it didn't reach her eyes, and it was accompanied by a small, almost hard laugh.

'Nope. The attention will be on Gemma and Alessio. Plus half the guest list are super famous, so I'll be able to fly under the radar.'

He studied her expression, saw that the words were sincere, but sensed that the idea of a celebrity bash wasn't the issue here. Which was odd in itself. What was bothering her? The fact that this day marked the end of their interlude? Did Gabby want to prolong their time together, too? If so, was that good or bad?

The questions tumbled around his brain.

'We'd better go in,' she said. 'You've got your best-man duties to attend to. I'll be fine with your family.' As they entered, she looked around. 'This is beautiful.'

Now he knew something was wrong—because this was way more than 'beautiful'. The Roman Baths were exquisite, magical with ambience, the stone walls and arches imbued with history. Guests milled around the edges of the deep blue rectangle of water that twinkled in the torchlight that cast a golden mist on the ancient surroundings. Yet Gabby's words sounded mechanical, flat—utterly unlike her usual self. And where were the facts, the research, the historical information?

But before he could respond, his family surged forward and the moment was lost. He and Gabby hugged everyone, and then he needed to go and help usher in guests with Alessio, who radiated happiness and joy.

'This beats anything! It's better than racing, better

than winning, better than being on the podium spraying champagne.'

'I'm glad for you—but you make damn sure you look after my sister, OK?'

'I will.' Alessio's tone was überserious now. 'I mean it, Zander. I promise. I'll be there for Gemma for the rest of our lives.'

The words twisted something in him, reminding him that once *he'd* believed that and been wrong. He hadn't been able to sustain love, hadn't been strong enough to figure out a way forward.

Then music struck up. The orchestra's notes hung in the air with a haunting beauty as Gemma walked forward on Frank Grosvenor's arm and all the guests fell silent. As he listened to Alessio and Gemma enunciate their vows, Zander hoped with all his heart that it would work out, that they could achieve what he hadn't been able to.

Once they had been declared husband and wife, and with the help of the ushers, Zander encouraged the guests up to the terrace, where waiters circled with drinks prior to the sit-down meal to be held in the Georgian grandeur of the Pump Room.

Then he moved across to where Gabby stood in the shadows, a glass of orange juice in her hand, staring into space.

'Hey. Are you OK?'

'I'm fine.'

'Well, you don't look it.' A slight sheen of moisture beaded her brow, and her skin seemed to have taken on a greenish tinge. 'You look like you need to sit down.'

'I said I'm fine.'

But she swayed, and he reached out to steady her, taking the glass from her hand and stepping forward to shield her from prying eyes. 'Are you going to be sick?'

'No... Oh, God. I don't know. Probably not...but maybe. I'll head to the bathroom.'

'I'll come with you.' His hand on her back, they wended their way through the guests to the restaurant, where the staff were scurrying in a hive of activity.

Gabby headed at speed towards the bathroom and Zander waited, aware of a tightness across his chest, an elusive feeling that he was missing something important.

When Gabby emerged she looked marginally better. 'I'm OK. I wasn't sick. Usually if I just sit down for a bit I can will it away.'

'"Usually"?'

There was a beat and then another. 'I meant whenever I feel nauseous...ever since I was a child. I'm fine now.' But her hazel eyes skittered away.

'OK.' Again there was that sense he was out of the loop. And now he went with his instinct. 'If you say so. But I don't believe you. I know something is wrong and I think you should tell me.'

'Stop...'

The word was too low, too urgent, and now real panic took hold of him. 'Tell me. Are you ill?' *Shades of Claudia.* He took her hands in his, shocked at how cold her fingers were. '*Tell* me. I'll sort it out.'

She gave a small half laugh. 'I don't think you can sort this out, Zander. Not even you.'

'Then I'll help. Tell me what it is.'

'I...I'm sorry, Zander. This isn't the time or the place, but...' Gently she took her hand from his. 'I'm pregnant.'

'*Pregnant?*'

The word echoed, reverberated up to the lofty grandeur of the ceiling, off the iconic Georgian chandelier and flew, *ping-ping-ping*, from one fluted pillar to the next.

It caused a sonic boom that vortexed around him, filled with the one word on repeat.

Pregnant.

It resounded in a sonorous toll.

Pregnant.

The meaning of the word sought entry to a brain desperate to block it out. Eventually he forced his vocal cords into action and looked down at Gabby, sitting on an elegant dining chair, surrounded by crystal and silver and pristine white napkins.

'But you can't be.'

He recognised the stupidity of the words even as he uttered them. Gabby wouldn't lie and she wouldn't make it up. Had Julia been right—had this all been an elaborate set-up? His own folly dawned on him. He'd accepted that she was on the pill, hadn't given any other protection a thought. Yet he couldn't believe he'd got it so wrong—anyway, she looked as shell-shocked as him.

'Well, I am. I told you the truth in Sintra. I am on the pill. It turns out that it's to do with that herbal remedy I was taking for anxiety—apparently in a low number of cases it can counteract the pill. It does say so in the small print. Ironic, really. All my research, all my planning, and I didn't read the small print.'

Zander wished he could think, but his brain felt as if it was encased in a gluey mix of sludge, each thought coming in slow motion. As she spoke, he had backed away from her and was now a foot away from the table. He recognised the stricken look in her eyes, looked away, caught a glimpse of his expression in an ornate gilded mirror. Horror had redrawn his features into a caricature of repudiation.

Too many emotions swirled inside him—along with the memory of Claudia, who had wanted a family. It had been Zander who had insisted on caution, on waiting. Now her voice echoed in his brain.

'Zan. I think we should go for it. I know we're young, but that's OK. Let's start a family—not a business.'

And he'd resisted, prevaricated, knowing his own dream would be given up, would flicker out before ever catching light. Then illness had struck and all their energy had been for the fight and then acceptance. Claudia hadn't ever got to hold a baby in her arms...and now Gabby would.

Gabby was carrying *his* baby.

The whole idea jarred in his brain and he felt something inside him shattering—illusions, plans, certainties. All were coated with a layer of guilt. It was all he could do to remain still, not to run from the room with its Regency splendour.

Gabby rose to her feet. 'I'm sorry. I didn't want to tell you now—not like this...not at the wedding. I know this isn't what you want.'

Her hand went to her tummy, lay flat over it almost as if she were protecting the baby from his reaction, from his words. The gesture dispersed the fog, cut through the sludge. None of this was the baby's fault. Zander's guilt and emotion, his past behaviours, failures and fears, had nothing to do with the miraculous being growing in Gabby's womb.

'Don't apologise. Of course you had to tell me. Why didn't you tell me before?'

'Because I didn't know how, and it didn't seem fair before the wedding. But...now you know. We're having a baby.'

Now he knew.

Images streamed through his brain. A baby with chestnut hair like Gabby's...another with dark blonde

hair like his, hazel eyes…blue, grey…so many permu-
tations and possibilities.

Then panic broke in, short-circuited the connection
and dispersed the images. How could he be a dad? He
wasn't a family man; he was a businessman. And in his
case the two were mutually exclusive. *But that wasn't
this baby's fault.*

He had to focus. This was his baby. That was the precious being he needed to think of now. Not himself. Right
now the two most important people on the planet were
Gabby and the baby.

'Now I know,' he repeated.

'Know what?'

A voice behind them. Zander spun round to see Julia
walking towards them, a vision in a red-and-black gown.

'Know that we need to be on wedding duty,' he im-
provised quickly.

'Yes, you do. It's time to move the guests in here for
dinner. I came in to double-check the seating plan.'

She moved back to the entrance and Zander took
Gabby's hand as she rose. 'We need to talk.'

Gabby nodded. 'But not now.'

'And, Gabs? Everything will be all right.'

Right now he wasn't sure how—all he knew was that
somehow he had to make it so. Even if he had no idea
how. Even if the idea of fatherhood was making his skin
clammy with sheer, unadulterated terror.

Gabby walked by Zander's side back to the gaiety and hum
of chatter and laughter, the pop of champagne corks, the
vibe of celebration, and tried to focus on the part she was
here to play. She was no longer sure what that even was—
everything was surreal as her emotions corkscrewed.

Sharing the news had brought a modicum of relief

along with a surge of misery. Saying the words had made it real, but the initial horror on Zander's face and his gesture of repudiation had hurt, even though she understood it.

He'd been taken by surprise. But he'd recovered enough to tell her everything would be 'all right'. Whatever *that* meant.

'Gabby, come over here for a photo,' she heard Gemma call out, and she walked over, pinned a smile to her face.

She looked at the Grosvenors with the sudden realisation that they were related to the baby growing inside her, and the idea sent her emotions into free fall again. But somehow she pulled herself together, and she kept herself together over the next few hours.

She tried to appreciate the grandeur of the Pump Room, the classical melodies played so beautifully by the orchestra, the Georgian banquet that drew gasps of awe from the guests.

Once the meal was over the guests moved into yet another room. Music struck up again and the bride and groom took to the floor. Gabby felt her chest constrict as she watched, seeing the love in Gemma's and Alessio's expressions, the protective, almost reverent way Alessio held his bride, and she blinked back tears. What if this never happened for her?

Then Gemma turned and gestured to her. 'Come on. Family on the floor next!'

Laura and Frank moved forward and started to dance, their movements so attuned to each other, the smiles on their faces only for each other. Julia was dragged forward by Freddy and Heidi, and soon the three of them were dancing, laughing together.

'Zander, come on!'

Gabby realised there was no choice, and put her hand into his proffered one. They stepped on to the floor. His arm encircled her waist and she felt his reaction, his small intake of breath, and knew he was realising the fact that inside her was the start of a baby. *Their* baby.

As they swayed together to the music, she allowed worry and anxiety to dissipate in the awe-inspiring knowledge that she and Zander had created the beginnings of a new life. She let him hold her close, and rested her head on the solid wall of his chest.

They stayed until the end, waved off the bride and groom, said farewell to the rest of the family, gave a hug to the sleepy children—and then they were back outside, where a chauffeur-driven car waited to take them home.

'What would you like to do?' Zander asked.

'We'd better stick to the plan. Go back to mine. But...' She hesitated. 'Would you mind sleeping on the sofa bed?' She might have no idea where they would go from here, but she knew the fun fling was definitely over. 'Tomorrow we'll talk.'

CHAPTER THIRTEEN

GABBY OPENED HER eyes and tried to orientate herself…
And then slowly memory seeped back in. She was pregnant. In seven or eight months she'd be a mum. In all
her dreams this was not how she'd imagined it. The plan
had been to find Mr Right, get married, buy a house—
provide her baby with two loving parents, security, a
happy family life, siblings…

Well, that plan had gone…dispersed into wisps of illusion. Touching her tummy, she pushed away the feeling
of inadequacy, of not being good enough.

'I'll figure it out, baby. I promise,' she said aloud.

And she would. Somehow. And the first step towards
that was to talk to Zander.

A tantalising aroma wafted into the room and she used
the bathroom, then pulled on her clothes with the realisation that she was ravenous.

Two minutes later she entered her lounge and crossed
the room to the kitchenette, seeing that Zander had already packed away the sofa bed in the lounge and had set
up the circular foldaway table. A vase of flowers was in
the middle, surrounded by slate place mats, knives, forks,
chocolate spread, fresh lemons… The air was permeated
with the smell of bacon sizzling.

Zander stood at the kitchen counter that separated the
lounge and kitchen areas, stirring a bowl of batter. 'Pancakes,' he announced. He glanced up at her, then back
down at the bowl, a faint flush on his cheeks. 'My dad
used to make pancakes every Sunday morning. I figured
we could start the tradition early—the baby eats what
you eat, right?"

The words brought a sudden sting of tears to her eyes but she blinked them away. 'Sounds perfect. I'll put the kettle on.'

Fifteen minutes later they sat down, a mound of pancakes between them, and Gabby dug in, relieved that the nausea seemed to have been flummoxed by the notion of pancakes. Maybe the baby liked them? The idea made her smile. Or maybe the baby liked the fact this was his or her first family meal.

Whoa—that idea wiped the smile from her lips. It was a stark reminder of what she'd wanted for her children— the real thing, a happy family...

She pushed her empty plate away. 'So...' she said.

'So,' he answered.

He looked a different man today, no longer shocked, no longer horrified. Instead his expression indicated a man in control of his emotions.

'First, I apologise for my initial reaction yesterday— you took me by surprise and I was utterly shocked.'

'I appreciate the apology, but I saw your face when I told you—that was more than shock or surprise. That was horror. I know you don't want children, and I don't want my baby to feel unwanted or unloved. I can't bear that thought.' She truly couldn't. A tear quivered on the edge of her eyelash. 'I *was* that baby—the unwanted one. The unwanted child. That will *not* happen to this baby. Not for a second. Not on my watch.'

His blue-grey eyes didn't leave hers as he reached out to cover her hand with his own. 'This baby won't be unwanted or unloved, and I swear to you that I regret my reaction. It wasn't horror. It was...' He hesitated. 'I don't know what it was. Disbelief, guilt, panic. You see, Claudia wanted to start a family. I was the one who held back— partly because I knew once we had a baby I would never be able to chase my dreams. Then she fell ill…never had a chance to be a mum.'

Oh, God. His reaction made sense now. The idea of fatherhood must seem almost like a betrayal of Claudia—an extra lash of the guilt he already felt.

'It's not your fault.'

But his set expression told her he thought it was.

'You didn't know Claudia would die so tragically young. You thought you had plenty of time. Maybe you weren't ready to be a parent so young, even if Claudia was. That is not a sin. Maybe in the end you'd have found a compromise between family and business—the tragedy is that you'll never have a chance to find out.'

'I know that logically, but if I had reacted differently, if I'd been a different person, maybe she could have held her baby in her arms. But, whatever happened with Claudia and I, this baby will *not* bear the brunt of the past. You're right—I didn't plan to have children, but now I want to be the best father I can.'

'I want to be the best mother I can.'

'And I know a way for us to do just that.'

'I'm all ears.' Lord knew she'd welcome a plan of action.

He inhaled deeply, exhaled, sipped his coffee and then said, 'I think we should get married.'

Gabby froze. 'Come again? You think we should *what*?' Frantically her brain tried to come up with words that rhymed with *married. Tarried… Carried…*

'Get married.'

'You and me?'

'Yes.' His tone held exaggerated patience. 'Seeing as *you* are pregnant with *my* baby—yes. You and me.' His gaze didn't leave hers; his blue-grey eyes were utterly serious. 'I know I'm not Mr Right, but it is the right thing to do.'

'But you don't want to get married. You don't want any sort of relationship.'

'I *didn't* want either of those things, but now the situation has changed. I didn't plan on being a father, but now that it's happening I want to do the best I can, and that means being there for my child.'

Gabby picked up her orange juice, put it down again, tried to work out what to say, what to do. Eventually she shook her head. 'No. I appreciate that you want to do your duty, do the "right" thing, but I told you—I never want this baby to feel it's a burden or a duty. You can be a good father without us getting married.'

'I believe I will be a better one if we are. I am doing this because I want to. For the baby. I know I don't have to. I accept that it is perfectly OK nowadays to parent separately. But that isn't what I want. I want to be there under the same roof, be there for the firsts, be there for meals, holidays, be there when he or she needs me. We'd be a *family*.'

Under the same roof... A family... The words resonated within her, made a sense of rightness course through her veins. Their baby would grow up with one proper home, the security of not having to move from house to house. But...

'Yes, we'd be a family, but our marriage wouldn't be—'

'It wouldn't be how you want your marriage to be. I know that. It would be different—based on liking and respect and physical compatibility.' His gaze skittered from hers for a moment. 'Not love. I understand that's second-best for you, that you hoped for a happy-ever-after with Mr Right, but you said it yourself—Mr Right may never turn up. I think we could be happy—or certainly not *un*-happy. You also said you wouldn't have children until you could offer them two loving parents and security. We can give our baby both those things. Together.'

Gabby's mind reeled. Thoughts ravelled and unravelled as she tried to think, to consider the ramifications of his suggestion. Because whatever she'd expected his reaction to be it wasn't this. Marriage was not what he wanted, and a marriage without love was not what *she* wanted—and yet he was right; the baby changed everything. All she'd wanted was for her mother to be willing to change her lifestyle for her. Zander had just shown that he was willing to do that for his child. Surely she was, too?

If they got married, their baby would have one home, wouldn't have to move from her home to Zander's in a constant cycle of change. It would have a family—Zander's parents, his sisters—he'd have cousins. And… A stray thought crept in… And so would Gabby. Sisters-in-law who might become friends, parents-in-law…

Gabby closed her eyes, contemplated all those solid tangible reasons for marriage. But… 'How would it work? In real life, I mean. Where would we live? What about my job?'

There was so much to think about. She loved her flat, but it wasn't big enough for a baby. She loved her job, but did she want to keep working? If she didn't keep working how would she support the baby? She wouldn't live off Zander. So that answered that. But then…

'Whoa, Gabby. *Stop*.'

Looking down, she realised she'd helped herself to the last remaining pancake and had been spooning sugar on to it in a continual stream.

'I know this is a lot to think about but we'll work it out. Do you want to live in Bath? Do you want to keep working?' he asked.

'Yes. And yes. I need to stay near Gran and I would like to stay on at least part-time.'

'Then we'll live in Bath.'

'But you'd have to commute.'

Zander's work ethos: another reason in favour of marriage. Zander's work was his life; if his child lived under his roof it would maximise their relationship potential.

'It's only an hour and a half by train. Or I could get a

driver...work in the car. That would be compensated for by all the other advantages. We'd be near my family, your job, your gran.'

'You'd do that?''

'Sure. It truly doesn't matter to me. A house is a house.'

'No. A house is a *home*—I want my child to have a home. *I* need a home.'

'Of course. I'll leave all that to you.'

The words triggered a sense of sadness, a reminder of the terms of this marriage—in her dreams of Mr Right they'd picked furniture together, debated every purchase, painted walls, chosen wallpaper for the nursery. This would be another fake relationship with Zander, but this time it would have no end date.

As if he'd picked up the motes of her dissolved dreams in the air he frowned, reached out and gently touched her cheek. 'We don't have to get married. I won't try to bull-doze you into it. I get that you may want to hold out for Mr Right, and I don't want to make you give up a dream if you'll regret it for the rest of your life. But if we do get married I will need an assurance that you won't still be on the lookout.'

Outrage jolted into a welcome spark of anger. 'I wouldn't do that. If I marry you, Zander, I'll honour my vows and my commitment—and I'll expect you to do the same.'

Unlike Miles and Steve. Another advantage to this type of marriage: it wouldn't turn her into an insecure, needy nutcase. There would be rules, a maintenance manual she would understand because she would help write it.

'I would. That's the point I'm making. This marriage can only work if we're both happy with its parameters and our expectations. There is no point getting married for the sake of our child if what he or she witnesses is anger or misery. And...' He gave a rueful shrug. 'And I don't want you to be angry or unhappy.'

'Ditto.'

'I truly believe we can make this work. Arranged marriages have worked throughout the centuries. Unions based on something other than love.' He leant back as if to give her space. 'So what do you think?'

What did she *think*? This was her chance to give her baby everything she'd ever wanted as a child. In truth she wouldn't have cared if her parents had loved each other or not as long as they had seemed happy; she had wanted love, a family life, a home and security. Her child would have all those things if she married Zander. So really it was a no-brainer. She had to try or she'd always regret it.

She just had to ignore that voice in her head that still argued…

'I think we should do it. So I suppose the next step is to share the news.'

'Agreed. I'll tell my family.'

'And I'll tell Gran.'

The next day
Bath, Lucille's house

Telling her gran had been much harder than Gabby had anticipated. At first Lucille had been genuinely thrilled about the baby, and definitely happy that Zander wanted to be part of the baby's life, but then Gabby had gone on. 'And we've decided to get married!'

For reasons she couldn't quite understand, her voice had come out overbright, high and squeaky, and her arms had, of their own volition, lifted to cross her chest.

'Why?'

There was no judgement in Lucille's voice, but worry clouded the blue eyes that just seconds ago had been bright with joy.

'Because we feel it's the best thing for the baby. He or

she will have both parents under one roof, won't have to move from house to house and will have a proper family life. It will work around Zander's work ethos, maximise his time with the baby, and I'll be giving the baby a family. If anything happens to me, he'll have *them*. The Grosvenors.' She came to a stop, searched her gran's face for approval that wasn't there. 'I don't have a choice.'

'There is *always* a choice.'

'Then I believe this is the right one. This baby deserves to have what you and Gramps gave me. A family—that is what is most important.'

'But *you* are important, too.'

'I know that. And if I loathed Zander, of course I wouldn't do this. But we like each other, we have mutual respect and he is a good man. I'll have a good life.'

'A *good* life—but will it be the best life you can have? It's your life. You only get one.'

'Yes. But I have to do what's best for my child—that is paramount.'

Her grandmother looked troubled. 'Of course your child comes first. But I don't think it's necessary to sacrifice your life.'

'It's hardly a sacrifice.'

Lucille sipped her tea. 'But it *is*. You are twenty-nine years old and you and Zander are making a decision to give up on love, never to have a marriage like I had with Gramps.'

'But I may *never* meet my Mr Right.'

'This way you definitely won't. Instead you will be making a commitment to a loveless marriage—in sickness and in health, for better and for worse.'

The words and their solemnity rang around the room, and Gabby scrabbled to scoop up the seed of doubt before it could take root.

'What if your child *knows* you got married only for him

or her?' Lucille continued. 'That you would have preferred not to? That's a burden for a child. I always worried when you were young that you thought your grandfather and I took you out of duty.'

Gabby closed her eyes. She *had* thought that, and it had been a horrible feeling—a precursor to guilt and self-reproach.

'We didn't. We took you because we loved you. Our biggest fear was that we wouldn't be allowed to keep you.'

'That was my biggest fear, too. That's why I want my child to have absolute security. I don't want him or her to move from home to home. That's worth the trade-off to me. I truly believe this is the right thing to do.'

Lucille hesitated, topped up her cup of tea. 'Gabby. Are you sure this is only about the baby?'

'What do you mean?'

'You and Zander have spent a lot of time together, and from all you've told me you've enjoyed that time—are you *sure* that you don't have stronger feelings for him?'

Gabby barely even waited for her gran to finish the sentence. 'I am absolutely sure. Zander is a good man, Gran, but he isn't my Mr Right.'

Too successful, too good-looking, too overwhelming. She wouldn't *want* to love him—she sensed that that way lay a path to doom, a return to neediness and insecurity.

'Then I will support your choice, even if I don't agree with it. And I will be the best great-grandmother ever.'

'I know you will, Gran.'

Bath, the Grosvenor home

Telling his family had been tough, but once they had established that he was planning on being part of the baby's life they did seem genuinely happy at the idea of an addition to the family.

But then he said, 'Actually, Gabby and I are getting married.'

Silence greeted the announcement—a silence so profound that annoyance surfaced, came out in his scowl.

'Don't all fall over at once congratulating me.'

His parents and Julia exchanged a quick glance, and as if by tacit consent his mum spoke. 'The thing is, Zander, you haven't mentioned the word *love*.'

Damn right, he hadn't. The word filled him with panic. Love would bring this marriage to its knees—he couldn't sustain it and didn't want to contemplate it. But the word also inspired guilt, because Gabby *did* want love and he couldn't give it to her.

'Gabby and I want what is best for the baby, and we like each other… We get on. There is no reason why it shouldn't work.'

'There are at least a dozen reasons I can think of,' Julia interjected. 'God knows, Zander, I think a child should have a father…' Her voice was touched with a seldom-acknowledged sadness; her husband had decided the whole family gig was too much for him and absconded over the horizon. 'But you can have joint custody—you will still be part of its life.'

'Not in the same way.' Zander turned to his parents. 'Tell me *you* approve.'

Laura and Frank exchanged looks. They had one of those telepathic methods of communication that seemed to be a product of all their years together.

Laura spoke. 'Darling, we will support whatever you choose to do, but I don't think I do approve. I want you to marry for love.'

'Dad?'

'I always hoped you'd find love again, Zander. I understand why you're doing this, but I believe you and Gabby can and will be fantastic parents whether you get married or not. We will welcome both Gabby and the baby into our family, regardless of your marital status.'

Zander looked around the table, then rose to his feet. It was time to go. In this instance his family was wrong. It was as simple as that.

'I love you all, but I want to be there for my baby as much as possible—and that means marriage.'

A few days later

Gabby surveyed her breakfast without appetite or enthusiasm and told herself that sugar-free muesli was good for the baby, who could not, after all, survive on pickled eggs alone. And she needed to hurry up. Zander would be here at any minute to take her on a day out—though he'd declined to say any more than that. Told her it was a surprise.

She spooned up the last unappetising mouthful and patted her tummy. 'Maybe there will be pickled eggs later, baby.'

As she finished speaking the doorbell heralded Zander's arrival. Gabby opened the door and her tummy looped the loop—was she really going to marry a man who did this to her?

Zander smiled at her. 'Ready to go?'

Gabby grabbed a denim jacket, tugged it over her T-shirt and jeans. 'I am now.'

Once in the passenger seat of his car, she turned to him. 'So where are we going?'

'I told you—it's a surprise.' He glanced at her before turning the ignition, and concern lit his blue-grey eyes. 'It's an hour till we get to our first port of call, so if you want to nap go ahead.'

She *was* tired. As soon as she went to bed each night questions marched behind her eyelids, along with doubts and worry as to whether she was doing the right thing for the baby. Yet now, when she closed her eyes, lulled by the movement of the car and his presence, she slept, opening her eyes only when the car came to a stop.

'Where are we?'

'A helipad. We're flying by helicopter to Cornwall and we're going to Tintagel Castle. I did some research and the flight is completely safe for the baby. But if you feel worried, obviously I'll change the plan.'

Helicopter. It occurred to Gabby that for Zander taking a helicopter was akin to hopping in a taxi. The realisation was a reminder of just how wealthy he was, and for a moment discomfort tugged at her chest.

She blinked to dispel the unease. Zander had planned this, and it would be churlish not to simply appreciate it. 'Let's go!'

Twenty minutes later they approached the craft and she gazed at it in surreal fascination. 'I've never seen one close up.'

'I'll climb in first and then help you. You need to use the footplates, and then there's a big step up to get in.'

Once inside she settled back, and soon the whir of the blades made conversation impossible.

The eventual take-off was completely different to that of a plane.

'It's as if we've just lifted and floated upwards,' she said.

Once they were airborne the noise abated a bit and she looked down over London, watching as it became smaller and smaller, the familiar landmarks looking like little toy miniatures.

'So why Tintagel?' she asked.

'I figured I owe you a castle after Sintra, and I thought it would be good to spend a day together away from familiar haunts. Give us a chance to centre ourselves. It's been a pretty momentous few days.'

The rest of the journey was spent watching the landscape. The aerial perspective of rich swirls of brown and green dotted with farm buildings, grey blocks of towns and cities, caught her breath with its sheer variety. Then finally there was the intense sweep of the sea that indicated they were nearly at their destination, a prelude to the helicopter's descent.

As they alighted from the craft, the Cornish breeze combined with the whir of the helicopter blades to lift her hair in a wild tangle and puff out her clothes so she resembled a fairground mirror reflection.

Once en route in the hired car, Gabby gave herself up to the sheer pleasure of watching the beauty of the Cornish countryside flash past. The fields were full of summer—the golden swish of corn, the deep brown loam of tilled earth—and stacked hay dotted the horizon. The drone of a tractor through the open window mixed with the buzz of insects, whilst cows and sheep watched their journey with placid interest. They passed a farmhouse, and then the green changed shade as the landscape turned to scrubland and then back again.

At the end of a half-hour journey Tintagel came into view, the ruined castle a craggy, impressive feature that loomed over the headland to the sea.

'Tintagel is where King Arthur is said to have been conceived—you can't get much more magical than that,' she said.

'Then let's go.'

As they walked from the car park Gabby had an urge to take his hand, but held back, unsure as to the etiquette. Somehow, to hold hands now they were getting married seemed to imply a level of intimacy unsuitable in an arranged union. Instead she allowed herself to enjoy the warmth of his presence, to appreciate the thought that had gone into this trip.

The short walk to the ticket office was achieved in

companionable silence and then they began the trek to the castle ruins, pausing as they looked across a wooden bridge and up…and up…at the steep ascent.

Zander frowned. 'I should have researched this better. I got hooked on historical splendour and magical legends. I'm not sure you should climb this.'

Gabby considered for a moment. 'The doctor said I'd be fine with exercise.'

'Hmm… Hang on. I'm going to call Julia for advice.' Minutes later Zander dropped the phone in his pocket. 'Right, Julia said she went rock climbing in her first trimester with Heidi and was fine. Her advice is to try it, but to turn back if there is any problem, however small, and to take it slowly.'

'Yes, sir!'

His concern made her feel…cared for. *Alert! Alert!* His care was, as it should be, for the *baby*.

As they walked across the bridge he stayed close to her. Every so often he reached out as if to steady her, and she smiled up at him as they paused, arm in arm, and looked over the rail at a sea that was a clear sun-sparkled turquoise.

He pointed downward. 'Merlin's cave.'

'I can almost imagine a dragon swooping down to visit him.'

Then came the stairs and, as instructed, she took them slowly, very aware of his focus, of the heat of his gaze as he made sure she was all right, his hand on the small of her back to help her.

And then they reached the top and she gasped in sheer awe. The ruins themselves were darkly atmospheric, though the arched doorway and slit windows were all that remained of the great hall. Low stone walls marked where houses, kilns and a chapel would once have teemed with people and medieval life.

But it was the view that literally caught at her newly

recovered breath. The headlands were a myriad of jutting rocks, in shades of green, brown and terracotta. And way below the sea crashed with all the force and power of nature against the rocks.

'It's a place where your imagination can swoop and soar... You can almost *taste* history.'

Zander's eyes rested on her face. 'I've brought something perhaps a little more sustaining if you want to picnic up here. I even brought pickled eggs.'

'That sounds wonderful!'

Soon enough he had unpacked a hamper bearing the logo of a famous London store and Gabby got down to the serious business of eating for two. Mini quiches, game pie, pâté and crackers, and, of course, the pickled eggs were all washed down with sparkling elderflower pressé.

Eventually she sat back, replete. 'Thank you. That was delicious and it has fortified me for the trek back down!'

'Before we do that... I thought it would be a good time to give you this.' Reaching into his pocket, he pulled out a small box, snapped the lid up and handed it to her.

A jolt of emotion shot through her as she saw the glint and sparkle of the ring embedded in velvet—a beautiful mix of an ice-white diamond and deep blue lapis lazuli set in white gold.

'If you don't like it we can change it.'

'No! It's stunning.'

Carefully she took it out, looked at it for a long moment. Suddenly the whole ambience of the day shifted, and as if in response a cloud moved across the sun for an instant.

Don't overthink it, Gabs.

Quickly now, she slipped it on to her ring finger—he didn't offer to do it and in truth it wouldn't have felt right if he had. Too much like a parody. After all, this ring was not an indicator of love, merely an intention of commitment without it. A prop rather than a symbol.

Holding her hand up, she watched as the newly reappeared sun sparkled in the stones' facets, causing motes of light to dance in the air. Yet for some reason her finger felt weighted.

'The central stone is a diamond, obviously, and the blue stones are lapis lazuli—the colour reminded me of the sea and Sintra, and the jeweller said they represent friendship.'

Now sadness truly prodded her—a definite sense of *This is not how it's meant to be*. Yes, the ring was beautiful, the idea brilliant, but the most important component was missing.

Stop it, Gabby.

This was not the time to be whiny or act the ingrate—Zander had gone to a huge effort and she should appreciate it. Because in their marriage friendship, not love, would be the cornerstone. Love for their child would be the bedrock.

'It's perfect,' she said. 'And thank you for making an occasion of it.'

'I thought it was important. After all, one day our child will ask us where we got engaged. My sisters were always asking Mum and Dad to tell their engagement story.'

'I used to love hearing Gran and Gramps's, as well. Gramps hired a tandem and asked Gran to ride through life with him. He said that he'd pedal harder when she needed to rest and that they'd always balance each other out on their journey through life together.' As always, the story brought a smile to her lips, though the memory was touched now by the sadness of missing him. 'What was your parents' story?'

Zander smiled in reminiscence. 'I told you Dad's an electrician? He rigged up loads and loads of fairy lights in their local park, hired a violinist and told her she was the light of his life. And she really is—his face still lights up when she comes into a room and vice versa.'

'And what about you and Claudia?' Gabby didn't know

why she'd asked that—perhaps because that was what a *friend* would ask.

The thought tasted bitter on her tongue and she picked up her glass and gulped at a swig of elderflower.

Zander hesitated. 'I was only eighteen and I went for the romantic cliché. I saved up, took her out for an expensive meal, gave her a red rose and a ring. All the other diners clapped when she said yes.'

She could see it now—the earnest youth he had been, at a time of life when he had still been struggling to come to terms with and conquer his dyslexia and all that had come with it. His dark blonde hair had probably been longer than it was now, flopping forward over one eye, and he would have been dressed up in a suit. Claudia, young and beautiful, would have been alight with the glow of optimism, hope and love.

His parents, her grandparents... Their proposal stories had been full of love—a foretaste of their hopes and dreams of going through life together with love to guide their movements. Whereas this...this was kind and thoughtful and...*all wrong.*

She wanted Zander to be down on one knee, slipping the ring on her finger for real. Because he loved her, not because it would make a good story for their child. She wanted love, not friendship, because she loved him and, dammit, she wanted this to be *real.*

Oh, hell. The drink suddenly tasted too sickly-sweet, cloying on her tongue. She loved him. She *loved* him. She loved Zander. Her Mr Wrong. *What to do? What to do?*

'Gabby? What's the matter?'

Panic, horror, terror—all fused into an icy coldness, enabling hard logic to overcome emotion. Whatever she did, she could not let him suspect the truth, learn of her misplaced, idiotic, unwanted love. A love he would reject just as surely as her mother had rejected her love all those years ago.

But now this marriage would be impossible. How could she hope to make it work when the rules and parameters had exploded? Even *she* couldn't live a lie, play a part for the rest of her life, day in, day out, yearning for what she couldn't have.

He mustn't know—must not suspect even the possibility that love had somehow had the temerity to take root and flourish within her for him. This wasn't his fault. None of it was.

So now she would have to play a different part—tell him the truth, but not the whole truth. Above all she had to make this work for the baby's sake. It was impossible for her simply to walk out of Zander's life, but somehow she had to figure out a way to rip this love out by its fledgling roots.

The glint of the ring was harsh now, carrying the weight of falsehood, and she tugged it off and held it out to him. 'I'm sorry, Zander. I can't do this.'

Shock etched his face, turned it white under the tan, and his body jerked backwards as an expression she couldn't interpret flashed across his blue-grey eyes. But his voice was calm when he spoke. 'Why not?'

Deep breath. *Careful, here, Gabby.*

'Because we would both be settling for second best, and that is not how I want to teach my child to live his or her life. It is not what a marriage should be. A marriage should at least start out like your parents' did, like my grandparents' did, like yours did. You don't want to get married. You told me that don't want to marry anyone, and you certainly don't want to marry me. You want to marry the mother of your child for your child's sake, and I honour that sentiment but it makes me second-best and secondary. I can't spend my life like that. I still want my shot at love with Mr Right.'

Those last words were the hardest, but she forced them out, knowing they would help her argument.

A small hope flared that Zander would step up, reach out, grab the ring and say, 'Gabby I love you. I want a marriage based on love, too,' then place the ring back on her finger as a gesture of loving commitment to her and the baby.

Her insides clenched and her heart pounded with a sheer yearning that the scenario would play out that way—that he, too, would have a eureka moment, realise that the past weeks had been more than a charade, more than just fun.

The seconds ticked on, each one full of anguish as she watched his face, saw confusion and pain. She wished so hard that he would love her back, *could* love her back. For herself.

Tick-tock. On and on.

Finally his lips opened and she braced herself.

'What about the baby?' he asked.

As hope died, crumbled to ashes, she stared down at the ring, at the lapis lazuli blinking at her in a kind of Morse code: *friendship, friendship, friendship.* That was all she could hope to have, and she would make that OK for the baby's sake. Before that, though, she needed space and time, to get her head together and bury this foolish love as in the past she had buried grief and anger. She'd learn her part and play it perfectly.

'First take the ring,' she said. 'Please.'

CHAPTER FOURTEEN

ZANDER STARED AT her outstretched palm. The ring glinted at him in all its suddenly cold hard beauty. He'd chosen it for Gabby; he didn't want it back. Staring at the blue stones, the white faceted diamond, he tried to think. But his brain had gone into shutdown mode, and the urge to sit on his hands, make her put the ring back on her finger, was paramount.

'What about the baby?' he repeated. After all, that was why they'd decided to get married. 'I thought we had agreed this was best for our child. The right thing to do.'

Now she winced, and a dark part of him was glad—because perhaps he could persuade her that marriage was the right option.

'We did.' Her voice low, torn, ragged with guilt. 'But I can't go through with it. I'm sorry.'

'I want to be part of this child's life.'

'You will be. I want that, too. Of course I do. I promise we can sit down and work out custody arrangements. I want this baby to have you and your family in his life.'

'And, like we've said, the best way to do that is if you and I and the baby are under the same roof. Instead of moving from house to house.'

Stop! The voice was a Klaxon in his head as he saw the look of pain on her face and knew his words had triggered memories of her own childhood, the packing of her suitcase…

But that had been his intention, hadn't it? Number one bastard that he was. How low was he willing to go in his belief that this marriage was right? And right for *who* anyway? Maybe it was better for the baby, but not at the cost of Gabby's happiness, her life. She deserved a shot at her Mr Right—someone able to believe in love and for ever, someone able to commit and not prioritise work over love.

Not someone like Zander, with a proved track record of failure, a lack of capacity to nurture love, to be satisfied with what he had. He was a man who revered ambition, craved success, and he would never be able to put a family first.

Yes, this marriage would suit *him*—because he wouldn't have to put Gabby first. He could have it all. So he was trying to bulldoze her into a marriage she didn't want, a life she didn't want. *No more.*

Yet as he prepared to speak, an inexplicable sense of loss tore into him. For a searing moment he imagined the life that had nearly been his—a life with Gabby, a family life, with trips to the supermarket, holidays, meals, laughter. He watched as the images of that illusory life faded and dispersed in the breeze. Because that wasn't reality. He couldn't offer her love because he knew that for him the emotion wasn't sustainable, knew that it couldn't coexist with his ambition. His plans revolved around his work, and he'd always known it wasn't possible to have a family, as well. Hadn't he?

'It's OK, Gabby,' he said, even as he knew it wasn't. It wasn't OK at all to have this dark bleakness descend on his heart. His arm felt heavy, inert, but he forced himself to reach out and take the ring. 'We'll make this work a different way.'

'How?'

'Tell the baby the truth. That we both love him or her...'

'But we don't love each other,' she broke in. 'That we're

friends. And maybe two homes will be OK as long as they're both full of love and security.'

'Yes.' He forced conviction into his voice and his expression, but inside a sudden bleak disappointment washed over him—a pain he didn't fully understand. 'So what now?'

Gabby hugged her knees, stared out to sea. 'Well, there are still seven months until the baby is due. If you want to attend antenatal classes with me, of course you can, and I'll keep you posted on how the pregnancy is going. But otherwise there's no longer any need for us to see each other. No more charade, no more engagement.'

No more Gabby.

As he sat there, so near her and yet so very, very far away, the bleakness increased. It felt like a jagged tear in his chest. He had a sense that he had failed, that he had missed something crucial. They sat in silence for a long time, both looking out at the crags and cliffs, the imposing Cornish coastline and the deep blue of the sea, until finally Gabby shifted.

'We should go,' she said.

Zander nodded, told himself it was for the best. He couldn't sustain relationships, and he didn't understand compromise. He would never again risk love because he knew he couldn't nurture it. On his watch it would fray, wither and fade away.

He told himself that now he could focus on work—take his company to even greater heights without any distraction for the next seven months. And after that he would work out a balance between the baby and work without having to factor Gabby in at all. It was all for the best.

So why did his very soul feel so heavy as they trudged towards the steps he'd climbed in such anticipation?

A month later
Bath, Lucille's house

Gabby smoothed her hand over her growing bump and smiled at her grandmother. The baby seemed to have rejuvenated Lucille.

'I'll be here on this green earth for as long as I can be. Here for the baby and for you, Gabrielle,' she said.

'I hope you're here for years and years, Gran.'

Thank heaven for Lucille—her family, her rock. And a welcome distraction from thoughts of Zander.

Gabby had hoped that a month without seeing him would at least have started a cure for love, would have stunted its growth, made it less intense. But with each passing day the sheer ache of missing him intensified until all she wanted to do was call him, just to hear his voice.

But she didn't. Her plan, such as it was, was to starve this love until eventually it would have to perish. She tried to ration even her thoughts of him—so far without noticeable success.

'Gabby?'

'Sorry, Gran. I was thinking.'

'So have I been.'

'About what?' Idly, Gabby reached out for one of the small square marzipan-topped cakes which were her current craving.

'Do you love Zander?'

The sheer unexpectedness of the question caught Gabby off guard and the cake dropped from her suddenly nerveless fingers, crashed on to her plate in a scatter of iced crumbs. 'Of course not.'

'Gabrielle. I'm an old lady, but I've known you all your life. Tell me the truth—I want to help and I know you aren't happy.'

'I *am* happy. I'm happy about the baby. A bit terrified, but mostly happy.'

'And what about Zander?' Lucille persisted. 'Gabby, you can tell me. That's what family is for.'

Gabby hesitated, and then the need to confide, to share the secret that burned within her with her gran, overcame her doubts. 'I do love him. But he doesn't know and he mustn't ever know.'

'Why not?'

'He doesn't want my love, Gran, and I can't face the humiliation of inciting his pity or compassion.' She couldn't take the rejection. 'Plus, it would make things complicated, and that's not fair on the baby. We've agreed to explain that we're friends, that we don't love each other but we both love him or her.'

Her gran frowned, her delicate skin creasing. 'But that's not true. You said you wanted to tell your child the truth, that you didn't want to live a lie by getting married. This will be living a lie, too.'

'For my child.'

'No, Gabby. It will be years before he or she is worried about the intricacies of the relationship between his parents. I don't think this is about the baby. I think it's about *you*. And, darling, I understand how scared you must be of having your love rejected again. Like your mother did. But I know that I would have told your grandfather I loved him no matter what. Because love should always be given a chance. And if Zander does reject that love I know you're strong enough to face it and move forward.'

The last words were slurred slightly and Gabby could see the forcefulness of her speech had tired her grandmother.

Quickly she poured another cup of tea, and then she

covered her gran's veined hand with her own. 'Thank you. I'll think about it. I promise.'

And later, when she had gone back home, she did. She would never break a promise to her gran, so she thought about it long and hard. Replayed every word Lucille had uttered.

She closed her eyes and cringed at the idea of the pity, the compassion, the sheer awkwardness such a confession would generate. Yet Gran was right—love deserved a chance.

Gabby stared at the ceiling and made her decision, then snuggled down under her duvet and told herself it was the right thing to do.

Zander drummed his fingers on the desk and stared at his phone, willing it to ring and for it to be Gabby. Saying what? He closed his eyes. They had said everything they needed to say. Antenatal classes didn't start for weeks, and until then the baby quite simply did not need him. Neither did Gabby—and he certainly didn't need her. Though it was galling to realise how much he missed her. Somehow during the charade Gabby had got under his skin, permeated his life in ways he hadn't foreseen and didn't know how to combat.

His intercom buzzed and his PA's voice rang out. 'Your sisters are here.'

'Both of them?'

For heaven's sake. Zander sighed. The Grosvenors were gathering for lunch at their usual venue of a London Italian restaurant to celebrate his mother's birthday. But the plan had been to meet at said restaurant, not at his office.

'Tell them I'll be right down.'

Zander rose and hitched his jacket off the back of his

chair, made his way to the marble-floored lobby where his sisters waited. 'Why the escort?'

'To make sure that you actually come.'

'I wouldn't bail on Mum's birthday.'

'Well…just in case. We haven't seen you since you emailed us that you and Gabby aren't getting married after all.'

'Work has been busy…' It was true enough. He'd thrown himself into work with a ferocious energy, even though he knew he could have delegated many of the tasks he had undertaken himself.

'How are you feeling?'

'I'm fine. It's all worked out for the best.' The words sounded so hollow they echoed.

His sisters exchanged glances.

'Are you sure?' Gemma asked gently.

'Of course I am.'

And if he wasn't fine now he soon would be. Of course he would. At some point surely the palliative effect of work would kick in, relieve these ridiculous symptoms.

The ache he felt in the morning when he woke up, the horrible emptiness of his apartment, the sudden sterility of the furniture he'd once barely noticed. The echoing absence of Gabby, the solitary meals. The obsessive checking of his phone and email in case he'd missed a message. The dreams, and the way his head would turn every time he saw someone who looked even remotely like Gabby.

What was the matter with him?

They approached the restaurant and he halted as he saw Alessio look up towards Gemma, saw the way his best friend's face softened, the sheer love in his eyes.

Suddenly—just like that—he knew exactly what was wrong with him, and came to a sudden halt.

The realisation transfixed him to the spot as knowledge flooded him with its truth. *Dear Lord.* He was an idiot, a fool...denser than platinum. He loved Gabby—*he loved her.* And he had to tell her right now. The urgency was illogical, but absolute. Even if she didn't love him back—and why should she?—he wanted to tell her. He wanted her to know.

Zander turned to his family. 'Sorry, guys. I need to make a call.'

Phone in hand, he raced out. Relief flooded him when she answered the phone.

'Zander?'

'Gabby—where are you?'

'Actually, I'm at Bath Station, about to get on a train to come and see you.'

'You are?'

'Yes.'

'That's brilliant. I'll come and meet you when you get in to London.'

'But—'

'I'll see you in an hour and a half.'

Which didn't give him long.

He raced back inside the restaurant. 'Mum, I love you. Happy birthday! Got to dash. It's an emergency. Not a work one.'

Gabby looked out of the window as the train pulled into the station, wondering anew why Zander had said he'd meet her. Presumably to save her trekking across London to his office? Well, she'd deliver her carefully rehearsed speech and then she could turn around and get on the next train back.

As she alighted from the carriage and headed to the barriers she frowned. That couldn't be Zander, could it? Every iota of her body identified him as the man she loved, but why would he be carrying an enormous bunch of heart-shaped helium balloons?

For a moment hope peeked up over the parapet of pessimism—until suddenly she remembered that it was Laura Grosvenor's birthday. They must be for his mum. Maybe Frank had asked Zander to pick them up for him, or…

Now she was through the barrier and there was Zander, looking dishevelled, as though he'd raced across London, his face flushed and his hair rumpled.

And so utterly gorgeous.

Her heart ached with love and she yearned to throw her arms around his broad chest. *Bad idea.* She needed to give her rehearsed speech and then leave. At speed. Preferably before he even had a chance to respond.

'Hey,' she said, keeping her eyes away from the balloons, deciding it would be best to ignore them. 'Thank you for coming to meet me. Especially on your mum's birthday. I am *so* sorry. I hope I haven't spoilt the plans?'

'Nope. You haven't. Not at all.' He ran his free hand through his hair. 'Gabby…?'

It was now or never, and she tucked a strand of hair behind her ear and tried to recall her carefully prepared speech. But her brain had become scrambled, messed up by his sheer proximity which seemed to have dispersed every rehearsed word.

The careful explanation, the caveats, the build-up. All gone. Instead, she said, 'I'm here because I love you.'

The words fell from her lips and she closed her eyes, unable to watch his reaction, braced for rejection.

'It's not a big deal. I'm not expecting anything back, and it won't affect how we bring up the baby. I totally get that you don't do love after Claudia.'

She sensed him right in front of her—so close she

could inhale his oh-so-familiar citrus smell, so close it took all her willpower not to touch him.

'Open your eyes, Gabby.'

His voice was gentle.

'Look at me. Please?'

The last word disarmed her and she obeyed, looking directly into blue-grey eyes that held a depth of seriousness, warmth and joy.

'I love you, too.' He gave an almost strangled laugh. 'Why do you think I'm standing here with a bunch of balloons?'

Disbelief warred with hope. 'But you can't... I don't understand...'

'I'll try to explain about Claudia. I told you that we had different dreams and ambitions. But it went deeper than that... Very soon into our marriage I realised that I'd made a mistake.'

His breathing was shallow and Gabby stepped closer to him, to offer what comfort she could, sensing he'd never admitted that before.

'We were too different... Perhaps we'd never really known each other. Then she fell ill, and in that awful time the only thing I am glad of is that she never knew. That she believed in our love to the end. And so did everyone else. Because I didn't want to betray her memory, because I felt such guilt.'

'Oh, Zander. I am *so* sorry.' She could see how the guilt, the secrecy, the living a lie would have eaten away at him. Topped up by the guilt at all his success after her death.

'It's OK. I'm telling you because I want you to understand why I believed that love wasn't possible for me. I believed it was *my* fault—that my ambition killed my love and that that would always happen, that it was a given.

I'd always put my wishes, my work first. You've made me see that it isn't true. You've made me look back on my marriage differently. Perhaps Claudia and I simply weren't suited and our love simply couldn't have survived our differences because we couldn't ever have worked out a compromise. You've shown me I *can* do that—that *we* can do that. You've shown me that work isn't the be-all and end-all of life, that I can achieve a balance.'

Joy lightened her whole body and she felt as if she must be radiating happiness.

'And you've changed *me*. Brought me out of my comfort zone, encouraged me to try new things and overcome my fears and anxiety.' Gabby grinned. 'You've shown me how to have fun, take some risks, to sing and be heard and seen. Before I set out today I even sent my book off to some agents. I spent so much of my childhood, my life, feeling afraid, thinking I had to be invisible or quiet or perfect. You've helped me figure out who I am. The real me. Made me see I *am* good enough, and that some things are worth risking rejection for.'

'I'm thrilled about your book. And this is what I hope we'll do for the rest of our lives. Grow together, learn together, discover new things. *Together.* I want to make a home with you. Ever since you entered my house I've realised how bland it is, how dull… I want a *real* home, full of love and clutter and…you.'

Gabby grinned at him. It seemed impossible to smile as widely as her happiness dictated. 'I'd love to take you shopping, to all the markets and places I love. We can choose colours together, paint walls, make the happiest home in the world.'

'I love you, Gabby. I love everything you've achieved. I love your courage, your loyalty and your love for your grandparents. I love the way you overcame your fears. I admire your resilience. I love the way you tuck your hair behind your ears. I love *you*.'

'I love you, too—your strength, the way you've coped with dyslexia, your drive and ambition, your love for your family, the amount you care… I just *love* you, Zander. This baby is the luckiest baby in the world to have a dad like you.'

'And a mum like you. So…now seems the right moment for this.'

Turning, he made a slight movement with his hands and suddenly from the crowds emerged a group of people holding instruments. Before Gabby even knew what was happening a jazz melody broke out, the strains upbeat and beautiful, and a woman began to sing, her voice rich and melodious.

And then Zander released the balloons and went down on one knee, pulling a box from his pocket.

'Gabby. Will you marry me and make me the happiest man in the stratosphere?'

'Yes, I will!'

And this time he slid the ring on to her finger and looked up with a smile. 'Diamonds, lapis lazuli and sapphires. Love and friendship for a lifetime. We are going to be the happiest family in the whole entire universe.'

And as he picked her up, twirled her around and then pulled her into a deep, soul-satisfying, toe-curling kiss, Gabby knew that they would be.

* * * * *

AN UNEXPECTED PARTNERSHIP

TERESA SOUTHWICK

To my friend Vicki Kahler Goeres. It seems like yesterday we were new neighbors who clicked immediately and bonded over our hair. We don't live on the same street anymore, but the friendship is still going strong. Thanks, buddy.

Chapter One

Tess Morrow needed to cry.

Grief had been trapped in her chest all day, and the pressure to let it go grew more painful by the second. She'd been strong during her grandfather's memorial service here at The Pub. All Patrick Morrow's friends had shared their stories of him, the funny, generous, kind man who'd raised her, and she hadn't shed a tear. People offered condolences and she gracefully thanked them. But if one more person said "I'm sorry for your loss," the composure that was making her face hurt would shatter. If the stragglers didn't leave pretty soon, she couldn't guarantee they wouldn't see her ugly, wet, snotty cry.

She both yearned and dreaded to be alone when it happened. Still, the sooner she sped up them up, the sooner she could mourn privately.

She walked over to the booth by the front window and smiled at the three men and one woman there. They were here to pay their respects. "Can I get you anything? Another beer? Glass of wine?"

All four shook their heads. They were older, longtime friends of her grandfather. Silver-haired John Alexander gave her a sympathetic look. "How are you holding up, honey?"

"Okay," she lied. "I learned how to be strong from him."

"That was Pat," he agreed. "Strongest person I ever knew."

The older woman sitting beside him touched his arm and gave the other two men a look. "We need to go. It's been a long day for Tess."

The others murmured their agreement and slid out of the booth. Every one of them asked if she needed anything and then hugged her. Made sure she knew to call if they could help her at all. Finally, blessedly, she closed and locked the door behind them. She lowered the shades on the big glass windows looking out on the nearly empty parking lot. Finally she was alone.

"Tess?"

She whirled around, heart pounding. "Dear God, Leo. You scared the crap out of me."

"Sorry. I didn't mean to."

"What are you doing here?" She blew out a long breath.

"I came to pay my respects to Pat," he said. "He was my friend."

"I meant *still*. What are you still doing here?"

"Just wanted to stick around. Make sure you're okay." He shrugged one broad shoulder.

Leo "The Wall" Wallace used to play professional ice hockey up until two years ago when an ankle injury ended his career. That sucked for him, but prevented female heartbreak in every major city with an NHL team.

He was a really big man, not just tall, but muscular, too. He had dirty-blond hair that insisted on curling and blue eyes that normally sparkled with mischief and flirtation. Right now they were somber and a little sad. Her grandfather had had a soft spot in his heart for this man. Tess's heart? Not so soft for him.

"Where did you come from?" Her pulse was finally slowing to normal.

"My favorite booth."

She glanced at it in a far, shadowy corner that Pat had

called the penalty box. In honor of Leo and his time spent in one during his hockey career.

"Well, I didn't see you." That was only half a lie. She'd ignored him, or tried to. He was a reminder of problems—personal and otherwise.

In the last year or so, bar revenue had declined. They were losing business to trendier establishments, and six months ago her grandfather had approached Leo about investing in The Pub. He'd introduced her and suggested lending Leo's celebrity name and a bit of capital to modernize and shake things up. She'd assured Pat that the two of them together could come up with a plan to make the place profitable again. But he was sick. Losing the man who'd taken her in when she was six years old hadn't been part of that plan.

Tears stung her eyes but she managed, just barely, to hold them back. "I'm fine."

He moved closer, stopping right in front of her. The man was like a mountain. Hence his nickname, "The Wall."

"Are you really?"

"I have to be." She looked up and met his gaze, trying to pretend her heart wasn't pounding too hard, and if it was, that it had nothing whatsoever to do with him standing so near. "Okay, thanks for coming. You can go now."

She turned her back on him and resolutely walked to the door and opened it. "Goodbye, Leo."

He hesitated a moment, then nodded and joined her at the exit. "Good night. I know how much you'll miss him. I'm very sorry for your loss."

His voice was so gentle, soft and sincere, yet somehow it popped the bubble of strength around her. She just couldn't keep it up any longer. Moisture blurred her eyes, and big, fat tears rolled down her face. Then the sobbing started, deep, wrenching cries that broke loose from inside her. She covered her face with her hands. If there was anyone she didn't want to see her like this, it was Leo Wallace.

"Tess?"

She couldn't answer, not even to tell him to go away and leave her alone. A moment later she heard the door close and the dead bolt click. Then she felt strong arms come around her and she was folded against his body. He made shushing noises, patted her back and mumbled nonsense about everything being okay.

Tess would never be sure when the closeness stopped being about comfort and turned into *awareness*. There was a reason women were drawn to him and right this moment Tess didn't have the reserves of strength to pretend she was different. No matter how ill-advised it might be.

The good news was that she had stopped crying. The bad was that she looked at him and their gazes locked, and suddenly it was hard to breathe. One moment they were staring at each other, the next he was kissing her. And she was kissing him back!

She opened her mouth and he didn't hesitate to accept the invitation. Their tongues dueled and breathing escalated. He threaded his fingers into her hair as their bodies strained even closer. She could feel that he wanted her and she wanted him, too.

"Leo…" There was no mistaking the pleading in her voice.

"Are you sure?" His eyes darkened with intensity as he searched her gaze. "Maybe this isn't—"

"Don't say it."

Right this second she didn't feel sad or lonely and holding on to that bubble of painlessness was vital. For as long as it lasted, she wanted passion to cancel out the grief. She didn't want to think about anything but this. She tugged him closer to the booth and her butt bumped up against the table. Leo lifted her onto it but there was still a question in his eyes.

"Yes," was the single word she said.

That was all he wanted to hear. As she leaned back onto the table, he slid the hem of her black dress up and hooked his fingers in the waistband of her panties. Quickly he slipped them down her thighs, over her knees, letting them fall down her legs until she kicked them off.

And then he was inside of her, filling her completely. There was no room for thinking; all she could do was feel and take what he offered. He moved slowly, thrusting in and out until she wrapped her legs around his hips to draw him in deeper. One more push and the knot of tension in her belly dissolved as pleasure roared through her. When her shuddering stopped, he thrust one more time and then went still, groaning with the power of his own release.

Tess lay there with her eyes closed. She could feel Leo standing between her legs, palms flat on the table. The only sound in the room was their mingled breathing slowly returning to normal. She didn't want to move. She didn't want to talk. She just wanted to hold on to the haze of pleasure and forgetfulness he'd given her.

"Tess?"

And the glow was gone. She opened her eyes and let him take her hands to help her sit up. He smoothed her dress over her thighs and bent to pick up her panties from the wooden floor.

He held them out. "I don't know what to say."

It was the first time she'd ever seen him less than cocky and self-assured. That was a surprise. "Just don't say you're sorry."

"Should I be?"

"No."

"Are you?" he asked. "Sorry about it?"

"It never happened." She so didn't want to talk about this. "You were never here. I don't want to hear about it. We will never speak of this again. And I don't want to ever hear anyone else talk about it. Is that clear?"

"With women nothing is ever clear," he said.

"Then let me point out that I'm not crying anymore." A vision of what she must look like flashed through her mind because she had ugly-cried. Snot and tears and sobs, oh my. "I'm sorry you had to see that."

"At least you weren't alone."

"It would have been so much better if I was." Oh, dear God, what had she done?

"So you do regret it." His mouth pulled tight for a moment.

"No. *It never happened.*"

"Or do you regret that it was me?"

She didn't want to hurt his feelings. Although he didn't seem to extend that courtesy to the plethora of women he took up with and threw away like used tissues. Still, he'd been considerate enough to pay his respects to her grandfather. Pat had always told her to be nice to Leo. He's not a bad guy. Tess could pull it together just this once. After all, there was nothing like hot, unexpected sex to take your mind off grief.

"Leo, it's just that you and I are like oil and water."

"A minute ago we mixed just fine," he said, the cockiness back in all its glory.

"Nothing happened," she reminded him. But heat crept into her cheeks and if there was a God in heaven, Leo couldn't see it in the dim light. Suddenly she was exhausted and her eyes felt puffy and sore from crying. "If it's all the same to you, I'd like to be alone."

"Whatever you want." For a second it looked as if he would say more, but then didn't. He straightened his clothes and went to the front door, steps away. After opening it he said, "See you, Tess."

"When hell freezes over," she whispered, locking the dead bolt behind him.

Six weeks later Leo was surprised when Tess called and asked him to stop by the bar. Where "it" had never happened. He was on his way there now and very curious about what was on her mind. After the night of Pat's funeral, he'd avoided The Pub, respecting Tess's wishes. But he missed the place, missed the older man who'd been more like a father to him than his own.

She wouldn't talk about whatever it was on the phone but he figured she wanted to discuss investing in her business. Not long before he died, Pat had told him it was in trouble and the best hope of saving it for Tess was to take on a partner. He'd heard what she said when he left after the memorial and figured hell must have frozen over. Her call came out of the blue and the only reason she would speak to him was finances.

He pulled his car into the nearly empty lot outside The Pub. The only other vehicle was a small, fuel-efficient one that had a few years on it. Probably Tess's. Anticipation hummed through him and adrenaline started to flow. Not unlike the way he used to feel before a hockey game.

After parking, he turned off the car and exited. "Let's see what the lady has to say."

He walked to the door, where the Closed sign was displayed. Peeking inside, he saw Tess behind the old-fashioned wooden bar with a brass foot rail. She was wiping everything down.

Leo would have to be a moron to miss the fact that she

didn't like him very much. Other than his ex-wife, who was a lying bitch, Tess was the only woman who'd given him the cold shoulder. Maybe he couldn't get her off his mind because she was a challenge. Without hockey to consume his competitive nature, he was channeling it to her.

That was as good an explanation as any because she wasn't his type. She was pretty enough, but not the kind of woman who gave men whiplash turning to stare. But there was something fresh and appealing about her brown hair and eyes, something friendly and inviting. For everyone but him. Until that night he'd never made a move on her. Why waste time on a woman who showed no sign of ever warming up when an abundance of ladies lined up to be photographed on his arm?

Except she did warm up to him that night. She could pretend it never happened, but he had the scorch marks to prove her wrong.

Time to get his head on straight and talk business. He tried the door and found it was unlocked. Tess looked up but her expression didn't signal that she was happy to see him.

"Hey," he said, closing the door behind him.

"Leo." She stopped wiping the bar and watched him walk over and sit on one of the stools in front of her.

He could almost feel the tension radiating from her. Maybe he could put her at ease. "I want you to know that I respect what you said that night—"

She held up a hand to stop him. "Don't."

"Understood." He met her gaze. "So, why did you ask me to come over and talk?"

"It's about The Pub—" Her lips trembled for a moment as grief slid into her eyes. She blew out a breath and

TERESA SOUTHWICK   15

continued, "I'm aware that Granddad came to you with a proposition to invest."

"That's right. I talked with him a lot when I suddenly couldn't play hockey anymore. About what I was going to do." That had been a personal low. He was dealing with an injury that forced him to retire prematurely from the sport that defined him at the same time his wife admitted she'd been cheating with a former lover. She announced she was leaving and taking their child with her. Leo had spent a lot of time at The Pub, drinking and spilling his guts to Patrick. "Your grandfather told me I needed an act two and I had a good head for business. He was right about both."

"He told me you bought the local ice rink and it was finally turning a profit."

"Yes. Among other ventures." All of them had been going down when he took over. Now every one of them was prospering.

"Before I make my pitch, you should know that The Pub was doing fine until Granddad got sick. The medical bills after he was diagnosed were substantial. Even then things were okay. But recently—"

"So you're letting me know you're a good manager."

"Yes. And the good news is that there's been an uptick in business."

"Yet you're approaching me, I assume for help, even though you fought Pat tooth and nail when he suggested I put up money and lend my name to improve declining revenue." At her surprised look he added, "Yeah, he told me you weren't in favor of partnering with me. So why now, Tess?"

"I had to let a full-time employee go and cut hours for others. That's enough to keep the doors open but not to grow." She didn't exactly answer the question of what had changed.

"Okay."

"This place has been my home since I was six and came to live with Granddad. I grew up here. Did my homework in the office in the back. Swept floors because I wanted to help. Did inventory. But there's a lot of debt from his cancer treatment and medical bills. I want his legacy to go on. I just don't want to see it turned into a sports freak show."

He winced at the dig to his former profession but sympathized with the sentiment. Or maybe the sheen of unshed tears in her eyes and the fierce pride on her face made him go soft.

"So, tell me what you're proposing."

She outlined the high points: an infusion of capital to update the place, a percentage of the business and a few other things. She finished up with, "If that's acceptable, I'll take you on as a silent partner."

What she outlined was agreeable to him and at this point in the negotiations it was probably best not to tell her "silent partner" was never going to happen. The thing was he really wanted to buy in. The place was conveniently located and had a lot of potential. Leo also wanted to preserve Pat's life's work.

"Do you have any objection to using my lawyer to draw up a contract?" he asked.

"No."

"Okay, then. I'll get in touch with her first thing in the morning."

"Figures your attorney would be a her."

"I didn't hire Annabel because of her gender. She's a damn good lawyer." And beautiful, too. But it was strictly business and a line he wouldn't cross even if there was an attraction between them.

"If you say so."

Tess was starting to get under his skin, and not in a good way. "Clearly you have a low opinion of me. Why is that?"

"The parade of women through your life for one thing. That speaks to being shallow, self-centered and commitment resistant."

Any guy would run in the face of commitment if he'd been through what Leo had. A guy would have to be an idiot to go through that again. Hockey had given him highs and lows—sanctuary from a lousy home situation, a college education and more than one Stanley Cup championship. The game was physically aggressive and injuries left marks. But they were nothing compared to what losing his career and family at the same time had done to him.

It was best to change the subject and get back to business. "You said The Pub was doing all right until recently. What changed?"

She suddenly looked nervous. "I probably should have led with this, but I wanted to get business details wrapped up first. Although if you have a problem with the fact that I didn't tell you this up front, feel free to change your mind about investing. You don't have to help if you don't want to."

He'd promised Pat he would look after Tess whether she wanted him to or not. There was no way to know what was going through Pat's mind when he made Leo swear, but a vow was a vow. If she was trying to scare him away, it wasn't going to work. "You're not making any sense."

"I know. I just want to make it clear that I'll figure out some other way. I could have worked eighteen hours a day with little pay before and it would have been all right. But things have changed. Now I have to—"

"Tess." That stopped her babbling but not the tension and nerves still making her twist her fingers together. "What's going on?"

She blew out a breath and stood a little straighter, as if bracing herself. "You know that thing we're not talking about that never happened?"

"For the record you can pretend we didn't have sex on that table over there. You can semantics the hell out of it, but that won't change anything. The fact is that we did it. You can bury your head in the sand but that leaves your backside exposed."

"You're not wrong about that." She looked everywhere but at him.

This was really starting to get on his nerves. "What's going on, Tess? Just spit it out."

"I'm pregnant."

He blinked at her and couldn't wrap his mind around the words. "I'm sorry. What?"

"I'm going to have a baby."

Bingo. That was the scariest thing she could have said to him. He couldn't believe it. No way this was happening to him. Not again. He wasn't getting sucked in for a second time by a woman who was lying about having his baby. Leo stood up and walked out of the bar.

Chapter Two

The door closed behind Leo, and Tess could almost feel the sting of a slap on her face. She couldn't decide if she was more shocked or angry that he'd walked out on her. And his child. This was the man her grandfather had wanted as a partner? She'd had her reasons for pushing back on that but none of them were about him not taking responsibility for his actions.

It was about the revolving door of females in and out of his life. Well-publicized, short-term affairs with actresses and models. Glorified one-night stands with glamorous women, rich and famous. Even the not so famous made headlines with him. But in all the publicity surrounding his "over in fifteen minutes" relationships, he'd invariably taken the blame for why things hadn't worked out. Always a version of "she's a great girl and I'm not good enough for her."

As much as she wanted to believe he had no feelings and hurt women from coast to coast when he threw them away, the only one he trashed was himself. One had to conclude he wasn't mean; he just had a problem with commitment. She wasn't into it either. That's what happened when the man you loved cheated repeatedly. He was a cocky college jock and that baggage had affected her opinion of Leo from the moment they were introduced.

In a way, Tess respected the way he characterized the

end of his affairs, even if she didn't condone "quantity over quality" behavior. So yeah, she was more shocked than angry right now. All the scenarios she'd imagined of how this conversation would go down never included him turning his back and walking away.

Tears filled her eyes and she didn't miss the irony. The last time she'd cried in this room, Leo had been there to comfort her and they'd had sex. Now there was a baby and he left her, taking his investment money with him.

Suddenly the door opened and Leo walked back inside. He stood there, staring at her, eyes narrowed dangerously. "A baby. You're sure."

"Peed on a stick and confirmed by a doctor." She had questions, too. "Why did you walk out just now?"

An angry, intense look pulled his mouth tight and made his eyes narrow on her. "I had to think before saying anything."

"Okay. So what are you thinking?"

"Is it mine?"

She was sorry she'd asked. The question tweaked her temper, implying that she was an underhanded opportunist. He was questioning her integrity, but she grudgingly admitted that he had a right to ask. "Yes."

"How do I know it's mine?"

"Because I said so and I don't lie." She glared at him.

He finally closed the door. "Right now, for the sake of argument, let's assume it's mine—"

"Stop calling me a liar. Of course this baby is yours. I've been pretty busy trying to save this bar, my grandfather's legacy. When would I have time to date?"

"You don't have to date," he said wryly.

"That's where you're wrong. I would have to date before doing…" As soon as she realized what was going to come out of her mouth, she stopped talking.

"You and I never went out before we…" He glanced at the booth by the door, where they'd done the deed. Then one corner of his mouth curved up as he looked back at her. "But wait, I forgot. That never happened."

"Obviously you don't intend to let me forget I said that."

"Not likely." He moved closer, stopping on the other side of the bar from her. "You're going to have it." It wasn't a question.

The part of her that wasn't super annoyed with him respected that he wasn't pushing for termination of the pregnancy. Truthfully, that had never entered her mind. "Not that you get to tell me what to do, but yes, I will have this baby."

"I need a test."

To make sure he was the father. As infuriating as it was to be doubted, she'd actually anticipated this. At her first doctor's appointment, she'd asked questions about prenatal testing.

"Before the baby's born it would require an amniocentesis to determine paternity. It's an invasive procedure that requires insertion of a needle to take amniotic fluid. This test poses the risk of miscarriage."

"Okay." His frown deepened. "So we have to wait."

"No. There's a blood test that can determine a very high probability that you're the father. Even though I'm telling you that."

"Like I said. I need a test. Let's do that."

"Okay." She folded her arms over her chest and met his gaze. "I'll set it up. We can have results in one to two days."

"Either you're a very good bluffer or—"

"I'm telling the truth," she finished for him. "Look, Leo, I didn't plan this."

"Okay."

"I can tell that's what you're thinking. I guess if I was in your shoes, the thought would cross my mind."

"Very understanding of you."

"I don't know what to say. I've never been in a situation like this," she defended herself. "It's not like I did it on purpose."

She glanced past him to the booth where it had happened. Heat slid into her cheeks as memories rolled through her mind. Those passionate moments in his arms were all that stood between her and the overwhelming grief of losing her grandfather. She'd never felt so out of control but she couldn't speak for Leo.

"You've had a lot more experience at that sort of thing than me. Since the responsibility should be shared equally, I won't ask why you never brought up the subject of protection."

He shifted his feet, the only sign that her comment struck a nerve. "That's fair. If—"

"I'm telling the truth," she finished. "I never planned to get pregnant. I was upset. I just buried my grandfather and that was a long, horrible day. I'm sorry I couldn't hold back the tears any longer. For the record I didn't ask you to comfort me. In fact I thought I was alone."

A hint of sympathy softened his gaze for a moment. "You weren't. And I assumed you were on birth control."

"I wasn't. And you know what they say about people who assume. Makes an ass out of you and me."

That was an understatement. He and his consolation had taken up every square inch of her attention. And now she was paying a really high price for it.

"I had a lot on my mind that day." She looked around the room. There were pictures on the walls of The Pub while it was being built. Opening day. The surrounding area before homes and businesses popped up. Her glance settled on the wood floor, the scarred bar between them, every mark with a story that was part of the history. "I grew up here with my grandfather. I live in the apartment upstairs. This is my home, as well as my livelihood. My business. My career. It's everything. You've got no skin in the game. Not really. To you it's just an investment."

"Which you're against."

"But Granddad trusted you. And I think you would understand why I feel that way if you were in my situation. For a few weeks after losing Granddad, my bottom line improved." Although that probably had more to do with cutbacks than actual customer expansion. "I thought I could make it. Cost reductions saved money but required me to work more hours."

"Then you found out you were pregnant."

She nodded. "I can't put in the time necessary to keep the business afloat. I have to take care of the baby. And I don't want my grandfather's legacy to disappear, but—"

"So it's the pregnancy that changed your mind about contacting me."

She'd vehemently told him she wasn't a liar. There was no point in starting now. "Yes."

"Because it's the only way to save The Pub."

"Maybe there's another investor I could interest. But Granddad liked you." She would give anything to know why. If only she shared the opinion. She didn't have a problem with him professionally. It was the personal that she was afraid of. Look what happened that night. But there was so much more at stake here. And she didn't have a lot of choices. The only thing she trusted unconditionally was her grandfather's judgment. Other than warm memories and this business, there was nothing left of him. And the thought of it ceasing to exist broke her heart. "Are you still going to invest in the bar?"

"You're having the baby."

"How many times do I have to repeat it? The child I'm carrying is the only reason I need your help. If I wasn't pregnant I'd muddle through without you. Yes, I'm having the baby."

"Then I'm definitely going through with our deal. I'll contact my lawyer to draw up papers."

"I'll make an appointment for blood tests at a private lab."

"Fair enough."

"Okay, then."

She said that with way more enthusiasm than she felt. He obviously didn't believe her about the baby, and the juxtaposition of his agreement implied that if he had no connection to the child, she and her business could dry up and blow away. He was sticking around just to keep her honest.

She couldn't wait to see the look on his face when he had to admit he was wrong about her.

Leo offered to pick Tess up for the meeting at his attorney's office to sign the partnership agreement but she politely declined. In a very cool and distant tone, she'd said it would be best to meet there. Fine with him. He hadn't seen her for a couple of weeks and that was for the best. A cooling-off period gave him time to brace himself to deal with her as they saved her bar. But out of sight didn't mean she was out of his mind. Her and the baby. Damn.

He rode the eight-story building's elevator to the top floor, where Annabel Sanders had her office. The doors opened into the reception area with a view of the whole valley. Huntington Hills in Southern California had a population right around two hundred thousand and was beautiful in the spring. Trees and flowers were blooming, and the vibrant colors of purple, pink and yellow stretched all the way to the mountains.

He walked over to the receptionist. "Hi, Geraldine."

"Mr. Wallace." The attractive woman was in her fifties and had stylishly cut short blond hair. Her blue eyes twinkled with humor. "And you know perfectly well the name is Geri."

"Right. I keep forgetting."

"It's a common problem with our former-hockey-player clients. Too many shots to the head."

"How many hockey-playing clients does Annabel have?"

"Only you. Thank goodness."

"Ah. Maybe I can shake the bushes, contact some of my teammates. Send some business your way."

"Please don't. You keep us busy enough. What with all the investment opportunities you're researching."

He had to make up for lost time. His career ended abruptly, and not long after his marriage ended, too. It was a dark period, most of which he'd spent in Pat Morrow's penalty box. He owed that man a lot for pulling his head out of his ass.

"You know you love me," he said. "If you weren't already happily married…"

She leaned back in her chair and looked up at him. "You're a shameless flirt. I should leave my husband and call your bluff."

"You should. But we both know you won't. You're way too smart to toss aside a good man for the likes of me." Leo felt someone behind him and turned. "Tess. Hi."

"Leo."

"I didn't hear you." No doubt she heard Geri calling him out on his crap.

She ignored him and smiled at the receptionist. "Hello. Tess Morrow to see Annabel Sanders."

"Nice to meet you." Geri gave her the friendly receptionist look. "Annabel is with a client. Her meeting is running a little late. I apologize for that. If you'll just have a seat in the waiting area, she'll be with you both as soon as possible."

"Thanks," Tess answered.

"May I get you something? Coffee?"

"No."

Leo noticed her already pale face go a little whiter. "You okay?"

"Fine." She smiled at Geri, then walked over to the cushy chairs by the windows and sat.

Leo followed and took the seat at a right angle to hers. Because she'd told him she was pregnant, he knew she was nauseated from morning sickness. He still couldn't quite wrap his head around the fact that the baby was his. Maybe.

"So, I got the results of the blood tests," he said.

"Me, too." There was a "told you so" look in her brown eyes.

"It's not conclusive," he pointed out.

"It conclusively confirmed you can't be excluded as the biological father."

She was right about that. He'd done the research. The most accurate results came from an infant's umbilical blood or tissue from the placenta, and that would have to wait another seven or so months. Fetal DNA could be observed in the mother's blood and rule out someone who absolutely couldn't be the father. Right now the test results were not admissible in court for purposes of custody or child support.

But they prevented a guy from getting emotionally involved for months only to find out he had no biological connection. And sometimes a man was led to believe he was a father for several years before finding out he wasn't. He didn't intend to be that naive a second time.

"Leo? Are you all right?"

"Hmm?" He met Tess's questioning gaze.

"You look weird."

Not surprising. He was remembering a weird, painful time in his life. It still hurt and he'd be damned if he'd let another woman pass off another man's child as his. "I'm fine. But I was going to say the same about you. You're a little pale."

"It occurs to me the term *morning sickness* is inaccurate. This icky feeling doesn't just happen in the morning. It can be anytime, day or night."

"So that's why you turned green when Geri mentioned coffee."

"I thought I did a good job of hiding it," she said.

"No." She might be concealing other relevant facts, but not her current distaste for coffee. "But you're not supposed to have it anyway, at least not much," he qualified. "It's not a complete no on caffeine, but it has to be less than two hundred milligrams a day..." He stopped because she was staring at him as if he'd grown another head. "What?"

"How did you know that about coffee during pregnancy?"

He knew because he'd married the last woman who said she was having his baby and embraced the experience with her. Along with the pain of finding out the son he loved more than life wasn't his, he remembered pregnancy do's and don'ts. "I guess I just heard it somewhere."

"You do meet a lot of women." There was sarcasm in her voice.

"One of the perks of being a hockey star," he said, hoping to change the focus of this conversation.

"Must be a difficult cross to bear." Now bitterness mixed with the sarcasm.

If he didn't know better, he would say she was a little bit jealous, but that proved again just how bad he was at reading women. She'd taken a dislike to him almost from the moment they met. There was definite female interest in her eyes, right up until Pat Morrow introduced him as a former professional hockey player. *An athlete*, she'd said, in a disdainful tone that lumped him in with litterbugs and dog haters. Neither of which he was.

He'd liked her from the first but she gave him the cold shoulder. Until the night of her grandfather's memorial service, when she was hot as hell and took him to heaven. She was right about one thing. He had had no room in his brain to think about protection that night. Holding her felt that good. *If* the baby was his, the blame could be shared fifty-fifty. But that night proved one thing. Tess was attracted to him even though she disapproved of him personally.

He met her gaze. "I do like women. That's not a hanging offense."

"No one said it was."

"You didn't have to say it. Judgment is written all over your face."

"Wow," she said. "Apparently my face gives away more than just the fact that the thought of coffee makes me want to barf."

"Was it coffee? I assumed it was the sight of me."

"Wow again. I'm surprised you could find a helmet big enough for your swelled head. Not everything is about you, Leo."

"And jumping to that conclusion just proves—"

"Hello, Leo." His attorney interrupted him. The pretty, green-eyed redhead smiled at Tess and held out her hand. "I'm Annabel Sanders. You must be Ms. Morrow."

"Tess." She shook the other woman's hand.

"I apologize for keeping you waiting. I didn't expect my last client to take as long as he did."

"I didn't see him leave," Leo said.

"I'm not surprised. You were having an intense chat." Annabel's eyes narrowed on him for a moment, and then she smiled at Tess. "It's nice to meet you."

As the two women chatted, Leo studied his lawyer. She was a beautiful woman. Spectacular curves were showcased in the body-hugging hunter green dress with the flaring skirt. She was also funny and brilliant but he'd never felt the slightest hint of attraction to her. Not once in the nearly two years he'd known her. Maybe because their relationship was professional.

"If you'll both follow me into my office, we can go over the agreement."

He let the women precede him into the large corner office with floor-to-ceiling windows on two sides. In one corner was a conversation area, defined by a leather love seat, two matching club chairs and a glass coffee table. The attorney sat behind her large desk. These digs were much nicer than the small, cramped office where they'd had their very first meeting.

Annabel opened a file on her desk and put on her lawyer face. "Tess, you got the email I sent with the attachment containing the agreement?"

"Yes."

"You had a chance to read it over and have your attorney look at it?"

"I read it," Tess said. "It looks fine to me."

Leo had clued Annabel in on the background that the partnership was a go because Tess was strapped for cash and trying to save her business. He could see her making that connection as the reasoning for not getting a second legal opinion.

"I can assure you that the terms are extremely fair," Annabel told her.

Tess nodded. "I agree."

"Do you have any questions?"

"No."

The attorney nodded. "Leo was very clear that he didn't want to take advantage of your grief and your grandfather's passing. My condolences, by the way."

"Thank you." Tess glanced at him and the paleness in her cheeks disappeared, replaced by a charming pink. Must be the "taking advantage" comment.

As he saw it, they'd had a mutual taking advantage, and the memories were never far from his mind.

"The thing is, Ms. Sanders—"

"Annabel, please."

"Okay. Annabel. Before he died, my grandfather approached Leo about the partnership because he trusted him. I have faith in his judgment. And I didn't see anything in the paperwork that changed my mind."

"Okay, then. We'll get this done."

She went through each page, having them sign and initial where indicated. It was a lot of paperwork, but finally they reached the end.

"Congratulations," the attorney said. "You two have a partnership."

"In business," Tess clarified.

"Yes." Annabel looked from one to the other. "By definition partners need to work together."

"Are you lecturing us?" Leo asked.

"No. Yes. Maybe." She looked at him. "I heard you talking in the waiting room and got the feeling there's an adversarial aspect to your relationship. If you're going to make a success of this venture, it's important to work together."

"Of course," he said.

"I mean it." She looked at Tess. "I don't know you, but I've worked with Leo for several years. He has an excellent head for business and a successful track record to prove it. Don't let his cocky attitude fool you."

"If you say so," Tess said defensively. "I should point out that I'm no slouch. I have a degree in business and I've worked at the bar my whole life. There's a loyal core of customers and we have to build on it."

"That's the plan," Leo agreed.

"Okay. I didn't mean to overstep, but I see the other side when things don't work out. I dissolve partnerships, too."

"Our joint venture will be fine," Leo assured her. It was also necessary. "So, Tess, I'll come by The Pub in the morning and we'll discuss strategy?"

"Fine."

"Is nine too early?"

"No." But she looked as if she had swallowed a worm.

He'd never expected to go into business with Tess Morrow. But now that she was allegedly carrying his child, it was the best way to keep tabs on her. If she slipped up, he would be around to call her on the deception.

The last time he got screwed, he lost everything. He wasn't so gullible now. He would do whatever he had to in order to protect himself.

Chapter Three

Morning sickness really sucked!

It especially sucked when Tess had to see Leo bright and early. The early part she could do. Bright? Not so much. But he would be arriving at nine o'clock sharp and she needed to look her best. Well, at least the best she could what with feeling like something the cat yakked up.

She showered, put on makeup and blew her hair dry. Unlike her unruly tummy, it cooperated, falling past her shoulders in its shiny straightness.

She stared at her reflection in the bathroom mirror and ignored the dark circles under her eyes. "You look fabulous. This will be the first of many productive and profitable meetings."

She managed to choke down a piece of toast with peanut butter. The doctor had said to eat lots of protein but she'd never expected that to be such a challenge. Five minutes before nine o'clock, she walked downstairs from her apartment. The staircase ended in a hall where a left turn went to public restrooms and the bar. Going right would put her in the office and storeroom, with high-capacity refrigeration, an ice maker and shelves. She went left.

In the bar, chairs were turned upside down on tables, where they always spent the night. There were two more rooms off the main area—one for pool and darts, the other with tables for a quieter space for grabbing a bite to eat. Some people might still enjoy eating even though she wasn't one of them right now.

A knock on the door pulled her from the brink of self-pity and she moved to let Leo in. "Good morning."

"Hi." He handed her a bag.

"What's this?"

"Thought these might come in handy."

She peeked inside and saw soda crackers. "Wow. Be still my heart."

"What were you expecting?"

"Nothing actually. So, thanks."

"Keep them by the bed and eat one before you get up. It helps with morning sickness."

"And you know this how?"

He shrugged. "I picked up the information somewhere."

"It's unexpectedly thoughtful, so I won't say anything snarky about your women clueing you in."

"That's very generous of you." One corner of his mouth quirked up. Then he indicated the briefcase he was holding. "I've been consulting with a building contractor—"

"Wait." She held up a hand to stop him. "We only just signed the papers yesterday."

"Since our verbal agreement, I talked to someone I've worked with on other business ventures. The guy is creative and does great work. He came up with some changes and I happen to think they'll be a better use of the space we have."

We? Apparently just signing the papers didn't make her a team player. But since she'd put her name on the bottom line, telling him to take a flying leap didn't seem like something she could do.

"Okay. Show me." She grabbed one of the chairs from a table to make room for a conversation with visual aids.

"You shouldn't be lifting things."

"Why not? I'm fine. Just pregnant—not an invalid." She rested her hands on her hips. "If not me, who's going to lift things?"

"Not while I'm around." He set down his briefcase, then removed the other three chairs.

"Thanks."

There he went being sweet again. That was twice in one morning. Tess didn't trust sweet. It was easy to heft chairs and bring crackers, but a man like him couldn't keep up sweet for long.

They sat and he pulled out his laptop, then set it on the table. He opened a file and then slid his chair closer to hers so they could view the screen together. He smelled good, disarmingly masculine. Some combination of soap and cologne that made her tummy flutter—with something besides nausea. It was attraction, damn him. That's what had gotten her into this mess in the first place, and still fascination survived. There was something seriously wrong with her that she couldn't shake this feeling.

"Okay. So, what am I looking at?"

"This is what the bar would look like with the two walls knocked out, making it one big room."

Not ten minutes ago she'd been thinking how cozy and perfect the setup was with quiet dining and game rooms separated. "But what about the pool tables and dart boards? And some people like a peaceful corner for food and conversation."

"A few customers might appreciate that. If they don't like the change, there are quiet restaurants to take their business. That isn't our core customer, not the clientele we want to attract."

"We can't afford to lose anyone."

"We'll more than make up for that with new business.

Look at the way Nate has it drawn out. The tables are still there. And we'll add an air-hockey table to the game area."

"We will?" She shifted and their arms brushed. The touch made her hot all over but he didn't seem to notice.

"Hockey is trendy."

"Pool is classic."

"We can do both. Open that customer-interest window wider." He met her gaze and something intense flared in his when his knee grazed hers under the table.

Not unlike the way he'd looked at her the night *it* had happened. She swallowed and forced herself to look at the computer screen. She pointed to the opposite corner.

"What's this?"

"We took some of the dining space for live music and dancing. On the weekends people want to de-stress."

"You mean relax."

"I mean let off steam. Loud music. Singing. Maybe karaoke. Watching games and yelling at their team or booing the opponent. Dancing. Contests. Promotions."

He was so enthusiastic but she was looking at the end of an era and it made her sad. "Did my grandfather know about any of this?"

"I talked to him a little bit. Brainstormed as ideas popped into my head."

"What did he say?"

"Pretty much what you are," he admitted. "But he didn't shoot anything down. He knew status quo wasn't working."

That was honest. He could have lied. Pat Morrow was gone and she'd never know what he thought. She couldn't dispute that the current situation was less than successful, but she wasn't ready to concede the point yet.

"Would you like some coffee?" It was a delaying tactic, giving her more time to think.

"Yeah. If it's not too much trouble."

"There's a pot right here." She needed to put some distance between them and was willing to risk the smell.

She went behind the bar and put water and grounds into the drip coffee maker, then hit the on switch. When there was nothing left to do but wait, she walked back to the table, careful to stand far enough away so that she couldn't be distracted by his body heat and manly smell.

As if there'd been no pause, Leo started talking. "We need to put in TVs around the room to show football, baseball, hockey games. Make this the designated place to watch my former team."

"Lend your celebrity name to bring in customers?" She meant women but kept that to herself.

"Yes. Anything that will get the word out there so people will give us a try."

"I don't know about this, Leo." She frowned. Apparently he'd forgotten what she'd said about turning her grandfather's legacy into a sports freak show.

"Look, Tess, I'm aware that this is an emotional time for you—"

"Hold the phone. Don't make my hesitation about me being pregnant. I have a business degree with a minor in marketing."

"That's not what I meant. Your grandfather just died and this pub was his baby. He put everything he had into every corner. But he knew that change isn't a bad thing. We can make it fresh and still keep his heart and soul. You just have to trust me."

And there was the problem. He was too much like the guy who had broken her heart, which made trust in his judgment hard to come by. But that was personal. This was business and his lawyer had assured her he was good at it. Plus her grandfather had chosen him to invest.

While they'd debated, coffee brewed and the smell of it was everywhere. Or maybe it was her supersensitive nose due to pregnancy. Didn't matter why, but the stronger the smell, the worse she felt. She fought back as long as possible but it was a losing battle.

"I'm—oh, God—I'm going to be sick."

She put her hand over her mouth and raced upstairs for the privacy of her own bathroom. She made it—barely—and lost her breakfast. No way the perfect Leo Wallace was going to see her toss her cookies.

"Tess?"

Dear God, no. He followed her! "Go away."

The next thing she knew, he was beside her, scooping her hair back from her face as she bent over the toilet. She'd be furious if she didn't feel hot, sweaty and humiliated. He held her hair with one hand and rubbed her back with the other.

No, no, no. "Go away. Please," she mumbled.

"Not happening."

Her stomach was empty but she waited a few moments to make sure it was over. With a shaking hand, she pressed the handle to flush and then straightened up. After closing the lid, she stood and sat down on it, refusing to meet his gaze.

"I'm okay now. Really. You can go. I'll meet you downstairs in a minute."

Her eyes drifted shut, but she heard the sound of running water in the sink. A moment later he pressed a cool washcloth to her forehead and rubbed it across her neck. It felt so good she could cry. That might be about gratitude, or hormones, or both.

"Stay here. I'll be back in a second."

Before she could pull together the energy to say "don't tell me what to do," he was gone. Several moments later he was back with the box of crackers. He opened it and one of the four individual packs inside, then handed her a salty square.

"This will help." He crouched in front of her so they were eye to eye. His were full of sweetness and sympathy.

"The last thing I want to do is eat," she said weakly.

"I know, but you have to. This will settle your stomach."

If she didn't feel so crappy, she would have asked how he could be so sure. Instead she gave him a skeptical look. "If you're wrong and I lose it again, will you promise to go away?"

"Cross my heart."

"Do you have one?" She took a small bite of cracker, chewed and swallowed.

"There's the snark I know and love. You must be feeling a little better."

When there was no adverse reaction to the single nibble, she took another and waited. It went down easily. Even more surprising, she was suddenly hungry. "Can I have another one?"

He handed her the package. "Knock yourself out."

She took small bites and chewed slowly. "You know, when I took the pregnancy test and it was positive, I couldn't believe it was true. There was nothing tangible to prove I was going to have a baby. Then bam. I feel like roadkill, proof that there are changes going on."

"Nature is pretty amazing."

She nibbled two more crackers and began to feel more like herself. She knew that because her defenses against him were going back up.

"You're being awfully nice to me for a man who doesn't believe this baby is his."

He looked down for a second, then back at her. There

was a glint of humor in his blue eyes. "About that... I asked around, to see if you'd slept with anyone else."

"You didn't!"

"Everyone said no. But you might have said it never happened."

"Okay. Now you're being a jerk so all is right with the world." But was it? Her heart seemed to swell a couple of sizes. "Make no mistake. If it gets out how sweet you're being to me, there will be hell to pay."

"Oh?"

"More women will throw their panties at you."

"More than zero?" He arched an eyebrow. "No one does that now."

"Like I believe that," she scoffed.

But she couldn't shrug off how incredibly nice he was being, even with questions still surrounding the pregnancy. She didn't think he had a sweet bone in his body. But she was wrong and that was a problem.

Leo stood outside The Pub, waiting for Tess to let him in for their meeting with the contractor. Nate Stratton would be here any minute, and Leo wanted a few moments to reassure her, yet again, that the changes would be profitable in the long run. Which was what her grandfather had ultimately wanted.

He hadn't seen her since the morning a couple of days ago when she'd tossed her cookies. She'd been a trouper then, no question. It wasn't often her vulnerability showed, and she probably hadn't been able to brazen it out. The pregnancy hormones were in charge after all. But, damn, seeing her toughness slip brought out a protectiveness he hadn't experienced since—

The door opened and there she was, looking so pretty and... Dare he say it? Glowing. "Hi."

"Good morning," he managed to say.

She glanced at the store-bought cups of coffee he was holding, one in each hand. "I hope you didn't bring me one. Not after last time."

"No. It's for Nate. So you don't have to make coffee." He'd expected her expression to soften or maybe get a hint of a smile, but her frown deepened. "What?"

"That was very thoughtful of you."

"Then why do you look like that?"

"Like what?" she asked.

"Like you want to brain me with a coffeepot."

"I didn't think it showed," she admitted.

"You lost me."

"You're being nice. Thoughtful. I don't trust it." She shrugged, defiance in her eyes.

At least she was being honest, he thought. "Well, I'm not sure how to defend myself against that. What if I promise not to be nice anymore?"

She nodded approval. "I'd appreciate that."

"Can I come in now?"

"Oh. Sure. Sorry." She stepped back and pulled the door wide. "It's half yours now."

And she wasn't happy about it. The tone, the body language, the glare she tried to hide. All of it said she wasn't yet reconciled to him being her partner. Only financial results would show her this was a good thing, and that wasn't going to happen overnight. Still, he did miss the sexy woman who'd clung to him and kissed him back. He was fighting that feeling because it was dangerous. It would be months until he knew for sure she was telling the truth about the baby. Speaking of which...

"How are you feeling?"

"So far, so good. Today. The crackers are helping."

"Glad to hear it."

"I'm really curious how you know so much about pregnancy nausea." She folded her arms over her chest and looked up at him as if he was breaking some rule.

The truth was his wife was pregnant when they'd married, and he'd gone through it with her. Reading the books. Researching on the internet. Catering to her cravings. It was hard to shake the bitterness about how that had all turned out. Tess's grandfather had helped him deal and obviously hadn't spilled the facts to her, treating Leo's story like attorney/client privilege. That was then; this was now and he didn't want to talk about it.

"I must have seen it in a movie." If only. Then it wouldn't still hurt like a son of a bitch.

"Anyway. Thanks for the tip." She glanced at the watch on her wrist. "Your friend is late."

"He's busy. I had to do some fast talking to get him to take us on." Although now that he thought about it, Nate's attitude had changed a little after meeting Tess and looking at the bar.

"No rush as far as I'm concerned." Translation: she didn't care if it never started.

"That's emotion talking. Because in your business classes I'm sure you learned that the sooner you start increasing profits, the sooner your business is out of trouble."

She nodded. "And the sooner you can turn everything over to me and we'll see less of each other."

Only if the baby wasn't his.

"Since we're going to turn this place into a sports freak show, I suggest lending my name," he said. "It's recognizable."

"To who? Besides your female fans, of course."

"I have two Stanley Cup rings." The look on her face

didn't change, so he said, "You do know the significance of that, right?"

"Actually, no."

"In hockey it's the equivalent of winning the World Series in baseball. Or the Super Bowl in football."

"Ah." She still didn't look impressed.

"And we came close to winning it at least five more times."

"So, lending your name. Does that mean we're going to call it Leo's Lounge or The 'Wall' Flower?"

"Funny." Until now he hadn't been aware that she knew his hockey nickname. "We can talk about names later. I'm more interested in getting the inside ready." He looked at his watch. "And if Nate doesn't get here soon—"

"Knock, knock." The door opened and in walked Nate Stratton, bachelor, builder, businessman. "Sorry I'm late. Had a crisis at another site."

"Glad you made it," Leo said.

"Hi." Tess smiled in a way she'd never smiled at Leo. It was a friendly look, but a little flirty around the edges. She held out her hand. "Nice to see you again."

"Same here." Did the guy hold her hand a little too long when he shook it?

Leo was aware that women found his friend attractive. They'd been each other's wingman more than once, and a time or two his date had made a move on the guy. It never bothered him before but it damn sure did now.

"So, what have you got to show us?" Leo wanted to move this along.

"I've got the plans on the computer." He put it down on the table without chairs on top of it. "Here we go. I think you're really going to like this."

Tess and Leo moved chairs and sat on either side of the contractor. Was she close enough to Nate that their arms brushed? he wondered. The thought did not make him happy.

Nate went through more detailed, three-dimensional plans from the initial one Leo had originally shown Tess. They *were* good. He could easily picture the changes opening up the interior of the bar and infusing life into the place. He glanced at Tess but had no idea what was going through her mind.

"This is just a thought," Leo said. "But since we're doing some makeover anyway, I propose we upgrade the kitchen. We can hire a chef and shake up the menu. Another marketing strategy."

Tess looked less than thrilled. "I feel everything my grandfather put into this place slipping away."

"I promise when I'm finished there will be a mix of old and new," Nate promised. "Not that I get a vote, but I agree with Leo about the kitchen. Atmosphere, fun and good food will bring in the customers."

"Nothing is sacred," Tess muttered.

"If you don't want—" Nate started.

She held up her hand to stop him. "No. If we're going to make changes, let's go all in."

"You won't be disappointed," Leo assured her.

"I agree." Nate looked at each of them. "Let's talk logistics."

The contractor explained how many weeks total for the work, the mess involved and the estimated time frame The Pub would have to close for construction. He gave Leo a copy of the plans on a flash drive and instructions to contact him after they had discussed everything. He would draw up a contract and give them a start date. Then he excused himself to go to another meeting he was already late for.

When they were alone, Tess met his gaze, her own worried. "I didn't think about keeping this place open during construction. Or that it would have to close."

"It's a lot to consider, but remember he said it would only close for a short time. When water and electricity would have to be turned off, we can't conduct business." Leo thought for a moment. "But before that stage, we can have a 'pardon our dust' promotion. Half off drinks and food. Extended happy hour. BOGO. See the before and after. Customers will respond."

"When life gives you lemons, make lemonade?"

"Exactly," he said enthusiastically.

"We can't afford to lose anyone."

"I know. It will be all right. But there's something else that concerns me more than that." He turned his chair toward her, the now-empty one sitting between them.

"What could possibly be worse than shrinking our customer base?" she asked. "Or losing four to six weeks of revenue?"

"Construction means dust and paint fumes in this building."

"Okay. We can utilize the patio area more. Use outside heaters if necessary until summer is here."

"No. I meant I'm concerned about you living upstairs during the demolition and painting. Plus if the water and electricity are off, you can't be here."

"I can make do. I'm tough."

"You're also pregnant. None of that will be healthy for you and the baby."

Now she looked uneasy. "I'll get fans and open the windows upstairs. It's spring. It will be fine."

"I'm not comfortable with that." No matter whose baby she was carrying, the scenario they were discussing was bad.

"It's where I live. What do you want me to do?"

"Move out."

"Where?"

"Can't you couch surf with friends?"

She thought for a moment and then shook her head. "Anyone I'd feel comfortable asking either doesn't have room or is living with a parent."

"Then an extended-stay hotel."

She shook her head. "I'll just have to make this work here at The Pub."

"Why are you pushing back so hard?" he asked.

"Because I don't have the money to stay somewhere else."

"I'll pay for it. The cost of doing business," he explained.

"I can't let you do that."

Her face was showing all kinds of stubborn kicking in, so he didn't pursue that approach. There was one more thing he could think of.

"Move in with me. I don't live with my parents." Heaven forbid. He couldn't wait to get out of that battle zone when he was a kid. "And I have plenty of room at my place. We'd probably never see each other."

"That's not a good idea."

"I disagree. It's the perfect solution. And it won't cost any more out of pocket. So everything is settled. It won't be for long. It'll be great."

The best part was that he could really keep an eye on her. To make sure she ate properly and took care of herself. If he could also see for himself that she wasn't going out with another man that would be okay, too.

Chapter Four

Leo finally wore her down and Tess agreed to move in
when The Pub renovation started. It moved quickly, and
two weeks later she pulled her small compact car into
his circular driveway and parked behind his big, expensive silver SUV. She'd always figured him for something
flashier but he'd said they were too small and uncomfortable. The thought of his broad shoulders squeezed
into a sports car made her heart flutter more than a little, which was disconcerting since she was practically
on his doorstep.

A very impressive doorstep, attached to a New England–
style house with gables and siding, surrounded by mani-
cured grass, bushes and flowers. She was a little nervous
about seeing the inside. Sharing living space with the man
whose outstanding shoulders had just made her heart flutter was definitely going to be something. Whether good
or bad was yet to be determined.

She didn't quite know what to make of his inviting her
to stay with him. He was right about the dust and paint
fumes, though. She'd checked with the doctor, who totally agreed with him. And anyone she'd felt comfortable
asking for temporary lodging would have been inconve-
nienced. Leo sure didn't lie about the size of his place.
He could put up the entire UCLA marching band here.

But she had a sneaking suspicion the offer had more to do with not trusting her than anything else.

Trust was a fragile thing. Once broken it was pretty darn hard to rebuild. She found it easiest not to believe in someone at all.

"Enough procrastinating," she said to herself. "Journey of a thousand miles. Single step and all that."

She popped the trunk on her car, then exited and went to the rear to get her suitcases. Before she could, the front door opened and Leo came out and jogged down the three steps.

"Let me get that stuff," he said.

"Thanks." She didn't push back, because somehow he always got his way. Without another word she grabbed a couple of grocery bags out of the rear seat and followed him inside. "Where's the kitchen?"

"Back there." His hands were full so he lifted his chin to indicate the general direction. "I'll take your suitcases up to the guest room."

"Okay. Thanks," she said again.

That was very sweet of him, and the more she got to know him, the more she actually liked Leo Wallace. Since they were now partners, that was a good thing, right? As long as it didn't turn into more than business. Although that seemed like shutting the barn door after the horse got out. And now they would be roomies. Eventually they'd be parenting together. Maybe they could be friends. She was beginning to think she could manage that.

The man had very good taste in houses but the jury was out on his decorating skills, what with the interior having very few furnishings. There was nothing in the living and dining rooms. In the kitchen there were white cabinets and gorgeous granite on an island as big as a Toyota.

The adjacent family room had a flat-screen TV above the fireplace and a brown leather corner group in front of it.

Tess set her bags of groceries on the island and went in search of her host. Walking up the curving staircase she called out, "Leo?"

"Up here."

Following the sound of his voice, she found him in the first bedroom off the upstairs landing. She walked in and looked around. Her suitcases were on a flat bench at the foot of a king-size bed. The spread had flowers and matching throw pillows. Somehow the decor didn't seem to fit a man whose nickname was "The Wall."

"This is a beautiful room." And she meant that sincerely.

There was a window seat that looked out onto the brick patio that surrounded a big pool. A door to her left led to the full bath and big walk-in closet.

"Somehow I didn't picture you as a flowered comforter kind of guy," she said as she turned to him.

He looked a little sheepish and awfully darn cute when he said, "I bought the furniture and bedding after we agreed you would move in."

Her chest tightened and she had the distinct feeling that her heartstrings were being tugged. He was telling her that this room had been empty and he furnished it with decor that was suspiciously similar to that found in her apartment. One could conclude that he'd done it specifically for her. But one really and truly didn't want to believe that.

"It's lovely. And very nice of you. But you promised not to be nice to me."

"Yeah." He shrugged. "I forgot. Want to see the rest of the place?"

"Yes."

She trailed after him from room to room as he explained where everything was and showed her the huge backyard. The grass area beyond the pool was big enough for a hockey rink, if it wasn't Southern California, where it was only possible to maintain indoor ice with equipment. He'd even made space for her in his downstairs office so she had somewhere to work.

Back in the kitchen he showed her around. Last but not least there was a rack hanging over the island with copper-bottom pots and pans dangling from it. The effect was all pretty perfect.

He noticed the bags of groceries sitting there. "What's this?"

"I'm making dinner. My way of contributing."

"You don't have to."

"Are you afraid I can't cook?" she challenged. "You were awfully quick to suggest hiring a chef for The Pub."

"It was just a thought. A brainstorming thing."

"Because the burgers, hot dogs, and fish and chips I make aren't fancy enough?" It was simple stuff and she wasn't the only one who did the cooking. Which reminded her. "It was generous of you to pay the employees while the renovation is underway."

"It's fair. Also smart business to retain good help. Cheaper in the long run since they're already trained," he explained.

"Still, it's appreciated."

He leaned back against the counter and slipped his fingertips into the pockets of his worn jeans. "So, what's for dinner?"

"You'll see."

"Can I help?"

She thought for a moment. "Maybe set the table. And there's stuff in the bags to make salad."

"On it," he said.

She'd brought everything necessary for chicken marsala, including the cooking wine. He gave her a funny look and she got it right away. "The alcohol will burn off in cooking. It's fine for a pregnant lady."

"Okay."

She found her way around his kitchen as if she'd set it up herself, which was a little disconcerting. Their minds, organizationally speaking, worked the same way. That saved her time in fixing dinner. When everything was ready she put the food out on the circular oak table, in a nook with a view of the backyard.

She cut a bite of chicken and nodded as the flavors hit her tongue. "It's not bad, if I do say so myself."

He tried it and met her gaze, surprise in his own. "Definitely a winner."

"Don't sound so shocked. I have skills."

"I'm aware."

There was a hint of something in his voice that she had a feeling meant he wasn't only referring to her cooking abilities. Best not to go there, so they ate in silence. He scarfed up everything on his plate, and then had a second helping. It made her happy that he enjoyed it. Maybe that had something to do with her nesting instincts, which had gone nuts so far in this pregnancy.

"This is really a beautiful home," she said to break the silence. "How long have you lived here?"

"Awhile," he said vaguely.

"Can we talk about how sparse the furnishings are?"

"Nothing to say," he told her. "That hasn't been a priority."

"What has?"

"Business. I needed something to fill my time when I stopped playing hockey."

A career-ending injury must have been hard, she thought. "So investing in businesses keeps you busy?"

"And pays the bills."

Still, she was curious. Was he deliberately not putting down roots? Less stuff equaled a fast getaway?

She wouldn't pry, but couldn't resist needling him about something else. Maybe it was payback because he'd initially walked out on her without a word when she'd told him about the baby.

"So, which room are you going to make the nursery?"

He stopped chewing, then slowly raised his gaze to hers. "What?"

"You'll want to have a place for the baby when he's with you. There are a lot of bedrooms upstairs. Which one are you thinking for him?"

"First of all—*him*?"

"I won't keep saying *it*. So *he*," she explained. "And which room were you thinking of for him?"

Something dark slipped into his eyes. He set his fork on the plate as if he'd suddenly lost his appetite. "I'll figure it out. If necessary."

"It will be," she assured him. "You can't just throw things together at the last minute. God knows I'm starting to freak out a little about all that needs to be done."

"Actually newborns don't need that much. One trip to the store and you're good."

"Really?"

"Yeah. Stuff to change diapers. Onesies. A few sleepers. If you breastfeed, you don't even need bottles. The rest of it you can get as needed."

"What about a crib?"

"Babies don't move around much for the first couple of months." He shrugged.

This made her more curious than the sparse furnishings in his house. Forget the fact that he provided soda crackers for morning sickness. "How do you know so much about babies?"

"Good question. Guys on the team had kids. I guess some of what they said sank in." The casual tone was forced and his eyes never lost their sort of tense, haunted look.

She didn't buy his explanation. In her experience men just didn't have much information about infant care. What was his story? As badly as she wanted to ask, she didn't go there.

She met his gaze and decided not to bring up breast-feeding. "We're going to need bottles for him. You'll need them when he's with you."

"If," he reminded her.

She was annoyed because she knew he was the only one who could be the father of her baby. But he was at a disadvantage; he didn't know for sure that she'd only been with him. So she cut him some slack.

"You're really stubborn. Your resistance to this child being yours is impressive."

"I'm not resisting, just waiting it out."

"Okay. But I'm telling you your life is going to change. Half the time you're going to be responsible for a baby. Feeding. Changing diapers."

"So will you," he said.

She didn't need the reminder. Nerves about how this was going to alter her life were already starting. She was just spreading the joy. "It occurs to me that at least half the time you're going to have to put the brakes on your love life. Assuming the flavor of the month isn't into children."

"Same goes for you." He wasn't smiling.

"I have no love life to interrupt," she told him.

"Really?" There was a glimmer of curiosity in his eyes that finally chased away the dark look. "I would think a lot of guys are interested."

"I meet a lot," she admitted. "It's part of the job. Some hit on me."

"And?"

"Nothing." She wasn't interested.

"Not that I believe it, but why?"

"It's like picking out a dog." She thought about how that sounded. "I don't mean all guys are dogs but when choosing, you don't want the one that's all over you. They're too eager. The one that hangs back is more calm and centered. Trainable."

"I see." He looked amused.

"My point is, are you sure you want me here? If you're bringing a woman home, you can just let me know. I'll make myself scarce."

"That won't be necessary," he said wryly.

"Right. Because you can always go to her place."

"No. Because there are no women."

When he got up and started clearing plates, it was clear the discussion was over. But that didn't stop her mind from racing.

Now that she thought about it, Leo had hung back until the night of her grandfather's memorial. To be fair, for some reason they'd both melted down simultaneously, and there was no explaining it because she would never be his flavor of the month. But they would always be connected by this child she was carrying.

And he knew an awful lot about pregnant women and infants. It seemed odd that he even knew what a onesie was. The man had a story, a secret, and she wanted to know what it was.

There was a woman in the house. Tess.

A woman he hadn't slept with the night before, which happened now and then. Leo wished he could say he had no interest in sleeping with her, except he did. But that wasn't an option because they were in business together. If that wasn't enough, sex would complicate an already bad situation. He didn't trust that she was telling the truth, even though she seemed completely confident that he was the baby's father.

In case she wasn't lying, he was going to make sure she didn't sleep in a building full of demolition dust and paint fumes. And that she ate well—for both her and the baby.

So this morning he cut up fresh fruit and made an egg, cheese and potato casserole. It was easy and good. He hoped Tess would like it. More specifically he hoped it wouldn't make her throw up.

He glanced at the clock on the microwave again and noted that the morning was slipping away. Did she normally sleep late? Possibly, since The Pub was busiest at night. But what if she wasn't okay? This house was big and he might not have heard if she needed help. Should he check on her? Maybe send a text? She'd taken her phone upstairs with her. If she didn't answer, he would go up and knock—

"Good morning."

He was checking on breakfast in the oven, and at the sound of her voice he closed the door and turned. "Hey, sleepyhead."

"I'm sorry I slept so late, but that bed is really comfortable. I was out cold."

That made one of them because the sight of her made him hot all over. "I'm glad. Not that you were out. That you slept well."

"I did." She sniffed. "Something smells good."

"Breakfast."

"A man who cooks," she commented.

"I'm a bachelor. Someone has to."

He told her what was in it and then studied her for signs that the scents of food were not adversely affecting her. He didn't see anything in her bright brown eyes and sunny smile that said she needed crackers. There was a fresh-faced prettiness about her that he'd liked the first time they had met.

And he was going to do his best to ignore how nice it was to have a woman here. He was also ignoring that this was the first time this house felt like a home. It had been a while since a woman spent the night, and he was going to chalk his feelings up to that.

"Are you hungry?" he asked.

"Yes."

"Smell's not bothering you?"

"No. And that's getting better. Everything I read about pregnancy said it usually does right about where I am now."

"Do you think it would be okay for me to make coffee?"

"Yes." She gave him a "don't go being nice to me" look. "Did you not make it because of me?"

"No big deal. I was going to stop by Starbucks later, when I went out."

"That's exactly what I didn't want," she said firmly.

"For me to go to Starbucks?"

"No. To change your routine because I'm here. Let me make coffee."

The determination on her face told him if he challenged her, he would lose the argument. "As long as you're not going to turn green."

"Can't promise," she said. "But if it happens I'll deal."

"Okay. Coffee is in the refrigerator." He nodded toward the machine on the counter. "There's the beast to make it."

"I'm on it."

then grabbed protective mitts and pulled the cast-iron skillet out of the oven.

"Do you have something to put on the table to protect it from that hot pan?"

"Last drawer," he said. "Some square pads."

She put them out. "There."

"Thanks." He set down the cast-iron skillet. "There's fresh fruit salad, too."

"I'll get it." She opened the refrigerator and then bent at the waist to retrieve the bowl.

He had a perfect view of her championship-quality butt and a stirring memory of cupping it in his hands to lift her onto the table in The Pub. In spite of the cosmic joke that was his life, he went hot all over, but most of the blood traveled south of his belt. Fortunately she didn't look at him when she closed the refrigerator door. She just headed to the table with the fruit bowl.

"Do you want coffee?" he asked.

"No, thanks. I'm not quite brave enough to risk that just yet." She glanced over her shoulder. "Can I pour you a cup?"

"Just sit. I'll get it."

He did and then joined her at the table where they would eat together again. For the first time since he'd lost his professional hockey career and his family, he felt the absence of loneliness. It seemed the darkness was no match for Tess's sunny disposition.

She took a bite of food, and almost instantly her eyes closed in ecstasy. It was so sexy, he thought there was a very real chance that his head would explode.

"This is so good," she said.

He took a bite and could barely taste it. Weird since this dish was one of his favorites. "I'm glad you like it."

"I do." Her eyes sparkled when she met his gaze. "You have skills, too."

He knew she meant cooking, but the way his body was responding to her made the words a double entendre. After a swig of hot coffee, his cynical side woke up completely and reminded him he was being the worst kind of dope. He needed to make sure his rational self stayed highly caffeinated.

"So, what's on your agenda today?" she asked.

"I plan to stop by The Pub and check on the construction progress. Then there's a pile of paperwork at the rink that I need to deal with."

"Sounds exciting."

He sipped more coffee. "What about you? This is kind of a forced vacation for you."

"I plan to inspect the destruction your contractor has done. What you so cavalierly call renovation." She held up a hand to stop his protest. "I won't stay long and Nate gave me one of those masks like the guys wear so I don't breathe in the dust."

"So he knows you're pregnant?"

"I told him, but he was too polite to ask who the father is. And I didn't volunteer the information."

He nodded, appreciating her discretion. "Still, do you think it's wise to go there? Even with the mask?"

"It will be fine. Especially since I'm seeing the doctor right after."

"Is something wrong?"

"No. Regular monthly check."

He was aware of that and also knew that during the last couple of months, the doctor visits would increase in frequency until the baby was born. But he didn't tell her he knew that, because she'd already asked a lot of questions about *how* he knew so much about pregnant women and infants. Since he was trying to forget it ever happened, he never talked about that time.

The pain of being shut out by the woman who'd deceived him never went away, and remembering just brought it all up after he'd struggled so long and hard to push it down. But he couldn't ignore the doctor's appointment for the baby that might be his.

"You weren't going to tell me about seeing the doctor today?"

"No big deal. This isn't my first visit. I didn't think you'd be interested in being there or that you cared at all about it."

"I do."

The words came out before he could adequately weigh how they would sound or what the consequences would be. The reasons he cared were complicated but that didn't mean it wasn't true.

"You're acting as if I'm pulling a fast one." She sounded irritated and he wondered if there was something she didn't want him to find out about.

"Are you?"

"Of course not. Would you like to come along?"

"Damn right I'm coming with you."

Chapter Five

Who knew Leo Wallace could cook? After an unexpectedly good breakfast, Tess went upstairs to get ready for her prenatal doctor visit. She took extra care with her makeup and hair, then added a navy blazer to her white T-shirt and jeans. If she was being honest, she was bothering with her appearance because Leo was going with her. He might think she was a lying weasel dog, but by God, she was going to be a well-groomed, attractive one.

To finish off the outfit, she stepped into three-inch wedges because Leo was really tall, and beside him she didn't want to look like a refugee from the land of the seven dwarfs. Now that she thought about it, maybe he wouldn't go in the exam room with her to meet the doctor.

That seemed unlikely, though, given his level of suspicion. She suspected this appointment, for him, was about gathering information to support his doubts about fathering her baby. How were they going to handle that?

"We have some talking to do, Leo," she said to her reflection in the bathroom mirror.

In her high shoes, she carefully walked downstairs and found him in the kitchen, leaning back against the counter, where a cup of coffee was close by. He was looking at his cell phone and glanced up when she came in the room. Actually he did a double take and that was like a blast of sugar to her carb-deprived ego. Worth it, she thought about her coiffing efforts.

"Are you ready to go?" he asked.

"Why? Do I not look put together?"

"No. You look—" He stopped and there was an approving gleam in his eyes. "Nice. Really nice."

"I guess that's marginally better than 'I thought you were going to do your makeup and hair.'"

"You always look nice," he said.

Typical guy. And she was stalling. "Look, Leo, we have to talk."

"About what?" A wary look replaced his approval.

"I don't know how to explain you." The words came tumbling out and he looked confused. Tess didn't blame him. "The thing is, I've been going to Dr. Thompson forever. I don't know what to say about you. Us. If you go into the exam room with me."

"That's the plan."

She'd expected a little squirming about breaching this totally female ritual. Maybe relief that she was giving him an out. Instead he looked ready to defend his stance. "How do I put it? '*I* know you're the father of my baby, but you have doubts about whether or not that's true.' That makes me look bad."

"Doesn't make me look too good either."

"So how do we do this? Should we tell her you're not sure about being the father?"

"You told me I am."

"Because you are. But do we share all that? Are we going to have this discussion in front of the doctor?"

"Do you want to talk about it with her?"

Her response was immediate, decisive and forceful. "Good God, no."

"Then you decide how we play this. The game plan is up to you."

"A sports metaphor?"

"It makes me happy." He shrugged. "What would make you happy?"

If it was true: that they were ecstatic about the arrival of their first child. She sighed. "Would you mind terribly pretending to be what I already know you are? The father of this baby?"

"I think I can manage that," he said.

"Okay." She nodded resolutely but was secretly relieved that he was going along with her suggestion. "Then we're going to be excited, expectant parents."

"Are you excited?" he asked.

"About pretending in front of my doctor?" The thought made her more nauseated than the smell of coffee.

"No. I meant about having a baby. Being a mom. You've never said how you feel about it."

"I wish I could say yes without reservations, but I can't."

"Why?"

"For one thing, I don't know if I'll be a very good mom. Mine wasn't, so zero role model there."

"What happened?"

Apparently her grandfather hadn't said anything to him. "When I was six, my mother left me with Granddad and never came back. Last I heard she's in Florida with some guy."

"What about your father?"

"He left her—pregnant and alone." She met his gaze. "If children learn what they live, that doesn't bode well for my being a good mother."

"I don't think there's anything to worry about."

"Easy for you to say. You're not the one giving birth."

"You're not alone." That might be a general reference to him sticking around, at least for the DNA portion of the program. "Besides, you're the most responsible person I know. And Patrick Morrow raised you to be that way."

"It seems prudent to point out that after my grandmother died, he raised my mother, too, and that didn't turn out so well. What if I take the easy way out like she did?"

"That's not who you are. The Pub is a perfect example. With profits down, it would have been easy to cut your losses and walk. But you're fighting for it."

"It's Granddad's legacy. And I love that place."

"You love your baby, too."

"I do." And that was the simple truth. "However as far as being excited, that's hard. The timing isn't good, what with trying to increase The Pub's customer base. And—" she watched him watching her "—the circumstances aren't exactly desirable, if you know what I mean."

Evidence of that was him saying "your baby," not "our baby." They had to get their act together before taking it on the road. "It's your baby, too. Our baby. In front of the doctor anyway."

"Right." He looked at the time on his phone. "We should probably get going. I'll drive."

"I can."

"We're taking my car. I don't fit in that glorified skateboard you call a car."

She looked up at him, then let her gaze linger on his wide chest and impossibly wide shoulders. The memory of being held in his strong arms was never far from her thoughts. She swallowed once and said, "I think you might be able to squeeze in but it would take the jaws of life to get you out. So you win."

"Funny." The tone was sarcastic but he grinned.

Wow, Leo was quite the handsome charmer when he

didn't scowl. Hopefully the doctor would see that man and not the one who kept reminding her he didn't trust her.

They made a quick stop at The Pub, and she was pretty vocal about the fact that tearing down walls was like ripping her heart out. So Leo hurried her back to the car and headed to the doctor's office.

The medical building was located on the west side of Huntington Hills, and Leo parked in the lot. They got out and walked to the door leading to the lobby. He opened it for her and they took the elevator to the second floor. Once inside the Women's Wellness Center, he slid his arm around her waist. It was like being on a movie set when someone yelled, "Action." He was ready to play his part, so let the pretending begin. But darn she liked him touching her.

After signing in they sat together on a love seat in the waiting room. Across from them was a very pregnant woman, and a man was rubbing her big belly and talking to it. She glanced up and saw Leo watching them, too. He didn't seem horrified. Another couple had a newborn in an infant carrier and the woman's not-yet-flat tummy was proof she'd recently given birth. Finally she noticed a toddler running around with her mom and dad in hot pursuit. They looked tired, probably from chasing their daughter around. People in various stages of having children. Being a family.

The door beside them opened and a woman in scrubs said, "Tess Morrow."

They stood and followed her, stopping at the scale in the hall. A note was made in her chart, and then they were moving again and she stopped at the bathroom, where she was instructed to leave her sample. After that Tess found the room and sat on the exam table, where her blood pressure was taken. The nurse informed them that she would be seen soon.

A few minutes later Dr. Thompson walked in and smiled. "Hi, Tess. How are you?"

"Good." She glanced at Leo who'd stood and was now beside the exam table, rubbing her back. "This is Leo Wallace, the baby's father."

"Nice to meet you. Congratulations."

"Thanks." He smiled at Tess. "I couldn't be here before, but I'm glad I could make this appointment."

"Leo and I met at The Pub," Tess said quickly. "My grandfather introduced us."

"And now you're having a baby together. It must be hard for you that Patrick isn't here. He'd be very happy for you."

Probably not, Tess thought, risking a glance at the man beside her. "Yeah."

"We couldn't be happier," he said. "It was a surprise, but definitely exciting. Can't wait to be parents."

Tess wondered if she was the only one who thought he was spreading it on a little thick.

"I told Tess but it goes for you, too," Dr. Thompson said to him. "Feel free to take any of the pamphlets on the wall there. They're full of facts and suggestions for pregnancy, links on the internet and books that I've vetted for my patients. With a lot of misinformation out there, these will save you time, effort and needless anxiety. Happy mother, happy, healthy baby."

"That's the plan." He settled his muscular arm across Tess's shoulders and gave her a hug.

"And I'm here. Anything I can do to help, just let me know. Okay, lay back on the table." The doctor put a small ultrasound device on Tess's belly and explained that it would identify the baby's heartbeat. She smiled broadly. "Sounds really good and strong."

Then she pulled a tape measure taut over Tess's abdomen to determine the baby's approximate size. "Definitely growing. Everything is normal."

"That's great." Leo was holding her hand and squeezed it before helping her to a sitting position.

The doctor frowned a little as she looked at the chart. "You've lost some weight. Are you eating right?"

"Morning sickness has been a challenge," she said. "Leo gave me crackers and that helped. But it's getting much better now."

"And I convinced her to move in with me," he added. "I'm making sure she eats."

"Good." The doctor beamed at them as if they were parental stars. "You make a beautiful couple and this is going to be one good-looking baby. I've known Tess since she was a teenager. It does my heart good to see her so happy now."

That was a leap, Tess thought, but no way she was calling the doctor on it. After all, that meant she was buying the excited, expectant parent act. Leo had pulled it off brilliantly, and that was a surprise, considering how he really felt.

Of course the doctor asked if they had any questions and Leo did. About her due date and the time frame for when she'd conceived. He did it diplomatically and unless one knew why he was asking, there was no way to tell he was anything but curious. And, gosh golly, the date of her grandfather's memorial was smack-dab center of the primary window. Tess shot him an "I told you so" look and he gave a small shrug.

They left the office and Tess was relieved that things had gone without a hitch. Leo was a really good actor and no one could tell they weren't a couple. When her next appointment rolled around, she hoped to be back in her apartment and coming here alone. And that's when she felt a hitch in her heart. A reminder that it wasn't a good idea to get sucked into the fantasy of them being a real, traditional family. It would hurt like crazy when she was by herself.

After dinner with Tess, Leo left the house and drove to the ice rink. The business was open 24/7 and he made it a point to stop by at different times to check things out. It had stopped hemorrhaging money after he had made some common-sense changes and hired a new manager who knew hockey.

Buying the rink didn't make a whole lot of investment sense, and it wasn't about ego or vanity from his player years. He loved the ice. It was a purely emotional decision, so he understood how Tess felt about The Pub.

Tess was something. Honest and straightforward. She could have said she was beyond excited about having a baby when he'd asked, but she had told him her misgivings. As she'd said, he wasn't the one giving birth, hence his body wasn't changing. But her facts were indisputable. They weren't married.

And being at the doctor's with her today brought back a lot of memories. Ones that had been good but now brought a wave of pain and emptiness that nearly sent him driving off the road. It seemed like yesterday that he and his wife were over the moon about her being pregnant. He was still playing hockey and the team had a home game, giving him a chance to be at the first appointment.

Once he'd found out he was going to be a father, he'd vowed to be better than his own. He and Nancy were going to be the best parents in the history of parenting.

But it hadn't turned out that way, and he carried the torture of that inside him every single day.

He didn't believe in silver linings, but he drew on that experience earlier. At Dr. Thompson's office he had tapped into those feelings to play the role of a man who was completely thrilled about becoming a father. The ob-gyn put the time of conception at right about when he'd been with Tess. Along with the blood test and her unshakable assertion that he was the baby's father, he was starting to believe it was true. So, what now?

He had to put off thinking about that because the ice rink was coming up on his right. He pulled into the lot and noted that there were a lot of cars, which meant business was good.

After finding a space, he parked and then went inside. Immediately the smell of cold hit him, and for a few moments there was a sensation of peace, home. When he was a kid and his parents were screaming hateful things at each other, the only sanctuary he could count on was the ice.

The area around the rink had rubber padding to protect skate blades when outside the rink itself. This time of night was a free skate, meaning no lessons or practices. Anyone could come in and rent equipment to skate around the oval. It was almost time for the session to end.

He turned away and headed to the office on the second floor. There was a big glass window that looked out over the facility, and a desk facing it. Metal filing cabinets lined the wall, along with a trophy case holding pictures and awards from winning teams sponsored by the facility. It had been a while, but he wanted to make Huntington Hills Skating Rink competitive again.

He walked inside. "Hey, Mark."

The manager turned away from the window and

smiled. Mark Reeves was in his midthirties, tall and muscular, with black hair and brown eyes. They'd been competitors in professional hockey, but off the ice were good friends. The guy didn't need the money from this job any more than Leo did, and had invested along with him. But he wanted to be involved at a grassroots level.

He stood and held out his hand. "Leo. How are you?"

"Good," he lied, taking the other man's hand in his own and shaking it. "How's our business?"

"Profits are up. Not as much as I'd like, but going in the right direction."

"That's what I want to hear." He glanced out the window and saw that the number of people was starting to thin out. "I like what I see. You've added a team to the under-sixteen age group?"

"Yeah. Community outreach is starting to pay off. Adding is good. We can't afford to lose a team."

"Yeah." Leo knew all about that. Ice time for practice had a rental fee. There was revenue from skating sessions like the one just winding down now. But all services—skating lessons, blade sharpening, the shop they'd opened for selling equipment and apparel—all of it added up. And every hour of the day, ice time had to be utilized to bring in profit.

He looked at his friend. "Is everything in place for the Sticks for Kids roller hockey event?"

Mark nodded. "I have the park permits and supplies. We'll be working on stick handling and drills to promote teamwork. Kids bring their own rollerblades."

"Good."

"I've lined up some players from the men's ice hockey team I coach to help with younger kids. Education is the cornerstone of everything. It creates buzz for the sport and hopefully interest in playing ice hockey."

"Sounds like you have everything under control."

He turned and looked out over the ice again. It was Thursday night and there were teenagers hotdogging in and out of families with younger kids. One little guy caught his eye, in between his parents and holding their hands as he walk-skated unsteadily.

If things hadn't gone to hell with his own family, he'd be doing that with Chad. Wondering how the boy was doing drove him nuts. Just then the boy in the rink fell and started to cry. His dad picked him up and brushed the ice off his pants, then comforted him. Exactly what a dad should do. The trio headed for the break in the wall around the rink and stepped off.

Dad was still holding the little boy and they headed for the exit. Probably going home for his bath, bedtime rituals and good-night hugs. Leo missed that time the most, and the small arms that had no chance of reaching around his shoulders but meant everything to him.

"Leo?"

"Hmm?" He turned away and met his friend's questioning gaze. "Sorry. I was thinking about something else. You were saying?"

"Are you going to be at the community event? People want to meet the highest-scoring defenseman who ever played."

"I'm planning on it." He rested a hip on the desk. "Every participant comes away with a free stick and ball, right? We have enough?"

"I think so. We'll use leftovers at the next clinic."

Leo nodded approval. "We might want to have that one on the other side of town."

"Sounds good."

"So, show me the new snack bar."

"We're getting positive feedback, pardon the pun." Mark grinned at his joke.

Leo groaned. "I hope the food is better than your sense of humor."

After following his friend downstairs, he noted the addition of more tables and chairs where customers could relax with a hot dog, a cup of hot chocolate or a soft drink. Soup, chili and taquitos, among other things, had been added to the menu. There was a teenage girl cleaning up and shutting it down. He'd interviewed her, but hadn't seen her in action yet.

Mark stopped at the counter. "Hey, Denise, how's it going?"

"Hi, Mr. Reeves." The pretty gray-eyed blonde looked at Leo. "Nice to see you again, Mr. Wallace."

"How's business?" She was a good hire, Leo thought. Smart, polite, pretty. Adults loved her because she was great with kids. And teenage boys would gather around her like bees to honey.

"It's really good," she said. "I was going to talk to Mr. Reeves, but since you're here, too…"

"What's up?" he asked. "Don't tell me you're quitting."

"No way." Her ponytail flipped from side to side when she shook her head. "Just the opposite. When school is out for summer, I was hoping to increase my hours. I only have one more year until I go to college, and I need to save all the money I can."

Leo looked at Mark, who gave a thumbs-up. "That would be great. We'll definitely work something out."

Possibly a rink-sponsored college scholarship, Leo thought.

"Thanks."

"So, you're closing up?" He noticed a foil-covered plate of food next to the cash register.

The teen followed his gaze, and what could only be guilt settled on her face. "It's leftovers."

Mark frowned. "No problem to take it. You'd just have to throw it out."

"It's not for me..." She stopped and, if possible, looked more guilty.

"What?" Leo nudged.

"I don't want to rat him out, but—"

"Now you have to tell us." Leo kept his voice light. He didn't want to scare her. "This business is our responsibility, and if something is going on we need to know."

"He's right, kiddo," Mark agreed.

She caught her bottom lip between her teeth. "I don't think it's against the law exactly. Maybe trespassing—"

"Why don't you let us decide," Leo said gently. Loyalty was pretty important to him but sometimes you needed to spill the whole truth. "No one has to know where the information came from. We'll keep your name out of it."

Her expressive face gave away the conflict raging inside her. Finally she nodded. "There's a boy from one of the teams. He slept here last night."

Mark looked surprised. "Whoever's working a shift is supposed to do rounds—"

It would be easy to hide, Leo realized. Men's teams rented ice time off-hours for practices and games. The place was big, with a lot of dark corners. Someone familiar with it could find a place to crash and not be noticed. And he was being fed.

Denise met his gaze, looking embarrassed and ashamed. "I know him from school, too. He's got problems at home and I felt sorry for him."

Déjà vu, Leo thought. "You did the right thing. And you're not in trouble. Just, if something like this happens again, come to us. We'll figure it out."

"Okay." She told them where to find him and gave Leo the plate of food. "His name is Josh."

Leo told Mark he would handle it, then went to the men's locker room. There was a small storage space and that's where he found Josh sleeping, using his bulky hockey bag for a pillow.

He turned on the light and the boy opened his eyes, then sat up. "Hi, Josh."

"How do you know my name?"

"I own this place. It's my business to know what goes on," he said vaguely. He handed over the plate. Teenage boys could eat more than half their weight in hamburgers and french fries, and it didn't matter whether or not the food was warm. "I thought you might be hungry."

The kid answered with a sullen, negative head movement.

"Why don't you let me call your folks? I'll even give you a ride home."

"No."

"What's your last name?"

"You own this place. I thought you knew everything."

They went back and forth for a while and he got no information. Clearly the boy didn't want to go home. Leo sympathized, but letting him sleep here was out of the question.

He decided it was time to get tougher. "You're trespassing, you know. I'll just call the cops. Let them get the information out of you."

"Go ahead," he challenged. "Anything is better than living with them."

Twenty years ago Leo was this kid. He hadn't run away from home but it had crossed his mind. What if someone had called the cops on him? There had to be a compromise. "Look, my name is Leo—"

"I know. Leo 'The Wall' Wallace. Highest-scoring defenseman in the NHL." There was a little bit of awe in his voice.

Maybe he could work that angle, Leo thought. Get Josh's trust and take him to the house. Tess was there. He liked the sound of that but hoped it had more to do with her as backup for this kid crisis than anything personal.

"What would you think about coming home with me?"

Chapter Six

Tess was sitting in the family room, idly using the TV remote to flip through channels while she waited for Leo. A part of her was really looking forward to seeing him, in a "crush on a boy" sort of way. The other part of her wanted to discuss the bar in a "what the heck are you doing to my grandfather's legacy" way. When she'd seen the demolition, her stomach had turned and it had nothing to do with morning sickness.

Oh, Leo had shown her the architectural plans and the computer images of how it was going to look, but now all she saw was an empty shell where there'd once been warmth and laughter. And maybe her imagination was working overtime, but tonight it seemed to her as if he'd been gone a lot longer than he'd led her to believe he would be.

Then she heard the front door open and angry voices drifted inside. He wasn't alone. Her first thought was that he'd taken her suggestion not to let her presence cramp his social life. That was followed by an unreasonable explosion of anger, with all the characteristics of jealousy. Seconds later it sank in that the person with him wasn't a woman. Curiosity got the better of her and she left the family room to meet him in the entryway and find out what was going on.

The heated conversation stopped when they saw her.

Leo had brought home a hostile teenage hockey player, if that oversize, smelly equipment bag was anything to go by.

She stopped in front of the newcomer, who didn't smell much better. "Hi. I'm Tess. Who are you?"

"You don't need to know," he said rudely.

"This is Josh," Leo said.

He was cute, she noted, in a purely observational way. Blond hair, green eyes, a little skinny but give him a few years and he would be a heartbreaker, just like Leo. Unlike her partner, he was anything but easygoing. Intensity rolled off this kid like sweat.

She looked at the other adult in the room. "What's going on?"

"Josh was crashing at the ice rink. Some beef with his folks. He wouldn't say what it was or give me any other information. I couldn't leave him there and the only other choice was to call the cops."

"Obviously there was another option because here you are with him," she pointed out. Her guess would be that Leo didn't want to call the authorities. That would have been easier, to let them deal with whatever was going on, but that's not what he'd done. The fact that he was getting involved gave her a sudden warm and fuzzy feeling.

"Are you hungry, Josh?"

"No." He tried to look sullen, but couldn't quite pull it off.

"It's a well-known fact that, at your age, boys are always hungry. I'll warm a plate in the microwave." She turned away. "Follow me. And leave that bag by the front door. It smells like a squirrel crawled in there and died."

Someone behind her laughed and it didn't sound like Leo. That was a start.

She knew her business partner well enough now to

know that he would have protested if he didn't approve of feeding this kid, so she led the way to the kitchen.

Tess pulled leftover baked chicken and fried potatoes, along with green beans, from the refrigerator and filled a plate before putting a cover on it. Then she put everything in the microwave and hit the warm-plate button on the panel. The light inside came on along with a low hum.

The kid was hovering in the space between the family room and kitchen island. He wasn't going to talk unless he felt comfortable and trusted them. How did they pull that off? She glanced at Leo and he looked uncertain, too. What would her grandfather have done?

Basics, she thought. "Okay, Josh no-last-name—"

"I have a last name," he muttered.

"Then let's have it," she said firmly.

"It's Hutak."

"Okay, Josh Hutak, there's a powder room down the hall. Why don't you wash up before you eat." She could see a protest forming and cut it off. "That's not optional and I recommend you don't even think about talking back. No wash, no food. Not negotiable."

Hunger must have won out because the kid turned without another word and did as requested.

When it was just her and Leo, she said, "What are we going to do with him? His parents must be worried sick."

"I would be." Something in those three words said he knew how it felt to be concerned about a child. He dragged his fingers through his hair. "I'm hoping I can get through to him and he'll voluntarily give up information. If he doesn't, that leaves no choice but to—"

"Call the police," she finished. "We could let him stay but the thought of what his parents must be going through makes me want to shake the information out of him."

"I know. But the way to a man's heart is through his

stomach, and all that. We'll keep this low-key if possible. I'd really rather not escalate the situation to that level."

Leo Wallace, heartless womanizer, was empathizing with this kid big-time, and Tess was curious. Clearly she knew nothing about this man beyond his lucrative hockey career and business pursuits, not to mention his pursuit of starlets and models. But she had a feeling there was a lot more to him than that.

The microwave beeped, indicating the food was warmed. At the same time Josh came back into the room.

"Have a seat at the table."

He did as instructed and she gave him utensils while Leo poured him a big glass of milk.

"Thanks," he mumbled before digging in.

Everything disappeared quickly, as he practically inhaled it all. She'd cooked that night and wanted to believe it was about her skills, but figured he just hadn't eaten for a while. That was concerning.

"Do you want more?" she asked.

"No."

She and Leo sat across from him at the table and waited for the kid to open up about his situation but he outstubborned them.

Finally Leo cleared his throat. "I didn't like my parents very much when I was growing up. They argued all the time. More than once, one or both of them screamed at each other that they wished they'd never gotten married. My mother and father were the poster couple for why bitterly unhappy people should not stay together and make everyone around them miserable."

"Are they still together?" Tess couldn't stop herself from asking. Where Leo was concerned, the list of questions was growing, and this seemed like the least intrusive.

"No. They split when all of us kids were out of high

school. But the damage was done. I have a brother and sister, and all three of us want no part of marriage thanks to them."

"It sucks." Josh's comment and emphatic tone indicated he was going through something similar.

Tess felt obliged to point something out. "Since we're sharing sucky family stuff, I need to tell you two it could have been worse."

"How?" Leo and Josh said together. They shared a fleeting grin.

"My father, the sperm donor, disappeared before I was born. When I was six, my mother and I came to Huntington Hills to live here with her father. She left to go to the store one day and never came back. So he raised me, but I didn't have either parent."

"You had your grandfather," Leo said.

"And he was awesome." There were times, like now, when the pain of missing him was hard to bear. "But I was different from most of the other kids at school. They all had a mom or dad, or both. No one I knew lived with a grandparent. It made me different that neither of my parents wanted me."

"I wish mine didn't," Josh muttered.

"Okay," Leo said. "I think we should declare Tess the winner of the 'worst parents ever' award. But, Josh, reading between the lines, I'm hearing that your mom and dad fight with each other but both care about you. I have a feeling you're getting flack for something. What's really going on?"

The boy stared at the empty plate in front of him, then looked up and glared. "I'm grounded from hockey."

"Why?" Leo asked.

"Because they suck."

"There's something you're not telling us." He didn't

flinch from the kid's hostile gaze. "I've been where you are. My parents didn't like each other but both of them wanted what was best for me."

"So you're saying it's my fault they fight?"

Leo's expression was bemused. "I'm not sure how you got there from what I said. No, their fights are with each other. I have a feeling they're in agreement about something that's going on with you. I can't help if you don't tell me what it is."

Tess was mesmerized by the gentle understanding in his voice. This was a side of him she had never seen before. It was a good side.

"Why did they take hockey away?" he asked.

Josh looked so achingly young and the pain on his face was tangible. There was also frustration and injustice tangled up in his expression. "I'm failing English. It's stupid. They know I want to play pro hockey someday but how can I if they won't let me be on the team now?"

"I see." Leo looked thoughtful. "So, what if you pull up that grade?"

"I'm back on the team," he grudgingly admitted. "But there's no way I can. I have to pass every quiz before the final and do an extra-credit paper on *The Great Gatsby* to pass the class. I'm just screwed."

"Maybe you could get a tutor," Tess suggested. "If your parents see that you're trying, you might be able to negotiate hockey reinstatement, pending your final grade."

"They'd never go for it."

"Well," Leo said, "running away from home isn't going to keep you on the team. It's an expensive sport."

The kid's gaze was full of desperation. "Maybe you could give me a job at the rink. I'll work for hockey expenses."

"That's an idea." Leo looked thoughtful. "But you're

underage. Without your parents' consent, I would probably be breaking a whole lot of laws."

"You don't understand—"

"I do. I went through the same thing. You've got no
choice," Leo said.

"What did you do?" Josh asked.

"I got my grades up in high school. There were hockey
scholarships for certain colleges, and I went after one and
played while I was going to school. Eventually scouts for
professional teams came looking. And I was drafted." He
stopped until the kid met his gaze. "But if I'd run away
from home, none of that would have been possible."

"My dad won't listen," he said hopelessly.

"I'll talk to him," Leo offered. "What have you got
to lose?"

Josh shrugged his shoulders. "Nothing, I guess."

"Good call. Why don't you give me your dad's number and I'll get in touch with him."

Josh thought that over for a few moments, then nodded his agreement. Leo dialed the number and introduced
himself when it was answered. From this end of the conversation Tess could tell that the man knew of Leo's superstar status.

When he hung up, he smiled at the boy. "Your dad is
on the way to pick you up. Let's wait for him out front.
It's going to be all right. I promise."

Josh nodded, then stood and thanked Tess for dinner.
After that he followed Leo out of the room and she heard
the front door open and close again.

Tess couldn't believe the man she'd just seen reasoning
with a teenage boy was the same one she thought had the
sensitivity of an alley cat. Now she knew why he found
marriage unappealing, and who could blame him. But for
reasons she didn't totally get, understanding why he was

that way didn't make her feel better. Because she actually liked him and that was more dangerous than simply being physically attracted.

Leo stood outside until the car's taillights disappeared. For that kid's sake, he hoped Josh's father had listened to him. He sighed and turned away, then walked back into the house, where Tess was waiting. He was glad she was there.

She'd cleaned up the kitchen from Josh's spur-of-the-moment meal and was sitting in the family room, staring at the TV, which was currently not on.

"Hey," he said.

She glanced over her shoulder to look at him. "I guess he got picked up?"

"Yeah." He walked over and sat on the couch, careful not to get too close. Being near enough to touch her wasn't a good idea.

"You were out there for a long time."

He met her gaze. "There was a little bit of a fanboy thing going on."

"So it's not just women?" she asked sweetly.

"I'm going to pretend you didn't just say that." He wished she would let that go.

"Okay. What did you say to his father?"

"I repeated the things Josh said, and Ed—that's his dad—admitted there's stress in the marriage and it could be handled better. They're in counseling."

"Good." She thought for a moment. "Did you suggest that Josh probably needs counseling, too?"

"I just met the guy," he said wryly. "It's something I'll save for our second conversation."

"His son ran away from home," she protested. "I think that's a cry for help."

"Yeah." He looked at her, all fierce and mother lion about a kid she'd just met. Maybe her instincts were on warp drive because she was pregnant. But whatever the reason, it was damn sexy. "I think his dad understands that."

"Are you sure?"

"We talked about the home situation and that Josh is caught in the middle. And the sport he loves is the only positive in his life right now. A place where he can just be a kid on a team, trying to put a puck into the other guy's net. It's a physical game but everyone is padded up and supervised. A safe place to release all those feelings you can't do anything about."

"How do you know so much about teenage boys?" she teased.

"I was one, remember?" He grinned briefly, then recalled what his life was like when he was Josh's age. "I wasn't exaggerating when I told him how it was with my family."

"Do you want to talk about it?" she asked.

"Is that your way of telling me I need counseling?"

"I would just say it straight out if I thought so." She shrugged. "All I'm saying is that I'm happy to listen."

He didn't think much about that time anymore, because he didn't feel trapped. He was a grown man and not stuck in a bitter, angry place. That was never going to happen to him again.

"Like I said, I wasn't being dramatic about my home being like a battlefield. There was no volume control. Either they were yelling at the top of their lungs or not speaking to each other at all. The tension was suffocating."

"That must have been awful."

"I didn't say anything unless absolutely necessary, for fear of setting off another round." He rested his elbows on his knees, clasping his hands together. "One time when they were wishing they never got married, I told them I wished they hadn't either. And maybe they should get a divorce."

"Uh-oh," she said.

"Yeah. He accused me of being ungrateful. She said I was selfish."

"Do you know why they didn't split sooner?"

"I asked my dad that once." He remembered bracing himself for an outburst of anger but that hadn't happened. His father had looked sad, which was worse somehow.

"What did he say?"

Leo saw sympathy in her eyes and wasn't sure how he felt about it. The look was just south of pity. "He told me they didn't want the family to be broken up."

"Oh, Leo." She sighed. "You were already broken."

"I know." And every time they'd screamed at each other about not wanting to be married, he'd vowed not to make the same mistake they had. But he had and it had been even worse.

"Do you see them much now?" she asked.

"Occasionally. He's in Washington state and she's in Florida."

"Did they pick opposite ends of the country on purpose?"

"A case could be made." He leaned back on the couch, stretching his arm across the back. With very little effort he could touch her shoulder and badly wanted to. A classic case of damned if he did, damned if he didn't. "Ironically, individually they are both nice people. But together they're like a bad chemical reaction."

"Do you think Josh's parents are like that?" she asked.

"Hard to tell. Ed seemed like a nice, reasonable guy. Worried about his son. Relieved and grateful to find out he was okay. Thanked me over and over for taking care of him."

"About that…" There was a sparkle in her expression, a look that turned the brown in her eyes the color of warm chocolate.

Leo was so used to her look of hostility and resentment, he didn't know what to make of this. "What did I do?"

"The right thing."

"Anyone else would have done the same," he said.

"Not everyone would have brought home a troubled teenage boy, let alone gotten involved in a family conflict." There was approval in her voice, something that wasn't there much when she talked to him.

He liked it.

"I didn't exactly get involved. But I did offer a piece of advice."

"Which was?"

"Don't take hockey away from Josh."

"And?" she asked.

"Ed explained that he couldn't do nothing and watch his son fail English. There had to be consequences. And that didn't mean taking away brussels sprouts."

She smiled at that and then said, "He's right."

"I agree. But I think I convinced him to make that a last resort. Give him a chance to bring up his grade, maybe with a tutor."

She nodded enthusiastically. "Now that's a really great idea."

"It was yours and I'm glad you still like it because I volunteered you. There's no time to mess around finding one and I know you like to read."

"I love to read, but—"

"Josh agreed. He likes you, by the way, and that's important. It might not work with anyone else. Ed is on board, too."

"Look, Leo—"

"I know I should have asked, but I needed to take a shot right then." Playing hockey, he'd learned strategy and setting up for a goal. No hotdogging. But sometimes you just had to swing away. A lot of times you missed the net, but every once in a while a player got lucky and scored. "I was in the zone with both of them."

"Another sports metaphor." She shook her head. "Reading between the lines, I'm going to assume you were taking advantage of your superstar reputation."

"Taking advantage sounds so harsh. I prefer to think of it as using my charm."

"Oh, please." But she didn't look upset. "Josh is such a fan, if you said jump, he'd ask how high."

"Then isn't it lucky I'm using my powers for good?" He gave her a pleading look. "Come on, Tess. It's not for long. Just help him write a paper and study for the final. The bar is closed right now anyway while the renovation is going on. So you've got the time. What do you say? This kid is at a crossroads and could go either way. Be a force for good."

She pulled her legs up to the side and angled her body toward him, sliding her shoulder out of his reach. "Are you implying that if I don't, Josh's life will be ruined?"

"I would never do that," he said virtuously.

"Oh, pull in your wings and halo, hotshot. Next thing I know you'll be walking on water." She met his gaze. "You didn't say it in so many words, but that's what I heard."

"So, what's the verdict?"

She stared at him for several moments, then nodded. "Okay. I'll help him. When do we start?"

"Tomorrow."

Her eyes widened. "Seriously?"

"He's going to meet you here after school to study for a quiz on Friday."

"I thought you said it would just be for finals," she said, pointing an accusing finger at him.

"He needs all the points he can get."

"Well, it's a good thing you didn't spring this on me. No pressure either," she said wryly.

"It's a tough time for him, Tess."

"I know. A cry for help. How can I turn my back?" Her voice softened. "I had my issues with not having parents, but in the long run maybe I was better off than you and Josh that they weren't around."

"Maybe." Thanks to Patrick Morrow, she'd turned out great. And Pat had helped Leo through one of the worst times in his life. He owed him.

"I'm tired. It's been quite a night." She stood and looked down at him. "I just have to say that you did good tonight, Leo. You're going to be a wonderful father."

He didn't say anything, just watched her leave as a too-familiar feeling of emptiness came over him. He'd been a good father once, until the kid he thought was his was ripped out of his life. That wasn't going to happen again. Not if Tess was carrying his baby.

Chapter Seven

Leo looked around The Pub and nodded with satisfaction. Plastic covers protected the booths, tables and bar. The changes were in the adjacent areas, and knocking out the wall had really opened up the place, made it brighter. In his gut he felt this was a good move and he really hoped Tess agreed. She was going to be here any minute and he was a little nervous about her reaction. The last time she saw it there was a devastated look on her face, and he couldn't make her feel better until the place was put back together. It wasn't yet. Still a work in progress.

This business wasn't just how she made her living; it was part of her history, and he'd come on pretty strong about modernizing. Doing nothing meant a slow, painful decline and eventual failure. It was the right thing to make sure this place was around for a long time to come.

The door opened behind him, and she walked in, looking so fresh and pretty, he wanted to just stare. It was a stupid reaction. He'd seen her a few hours ago at breakfast, when he realized he very much liked seeing her in the morning. And that was stupid, too. This living arrangement was temporary. And that's all it could be. He knew from personal experience not to get used to being happy, because the good stuff didn't last.

Tess was looking around and finally met his gaze. "Hi. So, it's still torn up."

"You're late." *Way to get her on your side, Wallace.*

"Sorry. I had to drop Josh off at home."

"How is the tutoring going?" Leo knew she'd been working with him twice a week for a few weeks now.

"He's a bright kid. He just doesn't like reading and writing." She shrugged. "We went through books on his suggested-reading list and I tried to steer him to one that might interest him. We're both going to read it so I can help him organize his thoughts to write the paper."

"Is he cooperative?"

"Very." She smiled. "He's polite and really funny. I enjoy tutoring him."

"Good." At least his idea for her to tutor had worked out. On the other hand, time would tell how the changes here would be. He glanced around. "So, what do you think?"

She walked around, studying the adjacent area in its rough stages. "With the wall gone, the bar will actually be in the middle of the room."

"Yeah."

"It's very open."

"Nate's guys are repairing wall board that was tweaked when the demolition was done. That takes the longest. Then there's paint."

"And when the fumes are gone, I'll be out of your hair," she said.

"You've really been a pain in the neck," he teased. The thought of her gone didn't thrill him, though.

"Speaking of finishing touches, I brought paint chips and some other decorating samples. We need window coverings and furniture."

"Let's see what you have."

She walked back into the old part and set her purse on a plastic-covered table, then pulled out paint charts in varying shades of beige, yellow, blue and green. Leo moved close to look at the colors, and their arms brushed. His gut clenched and tightened. The scent of her skin burrowed inside him and shorted out brain function until he couldn't tell the difference between gold and meadow green.

"I think we should go with earth tones," she said.

The card she held out had about six shades that went from nearly white to chocolate brown. And they all had names. He picked up another card with shades of blue.

"How about one of these?" He looked more closely. "The cerulean is eye-catching."

"Seriously?" The fact that her lips were curving up was a clue she didn't mean that in a bad way. "Hearing the word *cerulean* come out of your mouth just seems wrong somehow."

"I'm just reading the name." He pointed to it. "Seems to me this color will work with chrome and glass."

"Seriously?" This time she didn't smile.

"What?"

"Chrome and glass are only good if you want to get fingerprints at a crime scene." She held up a hand to stop his rebuttal. "Think about the time it will take to maintain. Not to mention it will completely alter the vibe. Goodbye, homey and cozy. Hello, dystopian society."

"Well, when Big Brother is watching, I hope it's here, with a game on one of our TVs."

"I'm serious," she said.

"Me, too."

"We have a core clientele that likes to come here and relax. I feel an obligation to them and their expectations. Plus we can't afford to alienate any segment of our customer base. It's like interviewing for a job. You have a small window of time to make an impression. Whether it's good or bad depends on appearance."

While listening to her passionate defense, Leo was more than a little preoccupied with her appearance. Her mouth, for one thing. He knew how good she tasted. And her hair. It was shiny and dark and pulled into a ponytail, with wisps curling around her face. She was wearing jeans that were getting tight, showing the baby bump where her stomach used to be flat. This wasn't the first time he'd noted pregnancy changes in a woman carrying his baby—at least he'd thought it was his.

"Are you listening to me?" Tess asked, breaking into his thoughts.

"Yes." Technically that was true, although he didn't really know what she'd said. Except she generally disapproved of his decorating suggestions. "Okay, how about a compromise? We continue the wood floor all the way through. Put in comfortable chairs with glass tables, a lounge feel for watching the game, as if you were in your own family room. Use earth tones in the original bar area and paint the new part a coordinating color of cerulean."

It was obvious that she didn't want to smile, but her lips twitched. When she answered, her tone was grudging. "That might work."

"Look at us. I think we just negotiated a peaceful settlement."

"It appears we have."

He grinned but it quickly disappeared. There was something else that he needed to bring up, and she was going to like it a lot less than chrome and glass.

"Tess, one more thing—"

Her expression turned wary. "Your tone isn't reassuring. You should work on that."

"Okay. But first we need to think about a new name for this place."

"What's wrong with the old one?"

"It sounds like it was made up by a man."

"It was. My grandfather." Her mouth trembled and she looked horrified when big, fat tears rolled down her cheeks. She covered her face with her hands and turned away from him. But her shoulders were shaking with silent sobs.

Leo couldn't stand seeing Tess cry now any more than the last time, right here in this room on the night of her grandfather's memorial. He put his hands on her shoulders and turned her, pulling her against his chest, then wrapping his arms around her.

"Hush. Don't cry." He patted her back.

"Damn hormones."

"It's going to work out. You'll see." That was something you said when the jury was out deliberating and you had no idea what the heck was going to happen. It was lame and all he had.

But damn, she felt good. If it made him a bastard for finding the silver lining of her distress, then so be it. Because he couldn't help the feeling. She felt even better than that night when they'd ended up having sex just a few feet from where they were standing right now. And he wanted her again. Even more than he had then.

When she abruptly pulled away from him, he was afraid he'd said that out loud. But probably not, since talking required air and suddenly it was hard for him to breathe.

Tess's hand was shaking when she brushed moisture from beneath her eyes. She drew in a deep breath, evidence that she wasn't unaffected by his touch.

"Sorry. I didn't mean to blubber."

"It's okay. I kind of surprised you by suggesting a name change. My bad."

"Would you mind if we take that up another time? I'm meeting my friends for dinner."

"No problem."

"We need to make final decisions on the finishing touches and it occurs to me that it might help to consult an interior designer. One of the regulars does that so I'll contact her and make an appointment. Let's coordinate our schedules so we can both be here."

When she pulled out her cell phone, Leo did, too. She started talking dates and he zeroed in on the current one. Between the bar renovations, the baby and thinking about Tess, he hadn't been paying attention to what day it was. But now the significance of this one sank in, making him feel as if he'd been bodychecked without hockey pads.

And for some reason, this year the pain of remembering was worse than ever.

When she walked into the restaurant called Burgers but Better, Tess was still quivering from feeling Leo's arms around her again. In the same room where they'd had sex. It would have been so easy to go there for a second time, because she wanted him. There was no denying the attraction, but acting on it would have been stupid. Once was a foolish mistake, but twice was a pattern and that was a template for heartbreak. They'd agreed not to mix business and pleasure, and she was sticking to that. Her priority was having her baby and saving her business, in that order.

And now she was going to put all that aside and have a carefree evening with her two BFFs. Tess had known Carla Kellerman and Jamie Webber since first grade. She'd come to live with her grandfather, and then her mom had split just before she started a brand-new school and knew no one. A terrified first grader had walked into the classroom and come out with two lifelong friends.

They'd been through a lot together—breakups with boyfriends, job changes, family problems and loss. There was no one she counted on more than these two women. It had been a while since she'd seen them, and since then Tess had gone through a lot of changes, life-altering ones. With The Pub closed because of the construction work, they were meeting somewhere different for dinner.

Tess got there first, which never happened because she normally got hung up at work, even before her grandfather died. But she wasn't currently working, unless tutoring counted, so that wasn't a problem. She was sitting at a booth in the brightly lit, casual restaurant when her friends walked in together and looked around.

She stood, waved and they came over. There were big hugs all around before the two of them slid into the space across from her in the booth. They smiled at each other for several moments, just happy to be together.

"The triumvirate of trouble together again." Jamie Webber was a pretty, blue-eyed brunette who labeled her hair mousey brown and her legs too short.

"That's what Granddad always called us. The last time we were together was at the memorial service." The pain of loss sliced through her. That was a sad day but she had a feeling what she would remember most was what happened between her and Leo. It was the day a life lost had been honored and another had been created.

"I miss him, too." Carla squeezed her hand for a moment. The redhead had a fiery temper and the biggest heart in the world. "A lot has changed for you since then. You're pregnant."

"Thanks for the newsflash." She'd told them about the baby, how it happened and who the father was.

"How are you feeling?" Jamie asked.

"Tired. Nauseated and generally in a state of doubt and fear. How are you guys?"

"Things are good," Jamie said. "I finally told Karl he was never getting out of the friend zone."

"How did he take it?" Both Tess and Carla had recommended letting the poor guy know sooner rather than later.

"I felt like I kicked a puppy. It was awful. You both know how I hate hurting anyone."

"We do," Carla confirmed. "And you're a brave little soldier. But letting it go on would have hurt him more in the long run. You did the right thing."

"I know." Jamie sighed, then looked sideways at Carla. "And what's going on with you?"

Tess pushed Leo out of her mind and focused on her friend. "Lots of changes, I hear. You're back home, where you belong, and have a new job."

"It's humiliating," Carla said. "Not the job. But leaving town. I can't believe I followed a guy to Denver, worked my ass off to help him get established, buy a house and then he dumped me. So now I'm back, forced to live with my mother in the house where I grew up. Full circle sucks."

"I'm sorry, honey," Tess said. "But selfishly, I'm glad you're back."

"Tell us about the job," Jamie urged.

"It's called Make Me a Match, as in matchmaking."

"So you're working at a place that brings couples together," Tess clarified.

"The irony is huge," Carla admitted. "I'm not the only one getting back on my feet. The company provides personal service and has been going through a rough patch.

The owner's nephew is some tech guy and agreed to help out for a limited time, make things run more efficiently."

"Sounds exciting," Jamie said.

"You should give us a try," Carla told Jamie.

"Actually I met someone. He's the reason I had to tell Karl how I felt. His name is Bill Para and he's in sales. Right now he's going back and forth between here and Seattle, but he's planning to move here. He says the weather is better in California."

"Can't argue with that," Tess agreed.

The waitress interrupted them and introduced herself, then took drink and food orders. It was—surprise—burgers all around. She pointed out the fixings bar that offered a plethora of items to make the hamburgers more exciting. Hence the name—Burgers but Better.

Drinks came quickly—wine for her two friends, club soda with lime for Tess. They clinked glasses.

"To the baby," Carla toasted. "I can't believe you're going to be a mother."

"Tell me about it."

Jamie turned serious. "I want to hear about this baby's father. Leo Wallace. I saw him at the memorial service and he seemed genuinely fond of your grandfather. What's he like?"

"Besides huge and hunky." Carla grinned.

"He's now my partner in the business for one thing." Tess knew that's not what they wanted to know but this was the simplest part of their relationship, and even that was complicated. "Apparently Granddad was fond of him. About six months before he died, he approached Leo about buying into the business."

"Knowing him, Pat wanted to make sure there was someone to watch over you after he was gone," Jamie said.

Tess nodded and explained about customer decline

and her reasons for going through with the partnership proposal.

"How does Leo feel about becoming a father?" Carla asked.

"That's a good question. He wants a DNA test after the baby is born. He made that very clear."

"Can't say I blame him," Jamie teased. "What with the way you sleep around. I'm surprised you could narrow it down to one guy."

"Funny girl." Tess was aware that her friends knew he was the one and only guy she'd been with in a very long time. They told each other everything. The only information she'd held back was her current living arrangement, and she wasn't sure why. But in a few weeks she'd be back in her apartment anyway. No harm, no foul. Getting serious again, she said, "He asked how I feel about being a mother."

"Wow, a man in touch with his softer side." Carla looked at Jamie and the two friends nodded at each other. "And?"

"I was honest with him. I'm nervous. It's a big change, not to mention responsibility. And I have a business to run, one that needs to grow to be successful. That means more hours at work, not less."

"Good thing you have a partner, then," Jamie said. "Is he excited about being a dad? Maybe having a new little hockey player?"

"Honestly, I haven't actually asked him how he feels about it."

"Because you don't want to know." Carla wasn't asking.

These two knew her better than anyone and would know if she was dodging the question. So she didn't.

"That's probably true. But it's a little freaky what he knows about pregnant women."

"Oh?"

"He brought me crackers when I was having trouble keeping food down." And he'd held her hair back when she threw up. "He insisted on coming to my OB appointment." But it seemed more as if he was keeping her under surveillance than anything else. "But he has a reputation with women, so—"

"So a sports guy who's a womanizer is a deal breaker for you," Jamie said.

According to Granddad, her father was the quarterback and captain of his high school football team, and he'd run out on his family. Tess's college love was a baseball player and he'd cheated on her. In Tess's eyes, athletes didn't make good husband material. She had to keep reminding herself there would never be anything, except this baby, between her and Leo.

The waitress arrived with their burgers and fries, and they took them to the bar for bacon, jalapeno, onions and just about any topping one could imagine. After returning to the table, there was nothing but silence because their mouths were too busy eating. It was a messy meal that required concentration and a bazillion napkins. Tess didn't complain because she was happy to no longer be in the spotlight, fielding questions she couldn't answer.

"That was super yummy," Carla said when she was finished.

"I'm a happy girl," Jamie agreed. "Tess, you're lagging."

All eyes were on her half-eaten hamburger. "My appetite isn't quite back to normal yet. I'll get a to-go box. Leo might like it."

"Oh? And why is it that he would be getting your left-overs?" Jamie asked, eyes narrowing suspiciously.

"What are you not telling us?" Carla demanded.

Tess had only said there were renovations going on at The Pub. Neither of them had asked if she was staying in her apartment while the work was being done. Now she had no choice. The cat was out of the bag and no way would they let this slide.

"I had to move out because of the dust and paint fumes. Not good for the baby."

"And what does this have to do with Leo?"

Tess looked at Carla. "He was actually the one who said it wasn't a good idea for me to be there. And that his house has lots of room."

"You could have asked me," Carla said.

"Or me." Jamie wore her heart on her sleeve, and clearly her feelings were hurt.

"Oh, honey." Tess reached across the table and squeezed her hand. "I couldn't impose on you in your studio apartment. There's not enough room." She looked at Carla. "And I couldn't ask you."

"Because I'm living with my mom. But you know we could make room."

"I didn't want to inconvenience anyone. Besides, Leo was pretty insistent." She held up her hand to stop the questions she knew they still had. "Separate bedrooms. That one time was, well, one time. A mistake. We're handling the consequences together."

"How very grown-up and civilized of you both." Carla's voice was wry.

"Okay." Jamie nodded. "As long as you know we're there for you. There's no favor you can't ask. Nothing we wouldn't do for you."

"Including hurting that big hunk if he hurts you," Carla

said fiercely. "Just so you know, I can be a father if he decides it's not for him."

"Sweet of you." Tess grinned. "But anatomically you don't have the equipment to be a dad."

"Still," she said, "I've got your back. Discipline is my middle name. I can be the bad cop."

"Me, too," Jamie chimed in.

"And I love you guys for that." Tess's vision blurred with tears. "Damn hormones."

"Oh, sweetie—"

They both reached over and took her hands. She sniffled and held on tightly. There was no doubt in her mind these loyal women would be there for her.

But Leo had surprised her. He had clearly connected with Josh and handled that situation extremely well. His fathering instincts were on full display and, in her opinion, he was going to be a terrific dad. He was also anti-marriage, flat out said as much because of his folks, but she was, too. They saw eye to eye on that.

It was just the business they seemed to butt heads on. "Thanks, you guys, for being my friends. I love our girls' nights."

"Me, too." Jamie squeezed her hand tight, then let go. She looked around the restaurant. "I sure do miss the bar, though. It's so friendly and comfortable there."

"Not for much longer." Tess thought about the meeting with Leo just a couple of hours ago. The one where she brought up wanting cozy and he pushed for flashy. She had a partner now and compromises had to be made. And more darn changes.

"What do you mean not for much longer?" Carla asked the question, but both women were giving her a skeptical look.

"The decor is changing—a mix of old and new. He wants it to be a sports bar. Do you believe that?"

"Guys like sports bars," Jamie mused.

Carla nodded thoughtfully. "Could be a good place to meet men. A fun place to suggest a first get-together for our Make Me a Match clients. So right there you've added another customer demographic. Women who want to meet men."

"Oh, brother." Tess already met a man and it was complicating the stuffing out of her life.

She'd be better off alone, but... Leo gave really good hugs. When he put those big, strong arms around a girl, she knew she'd been *hugged*. It made her feel better earlier, when she had cried.

But then it made her want sex. It made her not so sure mixing business with pleasure was such a bad idea. The more time she spent with Leo, the more she was leaning toward that very bad idea.

And now she had to go back to his place and see him.

Chapter Eight

Through his alcohol-induced haze, Leo was aware of someone shaking him awake. He opened one eye and decided it must be Tess, although she was really blurry, which was a shame because he liked looking at her. She was pretty. And his head was pounding, like a bunch of midgets were bouncing on a trampoline in his brain.

He focused a little and saw she was staring at him. "What?"

She held up a nearly empty bottle of scotch. "Did you drink all this?"

He struggled to remember, and then it came back to him why he'd deliberately gotten blind drunk in the first place. Holding out his hand he said, "Shame to waste that."

"I think you've had enough."

"Not even close."

She handed him a bottle of water instead. "Alcohol is dehydrating. You need to drink this. I learned a lot of useful stuff working in The Pub."

He sat up and the room started spinning, so he leaned against the back of the sofa again and rubbed the ice-cold water bottle across his forehead. The scotch would have been gone if she'd given him that instead. Anything to achieve a reprieve from the aching emptiness of loss. Just for this day. He wasn't entitled to much but surely it was okay to make the pain go away for today.

Tess sat on the coffee table right in front of him and set the liquor bottle behind her. He'd have to go through her to get the booze. As pleasant as that thought was, he couldn't do it and at the moment wasn't entirely clear on why.

"Have you eaten?" she asked.

He shook his head and, man, was he sorry. Pain exploded inside his skull and he winced. "Not hungry."

"Could you choke down some eggs and toast? Something light. It would make you feel better."

That's just it. He would never feel better. Not about this. "No. Just go to bed. I'm pretty bad company."

"So this isn't a good-natured bender you've got going on." She met his gaze. "I've seen a lot. I know the difference. If you were in my place, I'd be taking your car keys and calling an Uber."

"I'm not planning to drive."

He opened the plastic bottle and took a long drink of water. It helped some. But he still didn't want company. Conversation was the last thing he was looking for but she didn't budge. She had a look on her face, the one women get when they're determined to drag something out of a guy. And she didn't say a word. Another tactic to get him to open up.

"I'm not going to talk," he said stubbornly.

"Okay." But she continued to look at him.

Even in his semi-sober state he could tell this silence was getting awkward. He glared at her. "What is it going to take to get you to go away?"

"Tell me about Chad."

Hearing the name was like a two-by-four to the midsection. If her goal was to sober him up with an agonizing adrenaline rush, score one for her. And then something crept into his foggy mind.

"How do you know about him?"

"I don't. But you were mumbling the name and it sounded like a nightmare. You were pretty upset. That's why I woke you. Otherwise I'd have let you sleep it off."

"You should have."

"I couldn't." Her eyes took on a softness when she said, "Tell me. Who is Chad and why are you so upset about him?"

"Is there anything I can do to make you let this go?"

"Not even giving up chrome-and-glass decor for the bar."

Any other time he would have smiled at that, but not today. "It's Chad's fourth birthday."

"And you're not there. Is that your nephew? Godson?"

"He was my son. At least I thought so." He sat forward and rested his elbows on his knees.

"I don't understand."

He needed to start at the beginning, spit out the story and never speak of it again. "A woman I was seeing told me she was pregnant with my child. I wanted to do the right thing and asked her to marry me."

"Even though you saw your parents make each other miserable."

"Yeah. I thought it would be different for me. And it was." He met her gaze. "Just not how I expected. It was so much worse."

"What happened, Leo?"

"I supported her through the pregnancy. Made sure she scheduled all her doctor appointments when I didn't have a road trip, so I could be there."

"That's how you know so much about morning sickness and pregnancy."

"Yeah."

"Sorry. Didn't mean to interrupt. Go on," she urged.

"It was a textbook pregnancy and birth. I was there when Chad was born and over the moon in love with that baby boy. My son. I was a hands-on dad. Changed diapers, did nighttime feedings. Walked the floor with him when he was teething. I did all of it and loved everything. I was a good dad. Even Nancy—"

"Who?"

"My wife—ex-wife. She used to joke that I was a better mother than her." He sighed. "When I had to be away for road games, I missed him like crazy. Worried that he was all right. Hated that I might not hear his first word, see him take his first steps. All the milestones I wanted to be there for."

Leo remembered holding that tiny body right after he was born. He couldn't even put into words the power of the feelings that had rocked him to the core. Love, protectiveness, wanting to teach him everything. He was privileged to shape a little life and be a better dad than he'd had growing up.

"You said you *thought* he was your son. He's not?"

"For two and a half years I believed he was my child. She let me fall more in love with him every day." He met her gaze and wasn't sure why the pity in hers made him angrier. "When I broke my ankle in a Stanley Cup playoff game, I was almost happy. It ended my career but that meant I didn't have to be away from my son. I'd get an act two making a living but I'd never get back the moments in his life I missed."

"How did you find out he's not yours?"

"She told me."

"What?" Tess looked shocked. "Why after all that time would she?"

He shook his head. "She was leaving me because she

was having an affair. Seeing the guy when I was on the road, playing hockey. That was bad enough, but she admitted he was Chad's biological father. They were broken up and we were dating when she found out she was pregnant. I was the rebound guy who proposed faster than the speed of light and who made pretty good money in pro hockey. She knew she'd be well taken care of. Finally she told me the truth, said she had to be honest."

"Took her long enough. Two and a half years? The lying bitch." Tess was furious.

Somehow that made him feel a little better and he smiled at her fierceness. But it was gone in a heartbeat. "I couldn't stop her leaving and taking Chad with her. But she couldn't stop me loving him."

"What happened?"

"I hired an attorney and tried to get visitation with him. The problem is, I don't share his DNA so I have no legal rights at all. She took it one step further and got the court to order me to stay away from him."

"Oh, God, Leo. So you got the double whammy—your career was over and your family was gone." She moved to the sofa and sat close enough to put her arms around him. "And today is his birthday."

"A yearly reminder that I lost everything."

"I don't know how you survived that."

"Not well. It may come as a surprise to you, but this isn't the first time I've been drunk over what happened." The effects of the scotch were wearing off but the feel of her holding him was taking over for the liquor. "Your grandfather was the one who pulled me out of it."

She looked at him. "Really?"

"I lost myself for a while but he talked me back." He smiled a little, remembering Pat teasing him about getting a plaque with Leo's name on it for the chair he always sat in. "I was a regular. And it was like a therapy session. I talked about my problems and he told me how he felt about his daughter abandoning her child."

"It couldn't have been easy for him. Becoming responsible for a six-year-old girl." She looked a little guilty about it.

"What happened wasn't your fault, Tess."

"I know, but—"

"Hey, don't go there. I've got dibs on being the star of this pity party."

"Okay." She didn't look convinced.

"For what it's worth, he told me that raising you, having you in his life, was the best thing that ever happened."

"He was just saying that."

Leo shook his head. Still a big mistake. "No. He said you kept him young and he loved you so much. He told me he was sad for his daughter, your mom, because she was missing the joy of watching you grow up. To him, you were a gift."

"Sounds like him." She smiled a little, gave him a quick hug and then slid away. "He was a good man."

"The best."

"And so are you," she insisted.

"I don't think I'm even in his league." Leo missed her warmth. Missed it too much. "I'm not sure I would have gotten through all that without him."

"Fortunately you didn't have to. It's good he was there for you when you needed someone."

He'd needed someone tonight, too, and she was there. Just like her grandfather. Well, not exactly. Pat had never hugged him. But there was something in the Morrow DNA that was good and caring. He wasn't sure he'd have gotten through this painful anniversary without her. And that bothered him more than a little. He didn't want to need anyone.

* * *

The next morning Tess was awake early, or maybe she hadn't slept much. It was impossible to get out of her mind the complete misery on Leo's face from the sad anniversary he'd told her about. She was still trying to process what he'd gone through. Not in a million years did she think she'd feel sorry for cocky, confident Leo Wallace, but there was no way not to.

That witch had used him, then basically said, "Just kidding, you really have no right to love this child after all. It's time to stop now."

That was selfish and cruel, and he didn't deserve it. He'd done what he thought was right and married her, against his better judgment and negative feelings about tying the knot.

He hadn't offered to marry Tess and she actually *was* carrying his baby. Not that she wanted to get married but still... In his shoes, she would do the same thing—wait for conclusive DNA before becoming emotionally involved with the baby.

Speaking of shoes, she heard him coming down the stairs. A man as big as him just couldn't move silently like a cat burglar. He walked into the kitchen and his hair was still damp from a shower. His eyes were bloodshot and he hadn't shaved this morning. The stubble was pretty darn sexy and he looked a little dangerous. If anything it added to his appeal, and her heart skipped a beat.

"Morning," she said. "How do you feel?"

He winced and sat on one of the barstools lined up at the granite-covered island. "Is it necessary to shout?"

"Sorry."

"It's okay."

"Do you want coffee?" she practically whispered.

"Yes."

"Are you hungry?" She gave him a sympathetic look. "I got wasted in college just once. Now that I think about it, the next day was a lot like having morning sickness. Do you feel like eating?"

He held out his hand and rocked it back and forth. "Probably just coffee."

"I know what you need." She opened the pantry and got out a box, then set it in front of him.

He pulled out one of the packages of square soda crackers and gave her a wry look. "You probably think this is funny."

"No. And this is not a joke. It might help. Just sit tight. I've got you covered." She brought him coffee and a sports drink, since he always kept some in the refrigerator. Beside that she put two Tylenol on the counter. "Your electrolytes are out of whack, so this will help replenish them and flush the impurities out of your system. The crackers are bland and will go down easily."

"Okay." He took a square and bit into it with very little enthusiasm.

"I'll make you some eggs and toast, too. You need something light. Get calories into your body to reset your system."

While talking she quickly prepared some food and set a plate in front of him, then walked around the island and sat on the stool next to his. She watched him pick at the eggs and eat a triangle of the toast she'd cut diagonally. It must have helped because after that his plate was empty pretty fast. Now he was working on the sports drink.

"Can I get you more toast? Eggs?" she asked.

He shook his head and winced a little. "No, thanks. Maybe in a little while. Need to see how that settles first."

"Okay."

He studied her through narrowed eyes that were a little

less bloodshot. "Why are you being so nice to me? Obviously you don't approve of my dating style. I thought you'd be gloating. Thinking I got exactly what was coming to me. Poetic justice."

"So you do remember telling me about it." She hadn't been sure, although he'd been pretty articulate. Even with his voice slurred by the scotch. The day after a bender some people had no recollection of what they'd said. "I wasn't sure you did."

"Yeah, I remember." The dark look he'd worn last night was back.

"I can't believe you assume I'm the kind of person who would think what that woman did to you was okay under any circumstances. She lied to you and her child. That little boy thought you were his father. He bonded with you. And you with him." She shook her head at the injustice, disgusted by the deception. "There's no excuse for what she did. How confused that child must have been."

"Yeah. It wasn't a hallelujah moment for me either."

"Of course not. At least on some level you understood what was happening. But he was young. That's a blessing in a way. He probably won't remember." She stared at him. "There's less chance of that awful situation messing him up."

"Can't say the same for me. I remember it all." He wasn't drunk now, but the bitter, angry expression was still there in his eyes, on his face.

"What she did was despicable. Unconscionable. She deceived you in the cruelest possible way. On top of that she cheated on you..." Tess was momentarily at a loss for words that were bad enough to describe what happened to him. "I honestly don't understand how she could do something like that."

One of his eyebrows arched. "I was gullible. A sap. A fool."

"No." She was adamant. "Did you make the decision to date a woman who was a liar? If the answer to that question is no, which I'm sure it is, why in the world would you question whether or not you were the father of her baby?"

"I had no clue she wouldn't know the truth if it walked up and shook her hand."

"Then you're not a fool."

He looked surprised. "Don't look now but I think you just defended my honor."

"Guess I did." And didn't she feel just the tiniest bit sheepish and guilty. "I can see based on our recent history why it would come as a shock."

"Just a little."

"Well, brace yourself for another one. I understand why you're so determined to have a DNA test done when the baby is born. After going through that awful experience, I can't blame you at all."

"If that had never happened to me…" He cradled the mug of black coffee between his big hands and then met her gaze. "But it did, and here I am again. Trust is hard."

"I know." She nodded emphatically. "And we'll have to wait for proof. But for what it's worth, I can assure you that before my grandfather's memorial, I hadn't slept with anyone for a really long time. Over a year. Probably more. It's been so long, I can't even remember when I last had sex…"

Tess realized what she was saying, the intimate information she was revealing, and felt her cheeks burn with embarrassment. If only the earth would open up and swallow her right this minute. She couldn't even look at him.

"You're blushing," he pointed out.

"Thanks for stating the obvious."

"It's cute."

"Not if you're me. I don't suppose you'd like to share how long it had been since you'd had sex, before that night?" She met his gaze but he didn't respond. He simply looked amused. "I didn't think so. But I bet the women you go out with don't blush."

"So, we're back to that. I'm sorry you think so little of me." He sighed. "Full disclosure. Most of them are using me."

"Like Nancy?" Tess's gaze lifted to his. "And you're okay with that?"

"Not like her. No one is lying. Everyone's motives are right out on the table. They're mostly models and actresses looking for publicity to further their careers. I'm a bachelor who used to be in sports. I do endorsements, and a lot of people know who I am. When I'm photographed with a woman on my arm, the rumors and gossip go crazy. Inquiring minds want to know if this is the one who finally caught Leo Wallace. It gets her name out there. When they need a public-relations shot of adrenaline, the publicist calls with a heads-up that I'm 'dumping' them."

"And you're okay with being the bad guy?" she asked.

"Sure." He shrugged. "They always say nice things about me. Bottom line is that there's never anything serious. No one is hurt; no broken hearts. It's just words and if someone's career gets a bump out of it, I'm good with that."

Tess felt petty and small. "That's actually really nice of you."

"I keep telling you I'm a sweetheart of a guy."

Obviously her grandfather thought so or he wouldn't have wanted him to buy into the business and be her partner. Now Tess felt kind of awful. She'd been downright unfriendly to him based on what she'd read about him in magazines. In reality he was doing those women a favor. Since their guards were down at the moment, this might be a good time to explain her hostility.

"I was wrong about you." She met his gaze. "You may have noticed that my attitude toward you was a little cool."

"Really? That was you? I thought we were on the brink of another ice age." For the first time since he'd walked into the kitchen, there was a twinkle in his eyes.

It might be that he was feeling relief at unburdening himself. Or he was enjoying the prospect of her eating crow. Or both. Either way she was glad he seemed to be snapping out of the despondent mood of last night. If she had to grovel a little, that was okay with her. But it was important that he understand why she'd jumped to conclusions about him.

"In college I had a boyfriend."

"Only one? I would think a girl as pretty as you would have guys lined up."

The compliment made her feel warm and gooey inside, and then the painful memories threw a bucket of ice water on her amusement.

"There was a line all right, but not for me. He was an athlete, a star, and women couldn't seem to help throwing themselves at him."

"I'm guessing he didn't throw them back." His eyebrows drew together in a frown.

"I thought he did. At first. Then I caught him cheating and confronted him."

"So you cut him loose," he guessed.

"Not then. I gave him a second chance. And a third. Each time he told me it wouldn't happen again. He loved me and begged me to forgive him. I was in love so I believed him." She looked up and wondered what the expression in his eyes meant. "So I'm the gullible one. The sap. The fool who was drawn to the aura of the athlete and got squeezed out in the crush of adoring women."

"That explains why the first time we met you gave me a look that could laser the paint off a car."

It was her turn to wince. "I apologize for that. It was very unfair of me."

"Don't worry about it. Now I understand why. Guess we both have baggage." He put his big hand over hers. "But I want you to know that not all athletes are jackasses."

"Point taken," she said. "And not all women are lying bitches."

"Understood."

His warm hand felt so good holding hers. Every time he touched her, she felt breathless and weak in the knees. Sometimes he didn't even have to touch her. One look could render her tongue-tied and out of breath. In fact the look he was giving her right now, a combination of teasing and tender, was making her want to crawl into his lap and put her arms around him. That made it so much harder to say what she had to because it couldn't happen.

"We do have baggage," she repeated. "Trust is hard for me, too. My biological father abandoned my mother. Then she left me, too. And I took a chance anyway and ended up getting hurt. And you've made it clear you don't want a commitment." She slid her hand out from underneath his. "Clearly neither one of us wants to get personally involved."

"I couldn't agree more," he said. "Our partnership is business, not pleasure."

"Exactly." She nodded and smiled. "And when the baby is born and the DNA is done, we'll work out a parenting agreement fair to both of us."

"That sounds good."

It didn't feel good to her, though. They were staking out positions to clarify there would be nothing romantic between them. They were flat out saying that trust was an issue. Except that after what he told her about his past, Tess wasn't simply attracted to a handsome, sexy man. She found out he was someone she could like and really respect. How odd that she felt closer to him.

And still so very far away.

Chapter Nine

Josh was at the house for his tutoring session. The two of them were sitting at the kitchen table, and she was keeping him company while he took a mock quiz in preparation for his last exam on the Shakespeare play *Romeo and Juliet*. Leo was out doing whatever it was he did all day. Business stuff that kept him busy until dinnertime. She'd thought he worked a lot in his home office, but not since she moved in here. Was he avoiding her? It was a riddle for another time, and she wouldn't let the answer matter one way or the other.

Tess had talked to Josh's teacher and looked through previous tests to come up with study points for him to work on. While the kid agonized over literature, she brooded over Leo Wallace. It had been a week since his shocking revelation about his past. Seven days and nights spent under his roof while she looked at him in a completely different way.

He was a man who deeply loved a little boy he'd thought was his. Now he was under court order not to see this child and she couldn't imagine going through something like that. The poor man was entitled to a night of trying to forget.

After that everything had gone back to normal—whatever that was. She was still quarantined from the bar. Workmen were sanding walls and putting in new baseboards, getting ready for paint. That meant sawdust and fumes in the air. When the painters did their thing and it dried, she was going home. Oddly enough she wasn't all that anxious to leave. She was enjoying spending evenings with him—cooking, cleaning up the kitchen, watching TV (he was teaching her the basics of hockey) and just talking.

Clearly she'd been lonely, maybe even before her grandfather had died. Feeling lonely for someone her age to spend time with. Oh, who was she kidding? She had friends her own age—girlfriends. She hadn't spent time with a man in forever. That's all this feeling was. Friendship. With a man, a very good-looking one, who happened to be the father of her baby. The guy whom she hadn't liked very much and now found out she had been wrong about.

"This is stupid." Josh gave her a long-suffering and pitiful look.

She found out in their very first session that this was a recurring theme. "What's stupid?"

"Why do I need to know about Shakespeare? He's dead. For a long time now."

"I know. He was actually dead when I was in school. Back in prehistoric days," she said wryly. "When we wrote our papers with a hammer and chisel, on a rock."

He gave her an eye roll. "You're not that old."

"But by definition not that old means I am in fact old, though. Isn't that what you're saying?"

"Yeah." But he couldn't hide a grin.

"*Romeo and Juliet* is a classic. A tearjerker. The tragedy of star-crossed lovers."

"Because they were stupid," Josh said. "I don't get it. Why would a guy kill himself over a girl?"

"Why do you think?" Tess almost told him but this

should be a teachable moment. Even when he was rebelling against having to do work he hated.

"Because he didn't get the memo about her just being asleep and he thought she was dead. Stupid." He shrugged. "Romeo killed himself because he loved her?"

"Yes. And their families made it impossible for them to be together. And he didn't want to go on without her," Tess explained.

"What gets me is if he'd waited five minutes, she'd have been awake."

"So there's an argument for not making a hasty decision," she said. "Think things through and hang in there because it will almost surely get better."

"Are you talking about me now?" he asked suspiciously.

"Does it relate to your situation?" she asked.

"Maybe." He frowned for a moment.

"The truth is I didn't mean you. It was a note to myself."

"Why?"

Because it had been a rough year with her grandfather's illness and death. Financial problems with her business. Her unexpected pregnancy. Being off work. Worrying about money, especially with a baby on the way.

She met his impossibly young gaze. "Sometimes things are just hard and it feels like you can't catch a break."

He leaned back in the chair and stretched. "Yeah, tell me about it."

"The situation will get better. Sometimes doing nothing is best."

"That's what I did in English." He grinned.

Tess laughed. "And how's that working out for you?"

"Not great," he admitted.

"So sometimes doing nothing isn't an option."

"How do you know what to do?"

"Experience helps. Maturity. And—" she paused for theatrical effect then added "—reading and understanding Shakespeare."

He groaned dramatically. "It's so boring. I'd rather take Romeo's poison."

"Are you trying to tell me it's time for a break?" He had been working conscientiously since he'd arrived.

"Yes," he said simply.

"Okay. Are you hungry? Would you like a snack?"

"I could eat."

She stood and walked to the refrigerator. Because teenage boys had notoriously voracious appetites she'd stocked up on food. "How about a sandwich? Maybe fruit and some chips?"

"Yes. To all of it. I'm actually starving. And I have hockey practice in a little while."

Tess was dropping him at the rink because both of his parents were working. And they'd agreed not to take hockey away from Josh as long as he passed his classes. That was Leo's doing. He'd gotten involved with a kid on the edge, crying out for help. Because he'd been that kid. The thought of him paying it forward gave her a warm feeling, along with that weird sensation in her tummy every time an image of him popped into her mind.

She fixed Josh a ham sandwich on wheat bread, with mayonnaise, lettuce and tomato. After coring an apple and cutting it into slices, she put everything on a paper plate and brought it to him at the table, along with a bag of chips.

"Would you like water or soda with that?"

"Soda would be great."

She looked down at him, a lock of unruly hair falling over his forehead. She wanted to brush it back and wondered if that was her maternal instincts waking up. She hoped so. That would mean she had them, unlike her own mother, who had walked away and never looked back. From what he'd said, Leo would be a good dad. He didn't seem to have any doubts, but Tess had no frame of reference for this.

She grabbed a glass from the cupboard, put ice in it, then got a can of cola and poured it. After walking back to the table, she put it in front of Josh. He'd wolfed down the sandwich and was working on the apple.

"Leo is so awesome," he said.

"He seems like a good guy," she agreed.

"He's an awesome hockey player, too." He started spouting hockey statistics, records that still stood in that particular professional sport. "I'm going to be a hockey player just like him someday."

"That means playing in college." She remembered Leo talking about his trajectory to success.

"Yeah." Josh met her gaze warily. "You're going to tell me how I have to get my grades up so I can go to a school with a hockey team."

"It's like you can read my mind," she said.

"So, what's the deal between you and Leo?"

Apparently he'd decided on a quick change of subject, but the question caught her off guard. It shouldn't have. She was living in Leo's house with him, so she should expect curiosity. Along with the lack of a filter between the brain and mouth of a teenager. But the fact was she didn't have an articulate answer at the ready.

"I didn't catch that, what with your mouth full. Would you mind repeating?" she asked, stalling.

He chewed and swallowed. "I said—what's with you and Leo? Why are you living here? Are you guys a thing?"

"No," she said, dealing with the last question first.

But it wasn't that simple. They weren't dating, and never had. But there'd been sex—really wild, wonderful, quick and passionate sex. And she was carrying the baby to prove it. Her heart fluttered at the memory of being with him. More than once she'd thought about being with him again. In an actual bed.

"If you're not a thing, why are you staying here with him?" He took another apple slice and bit into it.

Just give him the facts. "I own a bar and Leo invested in it. He's now my partner." She sat across the table from him. "My apartment is above the bar and we're doing some remodeling. I had to move out temporarily and Leo offered me a room."

"Why?"

"So I didn't have to sleep on the street," she joked.

"No, I meant why did you have to move out?"

"Workmen were cutting wood. Sanding it. There's sawdust and other stuff floating around in the air. Plus there will be painting soon. So none of it is good if you're—"

"What?" he asked when she stopped.

She'd been about to say *pregnant*. Pretty soon she wouldn't be able to hide it, but that time wasn't now. The natural assumption would probably be that Leo was the father. But if she wasn't prepared to respond about her current living arrangement, she most definitely didn't want to talk about her condition.

Josh had some serious hero worship going on, and Leo was an exceptional role model. But this was a delicate subject. With luck she would be back in her place soon and there she could deal with it in her world, not Leo's.

But Josh had asked a question and needed an answer. "It's not good to be breathing that stuff in if you have pulmonary issues."

"That's like asthma and stuff, right?"

"And stuff," she agreed. "Allergies."

"Do you have that?" Josh bit into a chip and met her gaze as he chewed.

"No," she said honestly. "But Leo felt it was healthier for me to move out while the renovation is happening. And he has lots of room here."

"He's such an awesome dude."

"Yes, he is."

In more ways than she ever knew. She was teetering on the brink of a little hero worship of her own, and there was a problem with putting someone on a pedestal. The fall from said platform could be long and painful. And not just for the person on the pedestal. Whoever was feeling the awe could be in for a crash and burn, too.

Just because Leo wasn't a heartless bastard and was capable of genuine feelings didn't mean he could have feelings for her. He was pretty up front with the fact that he didn't plan on getting personal with her or having a relationship. For her own reasons she felt the same way.

A little while ago she'd told Josh that sometimes it was best to do nothing. She and Leo were a perfect example of that.

Leo was at the skating rink, in his office overlooking the ice. He was standing at the window, watching Josh's team gathering for practice. There were more parents than usual here with the kids—mostly moms, but dads, too. He knew something was going on that would affect this team and not in a good way. The adults were in groups, talking and looking very serious. The way a parent does when something negative is going to impact their child.

He saw Josh walk in, lugging his bulky hockey bag. Then he spotted Tess, just a step or two behind. He swore he felt his spirits lift and sort of levitate at the sight of her. Dropping the kid off was what she'd agreed to and he was getting a ride home with one of the other players. But Leo hadn't expected her to come inside.

Every protective instinct he had said not to go down there and talk to her. It was hard enough to pretend he didn't notice every sweet curve of her body when they were together under his roof. Nights were a spectacular challenge when he could picture her in a bed down the hall from his own. That should have been enough to keep him away.

Apparently it wasn't because the next thing he knew, he was heading downstairs, to where she was standing by the wall outside the ice.

"Hey," he said.

She smiled a particularly sunny smile. "Hey, yourself."

"How did tutoring go?"

"Oh, you know. Romeo and Juliet are dumb and English literature is boring."

He laughed. "I don't even know why I asked. If he was excited about it, his grades would be better."

"Yeah. But he's doing the work, which is the point. Someday he'll realize the importance of being a well-rounded human being but that's not today."

Leo watched the boys in their red-and-white jerseys burst through the opening in the half wall and onto the ice. School, family tension and all the bad stuff disappeared, and for the next hour it would be skating, teamwork and physical activity. "I was the same way at his age."

"He wants to be you when he grows up."

"God, I hope not. My life is a horrible warning."

"Not to him," she protested.

"If that's the path he chooses, he'll have to learn that hockey isn't everything." The pain of not seeing that certain little boy was with him every day. Wondering if he was happy. Did his biological dad love him enough? Did he even remember Leo?

Tess looked out on the ice, her gaze following Josh as he skated around. "I told him he better make Romeo and Juliet his new best friends if he wants to get into college like you did."

"Maybe that will help him see a point to the boring stuff now."

"Hopefully." She looked at the bleachers beyond the ice and at the facilities beyond the protective Plexiglas. "This is a nice place you have here. I planned to drop Josh off, not come inside. But I was curious."

"Would you like a tour?"

"Since I'm not working," she said wryly, "I've got nothing better to do."

"Try to keep the enthusiasm under control," he teased back. "It's not like I'm asking you to watch grass grow."

"Sorry. I didn't mean it like that."

"You should enjoy this time off. In about a week you'll be busier than ever and back home."

The thought of that didn't make him want to pump his arm in triumph. He must be more screwed up than he realized. Having her close put him on edge, and not having her around put him in a crap mood.

"I look forward to being busy again," she said. "So, are you going to give me the tour or not?"

"Follow me."

He showed her everything, starting with his office, which she called his window on the world. They looked at the skate-rental desk, then the equipment and apparel store. In the locker room she took one look at all the hockey bags and declared that a platoon of squirrels had crawled in there and the smell had killed them en masse.

In no uncertain terms she stated it wouldn't kill him to invest in a truckload of air freshener.

They ended up at the snack bar and he introduced her to Denise, who was working behind the counter.

"What can I get you?" the teen asked them.

"Coffee," he said. "Tess?"

"Hot chocolate." Her look was bittersweet when she added, "I don't think I've had it since I was a little girl and my grandfather made it for me."

"Anything to eat? Hot dog? Chili fries? Slice of pizza?" Denise asked him.

"No, thanks," he told her.

When she set the hot drinks on the counter, Tess started to pull out her wallet.

"It's on the house." Leo put his hand on hers, and a zap that felt a lot like static electricity zinged up his arm. It probably wasn't that but he didn't want to look too closely at why he'd felt it. Just another reminder that touching her was a no-no.

"Thanks." She took her cup and blew on the steam rising from it.

"Let's sit down over here. Unless you have plans." She'd told him that before the night of her grandfather's memorial, she hadn't been with a man in a very long time. That didn't stop him from feeling jealous about her with someone else in the future.

He didn't really believe Tess was lying, but it had happened to him once. Taking a chance on it not happening again was foolish.

"I have no plans." She picked a table and sat down on one of the chairs that faced the ice. "I like your place. But I'm wondering where the income stream is."

Leo took the seat across from her, his back to the practice going on. "Multiple sources. The snack bar, skate rental and sharpening. Even the equipment and clothing stores are all supported by selling time on the ice."

"How so?"

"There's admission for public skating. The hockey program is a big portion of revenue. Playing on ice is different from roller hockey. It's slippery."

"No kidding," she said with a laugh.

"Right. They have to learn to keep their balance."

"So the teams pay to practice."

"And play games." He glanced over his shoulder at the team now playing and frowned for a moment. "Every team is important to the bottom line. We do community clinics and giveaways at local parks to increase awareness of the sport and the team programs we offer. And it's not just business—it's a public service, in a way."

She nodded. "Because of kids like Josh."

"Yes."

She took a sip of her now-cooled hot chocolate. "It's also a safe environment with supervision, where kids can come and hang out."

"Yeah."

When his son was born—biology didn't matter; that boy would always be his son—Leo had been so excited about all of the things he would share with the little guy. He would take him on the ice and teach him to skate. Throw a football. Play catch with a baseball. So many hopes and dreams blew up in his face when he found out about the lie.

"I guess parental involvement is important," she said.

It was like she could read his mind. "Yes. Because of the expense, transportation and organization. Part of it is volunteer—coach, assistant coach, circulating information about practice and game times."

"That's quite a commitment."

A reflection of parents who loved their children. He knew the joy of that once, but now it was mostly pain. "Yeah. Without them the program doesn't work."

She nodded toward something going on behind him. "Don't look now but a whole bunch of those committed parents are headed in this direction. And some of the kids from Josh's team, too."

He turned and saw that she was right. Actually, he'd been expecting this. "Here we go…"

The group stopped in front of him and one of the dads stood a little ahead of the others. Leo guessed he was the spokesman.

"Hi, Mr. Wallace—"

"Call me Leo." He stood up and shook the man's hand.

"Okay." He cleared his throat. "Leo, I'm Bob Dempsey, assistant coach of the Predators. We've got a problem to discuss with you."

"Okay. What's up?"

"Our head coach. He had a job transfer, and long-distance coaching isn't going to work. As much as he regretted it, he had to quit. That leaves us in a bind." He blew out a breath. "I would take over, but the travel demands of my job mean half the time I can't be here for practices and games. If the boys don't have a coach, they have to forfeit."

"I know." Leo was looking at the boys and knew shock, anger and the unfairness of it all was cranking up all their youthful testosterone. He hated to see anyone not get to play. "What about one of the other dads? Or one of the moms?"

"No one else knows enough about the game or has the time, due to family and job obligations."

"That's a problem," Leo agreed.

"Josh Hutak came up with an idea and we thought it was worth a shot."

"Okay."

"Would you be willing to coach the boys? Obviously you know the game. You're one of the greats." Bob had a fanboy expression on his face. "You're here a lot. We were hoping you have the time and might consider doing it for them."

Leo had been afraid of this. It was true that he knew the game and had no family commitments. He glanced over his shoulder at Tess. At least not yet. Yeah, he'd reached out to Josh because running away from home made a big statement. But every one of these boys had a story. Every one of them could suck him in and they weren't his kids. He knew how it felt to get sucked in and lose out. His thing was to not get personally involved. The rink was just business. Being a coach was more.

"Look, Bob—"

The man held up his hand to stop the words. "Just think it over. Please. Don't say no yet."

He really wanted to say it, and the word was on the tip of his tongue. But Leo heard a chorus of voices and the words blended together into a pleading from the boys. The word *no* just didn't come out of his mouth.

He took the card with a phone number on it that the man held out. "Okay. I'll think it over."

"Thank you." Bob shook his hand again and led the group away.

He tucked the card into his shirt pocket for later. It would be easier to turn them down when he didn't have to look at their faces. Then he turned, and the look Tess was rocking told him where she fell on the issue.

"Don't you pile on," he warned her.

"I'm not sure what that means."

"It means that before our sports bar opens, I'm going to have to give you a crash course in the high points of sports." He put his hands on his hips. "I can't be their coach."

"You should."

"Why?" he demanded.

"You used to play hockey and know the game. You used to be coached, so there's that. You know how it's done." She tipped her head to the side and gave him what he thought of as her "kitten needing rescue" face. "You just told me that as far as revenue is concerned, you can't really afford to lose a team. And here's the big one. You told me that hockey was a lifeline when you were Josh's age. He's working his butt off to get his grades up so he can play. How do you tell him he can't because you're not willing to get involved?"

God, he hated how rational she was. She was using his words against him. But she'd never been more right.

He sighed. "Okay. I'll give Bob a call and tell him they've got a coach."

She smiled her approval at him. "You won't regret it."

He already did, because that smile touched him deep inside, in a place he'd sealed off to protect himself.

Chapter Ten

On the way home from the rink Tess stopped at the grocery store to pick up what she needed to make dinner. On the menu was oven-fried chicken, twice-baked potatoes and a salad with lots of fresh vegetables. When she got to Leo's house, he was on the phone in his home office so she jumped right into meal prep.

She wasn't working at her—correction *their*—business for another week, but at least she could make herself useful to earn her keep. After all, the man had given her a place to live.

She prepared the chicken on a cookie sheet after dipping it in egg, seasonings and cornflake crumbs. After putting it in the oven, she microwaved a couple of potatoes, scooped out the insides while saving the skin, and stirred butter, sour cream and chives into the mixture until it was just the right consistency. She sprinkled a little cheese on top and then slid them into the toaster oven to warm.

When the salad was made, she looked around the kitchen and realized she really felt at home here. And it had happened fast. The bar had been her home since she was six years old. Her apartment was cozy and you couldn't beat the commute to work. But it sure hadn't taken her long to settle in at Leo's house.

They said you didn't really know a person until you

lived with them, and she'd learned how true that was. She'd made it a point to get to know her baby's father. It was her obligation as a mother, right? Since she never really had one for most of her life, the fine print of the job was a little scary to her.

This kitchen was big, but felt even more ginormous without Leo in it. She wondered if he was still on the phone or just avoiding her. It was one thing to be lonely, all by herself in her apartment, but quite another when there was someone else here who sometimes treated her like an exotic-flu germ to be given a wide berth.

"I'll just go see about that," she said to herself. It was becoming a habit, talking to herself. And since he was here, she didn't have to. Not until she went back to her place.

She walked into his office, where he was actually still on the phone. While she waited, she settled into one of the chairs in front of his desk. There was a sheet of paper in front of him with a list of names and phone numbers. At the top it said "Predators Team Roster." Wow, Bob hadn't wasted any time getting out from under his coaching duties.

"The game is Saturday morning, at eight," he said into the phone. "I'd like Ethan to be at the rink thirty minutes early to loosen up, stretch and go over game strategy." He listened for a few moments and gave Tess a little wave. "Great. Oh, one more thing. Would you be able to bring water and energy drinks, maybe a snack?" He listened again and his mouth pulled tight. Classic Leo annoyance. "Okay. See you Saturday."

"I thought you were taking care of business in here," she said.

"I am. Hockey business."

"I guess you talked to Bob?"

"Yeah. He emailed the roster and game schedule."

"Since when is hours of phone time part of coaching?" She was feeling a little guilty for shaming him into this.

"What Bob failed to mention when he made his pitch is that the coach's wife was the team mom and did all the calls. So essentially we lost her, too."

"So you don't think she could be talked into staying behind to keep up the good work?"

He laughed. "Not likely, what with them being married and all."

"I had no idea this would be so time-consuming." More guilt crept in. "I'm sorry I said anything."

"That's right." His gaze narrowed on her, but his mouth curved up, a sign he was teasing. "You talked me into this. It's all your fault."

"Don't get crazy and say things you'll regret. Why don't you take a break. Dinner's almost ready."

"Something smells good," he said.

"It will be. You should have a beer. Chill out."

"That is a very good idea."

She stood and headed for the kitchen. "The least I can do is open one up for you."

"I'm right behind you."

Somehow she just *knew* he was staring at her butt as she walked away. Did he like what he saw? Did she want him to? Duh, no woman wanted a good-looking, former hockey-playing hunk of a man thinking her backside wasn't top quality. But did she want more? Could she ever risk that again? With something as important as a baby to worry about, she had an awesome excuse to put that question away, hopefully forever.

She opened the refrigerator and pulled out a longneck bottle of beer and then twisted off the cap. When Leo walked into the room, she handed it to him and he took a long drink of the cold liquid. In her line of work she'd seen a lot of men drink a lot of beers, but never was it as sexy as this. His neck muscles moved as he swallowed, and she barely held back a sigh of appreciation.

His big hand dwarfed the bottle he held. "This almost makes up for you getting me into this."

"I simply reminded you of what you already know."

"Sort of like my conscience talking." He took another drink of his beer. "And you're right about everything you said. I couldn't turn my back on Josh—or any of the other boys on the team, for that matter."

His words tugged at her heart. There was a time when she would have had a snarky comeback to everything he said, but now that she knew his painful past, her inner snark was rocking a whole lot of respect for this man.

It occurred to her—not for the first time—that he had way more experience with this parenting thing than she did. Since her résumé had zero kid know-how, of the two of them, he was practically an expert.

Once he knew for sure he was her baby's father, he was going to be a terrific dad. The question was, would she be a good mom?

"What's on your mind?" he asked.

She leaned back against the cupboards and folded her arms over her chest. As if that could stop him from seeing her deepest thoughts. "How do you know there's anything on my mind? I never said that."

"Your eyes are telling me."

She stared at him because she so badly wanted to cover her face with her hands. She was going soft on him and would prefer he not know how soft. The thing was, they were going to share a child, so there were fears she had that he would find out about anyway. She should probably confess.

"I think you're going to be a wonderful father," she started. "And you have no idea what a relief that is to me."

"Isn't that jumping the gun? First we need to have DNA done."

"Yeah, I get that. But it's going to be a match. That's not what worries me."

He set his beer on the island beside him, giving her and this subject his complete attention. "So, what is it you need to get off your chest?"

"I'm afraid I'm going to be a terrible mother." Her words came out in a rush.

"Are you mean to children? In the habit of tripping toddlers when they're learning to walk?"

"You tease, but this is a legitimate concern for me."

"Because your mother left you." It wasn't a question.

"Yes."

"But that's not all. And before you ask how I know that, your eyes are speaking volumes. Again." He shrugged. "I'm sensitive."

"Uh-huh. I wish my eyes would shut the heck up," she said wryly, then heaved a sigh. "But you're right. I'm a little nervous because everyone always said I look just like my mother. A clone. The spitting image."

"So she was beautiful, too." He leaned back against the counter as casual as you please. As if he told a girl every day that she was beautiful.

Well, that was unexpected. Nice, but still startling. And not her point. "She left me. A good mother doesn't abandon her child. The least she could do is stick around and take responsibility for screwing up her kid."

"You think you're messed up?"

"Don't you?"

"That's not the first thing about you that comes to

mind." His eyes went dark and intense for just a second. It was so quick, the change could be blamed on imagination.

Ignoring that was probably the best move, so she did. "What if I'm more like her than just looks? What if I can't handle the pressure of raising a child?"

"What if an asteroid crashes into the earth?"

"You joke, but I'm serious about this."

"I meant it in the context that you being a mom failure is about as likely as the asteroid/earth collision thing. Lighten up, Tess. You're going to do fine."

"How do you know?"

"Instinct."

"And yet there's still a doubt in your mind about whether the baby is yours." She held up a hand. "Scratch that. After what you went through, I can hardly blame you. But really—instinct?"

"If you weren't concerned, I would be worried. But you're all over this, which says there's nothing to worry about."

"I wish I had your confidence. And experience," she added.

"So get some."

"How? Rent a kid?"

"Funny," he said. "No, be the team mom."

"For your hockey team?"

"Yeah. You already know Josh. You've got time right now, until the bar's grand reopening."

Except for the fact that it could be a slippery personal slope working that closely with him on anything other than business, she didn't have a good reason to say no. "Other women get a plant or a dog to test their nurturing abilities but I get a hockey team?"

"Your mission, should you choose to accept it." He shrugged. "Deep end of the pool, Tess. Jump in."

"Okay. I'll do it." She blew out a long breath. "So, what are my eyes telling you now?"

He studied her closely. "Either dinner is ready or you want to choke me."

"How about both?"

"Good. I'm starving."

So was she. And hopefully he couldn't see how badly she wanted to kiss the living daylights out of him.

Leo had forgotten about the adrenaline rush of winning a hockey game. Since he broke his ankle, ending his pro career, he'd been trying to fill that void with women and sex. Watching the boys win was almost as good as playing on the winning team. Although as coach, technically he did, but he missed the rush of racing up and down the ice, working his ass off and the elation of scoring a goal.

Tess was standing beside him now, taking everything in with wide-eyed interest. She'd packed the ice chest with bottled water and energy drinks, and there was a bag with some empty-caloried treat that the kids would love. Parents and spectators were filing up the bleacher stairs, heading for the exit to wait for their kids outside, where it was warm. He watched the boys, now at center ice and skating slowly by members of the opposing team, shaking hands.

"Men are weird." With a puzzled look on her face, Tess stared at the team members passing each other.

"Should I be offended?"

"Oh…" She looked apologetic. "That didn't come out right."

"You think?"

"Sorry, it's just that I don't understand how one minute they're hitting each other, trying to take away that round black thing—"

"Puck," he said.

"Right. That. So they smack into someone—"

"It's called checking," he told her.

"Because that sounds so much better than *hit* or *smack*."

"It's a technical term. As in *checking* their forward progress down the ice."

"Anyway." She sighed. "They do that—checking—and knock each other on their butts. Now they're shaking hands and laughing. If that was me, I'd be so mad."

"Checking is part of the game. They all know it's not personal and when the game is over, it's over. Shaking hands teaches them sportsmanship. They learn to be gracious winners and good losers."

"Hmm. Lessons for being a grown-up," she mused.

"Exactly."

She nodded, then grinned. "I still think men are weird. Just saying."

"I could say the same about women, if I wasn't such a gentleman." He met her gaze and saw the teasing in hers. "You cry when you're happy or sad. Say 'fine' when you're anything but. And tell a guy you don't want to talk about it, then do a ten-minute monologue on why you're upset with a flower arrangement instead of a single rose."

"Because a single rose is more romantic," she said in a teasingly superior tone that also fell into the sassy range. "Everyone knows that."

"Guys don't."

"Because you're weird. I rest my case. Enough said."

She was a piece of work, and not in a bad way. After taking on team-mom duties, she'd jumped in with both feet. Phone calls got made, the kids showed up on time and she'd put together drinks and snacks for today's game. And that reminded him...

"Do not carry that ice chest back to the car."

"But it will be empty." Her face had the "men are weird" look on it again.

"I can't believe you were going to carry it full."

"It rolls," she defended.

"Not out of the car. Fortunately I was there." They'd come here together.

"I thought you had to get to the team and warm them up."

"There was time," he said.

"Well, I'm used to doing things on my own. And besides, I'm pregnant, not an invalid."

"Not a newsflash."

Before he could say more, the guys skated over and started taking bottled water and energy drinks out of the ice chest. It was too loud and raucous to have any conversation at all.

Tess watched the scene unfold, her eyes wide again. "They're like locusts, devouring every plant and blade of grass in their path. Leaving scorched earth behind."

"I think you're mixing your metaphors, but yeah. I can't argue with locusts." He took her by the shoulders and moved her several steps away. "Probably best to stand back, out of the way."

The kids thanked her politely, but as soon as they'd filed past, the roughhousing started up again. Good-natured arm punching, wrestling, grabbing someone around the neck. Guy fun. Male bonding.

Tess caught the corner of her bottom lip between her teeth. "Maybe I shouldn't have given them energy drinks. It looks like they have more than enough energy. Even after knocking each other down and chasing after that puck thing for an hour."

"Imagine if they hadn't released all that—let's call it youthful enthusiasm."

"Oh, dear God." She shuddered. "What you're telling me is that playing hockey is channeling their—let's call it vitality."

"Right. It has to go somewhere. This way they get exercise and learn how to get along with others, work together and handle disappointment when things don't go their way." God knew he'd needed that training when he had lost his family.

She was thoughtful for a moment, then said, "My grandfather took me to ballet classes."

"Last time I checked, that's not a team sport."

She laughed. "It checked all the same boxes as playing hockey."

"Still not a team endeavor."

"I beg to differ. There are other dancers in a production. Hello, *Swan Lake*. There's more than one swan." Her mouth curved up at the corners. "In case you're wondering, it wasn't Pat's idea. I begged him to let me do it and he finally gave in."

"Smart man."

"Yes, he was wise. But still weird like the rest of you," she said wryly.

"Are you ever going to let that go?"

"Maybe if this baby is a boy."

The baby. Even though her jeans were getting snug and she wore loose shirts, there were times he forgot she was pregnant. Like moments ago, when she teased and made him laugh. A few days before, she'd told him he would be a good father, and the words had made him feel good, before the pain of loss hit. He'd done his best with Chad because he loved that boy more than anything in the world. It wasn't enough and he was afraid to care that much again. To risk being shut out in the cold if it was taken away.

Tess shivered and she folded her arms over her chest. "I wish it was warmer in here."

"Hard to keep ice frozen that way." He grabbed his windbreaker off the bench and dragged it around her shoulders. "I should have warned you to wear a warmer jacket. Let's go get a hot chocolate at the snack bar."

"Twist my arm."

He called out to the boys hanging out on the bleachers nearby. "Good game, guys. See you at practice. Everyone clear on when it is?"

There was a chorus of "Yes, coach" and he nodded, then waved. Tess took the bag she'd brought the snacks in and used it to collect empty bottles and wrappers. Leo took the ice chest, and side by side they walked around the oval and over to the snack bar, where Denise was now working. He'd seen her just behind them in the bleachers, watching the game before she started her shift. He set the cooler by a table and then they walked up to the counter.

"Nice game, boss."

"The guys played well," he said, refusing to take any credit.

"Congrats on the first win of the season. This was the fifth game." She smiled. "So I think coaching might have made a difference."

He shrugged. "I just made a few adjustments in the lines. Spread around the stronger players. It was all them."

"If you say so. What can I get you?"

"A couple of hot chocolates."

"Make mine extra hot," Tess said.

"You got it." Denise walked away and came back with two coffee cups and protective sleeves. There was a generous amount of whipped cream on top of each. "Here you go."

Leo pulled out a bill to pay for them and she backed away.

"Seriously?" the teen said. "You're the boss. That should count for something."

"Let's just say I'm setting an example," he told her.

"I get it." She smiled as if suddenly understanding what the secret was. "You're trying to impress your girlfriend."

"What, I… No—"

"We're not a thing. Just friends." Tess jumped in to bail him out, but her smile was forced.

Leo knew that because she smiled a lot and he could tell real from fake. This was fake. And awkward.

"Oh. Sorry." Denise looked sheepish. "I thought I heard you say… Never mind. My mistake."

"That's okay." Tess took her cup, walked over to the table and sat down.

He waited for the sale to be rung up and get his change. He supposed anyone looking at them could come to the same erroneous conclusion that Denise had. After the game they'd been laughing and talking. He gave her his jacket, which was way too big for her. It reminded him how petite she was and how protective that made him feel.

The fact was, he was only her baby daddy. Maybe. That was yet to be determined. But was that all he was to her? Sometimes—a lot of times—it felt like more, and he was fighting the feeling with everything he had. But too often he got caught up in her and forgot to do that.

He sat down across from her. "Are you warmer now?"

"Yes. Thanks." She took a sip of her drink and there was a trace of whipped cream on her top lip.

This was one of those times when he did his level best to fight the urge to kiss that cream off her mouth. He blew out a long breath. "So, your first gig as team mom was a rousing success."

"Thanks." She smiled at the praise. "I brought drinks and snacks this week because soon I'll be back to work and won't be able to come to the games. Don't worry, though. I'll still make the phone calls, but I've assigned other moms and dads to snack duty, so it should be taken care of for you."

He nodded. "That means you'll be back in your place pretty soon."

Her bright look slipped for a second, then she regrouped and it was back with barely a flicker. "Yeah. I talked to Nate. One more day on the paint and two days to dry. He said one would be enough, but give it an extra day to be on the safe side."

Leo was all in favor of the safe side and getting back to it was what he wanted. He'd been thinking just a little while ago about trying to fill up the void inside him with women and sex. He'd had Tess only the one time, and then they had become business partners. Until today he hadn't given that void a single thought, and he had a bad feeling that was because of her.

"I bet you're anxious to have your own space back. Because, as you know, men are weird," he teased.

"I hope having me stay at your house wasn't an inconvenience for you."

It was, but not the way she meant. And soon there wouldn't be a problem. The sometime-feeling that they were more than friends would go away when she was no longer under his roof. But when he brought up the subject of her leaving, her smile disappeared. Real or fake, it was just gone.

And he didn't like that very much at all.

Chapter Eleven

Tess was at the bar, waiting for Carla. The workmen were gone for the day, which would disappoint her friend. She would miss seeing the brawny, tool-belt-wearing construction guys, but life was full of disappointments. Besides, her friend's job at Make Me a Match relied on algorithms and profiles filled out by clients, not face-to-face, man-on-the-street sightings.

The purpose of meeting here was to determine whether or not the paint smell was gone so Tess could come home. She'd asked Carla to come over and give her a second opinion. Nate thought it was fine but since he worked with it all the time, he had suggested she didn't take the chance that his sniff was sensitive enough for Tess's delicate condition.

There was a knock on the door before it opened and Carla poked her head in. "Hello."

"Hi." Tess walked over to give her a hug. "Thanks for coming by."

"No problem. There's no rush to get home. Mom is out with her friends from the Red Hat Society so she's not expecting me. I have a free evening."

"Translation—nothing better to do," Tess teased.

"Pretty much." She glanced around the now very open room. "Love what you've done with the place."

The cerulean walls looked pretty darn good if she did say so herself. "Really?"

"Yes." Carla studied her. "Don't you love it?"

"I think so. Hard to tell. I'm so emotionally connected that any change is like cutting my heart out. Leo assures me the modifications will make us competitive with the current trendy local hot spots."

"I can picture it." Carla looked around and nodded. "I like it for a meet for clients."

"Seriously? And we weren't on your list before?" Tess stared at her friend.

"Since I recently started working there after returning home in humiliation, it wasn't my decision." Carla looked sheepish. "I don't want to hurt your feelings, but before the renovation, this was a place the Red Hats would go, and those ladies are over fifty."

"And you don't have clients in that demographic?"

"Some," Carla admitted, "but our target clients are not retired or even close to it. They're high-powered professionals who want to find someone but are so wrapped up in their jobs, they're too busy to go through the time-consuming trial-and-error dating process to find that one special person."

"And you think *now* my business will measure up to your exacting standards?"

"Come on, Tess. Don't be that way. Change can be good. Shake things up."

"You sound like Leo," she grumbled. In her world things were shaken up quite enough, thank you very much.

"If everyone liked the same thing, all businesses would be just alike. Variety is key to finding your niche clientele. Different strokes for different folks. And all that."

"I thought you loved my grandfather's place."

"I do. And some of that is preserved." She looked at the bar that hadn't been touched in the renovation. "That doesn't mean it can't be made better. Keep what's working from the old and change what isn't to make it new."

"It's like you're channeling Leo right now," Tess said drily.

"Is that bad?"

"It's not good," Tess said.

Carla's eyes narrowed on her. "What's going on? Don't tell me nothing. Besides the fact that I know you practically as well as I know myself, you didn't ask me to meet you only to get my opinion on lingering paint fumes. Which, by the way, there aren't any. At least down here."

"Let's go up and check the apartment."

"You're stalling me, but okay."

Tess led the way upstairs, noting that there was no trace of a paint smell. She unlocked the door and stepped into her home. It felt as if she'd been gone years instead of weeks. And the space she'd always thought of as a warm and cozy haven smelled of loneliness. All she could think was that Leo's wide shoulders would barely fit in here.

"Can I get you anything?" she offered.

Carla shook her head. "It's sweet of you to offer, but you've been displaced and probably don't actually have anything."

"There is that…"

"So…" Carla settled herself on the floral-patterned love seat that separated the living area from her tiny kitchen.

It looked like Barbie's dream kitchen compared to Leo's ginormous one.

She sat in a club chair at a right angle to her friend. "Yeah, so…"

"What's got your pregnant panties in a twist?"

Leave it to her newly minted matchmaking friend to zero in on the heart of the problem. "Leo is coaching a teenage boys' hockey team. He stepped in when the existing coach had a job transfer. And I offered to help him because he also lost the team mom. She's married to the coach. Are you following?"

"Yeah. So far no problem. I guess there must be more." Carla had a knack for stating the obvious.

"I'm getting to it." She took a long breath. "After the game, Leo and I got hot chocolate at the rink's snack bar. The teenage girl behind the counter asked him if I was his girlfriend."

"And?"

"I told her I'm not."

Carla shrugged. "Still not seeing the problem."

"I'm still getting to it. So, here's the thing, I'm four months pregnant and still able to hide it with loose shirts. But I won't be able to do that much longer."

"Those of us who know and love you think you already aren't hiding it very well," her friend pointed out.

"Great. You get it, then," Tess said.

"No, not really."

"Okay. Let me spell it out for you. Very soon, when I'm out to here—" she held out her hand about a foot from her belly "—everyone will assume the baby is his."

"At the risk of stating the obvious," Carla said, her voice leaning toward sarcasm, "it is his."

"But we're not together," Tess cried. "What does that say about me?"

"You're human?" Carla gently suggested.

"Or I'm a slut."

"Stop it. Anyone who really knows you wouldn't believe that. And anyone else doesn't matter. They can go jump in the lake."

"I love you for that."

"I know." Her friend smiled. "Problem solved."

"No. It will soon be obvious that I'm going to have a baby. People will start asking questions. Like who's the lucky father? How do I answer that without lying? How do I say it was a big mistake and we're not together?"

"Do you want to be together?"

"What? Why would you ask that?" Tess said.

"Hmm. When someone answers a question with a question, something is definitely up."

"How do you know?"

"Questionnaires are a big part of my job. Individual answers to pair up people who we believe will make a personal connection. Sometimes the questions not answered reveal the most." There was a confident expression on her face. "I'm getting a vibe that you wouldn't mind being together. With him."

"As much as I hate to be the one to tell you this, your vibe can be wrong. You're not infallible."

"Agreed." Carla wasn't offended in the least. "But I'm right about this."

"No, you're not." Tess folded her arms over her chest.

"Hmm."

"Oh, brother. You're reading my body language, aren't you? You're going to say this is a classic protective pose and I'm closing myself off. Go ahead. Say it."

"I don't have to now." Her friend's grin was all-knowing. "Instead of putting you on the defensive, why don't you tell me about him. They say you never know someone until you live with them, so what's he like?"

"Different from what I first thought," Tess admitted. "He's not selfish, smug and arrogant."

She told her friend about him growing up in a home filled with conflict and unhappy parents. How his time on the ice was pretty much the only positive in his life. The way he'd taken Josh under his wing and prevented losing the hockey that he loved from becoming his punishment for a poor English grade. Tess felt the part about his wife cheating and taking away the child he loved like his own son was too personal to share. But what she told her friend was a pretty good sampling of reasons why she no longer believed he was a cocky, sweet-talking heartbreaker.

Carla nodded. "I wish you could have seen yourself just now when you were talking about him."

"If there's anything on my face, it's from lunch." Tess hoped saying so would make it true, because she didn't like where this conversation was going.

"Sorry, sweetie. You were trying to convince me of all his good qualities, wanting to persuade me he's a really good guy. There's absolutely no reason to do that unless you have feelings for him. Unless you like him."

"I do. But just as a friend." Tess tried to keep her voice neutral and not let on how desperately she hoped that statement was the truth.

"Okay."

"You don't believe me."

Carla's look was sympathetic. "I believe that you believe it's true."

"How can you know? The people you work with have filled out profiles because they're looking for love, not trying to avoid it."

"You would be surprised. Despite our best efforts, some matches don't work out. I keep a very large supply of tissues on hand for those occasions. There are times I feel like a counselor, helping someone get to the bottom of their relationship hang-ups."

"That's not what's going on with me."

That was exactly what was going on with her. She didn't believe Leo was like the boyfriend who cheated on her over and over. But Carla was confirming there were a lot of ways to be hurt.

Leo had said that she must be anxious to return to her own space. What she heard was that *he* was in a hurry to have his space all to himself again. It was time for her to move back and it was probably happening just in the nick of time. There was still a chance she could keep her heart in one piece.

Ever since Tess had moved into his house, Leo drove home with a sense of heightened anticipation. It was official. He couldn't avoid the fact that he looked forward to seeing her at the end of the day. It wasn't just about having someone there and not being alone. It was specifically *her*.

The renovations to the bar were finished except for a few minor details, and there wouldn't be any reason for her to stay with him. A couple days ago, after the boys' hockey game, he'd casually suggested that she must be anxious to be back in her space and maybe he'd been hoping she would say not really. That she was enjoying being with him. But she hadn't.

Leo liked being with her, talking about things. She had a quirky take on the world and made him laugh. Meals were eaten at the table, not in front of the TV, and there was conversation, too. They weren't having sex and that was killing him. He saw her every day and held her when she'd cried over changing the bar's name. At night, to know she was just down the hall and not be able to touch her was tearing him up. In spite of that, he still liked having her around. That got into tricky territory.

With all those thoughts running through his mind, the drive home from the ice rink seemed to flash by in seconds. Leo pulled into the driveway and noted that Tess was at the house. It was lit up like a church for Christmas services. A sigh of something that felt like contentment escaped him as he exited the car, and he tried not to hurry inside.

He told himself that he wasn't getting used to having her there, just enjoying the company while it lasted. And he really liked when he opened the front door and smelled something good cooking. His mouth started watering and he realized he was hungry, but not just for food.

Leo walked into the kitchen, where Tess was bent over in front of the oven, reaching inside to slide something out. He was treated to an amazing view of her butt. If only it was slightly less spectacular, he might want her less. Maybe.

He cleared his throat, partly not to startle her, but mostly because he wasn't sure he could speak in a normal voice. "Hi."

She straightened and glanced over her shoulder, then set a casserole on top of the stove. "There you are. I was wondering when you'd show up."

"Hockey practice went a little long."

She took off the oven mitts and faced him. "Those boys probably don't know how lucky they are that their coach owns the rink. I've heard that ice time is expensive. And they just got some at no extra charge."

"I wasn't late just because of practice. I stopped to talk to Josh while he was waiting for his dad to pick him up. Check on how he's doing."

"And?"

"School is better and his parents are...trying."

She frowned. "What does that mean?"

"I guess there's less tension in the house, at least in front of him. They've eased up on him about his grades. Oh, he said to tell you thanks for the help. He still doesn't like tutoring, but he passed the stupid *Romeo and Juliet* test."

"Shakespeare would be so flattered." She laughed.

He'd come to realize that the sound of her laughter magically relieved a long-day's worth of tension. The tightness in his neck and shoulders relaxed. He could only imagine what a "honey I'm home" kiss would do.

Enough with those thoughts.

"He's also embracing your philosophy."

"I have so many. Which philosophy would that be?"

"The one where you only have to remember this junk until the test and not for the rest of your life."

"Ah, that one. Heaven forbid." She nodded knowingly. "I left out the part where he probably can't delete it all from his brain as easily as he can from the computer."

"So he'll curse you when someday the words come out of his mouth, 'But soft, what light through yonder window breaks.'"

"'It is the east and Juliet is the sun,'" she finished. "So, you know from personal experience that no matter how hard you try, it will never leave you. I'm impressed."

"You remembered it, too."

"Only because I saw it recently from tutoring Josh." The expression on her face turned teasing. "In your case, maybe it's a pickup line."

Leo laughed because he'd never used that one and couldn't remember the last time he even needed a smooth opening with a woman. Then he stopped laughing when he realized he didn't even want to meet anyone new. Not since…

Tess interrupted that thought. "I was kidding. That wasn't a judgment on your social life. I don't think you're that guy."

"I know you don't." He had been, but wasn't now. "What's for dinner?"

"Shepherd's pie."

It was one of his favorites. "You remembered."

"I did."

"Hope it wasn't a lot of work."

"Not bad. And I made two. Froze one." She shrugged as if it was no big deal.

"Excellent." He looked around and the table was already set, a salad made. "Is there anything I can do to help?"

"Just have a seat and enjoy."

Leo enjoyed just looking at her, and it fed him somehow. If he was the kind of guy who was in touch with his feelings, he would say something about his soul. But he didn't even want to think that. Getting in that deep was a major violation that could land him in the penalty box for life.

Before he said something he would regret, he sat at the table and Tess brought over the casserole, then the salad. As usual she took the chair across from his. "So, what did you do today?"

"A lot of paperwork. Looked over reports for potential business investments."

"Really?" She put food on her plate and took a bite.

"Yeah. I have capital on hand and I'm hoping to find something that will give me a good return on the money."

"So the bar, ice rink and all your other financial projects aren't enough?"

"I like to keep busy. And this is my act two. I want to make it a success." He put food on his plate and tasted the shepherd's pie. The combination of beef, carrots, peas and mashed potatoes on top was heaven in his mouth. "This is really good."

"I'm glad you like it."

They ate in silence for a few moments. It was almost embarrassing the way he shoved food into his mouth but this sure beat anything he could have cooked. He was embracing the attitude of enjoying it while he could.

When the worst of his hunger was taken care of, he realized he hadn't asked what was going on with her. "How was your day?"

"Good." She finished chewing and swallowed. "I went by the bar."

"And?"

"It looks good." She met his gaze. "My friend Carla met me there and she likes it a lot. Better than before."

"Oh?"

"Yeah. She said the old atmosphere only appealed to members of the Red Hat Society."

"The who?"

"It's a group of women over fifty who get together for various activities. They all wear red hats." She frowned. "I never knew Carla felt that way about Granddad's place."

"Don't…" He stopped and looked at her.

"What?"

"I was going to say don't take it personally—then I remembered I was talking to you. It is personal."

She nodded. "But apparently you were right about it needing a makeover. And it looks good."

"So you wanted your friend's opinion on the results?"

"No. On the paint smell." Her much smaller portion was mostly gone but she speared a stray carrot with her fork. "To make sure it was okay for me to go back. I checked with Nate and he advised a second opinion because he smells it all the time. He's not sure his nose is as sensitive as someone who doesn't do that for a living."

"What's the verdict?" He kept his voice normal, natural, neutral. But it was an effort.

"Got the all clear." She set her fork on the plate. "I'm all packed and the guest room upstairs is all cleaned. After dinner, I'll tidy up the kitchen and then move back to my place."

If she'd smacked him in the gut with a two-by-four, he couldn't have been more surprised. But why? He'd known this was coming. He'd been aware it would be soon. And he should be happy, what with thinking about all that soul stuff just a while ago.

This time he forced a normal, natural, neutral expression on his face, then smiled. "You'll be happy to get back home, I'm sure."

"Yes." She sighed and looked around, maybe with a little longing in her eyes. "But this house is really nice. Although it wouldn't kill you to use some of that investment capital to invest in some furniture for the sad, empty rooms."

It was on the tip of his tongue to ask her to help him with that, but he held back. Because that would feel too much like decorating it for *her*. And this wasn't permanent. It was only ever meant to be temporary.

"I'll get around to finishing things around here one of these days."

"Admit it. You'll be glad to get rid of me and have your privacy back." She folded her arms on the table. "Then you can bring your dates back here for—whatever."

A few minutes ago she'd said she knew he wasn't that guy, and he knew the remark was meant to distance herself. It ticked him off when he should be grateful. A shrink would have a field day with him.

"I'll do that." He pushed his plate away with food left

on it. His appetite was gone. "And you don't have to clean up the kitchen. I can take care of it."

"I knew it," she said, pointing at him. "You *are* in a hurry to get rid of me." It was almost teasing, but that sentiment didn't quite reach her eyes.

He could do banter, too. It was a good place to hide and not let her see how he really felt. "Yeah. I didn't want to make you feel bad, but having you around has really been tough. And can we talk about your cooking?"

"If you hated that," she said, "you're going to hate the one in the freezer, too. At least it will remind you of how glad you are that I'm gone."

As if he needed reminding. Not that he was glad, but just that he should be. "What a relief that will be."

"Seriously, Leo. It was very gracious of you to give me a place to stay. I thank you, and your unborn child thanks you."

She stood and cleared her plate from the table. Leo did the same and together they did the dishes and put everything away as if she'd never been there.

"This is it." She looked up at him. "I'll go upstairs and get my suitcases."

"No. I'll get them. You shouldn't carry heavy stuff down the stairs."

"But I have to. My apartment above the bar is upstairs. It will be fine."

"I'll follow you over and bring them up for you." He held up a hand to stop her protest. "You can argue if you want, but it's a waste of breath. I won't take no for an answer."

"That's really sweet of you."

It wasn't sweet; it was crazy. He was a lunatic to prolong this. But maybe that was the point.

She actually had two suitcases and he carried them

both downstairs to her car. He followed her to the bar, where there was an outside entrance up to her place. After bringing everything inside for her, he stood just outside her door.

"So, I'll be seeing you," he said.

"Yes, you will. Good night, partner. And thanks again."

He nodded and turned away, jogging back down the stairs. No long goodbye. Simple, uncomplicated. And if that was the truth, why did he feel like crap for making it so easy for her to leave?

Chapter Twelve

Tess had agreed to tutor Josh and she intended to keep her word whether she was living under Leo's roof or not. And now she was not. But she wouldn't let a kid down just because she was missing his coach. A lot. It felt like more than a couple of days since he'd insisted on following her home and carrying her things upstairs. She felt out of sorts, as if she needed to do something. Like fix dinner and wait for him to come home.

Instead she was waiting for Josh. School got out a little while ago and he would be here soon to go over the paper he'd written about *The Great Gatsby*. This was certainly something his parents could handle, and Tess had talked to them to make sure they still wanted her involved. They did. He was sullen and abrasive when they tried to help so if she was willing, they couldn't thank her enough.

So Josh had emailed her the paper and she'd critiqued it after skimming the book she hadn't read since she was in the tenth grade. Leo was going to swing by and pick him up for hockey practice. It had all been arranged. At a given time he would be there, waiting in the parking lot so she wouldn't even see him. It was annoying how much that depressed her.

There was a knock on her door with the half window on top. Through the slit in the cotton curtains she could see it was Josh. He was on time. She opened the door to him and the hockey bag that was big enough for its own zip code.

She looked at it, then him. "Seriously?"

"I can't leave it outside. It might get ripped off and this equipment is expensive."

"But it's going to stink up my apartment," she said.

"Leo said he'd buy you a case of air freshener." The teenager had the audacity to grin.

"He already discussed this with you?"

Josh nodded. "Since you were back home, he told me to leave the bag outside. Then I reminded him that someone could take it in such a public place and he said that was a problem. Because the pads and skates and my helmet aren't cheap. My parents would kill me."

"And being dead would make it hard to play hockey," she said wryly.

"No kidding. That's when he said bringing it inside wasn't something that air freshener and open windows couldn't fix."

"He's very practical." She motioned him inside and pointed to a spot just beside the door for the bag. It was as far away from her as possible.

Josh did as instructed and then shut the door.

She said, "Would you like a snack?"

"If it's no trouble."

"I've got fruit and frozen taquitos. Some chips, too." She'd been grocery shopping and picked up extra that she knew he liked.

"Sounds awesome."

"Have a seat at the kitchen table. I've got your paper there. You did a good job. I just tweaked it. I used track changes and printed it out, then made some written comments in the margin. Mostly suggestions for different words, eliminating *stupid* and *dumb*, which are your favorites."

Instead of being offended, he grinned. "Well, those people in that book are dumb."

"I agree. They're also selfish, self-centered, deceitful characters who don't think about the consequences of their actions."

He looked pleased that she agreed with him. "And if they weren't so dumb, Gatsby wouldn't have gotten shot in his pool."

"It was a tragic end for a man who was simply desperate to fit in and be with the woman he loved."

"Like I said—dumb." He sat down at the table. "Just like *Romeo and Juliet*. Love made everybody stupid."

The kid was kind of insightful, she thought, setting some taquitos on a sheet of foil before sliding it into the toaster oven on the counter. "I guess that's pretty true."

"Why do writers write about people being morons?"

She gave that a ponder before answering. "I suppose it would be boring to read about a character who was perfect and never made a bad choice. Besides that, human beings are flawed."

"I guess."

She set a glass with ice and soda in front of him, then a plate with apple slices. Whether or not he'd enjoyed the book, at least he was thinking about it. And wasn't that the point? Maybe not the only one. "Great literature makes the reader feel something. Or should. Happy, sad, angry."

"I don't need to read for that to happen," he said. "My mom and dad do that all the time. Mostly the sad and mad part."

The timer went off and she took out the taquitos, put them on a plate and brought it over to the table before sitting across from him. "What makes you happy?"

"Hockey," he answered without hesitation. Then he started consuming apple slices while he looked thoughtful. "If it weren't for Leo, I wouldn't be able to play."

"He had a little help," she said wryly.

"Yeah. And I appreciate what you're doing. But he made it happen."

She couldn't argue with that. When Leo found this boy in the locker room at the ice rink, he could have called the police and social services. Somehow he knew that would have made things more messy and complicated. Instead she had suggested tutoring and he had talked her into being the tutor. Josh was on parental academic probation and was now bringing up his grade without giving up doing what he loved.

"He really did save your bacon," she agreed.

"And now he's my coach. And he's awesome. He just knows when to change up our lines for a game. When to bench a guy because his head's not in it. He takes the time to talk to me, explain stuff. And not just me. He does that with all the guys."

"That's really nice of him."

"It's not nice." He glanced at his paper with her handwritten comments. "Like you said there. That's a bland word."

So, he'd looked through it. She pressed her lips together to keep from laughing. "How would you describe him in one not-bland word?"

"Awesome." He didn't even have to think about it.

"That's a cliché," she said. "That's in your paper, too. Many, many times. There's this wonderful thing called a thesaurus that can supply various words that mean the same thing. Use your phone for more than playing games. I challenge you to give me something besides *awesome*."

He frowned thoughtfully as he ate. Finally he said, "I can't think of one. But he really cares. He *gets* me."

"Leo would like that. And I can't think of higher praise than—" Tess stopped because unexpected emotion clogged her throat.

"It's the truth. My parents don't understand anything."

"I'm going to stop you there, Josh. Your mom and dad love you or you wouldn't be here now to look over this paper with me. And if they hadn't agreed to this, you could kiss hockey goodbye."

"But all they do is lecture. Leo is cool about everything."

"He cares, but you are your parents' baby." She moved a hand protectively over her belly, where her own baby was growing. "He doesn't have the same emotional investment as they do. He came up with a solution that works for everyone. A compromise."

"He doesn't tell me what to do all the time."

"He actually does," she said. "It just doesn't feel that way."

"Maybe. He's just the best." Josh chewed and swallowed the last of his snack. Then he looked at her, and with all the angst of a fifteen-year-old in his eyes said, "I wish he was my dad."

And the hero-worship train kept on rolling, she thought. Maturity would give this teenager a different perspective on his parents and how much they cared. He didn't know yet how lucky he was to have both a mother and father who were there for him. If not for her grandfather, she didn't know what would have happened to her. And none of that minimized Leo's valuable contribution to Josh's future at a crossroads in his life.

Tess hadn't chosen to get pregnant and hadn't deliberately picked Leo for sex. It just sort of happened that night he'd put his arms around her, just being nice when she was crying. But even if she'd consciously put thought into the decision, she couldn't have selected a better man to be the father of her baby.

"Okay, fanboy," she teased, "let's dissect this paper and get you a really good grade on it."

For the next hour they went over each sentence, one at a time until every paragraph supported the one before it. They talked about more appropriate words and tightening the structure, eliminating content that was deadweight.

There was a knock on her door just as they reached the end of the paper. She glanced at the digital clock on the microwave. "Time flies when you're having fun."

"It's Leo," Josh said, looking through the window. "Oh, man, I'm late."

It was definitely Leo, and her heart responded the way it always did when she saw him. There was a painful squeeze and her belly tightened. Before she could make a move, Josh jumped up to open the door.

"We were working and I didn't notice the time. I should have been waiting in the parking lot. I'm sorry."

"No big deal, kid." Leo looked at her, then back at Josh. "Tutoring must be going well if you forgot to watch the clock."

The teen shrugged nonchalantly. "It's okay."

"I refuse to take that personally," she teased. "If I say so myself, it was awesome."

"Cliché." Josh pointed at her.

"I rest my case," she told Leo. "Now he's the language police. I think his paper will earn a good grade and raise his overall score in the class. In my humble opinion his hockey career is saved. My work here is done."

"Good." Leo glanced at the ginormous bag by the door.

"Hey, kid, why don't you grab that and meet me at the car."

"Okay." He started to, then turned back to Tess and gave her a spontaneous hug. "Thanks for everything. And the snacks were really good, too."

"You're welcome."

He scooped up the handles and hefted the bag over his shoulder, then waved and walked out the door.

Tess was going to miss him. She sighed, then met Leo's gaze. "I'm sorry you had to come up."

"I needed to talk to you anyway."

"First, where's my case of air freshener?"

He grinned. "It's on order."

"That does me no good. I'll just have to open windows." She leaned against the open door. "Okay, your turn. What did you want to talk about?"

"I can't right now. There are a bunch of fourteen- and fifteen-year-olds waiting for me at the rink and they need supervision."

"Right, so—"

"I wanted to set up a time to meet. We're having a grand reopening soon and we need to nail down some things. Are you free in the morning?"

"Yeah. I'll be here waiting for the new furniture to be delivered."

"How about ten?"

"Works for me," she said.

"Good. I'll see you then." He glanced outside. "I have to go."

"Right. Have a good practice. See you tomorrow."

The thrill of anticipation coursed through her until she checked the feeling. It felt a little like that scene from the movie *Oliver!* with the titular hungry orphan holding up his empty bowl and asking for more, please. How pathetic was she?

A short time ago she'd thought about what a great father he would be. And he would. But that was all about the baby. It had nothing to do with her. And wasn't it unfortunate that the two of them had more personal baggage than would fit in Josh's hockey bag? Neither of them wanted a relationship. And that was a darn shame because she'd always wanted a traditional family.

While living with him, she'd begun to think there was chemistry between them. That hope imploded when she saw how happy he was for her to go back home.

It was for the best. Josh's study of literature led him to the conclusion that people did stupid things because of love. No way was she going to be dumb again. So, she and Leo and the baby wouldn't be the traditional family she'd always dreamed of, but there would be a mother and father in the picture. That was more than she'd had. It would just have to be enough.

Leo couldn't put it off any longer. The grand reopening of the bar was happening soon and they needed to decide on a name. That's the main thing he'd wanted to talk with Tess about today, and he was on his way over there now. As much as he was looking forward to seeing her, no way he wanted her upset. And he knew this discussion would do that. When he had raised the subject, she had cried and he hadn't been able to ignore the compulsion to protect and comfort her. The first time it had happened was the reason he was in baby-daddy limbo now.

He drove into the parking lot and saw a big delivery truck backed up to the door. Tess was talking to two big, burly guys and pointing at something inside. She was wearing black yoga pants and a tank top. The outfit highlighted that her belly was growing rounder every day. The baby was getting bigger and would be here soon. And Tess looked both cute and sexy as hell.

It was a damn good thing he wasn't going to be alone with her because if she shed tears, he was going to comfort her. If he put his arms around her, he didn't think he would be able to resist kissing her. But there was no point in borrowing trouble. Maybe she would be okay with this change.

He got out of the car and walked over to her. "Morning."

"Hi, Leo." She looked up at him and used her hand to shade her eyes from the sun. "The new furniture is here."

"I noticed, what with the big delivery truck and all," he said wryly.

Side by side they watched barstools, love seats, club chairs, end tables and dining sets being taken off the truck.

"How was practice?" she asked.

"Good. I see improvement."

"That's great. Josh was singing your coaching praises yesterday. He talked about changing up lines and knowing when someone's head wasn't in the game."

He met her gaze. "There are a lot of factors that go into pulling a team together. This one has a lot of potential. No offense to the last coach, but it helps to have played the game."

"Probably, but you also have to be a leader, one the kids respect, or there's no way you're going to pull them together." She smiled. "According to Josh, you have wings, a halo and you walk on water."

"Fortunately it's frozen or I'd sink like a stone."

She laughed. "FYI, some of Nate's guys are here tying up loose ends. They're putting up all the flat-screen TVs."

"Yeah, he called me."

After a few moments of silence she said, "Enough small talk. What's so important that you had to make an appointment to talk about it?"

"Hmm?"

"Yesterday, when you picked up Josh, you said we needed to discuss something."

He actually remembered and was merely stalling. "Right. It's just last-minute details. It can wait until this is done." He angled his head toward the growing array of eclectic furniture accumulating on the sidewalk.

Nervously, she caught her top lip between her teeth. "I hope everything looks okay when they get it inside. Now that I see it, I'm not sure the furnishings all go together. Maybe blending new with what was already here was not the best way to go. I don't want to let my grandfather down."

"You won't," he reassured her.

"How can you be sure?"

"Because I won't let that happen. He knew that when he asked me to invest. This is going to be the 'in spot.' The happening place for all occasions."

"Date night and bachelor parties? Seems like sort of a conflict of interest to me."

"We've opened the window wider to appeal to a more diverse clientele. Birthday parties, family reunions, bachelorette parties, too."

"Baby showers?" She looked ruefully at her tummy.

"Why not?"

"I'm not sure we can handle the food for those types of events. I know I gave you a hard time about a chef, but you might be onto something."

"We can cater at first, if necessary," he said. "One of our first new hires should be a chef. Someone creative with food, who can turn pub cuisine into something special."

"What do you mean 'first hires'?" she asked. "You kept everyone on the payroll during renovations. And I promised Brandon he had a job when we reopened. He needs it until he gets his business degree from UCLA."

"I'm counting on him," Leo assured her. "But he *is* going to graduate next year and will probably leave. We need to train someone now to take over. And then there's replacing you."

"Hey, I'm a partner." She stared at him. "Not going anywhere."

"But you're having a baby." He indicated the bump of her tummy that proved his point. "You won't be able to fill in. At least not at a moment's notice anyway."

Leo remembered the turmoil of having a new baby in the house. Sleepless nights. Colic and crying. Teething and crying. The needs were varied, immediate and required attention. When he had to be out of town for games or other professional commitments, guilt and worry became his new best friends. His ex-wife wasn't a bad mother, but her parenting philosophy allowed for more crying and less cuddling. His way of thinking was just the opposite.

It was on the tip of his tongue to ask Tess's opinion until he reminded himself he didn't have to. Not yet. Not until the baby was born and he had proof that he was the biological father. The only privileges he had now were what she allowed. He wasn't going to get sucked in and care until a test said he had as much right to the child as she did.

All the furniture was finally out of the truck, and one of the delivery guys asked her a question about where to put it.

"Let's start with the barstools. The new ones will be intermingled. Take away half of the existing ones and place them old, new, old, new."

"You got it," number one big guy said. "You want us to take away the old ones?"

There was regret in her eyes when she nodded. "But save two. I'm going to put them upstairs in my apartment. Keepsakes."

"Will do," he said. "I'll have Vince carry them up for you."

"That's all right. I can do it."

"Lady, in your condition you shouldn't be carrying stuff like that at all. Especially up the stairs."

"He's right." Leo made a mental note to give these guys a nice tip.

Tess turned on him. "Did you say something to them about the baby?"

"I just got here. And, no, I didn't make a phone call. It's obvious."

"On the up side, at least they didn't assume I was just putting on weight," she said.

Not a chance, he thought. She was still curvy in all the right places, all the best ones. He would give almost anything to explore them. Just the fact that idea crossed his mind made him double down on his promise to not go to hell where Tess was concerned.

He instructed them to work around the two men hanging the flat-screen TV. Then they followed big guy number one and Vince inside, and Tess showed them how she wanted the lounge furniture arranged. She pointed out the dining area, where the tables and chairs would go, and studied the center bar with a critical eye, particularly the blending of chairs. "I wasn't sure these would work together, but it's okay."

Kind of like the two of them, he thought. "It looks better than okay."

They observed as the lounge took shape and there was a smile on her face. It didn't take long to arrange the tables and chairs in the separate dining area. She walked around the place, nodding her approval.

"It's not awful," she told him.

"High praise coming from you. I guess that's a hat trick for me." He saw her blank expression. "Hockey term. Three goals by one player in a single game."

"Okay, then. You get one of those."

While Vince took her keepsake barstools up to her apartment, big guy number one came over with a work order that needed a signature. Leo did that and gave him a check and a generous tip. "Great job."

"Thanks."

They shook hands and the men left the building just as Nate's construction guys came out of the lounge and left.

Tess was still strolling around, taking stock of the interior, as if she'd moved into a new house. "The walls are so bare. It looks so different."

"Good different or bad?"

"Not sure yet. But I guess it is what it is."

"Yeah, about that—"

"Now you can talk to me about whatever it is you didn't want to bring up in front of strangers." She met his gaze and there was nothing in her expression that hinted at what she was thinking. "It's about the name change, right?"

"Yeah. We need to make a decision. It should be on the window when we reopen."

"I know." There was a trace of sadness in her voice.

"What are your thoughts?"

"Keep the old one." Her tone was part teasing, part hopeful. "Just kidding. Mostly."

"I know this is difficult." The last time he brought it up she cried and he hated that.

"At least you warned me. And your reasoning is sound." She sighed. "So, I've been thinking... Here's my list, in no particular order and not especially good. The Corner Pub. Pub on the Corner. Cheers. No One Knows Your Name. No Name. Tess's Tavern. Tess and Leo's Tavern."

"Hmm." At least she hadn't left him out, much as she probably wanted to. "I know we're mixing old and new but I think those are a little too much on the new side."

"Do you have a better idea?"

"I think so." He hoped she approved, because he had work orders pending with a tentative new name. "What do you think about Patrick's Place?"

She didn't say anything, just let the words hang there in the air, where her grandfather had built his business from the ground up. Her eyes glistened with unshed tears and he was about to take it back.

"You don't like it. No problem. We can brainstorm some more. I have a list, too—"

"No." She put the tips of her fingers over her mouth for a moment. "It's absolutely perfect. Granddad would love it."

"Okay, then," he said.

That was a relief, until it wasn't. His arms ached to hold her. He'd almost counted on it but didn't have to after all. What kind of a scumbag was he for wishing she had cried? Now there was no excuse to hold her. Even worse, he wanted to kiss her. Not only was he a scumbag; he was a stupid one. He was on the verge of breaking his rule about getting personally involved.

The definition of *insanity* was doing the same thing and expecting a different result. Thank goodness the busywork to get Patrick's Place open was almost done. As soon as the doors were open again, he could back off and let her run the show.

He wouldn't have to see her, and eventually she would be out of his system.

Chapter Thirteen

"What if no one shows up?" Tess said to Leo. They were standing by the bar, staring at the front door that hadn't budged, even though they'd only officially reopened thirty seconds ago.

Patrick's Place was more than ready and she was primed for action, but panic was setting in. "What if this is an epic fail and we go bankrupt? I'll be an unemployed single mom. What am I going to do then?"

"Take a breath." He put his hands on her upper arms and gave her a reassuring squeeze before letting her go. "One step at a time. We've made all the right moves. Advertising in the local paper and TV spots. Coupons. Invitations to friends and former customers. They'll come. We'll have at least one spectacular night."

"You're being way too rational," she said before his words sank in. "One? Oh, God. What if no one comes back ever? Without repeat business, we'll fall on our faces—"

"This is just wrong," he said. "The world has gone mad. Everything is turned upside down."

She blinked at him. "What are you talking about?"

"I'm usually the 'glass half empty' guy and you're Priscilla Perky. What's up with this reversal of roles?"

Tess realized he was right. "I'm sorry. I just don't want to let Granddad down."

Hanging on the wall behind the bar was a grouping of

framed photos. One of a young Patrick Morrow with a shovel in an empty lot. Another picture was Pat and her grandmother, Mary, staring lovingly into each other's eyes, right here where Tess was standing with Leo. Still another showed her grandfather with his arm around her shoulders when she'd turned twenty-one and could actually work with customers.

"I don't want to disappoint him." Her voice was thick with emotion.

"That could never happen." Leo moved closer and gently nudged her chin up so she'd look at him. "He loved you more than anything in the world. You never disappointed him, then or now."

"I miss him."

"Me, too. But I believe he's here, Tess. Watching over the place. And you."

She nodded. "Thanks for the pep talk. I bet you're a really good coach."

"I am. Humble, too." His charming grin unleashed nerves of a different kind.

"It's showtime." Brandon walked behind the bar and dumped a bucket of ice into the sink back there. "The caterer and servers are ready to do their thing."

She and Leo had decided to hire someone for this event so Tess could schmooze. Bridgette Mansfield had been hired as the chef and would be helping out tonight, then take over during regular business hours. For now there were a couple of new menu items, and she was developing more.

The front door opened and in walked Carla and Jamie. They both gave her a hug, then stared at Leo.

"Are you going to introduce us?" Carla asked with her customary directness.

Tess couldn't believe her friends hadn't been introduced to him. But the memorial was the only time their paths had crossed, and she hadn't been at her best that day.

Carla spoke up first. "You were at Pat's memorial, but we didn't speak. I'm Carla Kellerman."

"Jamie Webber." Her other friend shook his hand.

"Nice to meet you both." Leo grinned. "I was just telling Tess that her friends wouldn't let her down."

"Speaking of letdowns," Jamie said, "I invited Bill to come tonight, but he was called back to the Seattle office."

Before Tess could respond with sympathy, the door opened again and a group of people walked in. They looked around and then headed to the bar, where Brandon was waiting for them. She recognized a few who were regulars when her grandfather was still alive.

"I'm going to mingle." Tess hugged both of her friends. "Bless you both for coming tonight. Leo will give you the tour."

"Happy to."

He gave them his most charming smile and had never looked more handsome. In jeans, a powder blue dress shirt and navy sports jacket, he was every hunky inch the successful financial professional. She remembered her friends saying that a sports bar would be a good place to meet guys. A flash of irritation jolted her and she recognized it as a bit of jealousy. Not for Carla and Jamie. But other women.

It was inevitable that there would be, because his marrying mind-set had been annihilated by the bitch who had lied about being pregnant with his child. His parents hadn't helped either. And it was incredibly sad because he was a decent, wonderful man with a giant capacity for caring. He deserved better; he deserved to be happy.

"Tess Morrow—"

She tore her gaze from Leo's back and looked toward

the bar. She smiled at the familiar face of an older man who had his choice of seats and had picked one of the old barstools. She walked over and hugged him. "John Alexander."

"Hi, honey. Good to see you again."

The man was a silver-haired widower in his sixties. Her grandfather had befriended him after his wife had died. He was lonely and came in frequently for a beer and conversation. Group therapy for the two of them, Pat had always joked.

"It's good to see you," she said. "Thanks for coming."

"Wouldn't miss it for the world."

"I have to admit to a little anxiety about this grand re-opening. I was afraid it would go down in flames." She looked around the room that already held a respectable number of people. The place was big but from where she stood, she could see what was going on. Patrick's Place was filling up nicely.

The door was opening every few minutes to admit more customers. The temporary help was circulating with appetizers, taking orders and serving drinks. Some people were at tables in the dining area while others made themselves comfortable in the lounge to watch the hockey game on TV. Stanley Cup playoffs, Leo had told her.

"I don't think there's anything to worry about," John said. "For what it's worth, I think Pat would have really liked what you've done with the place."

This man had known her grandfather pretty well and his opinion mattered very much to her. "Really?"

He nodded. "Without a doubt."

"It makes me happy you'd say so."

"It's like home away from home. Companions. A meal. Watch some sports with other fans, let off a little steam." He nodded again. "The Pub always had it but now there's a more with-it, welcoming vibe, if you know what I mean."

"Thanks to Leo." This was his idea. She glanced around and spotted him chatting up the hockey fans watching the game and requesting his autograph, which he scribbled on the cocktail napkins prominently displaying the name Patrick's Place.

"It doesn't hurt that your partner is Leo 'The Wall' Wallace."

"I see you've heard of him."

"Anyone who follows the sport has." John took a sip of the beer Brandon had put in front of him. "It would seem congratulations are in order on another front, too."

She dragged her gaze away from her gaze-worthy partner. "Hmm?"

"The baby."

Holy crap!

With everything else on her mind, she'd forgotten. And when she'd thought about the baby earlier, she'd assumed her loose white blouse over jeans would conceal her condition. Apparently not. And there was no point in blowing off the comment. He was a loyal customer who would be back, and the baby was going to grow until there was no way to hide it.

"Thank you," she said. "It was a surprise."

"Is Leo excited about becoming a father?" There was a twinkle in the older man's eyes.

Double holy crap! He couldn't possibly know. The question was—why in the world would he jump to that conclusion? She looked around and then lowered her voice so no one nearby could hear. "Why in the world would you think it's Leo's baby?"

"A feeling." He smiled. "Because of the way you keep looking at him."

"Oh?" Play it cool, she told herself. "How am I looking at him?"

"The way I did at my Janie. And Pat looked at your grandmother like that, too." He shrugged. "So maybe it's more of an educated guess."

"Anyone who knows me would be surprised by this, but I really don't know what to say." No way would Leo want this talked about. Maybe after a DNA test confirmed the truth, but definitely not here or now.

"Pat would be proud to be a great grandfather. He was fond of Leo, like a son—or grandson."

That made her so happy, and weepy, but she had to keep that part inside. "John, I don't—"

"Don't worry, honey. Your secret is safe with me." He lifted his beer glass. "Let's drink to the success of your new endeavor."

"To my endeavors," she echoed. Which included the business and the bun in the oven.

Tess kissed his cheek, then moved on. She greeted familiar faces and planted the seeds of friendship with strangers. Leo had been right. The place was crowded and everyone seemed to be having a good time. Until closing, Tess and Leo circulated, shaking hands, serving appetizers and drinks, making conversation and welcoming customers they hoped would become regulars.

After the employees cleaned up, they urged them to go home and get some rest, then locked the place up. She was alone with Leo, standing by the front door. Again.

He looked down at her. "I feel as if I just played a hockey game with double overtime."

Tess understood the sentiment even though she had no frame of reference for it. "Being nice to people is exhausting, but I'd say it went well."

"You were amazing."

"Thanks. You weren't so bad yourself." She looked down at his big hands. "Did you get carpal tunnel from signing autographs?"

He flexed his fingers. "Nope. All good."

"I heard from a lot of people—new customers—that they came in just to see the legendary Leo Wallace."

"Really?" He pretended surprise and it was the cutest thing ever.

"Own the honor, Wallace. You can't really pull off humble, so… Just saying."

He grinned. "I feel so used. Nothing but a marketing tool."

She laughed, but a yawn took over in spite of her efforts to suppress it. "Sorry. It's not the company. Just a long, busy day."

"And you're pregnant."

"Not breaking news." Not to her, but John had guessed.

"How are you holding up?"

"Not too bad. Although my feet hurt and I'm afraid to sit down because I may never get up."

"You need to go upstairs," he said. "Get some rest."

"I will. As soon as my feet stop throbbing. Go on home. I'll turn out the lights."

"As soon as I know you're settled upstairs." He moved closer, then scooped her into his arms.

Now it wasn't just her feet throbbing. Her pulse was going a mile a minute and she could hardly breathe. This was super dangerous—to her heart and his back.

"Put me down, Leo." Right words but there was no oomph behind them. She slid her arms around his neck.

"I will. As soon as you're in your apartment, safe and sound."

He carried her up the stairs as if she barely weighed anything, though the scale at the doctor's office told her once a month that that wasn't true. Stopping at her door, he removed his arm from beneath her legs and let them slide to the floor.

"Do you have the key?"

Right! He couldn't open it with his arms full of her.

"In my pocket." She fished it out and opened the door. "That was very chivalrous of you. Foolhardy but so gallant. Thanks."

"You're welcome."

The deep voice and completely adorable smile made her stomach flutter. Then she realized it wasn't *that*. The baby was moving. "Oh, wow—"

"What? Is something wrong?"

"No. Just the opposite. The baby moved. He's doing that a lot now. Feel." She took his big hand and put it on her abdomen. As if on cue, the baby moved again and it felt like big bubbles rippling inside her. "Did you feel that?"

"Yes."

His voice was ragged and at first she thought he was irritated that she would assume he wanted to feel the baby kick, or be involved at all. But that was before she saw the intensity on his face, read the hunger in his eyes and *knew*. Her heart started hammering.

And then he kissed her.

Leo ached to have her. When she took his hand and he felt the baby move, probably his baby, it was more than he could stand. His choices were to kiss her or implode. So he kissed her.

Those full lips were even softer than he remembered. He tunneled his fingers into her hair and cupped her cheek in his palm. When he traced her lips with the tip of his tongue, she opened to him and he explored the sweet moistness as his breathing escalated.

Tess put her arms around his neck and pressed herself closer to him. What with the pregnancy, her belly was more rounded now and her breasts fuller. Sexy curves made even sexier by the life growing inside her. More than his next breath, he wanted to hold her naked body against his own.

"Tess?" He took her arms from his shoulders, but couldn't end the contact and held her hands. "Should I not have done that?"

"What? Kiss me?"

He nodded. "Did I overstep? Read this—whatever it is between us—wrong? If you don't want this, I'll back off and we never have to mention it again."

"Are you saying you don't want me?"

"God, no." He squeezed her hands just a little tighter, as though she'd pulled away and he couldn't let her go. "I just wanted to… It's just that we agreed… You know, that this would be all business, no pleasure."

Her dark eyes sparkled with humor and passion, and she had never looked more beautiful. "Then we will take no pleasure from it."

Oh, thank God. He grinned. "Agreed."

Leo touched his mouth to hers again, trailing kisses over her cheek and neck, then nibbling her earlobe. She gasped and shivered, and tilted her head to the side, giving him license to take what he wanted. And he did. Until he couldn't stand it anymore.

"Where's your bedroom?" he asked.

She stared at him with glazed eyes. "What?"

"Room? Bed? Don't get me wrong. The table wasn't bad. But this should be done in a proper bed."

"Hmm. I never thought of my bed as proper." She

grinned and took his hand. "Let's go find out if you're right about it."

Tess led him through a doorway and into the next room. The bed was big, fluffy and feminine, with a flower print on the spread. Throw pillows of all sizes and shapes, in shades of pink, green and maroon, were neatly displayed. And not so neatly tossed aside when she started to pull down the covers, spread and all. Light trickled in from the other room, enough for him to see her slide her top over her head and drop it on the floor. From the waist up all she had on was a lacy white bra.

Leo was afraid he'd swallowed his tongue. She was so beautiful. He reached out and cupped her breasts in both hands. Through the lace, he brushed his thumbs over the tips and she gasped once, then moaned with pleasure. She was sensitive and responsive to his touch. And he was sensitive and responsive to the sensual sounds she was making.

His hands shook when he reached behind her and released the hooks on that sexy little scrap of material. The wisp slid to her feet and he stared at the beauty of her.

Her breathing was unsteady when she said, "You look like you're taking pleasure from this."

"No. I swear. Not enjoying this at all." He could barely get the words out and heard the ragged edges of his own voice.

"Okay. Just checking," she whispered. "And I'm not going to like this at all either."

She reached out and undid the buttons on his shirt, one by one, with excruciating slowness. It took every ounce of his willpower not to push her hands aside and rip the thing over his head. Finally the front was open and she rested her palms on his bare chest, touching him the way he'd touched her. It had been months since he'd had sex with her and he was afraid if he didn't hurry things along, this would go very badly.

"I'm hating this so much, but can we get to the part that is the least pleasurable?"

He wasn't proud of the desperation in his voice but it couldn't be helped. He kicked off his shoes, took off his socks and unbuckled his belt before sliding off his jeans and boxers.

Her eyes widened in approval as she gave him a once-over, then fanned herself by waving a hand in front of her face. "At the risk of totally blowing our agreement, you are not hard on the eyes."

"I aim to be adequate."

She smiled, then slid off her pants and stood in front of him without a stitch on. Leo could hardly breathe. Her legs were long, smooth and shapely. The rounded belly and full breasts were the essence of femininity and the most beautiful sight he'd ever seen.

"Say something."

"Not sure…" He cleared his throat. "I know we agreed no pleasure but you are—"

"Don't say it."

"Wait. First you tell me to talk—now I can't?" He shook his head. "I have to tell you. You are exquisite."

Her eyes filled with tears. "Thank you."

He tugged her into his arms and couldn't believe how soft her skin felt, how sweet her curves were against his chest. He kissed her long and deeply as he swept his hand over the curve of her waist and thighs. Slowly he moved his palm over her abdomen, lower to that place between her legs and slid one finger inside her.

She cried out with desire and her knees buckled. "Oh, Leo, I need you. Now."

Didn't have to ask him twice. He swung her into his

arms and settled her in the center of her big, soft bed. He got in beside her and pulled her close, touching her everywhere, kissing her until they both couldn't bear it another second.

He rolled over her, taking his weight on his forearms, and she opened her legs without hesitation, welcoming him to her. He entered her slowly, willing himself to take his time, but Tess was impatient. She arched her hips and wrapped her legs around his waist, urging him to go faster. He thrust once, twice and then she cried out and clung to him, her body trembling with pleasure.

The thought made him smile as he held her until the shudders subsided. Then he thrust slowly into her again, but there was no holding back now and his own release rocked him to his core. He buried his face in her neck and they held on to each other for a long time.

When he could think clearly, he rolled off her. "I must be crushing you."

"No." She snuggled in and rested her arm across his abdomen. "I'm fine. Better than fine, if I'm being honest. Finer than I've been in a long time."

"Me, too." He pulled the sheet up over them.

"It's a shame neither of us took pleasure in that at all," she said. "None. Zero."

"Yeah." That was probably the best pleasure he'd ever experienced, and for the life of him he couldn't explain why.

"For the record, my bed? Not proper. And it has to be said that proper is highly overrated."

"You and I have disagreed about many things, but that statement is not one of them."

Other than a nod, Tess didn't seem inclined to move, so Leo wasn't going to push it. Holding her felt too good after wanting her so badly for so long. Neither of them spoke, as if simply using their bodies to communicate contentment. He hadn't experienced it often in his life and savored the feeling now.

They might have dozed, because there was no telling how much time passed before Tess whispered, "Leo? Are you awake?"

"Yeah. You?"

She laughed and rubbed her cheek against his shoulder. "I've been thinking."

"I thought I smelled something burning."

"Very funny." She lightly tugged one of his chest hairs. "Ow."

"Serves you right." She sighed then and the expression on her face was thoughtful. "I want to apologize."

"Why? That was awesome. Perfect." And he sincerely meant those words.

"I know. It really was." She didn't say anything for a few moments, as if choosing her words carefully. "I just want to say that I really misjudged you."

"What? How?"

"When my grandfather introduced us. The thing is, I'd heard about you, your reputation with women, and figured you were a cocky, arrogant player."

"A sports jerk like your ex." When she'd told him about that, he understood where she was coming from. "We've been through all this. It's water under the bridge. There's no reason to bring it up again."

"I just need to say this. Since we became partners, I've really gotten to know you."

"And I've gotten to know you. It's all good."

She looked up and met his gaze. "You're not an arrogant, cocky player at all. You are conscientious and caring. You're a really good man."

"Don't spread it around," he teased.

"I don't have to. Your actions speak louder than words. Working with the kids on the hockey team. Taking a personal interest in a troubled teenager. Being there for me. Talking me through my panic tonight. What would I have done without you?"

"Not a doubt in my mind that you would have moved forward and been just fine."

"Maybe. But it was fun experiencing the grand reopening of Patrick's Place with you. It was special because of you."

"It was special, but not because of me. You're the heart and soul of this place now," he said.

As partners went, she was the whole sexy package. Don't look now but he was successfully mixing business and pleasure with a woman who was as dead set against commitment as he was. How perfect was that? Contentment spilled over into happiness territory.

"I have to tell you something."

"You just did. And we're good."

"No, this is different," she insisted.

"Okay." But he looked at her shining eyes and suddenly got a very bad feeling. "What?"

"I'm in love with you, Leo."

Chapter Fourteen

Leo knew his reaction to Tess's declaration was going to be bad but that didn't begin to describe how much worse everything was from what he'd expected. First of all the words *I love you* almost came out of his mouth, too. Fortunately he stopped just in time. Things between them were pretty damn good, and the last thing he wanted was to screw it up with a responding emotional statement. But she'd put it out there. Now what was he supposed to say?

Why in God's name had he let her touch him? To feel the baby move. Damn it.

"Leo?" She sat up in the bed and held the sheet up to cover her breasts. "I'm sorry. The words just popped out. I didn't mean it."

Really? So she said that to every guy she slept with? He experienced an unexpected and uncomfortable spurt of jealousy at the thought of her with another guy. Good God. This was crazy and he was insane. Except she didn't sleep around—or so she'd told him. Could he believe her? A woman he thought he knew had lied to him before. He hated that but never more than he did right this minute. Destroying his ability to trust was the worst kind of betrayal.

And he couldn't think of any good response to Tess's words. So he simply said, "Don't worry about it."

"Can't help it. You look weird." She was staring at him. "Let's just pretend I never said those words."

"Done." He smiled at her but it was forced. The worry darkening her eyes told him she wasn't buying his answer. "Now you look weird."

"I wish I could take it back."

Unfortunately he couldn't unhear the words any more than he could undo getting her pregnant the first time they had sex in this building. He almost smiled remembering what she'd told him then. Saying it back to her now was worth a try.

"It never happened," he told her.

"Okay."

"We will never speak of this again." Her words, but life hadn't cooperated then, he thought.

Tess nodded but there was a sadness in her expression that ripped his heart out. He needed to get back on solid ground, back to the business, and their partnership was the way to do that. "The grand opening of Patrick's Place tonight was even better than I had hoped. Pat would be proud of you."

"Would he?" She was naked under that sheet and her hair was post-sex messy. "I'm not so sure."

She was making this personal. He couldn't really blame her. That tendency was hardwired into women. But he couldn't get sucked in. Trusting unconditionally once before had set him up to be knocked flat. The only thing that got him up again was the vow forged by fire in his soul, to never care that deeply again. And he was on the verge of breaking that vow. If she kept looking at him that way, with her eyes all soft and sexy, he was going to cave.

"It's late," he said. "And I have an early meeting tomorrow."

"Yeah. You should go."

Leo wasn't going to wait for her to say it again. He slid out of bed and quickly dressed. She didn't move and he had the uneasy feeling that if he touched her, she would shatter.

But he couldn't stop himself from kissing her on the forehead. "I'll lock the place up on my way out. You get some rest."

"Don't worry about me."

He couldn't help it but didn't say that out loud. "Good night, Tess."

He left before she could respond, urgently needing distance to take a deep breath. Hit the pause button and find a way to protect himself. Words meant nothing unless they were in writing.

Tess had never in her life regretted having a big mouth more than she did that night when she'd told Leo she loved him. Just because she felt it didn't mean she had to say the words out loud. It was just that the feeling was so big, she couldn't hold it back. Unfortunately he had looked as if he'd swallowed a bee and it was stinging all the way down.

And it wasn't as if it was entirely her fault. Their all business, no pleasure vow had exploded when he had kissed her. The problem was that her announcement about being in love with him had taken things to another level of awful.

The worst part was she hadn't seen him since that night a week ago. They'd texted, mostly about business. She'd reminded him of her upcoming doctor's appointment but he claimed he had a meeting. It hurt that he wasn't even giving her an opportunity to show him she could ignore what she'd said, to repair the damage she'd done to their business relationship.

It was late in more ways than one. The bar was nearing closing time, and Brandon was wiping down and tidying things while a few customers finished up their drinks. The dining area was closed and shut down, with the lights dimmed.

One of the last-call customers was John Alexander, the man who'd noticed she was pregnant and jumped to the correct conclusion that Leo was the father. In the last week, she'd had a lot of time to wonder if the older man's observations of her romantic feelings for Leo had compelled her to put the words out there. Not that she blamed John. The colossal error in judgment had been hers alone.

But she hadn't gone out of her way to speak to him tonight, so a case could be made that part of her did hold him responsible, and that wasn't fair. She was behind the bar and walked over to stand in front of him.

"Hi, John."

"Hey, Tess. How are you?"

"Good." It wasn't a complete lie because in time she would make things good again. She'd prove to Leo that she was trustworthy. "How about you? Doing okay?"

"Oh, you know." He toyed with the half-empty beer glass. "The missing her never really goes away."

The "her" he meant was his wife, and that meant he was still in love with her after all this time. Not what Tess wanted to hear. It wouldn't be that way for her; she wouldn't have to miss Leo, because he would come around. And what was so wrong with saying she loved him? A lot of people actually *wanted* to hear those words. But now she knew his story, knew he believed love brought pain and loss. Somehow she would convince him it wouldn't be that way with her.

She looked at the older man. "Do you wish you'd never fallen in love?"

"No. I wouldn't trade missing her now for never having loved her. Not in a million years." He met her gaze and his own was sad, although surprisingly peaceful. "She was the best thing that ever happened to me. She gave me the most precious gift of all. Our children."

"That's beautiful." She blinked at the tears stinging her eyes. Then she felt her baby move and pressed a hand to her abdomen. "Children are a blessing."

"True enough." He took a swallow of beer and stood. "It was last call a while ago and I'm sure Brandon wants to close up."

"Yeah."

"And you need your rest, young lady." He pretended to be stern but the twinkle in his eyes gave him away. Then he grew serious again. "Don't worry, honey. Whatever's going on with you and Leo will work itself out. Just wait and see. Things will be fine."

"How did you know there's something going on?" She shook her head. "I think you're psychic."

"Just observant. And only with people I care about." He smiled fondly. "Good night, Tess."

"See you soon."

A little while later everyone was gone, including Brandon. She was about to lock up when a familiar car pulled into the lot and parked outside Patrick's Place. Leo got out and walked to the front door, which she then opened.

He was literally a sight for sore eyes. As much as she'd told herself not to, she'd shed a few tears over him. And why did he have to look so darn handsome? So masculine. His worn jeans with that white cotton shirt, long sleeves rolled to mid-forearm, made her heart flutter. And she knew how the muscles under those clothes felt to the touch.

She could hardly breathe, but managed to say, "Hi."

"Sorry to show up so late."

"No problem." She hadn't expected him to show up at

all and wanted to say how happy she was. But she didn't
want to compound her last mistake, so she kept the words
bottled up. "Come on in."

He walked past her. "You probably want to get out of
here and relax, so I won't keep you long."

"Actually I was going to look over today's receipts.
What's up?"

"A couple of things. I have some papers from the lawyer and I had a meeting today with my accountant about
Patrick's Place."

"And?" Side by side they walked over to the bar and
she sat on one of the stools.

Leo set his briefcase on the chair next to hers, then
met her gaze. "The accountant did revenue comparisons."

"Don't keep me in suspense. What did he say?"

"We're up 10 percent over last year, and business has
currently increased by a lot—even when he backed out
the numbers from the night of the opening." He smiled
but it was surprisingly tense. "The bottom line is better
than he'd hoped but he still cautioned that it's early. No
high-fiving just yet."

She was working in the trenches, so to speak, and knew
foot traffic was heavy. But it was a relief to have the numbers confirm her feelings. "That's fantastic."

"Yeah."

And yet his expression didn't match the sentiment.
"So why do you look like someone just used your hockey
stick for kindling?"

"For starters, I don't think a hockey stick is a good way
to start a fire. They're made of fiberglass as a compos-
ite with wood, graphite or Kevlar. I'm not sure it would
burn."

She didn't need to know that. He was procrastinating.
What did he not want to tell her? "What's wrong, Leo?"

"Nothing's wrong. It's just… I have papers."

Probably some rider had kicked in from the partnership papers they'd originally signed. "From the lawyer, you said."

"Right." He pulled a manila folder out of his briefcase, set it on the bar and slid it closer to her.

Tess pulled out several long sheets of paper with dense legal paragraphs and glanced at the top—Custody Agreement and Child Support. She went ice-cold. "What is this?"

"I had Annabel draw it up. It spells out a joint-custody arrangement, if I'm the baby's father. And there's generous child support specified, too."

Since she told him he was going to be a father, he'd been okay with waiting until the baby was born to get DNA results and work things out then. Now he'd gone to his attorney to get papers drawn up for her to sign? "All of a sudden you need something carved in stone?"

"It's my bad. I should have done this right away."

"But you didn't. And the only thing that has changed is I told you I love you."

He shook his head. "This is about protecting the baby."

"Really? Come on, Leo."

"There's no other reason."

"If you truly believe that, you're burying your head in the sand." She refused to look away. "This is about me saying I love you."

"No—"

"Oh, please. It couldn't be any more clear unless you put up a barbed-wire fence to keep me out. You think my signing a piece of paper will prevent you from getting your heart broken again."

"You're wrong." His tone was hard and his expression grim.

"Am I?" She knew she wasn't but he needed to hear this. "Everything was fine and dandy until I had the audacity to tell you how I feel. Now you have a legal document for my signature. What would you think?"

"It's my goal to protect everyone. To have everything spelled out in black-and-white. If the baby is mine—"

"I'm going to say this one more time. The baby is yours. And if you believe I would keep your child from you, you don't know me at all. Every child deserves to know their parents. So you just wasted a lot of money on a lawyer and an agreement you really don't need."

She slid off the stool and walked around behind the bar, where there were pens for signing credit card receipts. When she found one, she looked him straight in the eye before scratching her signature on the line where indicated.

"There. Just so you know, I signed this because I know you're afraid. I hope it gives you peace of mind."

"Tess, I—"

"No. There's nothing more to say." She started toward the hall and the stairs leading up to her apartment. Then she stopped. There was one more thing and he wasn't going to like this either, but how much more paperwork could a lawyer draw up to protect him? She turned back and said, "I'm not her, Leo. I'm not going to lie and cheat. I think you know that. And you're a fool if you walk away from what we have together. But I think you know that, too—"

Emotion choked off her words and she turned away to hurry upstairs. Every time he saw her cry she ended up in his arms. He made it clear he couldn't love her. She could read between the lines of that damn legal agreement. So there was no way she would let him see her cry. Not again.

* * *

When Tess signed that stupid agreement with tears glistening in her eyes, Leo knew he'd royally screwed up. It wasn't the tears that had convinced him, but the way he wanted to kick himself into next year for hurting her. Then he had ached to hold her and make it better, but she had walked away before he could.

He couldn't blame her. She'd nailed it when she accused him of being afraid. He wanted nothing to do with love, but he cared about her. There was no reason to put a label on it. Thinking about it had kept him awake a lot for the better part of last week, and he'd come to the conclusion that she was right about everything. He didn't believe she would lie and cheat. For several days he'd been trying to tell her that, but she was giving him the cold shoulder every time he came into Patrick's Place.

Now he was here to try again. He parked in the lot and walked inside, then looked around. Finally he spotted her behind the bar, drawing a beer. It was happy hour but he wasn't feeling especially happy. She was smiling when she set the frosty glass on a napkin in front of a customer. Leo really liked her smile and missed it aimed in his direction.

"'Winners never quit. Quitters never win,'" he muttered to himself as he headed in her direction.

He sat down at her end of the bar. Brandon was on the far side, pouring liquor into a shot glass for a cocktail, then adding a lot of olives. He delivered the drink to a very attractive twentysomething blonde who smiled and flirted with the young man. Being a bartender had its perks. Being a bar owner who was getting the cold shoulder from his partner did not. It was time to make things right between them.

Tess had her back to him, washing glasses and wiping

down counters. When she turned, he noticed that the pregnancy was really showing. There was no way she could conceal it now. And she looked more beautiful than he'd ever seen her. Glowing even.

Until she focused on him and her expression hardened into ice.

"Tess—"

"Do you want a drink?"

No. He wanted to talk to her but he had a feeling ordering something was the only way to make that happen. "Yeah. Can I get a beer?"

Without a word she moved to get him a frosty glass, then held it beneath the tap and pulled the handle. She tilted the glass to keep the foam to a minimum, then leveled it at just the right moment. She grabbed a napkin and set it on the bar, in front of him, with the glass on top.

"Thanks. How are you?"

"Fine." She was treating him like a stranger.

That wasn't actually true. A stranger who came in for a beer would get a warm smile and an enthusiastic welcome to Patrick's Place. He longed to be a stranger.

"I'm sorry I missed the doctor's appointment. There was a crisis. Pipe broke in one of my buildings. Is everything all right with you and the baby?"

"I'll let you know after the birth, when the DNA test results are in. According to our legal agreement, that's when it will be okay for you to start feeling anything."

"Come on, Tess. Can't we talk about this?"

"Call your attorney. Get her to draw up more paperwork. I'll look at it."

Before he could come up with a response, she walked away. She stopped to talk to Brandon, who nodded, and then she left the bar and went upstairs to her apartment.

"That went well." Now he was talking to himself.

He would keep talking if he had any helpful advice to give to himself, but that well was dry. Everything he'd tried so far wasn't working. So maybe he needed to talk to someone else. Tess's sarcastic comment was still ringing in his ears. *Call your attorney.* Annabel did legal work for him but was also a friend. So that was actually a very good idea.

He took out his phone and looked through his contacts. She was probably still in the office. It went straight to voice mail, so he texted her a brief message. 9-1-1. His phone rang moments later.

He answered and said, "Annabel—"

"What's wrong?"

"I need to talk," he said.

"Is this a legal matter?"

"Sort of." It was a result of the document she'd pulled together for him. "Are you with a client?"

"Nope. No more appointments. I'm at the office, catching up on paperwork."

"Can I come over?" he asked.

There was a brief pause before she said, "Okay."

He clicked off and headed for the door. There were four guys sitting in a booth and one of them called him over.

The man was balding, in his fifties. "Aren't you Leo 'The Wall' Wallace? The hockey player?"

"Yes, but—"

"Can we get your autograph?" He lifted his beer from the cocktail napkin and pulled a pen from his shirt pocket.

"Sure." Leo signed his name and handed it back.

"How's retirement?" one of the other men asked. "Do you miss playing? Games? Glory? Girls?"

He thought about the question and realized he hadn't missed those days for a long time. Life was filled with work. And Tess. She had brought joy and purpose to him, to his life. And soon there would be a baby. His baby.

"Everything I want is right here." Except Tess. He glanced at the four men. "Sorry to cut this short, but I have a meeting. Hope you'll come back in. I'd love to chat with you."

Everyone smiled and assured him he could count on their business. He waved on his way out the door and twenty minutes later he walked into the building where Annabel's office was located. He took the elevator to her floor and when it stopped, he headed down the hall. The receptionist was gone so he walked into the inner sanctum, where Annabel sat behind her desk.

"Where's the fire?" She didn't bother with pleasantries.

For some reason that irked him. "Hello, Annabel. How are you?"

"Annoyed. That's how I am. You said this was an emergency. To me that means someone—you—is either bleeding or on fire. If you are, it doesn't show."

That's because it was all happening to him on the inside. "I needed to talk."

"You could have called the office tomorrow and made an appointment."

"Since when do friends have to put a date on the calendar to talk?"

"So, we're friends."

"Of course we are. You know that." He felt like a lawyer presenting an argument in court. "I need to talk to you about something. You're logical and you're a woman."

"Oh, boy." She sighed and put down her pen. "This isn't going to be quick, is it?"

"No."

"Okay."

He counted on his friend's professional advice and

knew she would give him the truth. Always. They never mixed business and pleasure. But he'd crossed that line with Tess. Touching her made his willpower evaporate and he'd kissed her. He was a goner. And then she'd said what she'd said, and he ran for cover. He had to make things better, and not just so they could work together.

"Sorry. I'll buy you dinner later."

"Maybe. If I'm still hungry after you're finished confessing how you've been a jackass. After which I will give you outstanding advice on how to make up for your insensitive behavior."

"Wow. That's harsh," he said.

"Tell me I'm wrong."

"After you tell me how you know this." He sat in one of the club chairs in front of her desk.

"Seriously?" She sighed when he nodded. "I drew up that completely unnecessary agreement for you after you insisted you had to have it."

"How do you know it's unnecessary?"

"First of all I've met Tess. I like her and I'm an excellent judge of character. She is sweet, honest and oozing integrity."

Leo could not argue with that assessment. And she was so much more, too. Hot, sexy and smart. Prettiest pregnant lady he'd ever seen. She kept him on his toes. "What else?"

"How do you know there's more?"

"You said 'first of all.' That implies you have more criteria for your conclusion."

"Okay. Yeah." Annabel leaned back in her chair. "You had a verbal agreement with Tess to have DNA testing done after the baby is born. So there was no reason to have anything in writing right now." She met his gaze and frowned. "Unless something happened. Is Tess okay? The baby?"

"Both fine." At least that's what she'd said.

"For some reason you felt threatened. Because everything in those papers was about your rights being protected." Her eyes widened in comprehension. "She told you she has feelings for you, didn't she?"

Leo considered lying but there was no point. Besides, he'd 9-1-1-ed her and rushed over here to talk. "Yes. She said she loved me."

"Great." She looked pleased, then studied his face. "Or not."

"Come on. You know what happened to me. I fell in love, got lied to and lost my kid. If I hadn't fallen for her…" He shook his head. "Love is the last thing I want."

"Tess isn't your ex." Leave it to a lawyer to state the obvious.

"That's what she said."

"And letting her go because of your personal baggage makes you an idiot."

"She said that, too. Only she called me a fool."

"That works." Annabel glanced away for a moment, then met his gaze. Her own was intense. "A fool who's taken one too many shots to the head playing hockey."

"What does that mean?" He held up a hand. "I don't mean that literally. Why in the world would I take another chance in my personal life after what happened to me?"

"Because by some miracle of banked karma, you knocked up a really wonderful woman who is the one for you. God knows why, but she genuinely cares about you. And you made her sign something that proves you don't trust her."

It sounded really bad when she put it like that. "I guess I could have handled it better."

"You think?" Annabel gave him her patented "men are morons" look.

"Okay. Already established. Asked and answered, as you lawyers like to say. What do I do? How do I fix this with her?"

"Did it occur to you to say you're sorry?"

"Of course. I tried. I've *been* trying ever since I messed up."

"Not going well." Again stating the obvious. It sure looked as if she was taking a whole lot of satisfaction from that.

"If it was all sunshine and roses, I wouldn't have called you. Are you going to keep making fun of me? Or are you actually going to give me some common-sense suggestions to fix this problem?"

"Poor Leo." She tsked and her expression was a little condescending. "I'm sorry you're hurting. Truly. I just couldn't resist."

"Try harder. Tell me what to do."

"You, sir, need a very big gesture. Flowers. Jewelry is always nice. Expensive. A conciliatory billboard on Huntington Hills Parkway."

"That's the most congested intersection in town," he said.

"Like I said—very big gesture. Very public, too. Followed by a great deal of sincere groveling," she added.

"I was afraid you were going to say that."

"Telling her you were wrong will work wonders. You'll see. I promise."

"How can you be so sure I'm going to do this?"

She smiled now, a look without a hint of sarcasm or female satisfaction over a man's confusion. This was sincere and heartfelt. "I know you will because you're crazy about her."

At least she hadn't used the *L* word, but it was sounding pretty good to him. And she obviously knew him well. Because he was going back to the bar and this time he was going to make Tess listen.

Chapter Fifteen

When Tess heard the knock on her apartment door her heart jumped. Maybe Leo had followed her. But when she opened up and saw her friend Carla, she realized the word *maybe* was the cruelest, most painful one in the English language.

She forced herself to smile and hugged the other woman. "Hi."

"Hi, back." Carla held her at arm's length, studying her. "I was going to ask how you are, but you look tired. Are you eating? Sleeping? Taking care of yourself?"

"Of course." She shut the door. "To what do I owe this unexpected visit?"

"I haven't heard from you in an uncharacteristically long time." She shrugged. "They don't call. They don't write. They don't—"

"You've made your point. I've been busy with work."

"Aren't we all," Carla said wryly.

"So you came by yourself. Where's Jamie?"

"Bill is back in town." Carla had a look on her face, as if she'd eaten bad sushi. "She sends her love and made me promise to give her an update."

"What's wrong?" Tess asked. It was a relief to be talking about someone other than herself.

"I don't know how to tell her, but I think Bill is a two-timing, scum-sucking, cheating bastard."

"What are you talking about?" Tess asked.

"I'm pretty sure he's married."

Tess pointed to the kitchen. "Can I get you a glass of wine?"

"Sure. I could really use one."

Tess led the way and took a bottle of white wine from the refrigerator that she kept chilled for her friends and opened it. Reaching up into the cupboard, she took down a stemless glass and poured the golden liquid into it, then handed it over. She took out a bottle of water for herself.

"What makes you think he's married?"

"The signs are classic. He shows up unexpectedly and she has to drop everything to see him. The pub reopened and he's suddenly called back to the home office. And yes, I do mean that as a double entendre. She suggested the two of them take a romantic getaway to San Diego, but he wouldn't hear of it." Carla took a big drink of wine. "I just have a feeling and I don't want her to get hurt. But I'm afraid if I say something, she'll be mad at me."

"If he is, she's going to be hurt anyway. Wouldn't it be best to gently ask some questions? Maybe lead her in that direction without actually putting it out there?"

Carla nodded. "That's a good idea. It would help if you're there when I bring it up."

"Count on it." Tess hated to see her friend hurt, especially because she knew how bad it felt. The best thing she could say was that Leo hadn't lied to her, probably because he'd been lied to so horribly. She wanted to change the subject. "So, what's new? How's the matchmaking business?"

"Things are looking up since Gabriel Blackburne is temporarily helping out his eccentric aunt, who owns Make Me a Match."

"Isn't he in the tech business?"

"Yes, but the place desperately needed organization. Lillian is emotional and intuitive, super good at pairing people. He's analytical and brings balance." Carla took another sip of her wine. "It's amazing how many people would like to find someone but are too busy to look."

Tess hadn't been looking. It had just happened, damn it. Everything led back to Leo. She saw that Carla's wineglass was empty. "Can I refill that for you?"

"Since you're pregnant and can't have alcohol, does that mean I'm drinking for two?"

"Whatever you want. And you don't have to drive home. You can spend the night here."

Carla's eyes widened questioningly. "I suppose that means there's no chance you're going to have male companionship this evening."

"Why would you think that?"

"I saw the way you were looking at him when Patrick's Place reopened," Carla said.

"Are you talking about Leo?"

"Is there someone else I don't know about?"

Tess hadn't talked to her friends about the agreement he'd had drawn up for her to sign. Was there such a thing as being too heartbroken to even discuss it with the people you trusted most in the world? She'd been trying to pretend things were fine. The "never speak of it again" solution to her pain was working, just barely. And she wanted to keep it that way.

"Honestly, you don't even know about Leo."

"What don't I know?" Carla took the refilled glass.

"There's not much to know," she insisted.

"Well, I know you and your eyes are telling me that there's a lot on your mind. My matchmaking instincts are telling me it's all about one hunky hockey-player partner of yours."

"How long have you been working at this new job?" Tess asked.

"That's irrelevant." Carla waved a hand in dismissal.

"A couple of months gives you a matchmaking sixth sense?"

"Are you ever going to let me forget that before I hated him for hurting you, I actually liked Alan, the college athlete and first-class jerk?"

"I'm so over that." But Tess had a bad feeling that getting over Leo was going to be a lifetime struggle.

"We've known each other how long?" Carla asked. "Do you seriously think I can't see that something is up? If the shoe was on the other foot, would you not badger me until I came clean?"

"God, I hate it when you're right." Tess sighed. "Leo and I slept together."

"Old news, sweetie." Carla's gaze dropped to Tess's growing baby bump. "You're the cutest darn pregnant lady I've ever seen."

That made Tess smile. Thank goodness for her friends. She was being stupid by keeping this to herself. They'd helped her through every crisis, and this one would be no exception, because shutting them out wasn't an option. It would not be allowed.

"Let's sit," she said.

"Are you uncomfortable?" Carla looked concerned.

"A little. Feeling some pressure but that happens if I'm on my feet a lot. It goes away when I sit."

"Okay, then." Her friend moved to the love seat that separated the living area and kitchen. "Take a load off right now, missy."

Tess did just that and sighed before meeting the other woman's gaze. "The thing is, we had sex again, about a week ago, and—"

"I knew it! Like I said, off-the-chart chemistry between you two that night." There was an "I told you so" gleam in Carla's eyes. "Jamie and I talked about it on the way home and she saw it, too. My matchmaking mojo was crackling when I saw the way he was looking at you." She took a breath, then a sip of wine. "How did he propose? Was it romantic? Rose petals and champagne—well, not for you. But knowing you as I do, you're going to make love complicated because of the past. Please tell me you didn't turn him down flat."

"Things are definitely complicated, but not because of me." Tess held up her left hand and pointed out the bare ring finger. "He didn't propose."

"What's he waiting for? The two of you are clearly nuts about each other."

Nuts described Tess. She'd been deluded enough to fall for the guy, even though she knew it was a really bad idea. But that implied she'd had a choice. It had just happened. She hadn't wanted to lose her heart. Tears filled her eyes and that's why she'd resisted talking about this. But no way would her friend let this pass without hearing details.

"Tell me, Tess. What's wrong? Was it the sex? Bad?"

"No. It was really, really awesome. And I don't care if that word is overused." She sniffled. "And I was so in the moment. And the feeling was so big, it spilled over and—"

"What?" Carla demanded.

"I said it. I told him I love him."

"But that's a good thing, right? Tell me it is. For the sake of my career in bringing people together to find happiness. Which isn't easy, by the way." Carla looked worried. "Did he say it back?"

Tess shook her head. "He had his lawyer draw up an agreement for joint custody and child support *if* DNA proves the baby is his. He doesn't trust me, and that makes love impossible."

"But why? How could he not believe in you? You're the most honorable person I know. Besides Jamie, of course. What's wrong with him?"

"He wants no part of love." A tear trickled down Tess's cheek.

"Coldhearted jerk." Carla's eyes blazed and angry red blotches covered the fair skin of her face. "I'm going to hurt him—"

"No. He has a very good reason for feeling that way." Tess told her friend everything. "He never promised to love me and hasn't done anything wrong. The mistake is mine."

"Well, that really bites. And I can't even be mad at him." Carla put her glass on the coffee table, then reached over and squeezed Tess's hand. "What can I do?"

"Same as you always have. Be my friend." That did it. The sobs she'd been holding in fought their way out as tears spilled down her cheeks. She buried her face in her hands and let all the pain come out while her friend held her.

"It will be okay, honey. I promise. You're not alone. Not ever."

Tess had no idea how long the storm lasted but eventually there were no more tears left to shed. No offense to her friend, but it was a lot more comforting when Leo held her while she cried. Guess that was over, too.

She brushed the wetness from her cheeks and tried to smile. "Sorry about that."

"Don't be silly. You should have told me sooner, you know."

"Yeah." Tess nodded. "But it was hard. I hope you never have your heart broken, but if you do, I'll return the favor and hold you while you cry."

"Are you kidding? I'm never going to fall in love ever again."

"Yeah, that's what I said. Famous last words. And isn't that attitude a violation of the matchmaker code of conduct?"

"The business is about facilitating meetings for people who are looking for someone. The love part is up to them. Or not. My background in psychology is helpful. From reading profiles, it's a tool in pairing up people, but there's no way to predict what happens face-to-face. It's a job and I needed one badly after what happened with you know who."

"Good for you moving past all that. I'm glad I don't have to worry about you being an idiot, like me—" Her voice broke. "Damn hormones."

"Go into the bathroom and wash your face," Carla ordered. "Put a cold compress on your eyes. That was an ugly cry. You'll feel much better. No argument. Go."

Tess did as instructed and went to the bathroom right off her bedroom. She splashed cold water on her face, then wet a cloth and wrung it out before pressing it to her eyes. It did make her feel better. After a while she started to feel guilty about leaving her friend alone for so long. But before she went back out, it would be prudent to use the facilities.

When she sat, something on her panties caught her eye and she gasped. "Oh, God—"

There was a knock on the door, followed by Carla's voice. "Are you okay in there?"

"I'm bleeding, Carla. The baby…"

Leo left his lawyer's office and went straight back to Patrick's Place. Annabel had obviously gotten through to him pretty fast because the four hockey fanboys were still sitting in the same booth. He waved to them on his way past. Another time he would chat them up, but he was a man on a mission. He needed to find Tess ASAP.

He scanned the crowded bar area, the filled-to-capacity lounge, where a baseball game was on, and then the dining area. There was no sign of her. To get a better look, he walked closer, making sure he hadn't missed any corner. He hadn't and was surprised she wasn't here. Every night she poured drinks or visited with customers and worked harder than anyone. Because this investment was personal and emotional for her.

It was possible she was still avoiding him, but she wouldn't do that at the expense of her business.

"Brandon." He stepped up to the bar, where the young man was standing.

"Hey, Leo. I thought you were gone. It's been a busy night. I think you'll really be happy when you see the—"

He held up a hand. Wow. Did everyone think he was only about business? "Take a breath. I'm not here to check up on you."

"Okay." He smiled a little sheepishly. "How are you?"

"Been better. Is Tess around?"

"I haven't seen her for a while. Come to think of it, the last time I saw her was when you were in here before. I think she went upstairs then."

"She didn't tell you she was taking the rest of the night off?"

"No."

Leo knew she would have so she must be in her apartment. "Thanks, Brandon. By the way, you're doing a great job and when we open the second location of Patrick's Place, you're my first choice to manage it."

"We're expanding?"

"If things keep going the way they are—yes."

Brandon smiled broadly. "That's great news."

"See you later. I'm going to talk to Tess now."

"Okay, boss."

Leo headed for the hall and took the stairs two at a time. He knocked on the door and moments later it was opened. By Tess's friend Carla.

He smiled at her. "Hi—"

"Leo, thank God." She pulled him inside and was surprisingly strong for a small woman.

"What's up?"

"It's Tess."

The woman was clearly shaken, and fear sliced through him. "Where is she?"

"In the bedroom. I—"

He didn't wait for the rest and hurried past her. Tess was stretched out on the bed with her eyes closed. She looked small, fragile and tense. He moved closer and said, "Tess, what's wrong?"

Her eyes popped open. "Leo, I'm bleeding. It shouldn't be happening—"

"Okay." The fear got bigger but he forced calm into his voice.

"Carla made me lie down."

"Good." He knelt beside the bed. "But I think you should be looked at."

"I'll wait and see if it stops. I'll call the doctor—"

"Carla can do that and let her know you're at the emergency room."

"What are you saying?"

"I'm taking you to the hospital. Now."

She caught her top lip between her teeth and then nodded. "I'll get up and—"

"No." He stood, then scooped her into his arms as

gently as possible. "I'll try not to jostle you too much but this is the fastest way."

She was scared. He knew that because she didn't protest. He really, really wished she was arguing with him right now.

He met her gaze and tried to look more reassuring than he felt. For her sake. And the baby's. *His* baby. "Here we go. You ready?"

"Yes." She put her arms around his neck and hung on.

He carried her through the apartment, and Tess told her friend where to find the doctor's number and to call the answering service right away. Leo asked her to let Brandon know he was closing up tonight. He didn't want Tess to worry about it.

At the car he set her on her feet in order to fish the keys out of his pocket, hit the fob to unlock the doors and then opened the passenger side.

When he started to lift her again she said, "I can handle this."

Five minutes later they were at the hospital's emergency entrance, and he found a parking space close to the automatic doors. This time he ignored her protest that she could walk and carried her inside to the check-in desk. The staff got her into an exam room right away, then shooed him into the hall while they got her hooked up to monitors.

The door opened again and he was allowed back in. Tess was in a patient gown and the machines were rhythmically beeping. He was going to believe the sounds meant all was perfectly normal. She was still pale and scared, but looked a little calmer.

Leo pulled a chair over and sat. "What did they say?"

"Nothing. I'm waiting for the doctor. She's here for a

delivery. Isn't that lucky?" Her mouth trembled and her eyes filled with tears. "I'm so scared. My baby—"

"It's okay. Everything is going to be fine."

"Is it? You don't know that."

"You have to believe, Tess."

"Really? How can you even say that to me with a straight face?" With shaking hands she brushed the wetness from her cheeks. "You've never believed this baby was yours."

"It's mine," he said firmly.

"You don't have to say that because I'm in the ER. Don't you dare feel sorry for me."

"Nothing could be further from the truth." He took her hand and held it in both of his. "And you're wrong. I believed from the beginning that this is my baby."

"Oh, please."

"It's the truth," he insisted. "Deep down I knew it because Patrick Morrow's granddaughter was raised to be scrupulously honest. But after what I went through, I was trying to protect myself and denial was the best I could do."

Her face softened. "Then why make me sign those papers?"

"You said you love me and I went into survival mode again. Fight-or-flight."

"Then you get a gold star for that. Because you did both at the same time. An awesome multitasker." There was a little sass back in her voice.

"That's me. Overachiever at the worst time."

"Why worst?" she asked.

"It's the last thing I should have done. Because I love you."

"You have a very funny way of showing it," she scoffed.

"What can I say? Lack of a positive male role model. Except your grandfather. He showed me what love looks like."

"Me, too," she said sadly.

Leo nodded. "I have a sneaking suspicion that he was pushing us together."

"What?"

"He knew a lot of people who could have invested money in his business but he picked me. I think somehow he knew I was in love with you even then."

"He picked you because…" She stopped when his words sank in. "What? Are you really saying you love me?"

"I fell in love with you the first time I saw you."

She looked skeptical and had every right. "That's a very romantic thing to say. But—"

He put a finger to her lips to stop the words. "No *buts*. It's the truth and everything is going to be okay. We'll get through this together."

"Men always say that but don't mean it."

"I promise I mean it."

The door opened then and Dr. Thompson came in. She was wearing blue scrubs and a white lab coat. He felt better that she was here even though she threw him out of the room to examine Tess.

Leo paced the hall like a caged tiger. Or expectant father. It felt like a lifetime before the doctor let him back in. She was very reassuring and told them it wasn't unusual for spotting to occur. But she had no doubt that the baby was absolutely fine. Tess was to stay off her feet and take it easy for a few days, and Leo intended to see that she followed the doctor's orders.

After she was discharged, he drove her home and insisted she go straight to bed. Then he fixed her something light to eat and made sure she ate it.

"Is there anything else you need?" he asked.

"No." She smiled. "Thanks for everything. You should go home and get some rest. You must be tired."

"I'm not. And I'm not leaving." He sat in the chair near the bed and put his long legs up on the ottoman.

"What are you doing?"

"I told you we're going to get through this together. I'm settling in for the night."

"Why?"

"Clearly I have my work cut out for me to prove that I mean what I say. But I will prove it. And after I do, I'll convince you to marry me."

A sweet smile curved the corners of her beautiful mouth before she sat up in the bed. "Yes."

"Yes, what?"

"Yes, I'll marry you." She patted the empty space beside her in the bed. "Because, as you know, I love you. Very much. And I would never let my fiancé sleep in a chair."

Happiness and relief poured through him as he slid in beside her. He pulled her into his arms and kissed her gently. "This was the worst and best day of my life."

"Oh?"

"Our baby is fine. You love me. And we're getting married. A personal hat trick."

"I love it when you talk hockey to me." She snuggled close and rested her cheek on his chest. "And now you can do it for the rest of our lives."

That was the game plan.

Epilogue

Tess stood in the doorway of the baby's nursery and watched Leo holding their little girl. Leonore Patricia Wallace. The sight of her handsome husband—Leo "The Wall" Wallace—so gentle and sweet with that tiny bundle of pink preciousness, was too *everything* for words. She pulled her cell phone from the pocket of her jeans and snapped a picture. This was something she'd done countless times in the month since she gave birth. And every single picture was priceless.

Leo looked away from the baby and smiled. "Hey, Mrs. Wallace."

"Hey, Mr. Wallace."

Her heart was so full of love for this man, she was afraid it might explode. Many times over he'd convinced her that he was there and they'd see things through together. He'd been the best coach ever during labor and delivery. He was her rock, her love, her heart. And she was his. She remembered when this house was barely furnished, but not anymore.

"I love this room," she said, looking around.

"Me, too."

They had chosen not to know the sex of the baby and had decorated in gender-neutral colors and theme. The walls were cream with white trim. Framed prints of animals— pudgy hippos, elephants and giraffes—were on the walls.

The chest of drawers that also served as a changing table was cherry wood, as was the crib. Not that Leonore would use it for a while, what with the cradle in the master bedroom. Both she and Leo wanted the baby in their room until she was bigger.

Tess came closer and studied the tiny girl peacefully sleeping in her father's arms. "I think she has your chin. I love that little indentation."

"Mine or hers?"

"Both."

"She definitely has my disposition," he said proudly. "Mellow and serene."

Tess couldn't make a comparison since this was her first baby. But Leo had been through this before, a seasoned pro at this whole infant thing. She was wondering how he was feeling about it.

"Are you okay?" she asked.

"Yes." He looked up at her and seemed to know what she was thinking. "I will always love Chad and hope that he's healthy and happy. That his parents are good to him and he grows up well. But the emptiness I had inside for so long was gone the day you married me."

"Yeah. That was a good day." As was every single one since.

Their wedding happened not long after the night he'd carried her into the emergency room. After that, he was in a hurry not to waste time, but would have waited if she'd wanted to do it after giving birth. Have the dress, reception—the whole nine yards. Tess didn't care about anything except him and their baby.

They'd closed Patrick's Place for a night, found a minister and taken vows in front of close friends. No family, at least not living and breathing relatives. She was convinced her grandfather was there, watching over them, happy that the two of them had been smart enough not to blow off his matchmaking efforts.

"Are you okay?" he asked.

The discomfort of birth had faded and she was tired, what with having a newborn and being up at night. But she'd never dreamed happiness this complete was possible.

"I'm so good, it's scary," she said. "I have everything I've always wanted. You. Our baby. A family."

"I feel the same way." The baby started squeaking and squirming, so he shifted her to his shoulder.

Sometimes Tess still felt awkward doing that, but he was confident and sure of himself. His big hands were exquisitely gentle with their tiny human.

He smiled up at her. "It occurs to me that we're rich in family."

"How do you mean?"

"Think about it. There's you, me and Leonore. Then we have our Patrick's Place regulars."

"Yeah." Her gaze slid to the stack of baby gifts still in the corner of the room from all of their customers. Sitting on top of the pile was a small pink helmet, a gift from Josh and all the guys on the team. "And we have our hockey family."

"Exactly." He stood when the baby started to fuss and handed her to Tess. "That's her hungry cry."

"How do you know the difference between that, the one when her diaper needs changing and the general one when she's bored and needs to be held?"

"It's a gift." He shrugged.

"You're going to make me look bad. If you had the right equipment I'm sure you would feed her, too."

"I would go to hell and back if it meant my daughter would be happy," he said.

She kissed the small cheek, then smiled at him. "You are the baby whisperer."

"I'm a very lucky man."

"You didn't feel that way when I first told you I was pregnant." She laughed, remembering that conversation. And everything that happened afterward. "Maybe we should have named our little peanut Cupid."

"Because she brought us together." He put his arm around her shoulders, hugging them both.

Because of how close they'd come to missing out on this happiness, Tess would always believe that her grandfather was watching over them. "We are very lucky."

"I couldn't agree more."

Tess had the traditional family she'd always wanted, and the dream had started in a nontraditional way. They'd gone from conflict to contentment all because of an unexpected partnership.

* * * * *

MILLS & BOON

Coming next month

FROM HEIRESS TO MUM
Therese Beharrie

'Still can't get used to this view,' Hunter said quietly as she stopped next to him.

Autumn followed his gaze onto the city of Cape Town. When she'd moved out of her family home—the Bishop mansion, as some people liked to call it—she hadn't tried to find somewhere outside the city she'd grown up in to live. She'd merely been drawn to the Bouw Estate.

It had green fields that exploded with wildflowers; rolling hills beyond the fields; a river that surrounded the estate. The old manor and barn on the property had been renovated into what were now her home and her bakery, respectively.

'You didn't come here at eleven at night to talk about this view.'

His eyes slid over to her, the brown of them a well of emotion, before his head dipped in a curt nod. 'You're right.'

She gestured to the outdoor table she'd lovingly selected when she'd furnished her house. 'Shall we?'

He nodded, pulled a chair out and stepped back. With a sigh, she sat down, thanking him when he pushed it back in. She waited as he sat down opposite her. A long silence followed. She used it to study him. To watch the emotions play over his face.

When his eyes met hers, she caught her breath, and wished she had something to drink to distract herself from how vulnerable all of this made her feel.

'I don't know how to say this,' he admitted eventually.

She let air into her lungs slowly. 'Just…get it out.'

He angled his head, as if accepting her suggestion, but didn't speak.

'Hunter.' She paused. 'Are you in trouble?'

He opened his mouth, and Autumn could almost see his lips forming no, but then he closed it again. Rubbed a hand over his face; took a deep breath.

'I am.'

She straightened. 'Yeah? You're in trouble?'

His eyes shone with an emotion she couldn't quite define. It disturbed her. She'd dated him for two years; they'd been friends for one more. She should be able to tell what he was feeling.

'Yes.'

After a brief moment of hesitation, she laid a hand on the one he'd rested on the table. 'What's going on?'

He took a breath, then exhaled sharply, his gaze lowering.

'I'm a father.'

Continue reading
FROM HEIRESS TO MUM
Therese Beharrie

Available next month
www.millsandboon.co.uk

COMING SOON!

We really hope you enjoyed reading this book. If you're looking for more romance, be sure to head to the shops when new books are available on

Thursday 2nd May

LET'S TALK
Romance

For exclusive extracts, competitions
and special offers, find us online:

f facebook.com/millsandboon

𝕏 @MillsandBoon

⊙ @MillsandBoonUK

Get in touch on 01413 063232

For all the latest titles coming soon, visit
millsandboon.co.uk/nextmonth